Praise for *Mistletoe Man* . . .

"Ms. Albert artfully uses Texas language patterns to bring the down-home town of Pecan Springs alive with eccentrics in abundance in this colorful Christmas story."

—*The Dallas Morning News*

"China proves herself intelligent, independent, persistent and compassionate . . . This is a funny, human story that will give Albert's admirers a ringing jingle bell romp."

—*Publishers Weekly*

Raves for
SUSAN WITTIG ALBERT'S
previous China Bayles mysteries . . .

LAVENDER LIES . . . "Realistic, likable characters."

—*Chicago Tribune*

CHILE DEATH . . . "Satisfying . . . Not too spicy, just right."

—*Publishers Weekly*

LOVE LIES BLEEDING . . . "The best yet in an appealing series." —*Booklist*

RUEFUL DEATH . . . "A page-turner." —*Publishers Weekly*

ROSEMARY REMEMBERED . . . "Memorable, indeed."

—*Publishers Weekly*

HANGMAN'S ROOT . . . "Fine observations and sly humor."

—*Wilson Library Journal*

WITCHES' BANE . . . "A delightful cast of unusual characters."

—*Booklist*

THYME OF DEATH . . . "Lively and engaging."

—*Fort Worth Star-Telegram*

China Bayles Mysteries by Susan Wittig Albert

THYME OF DEATH
WITCHES' BANE
HANGMAN'S ROOT
ROSEMARY REMEMBERED
RUEFUL DEATH
LOVE LIES BLEEDING
CHILE DEATH
LAVENDER LIES
MISTLETOE MAN
BLOODROOT

With her husband Bill Albert, writing as Robin Paige

DEATH AT BISHOP'S KEEP
DEATH AT GALLOWS GREEN
DEATH AT DAISY'S FOLLY
DEATH AT DEVIL'S BRIDGE
DEATH AT ROTTINGDEAN
DEATH AT WHITECHAPEL
DEATH AT EPSOM DOWNS
DEATH AT DARTMOOR

Nonfiction books by Susan Wittig Albert

WRITING FROM LIFE
WORK OF HER OWN

MISTLETOE MAN

Susan Wittig Albert

BERKLEY PRIME CRIME, NEW YORK

Dedicated to the memory of
Marge Bell Clark

This is a work of fiction. Names, characters, places, and incidents either are the product of the author's imagination or are used fictitiously, and any resemblance to actual persons, living or dead, business establishments, events, or locales is entirely coincidental.

MISTLETOE MAN

A Berkley Prime Crime Book / published by arrangement with the author

PRINTING HISTORY
Berkley Prime Crime hardcover edition / October 2000
Berkley Prime Crime mass-market edition / October 2001

Visit our website at
www.penguinputnam.com

ISBN: 0-425-18201-0

Berkley Prime Crime Books are published
by The Berkley Publishing Group,
a division of Penguin Putnam Inc.,
375 Hudson Street, New York, New York 10014.
The name BERKLEY PRIME CRIME and the BERKLEY PRIME CRIME
design are trademarks belonging to Penguin Putnam Inc.

PRINTED IN THE UNITED STATES OF AMERICA

10 9 8 7 6 5 4 3 2 1

ACKNOWLEDGMENTS

Thanks to Pamela and Frank Arnosky, of Texas Specialty Cut Flowers, in Blanco, Texas, for their fascinating and informative articles in Lynn Byczynski's newsletter, *Growing for Market*. The Arnoskys' articles have given me useful information about the challenges and rewards of growing flowers for market in Central Texas.

Thanks to Bill, who makes it all possible, day after day. And to expert herbalists Theresa Lowe, Carolee Synder, Pat Reppert, Sybil Kunkle, Betsy Williams, and Deborah Cravens: E-mail friends who are generous with their advice and support and who surprise me, over and over, with their adventures and insights into the magical, mysterious world of herbs.

And speaking of herbs, I must add this caution to all readers:

Please don't use this novel as your herbal guide to good health. While both China Bayles and I have a great deal of confidence in medicinal plants and frequently use them ourselves, neither of us would presume to prescribe them as a treatment for your ailments.

The Druids hold nothing more sacred than mistletoe . . . and when it is discovered, it is gathered with great ceremony, on the sixth day of the moon, which for these Gallic tribes constitutes the beginning of the months and the years. . . . Hailing the moon in a native word that means "healing all things," they prepare a ritual sacrifice and banquet beneath a tree and bring up two white bulls. . . . A priest wearing white vestments climbs the tree and with a golden sickle cuts down the mistletoe, which is caught in a white cloak. Then finally they kill the victims, praying to their god to render his gift propitious to those on whom he has bestowed it.

Pliny the Elder (C.E. 23–79)

CHAPTER ONE

There are three species of mistletoe, one European, the other two American. All three are parasites that invade a host tree and feed off its nutrients. European mistletoe (Viscum album) *the legendary "Golden Bough," was believed to cure epilepsy and ulcers, encourage fertility, banish evil spirits, promote peace, and serve as an antidote to poisons. American mistletoes* (Phoradendron sp.), *which are widely collected as Christmas decorations, have been used to treat cholera, hysteria, heart problems, and nervous conditions. Western dwarf mistletoes* (Arceuthobium sp.) *are deadly tree pests whose infestations threaten whole forests. Their leaves have no decorative or medicinal value.*

China Bayles
"Mistletoe Magic"
Home and Garden page, Pecan Springs *Enterprise*

I said goodbye to Rowena Riddle and put the phone down with a bang.

"Uh-oh," Laurel Wiley said. "Doesn't sound good."

"It isn't," I said grimly. "The Christmas Tour of Homes is only a week from tomorrow, and I haven't even started to clean house, much less decorate. Now Rowena wants to know what sort of herbal goodies I'll be serving to the guests, so she can put it into the program." I made a face. "She wants to know what my theme is, too."

It was still a few minutes before nine, and the pale winter sun was just beginning to slant through the window. But Saturday's a big day at Thyme and Seasons, especially during the holiday season. Laurel turned the CLOSED sign to OPEN and straightened the Christmas wreath on the front door. She has been my full-time shop assistant since last spring, when I had to take time off to deal with a major crisis in my personal life. Part Cherokee, Laurel has a wide streak of earthy common sense.

"Seems like a reasonable request to me," she said. "What *are* you serving?"

I retrieved the cash drawer from under the dust rags. "Hey, give me a break! The Thanksgiving turkey is hardly cold on the platter. We're still eating leftover stuffing." I shook my head disgustedly. "Whatever made me agree to have the house included in that stupid tour, anyway? Everybody else has a theme, or a color scheme, or they're decorating ten dozen angel cookies. I haven't done the laundry since Halloween, much less decked the halls. It'll be a disaster!"

Laurel flipped her long brown braid back over her shoulder and began to straighten a rack of herbal recipe books. "If it wasn't the tour, it'd be something else," she said pragmatically. "A crisis in the tearoom, maybe, or a case of the flu. Nobody ever gets through the holidays without at least a couple of disasters." She grinned. "Especially not you, China."

Khat, the elegant Siamese who lives in the shop, sauntered in and leaped up on the counter for his morning stroking. I shoved the cash drawer into the register and checked to see that the tape was working. The register is a genuine antique—I bought it when Drews Dry Goods went out of business after seventy years at the same location on the square—and it loves to eat the paper tape. But it functions when the electricity goes out (which is more than you can say for computerized registers), and the old bell's satisfied jingle makes customers smile.

"Let's not talk about a crisis in the tearoom," I told Laurel firmly. "Let's not even *think* about it."

Thyme for Tea, which Ruby Wilcox and I opened in late September, has outstripped even Ruby's wildly optimistic financial projections. In late October, the annual Pecan Pageant attracted flocks of tourists to Pecan Springs, and we were far busier than we'd expected. The weekend after that, the Herb Fair brought in customers from as far away as Dallas and El Paso, all of them wanting to sample our menu. And then, to make a good situation even better, Mrs. Kendall appeared out of nowhere and offered her services as a part-time chef—a superb chef, as we learned to our great delight—which has given us a little breathing room. But Thyme for Tea is not even three months old, and it's too soon to congratulate ourselves. I didn't want to think about a crisis there, or anywhere else, for that matter. I was ready to settle in for a happy and restful Christmas season, the first that McQuaid and I would spend together as a married couple.

If you're new to Pecan Springs and are feeling a little lost, let me help you get your bearings. My name is China Bayles, and I own Thyme and Seasons, which is located in a century-old stone building at 304 Crockett Street, just east of Guadalupe and a couple of blocks from the courthouse square. In the same building, adjoining Thyme and Seasons, is the Crystal Cave, a New Age shop owned by Ruby Wilcox, my tenant and best friend, where you can buy crystals, weird music, tarot cards, and books about Wicca or astrology or healthful living. In the space behind both shops, where I used to live, we've located our new joint venture, Thyme for Tea. At the back of the large lot is a remodeled stone stable where Ruby and I hold classes (I teach herb cookery and crafts, Ruby teaches meditation and astrology and other mystical stuff). Both buildings are surrounded by a maze of small gardens, which you really must visit the next time you're here. I'm especially proud of my apothecary and culinary gardens, as well as the butterfly garden, the moon garden, and the Shakespeare garden, green and pretty even in winter. People can buy herbs and potpourri and New Age music at Wal-Mart or the Big Thrif-T on Nueces Street, but they come here because of the gardens and the herb classes and workshops, and because Ruby and Laurel and I are passionate about what we do. And also because Wal-Mart does not have a Khat.

Like most small business owners, I spend enough hours in the shop and the gardens to qualify as a full-time resident, but I no longer live on the premises. About eighteen months ago, I moved in with Mike McQuaid and his thirteen-year-old son, Brian, and at the end of September, a couple of weeks before Ruby and I opened Thyme for Tea, McQuaid and I were married. We live a couple of miles west of town in the big white Victorian house on Lime Kiln Road—the one with the Christmas Tour of Homes sign out in front and the elderly bassett hound sleeping under the front step. (The bassett, who is a grumpy old dog, is the reason my Siamese, Khat, elected to live at the shop.) Around the first of January, if all the paperwork goes as it's supposed to, McQuaid and I will no longer be renting this marvelous house—it will be *ours*, a thought that both comforts and unnerves me at the same time.

If you think that all these changes have come easily, think again. Independence, autonomy, and privacy have always been at the very top of my list of personal issues (right up there with being my own boss and loving what I do for a living), so it was pretty tough to give up my nifty one-person apartment and become McQuaid's roommate and Brian's surrogate mom—even though I loved both of them enough to give it my best shot. It wasn't a whole lot easier to agree to Ruby's proposition that she should invest the income from her big lottery win in the tearoom. We've been friends for a long time and I knew I could trust her. I was grateful for her generosity, too—without it, the tearoom wouldn't have been possible. But I didn't want to be financially dependent on Ruby or responsible for her financial investment, and I couldn't help feeling that taking a partner would compromise my autonomy, not to mention my privacy. You don't keep secrets from your business partner—not if you want the business to survive. It was a while before I could bring myself to agree, and I'm still second-guessing my decision.

Toughest of all was the decision to marry McQuaid. I agonized over it, afraid that marriage would erode a relationship I had come to value. Worse, I feared that the daily, inevitable compromises of married life would gnaw away at my last shreds of autonomy and send me hurtling down a slippery slope to total personal and financial subjugation. (This may sound a bit over the top, but that's how I was feeling about it.) However, events—not the least of which was McQuaid's getting shot last February, when he was working undercover for the Texas Rangers—persuaded me that marriage was the right thing and now was the right time. The shooting left McQuaid with a lingering paralysis and, for longer than I like to remember, a fierce and anguished despair. His recovery has been a painful struggle to regain his physical strength and mobility as well as his old optimism. Right now, he's on sabbatical leave from Central Texas State University, where he teaches in the Criminal Justice Department, and the time off has helped him cope with the lingering effects of the shooting. Our marriage has helped too. Now that we've made the commitment, we're both beginning to heal, he from the physical disabilities that nearly crippled him, me from my crippling fears of intimacy. He'll probably get well before I do. I might get the hang of it after a couple more centuries of practice.

Laurel broke into my thoughts. "Why not ask Mrs. K?" she said. She poured lemon oil on a dust cloth and began to polish the wooden counter. Khat purred and arched against her arm, asking her to rub his ears.

I'd lost track of the conversation. "Ask Mrs. K what?"

"To make goodies for your Christmas tour guests. She could bake those terrific fruit cake cookies she just added to the menu, or the lemon thyme bars that everybody likes. She could use the kitchen here, and leave you free to concentrate on the laundry and the Christmas decorations." Laurel grinned. "And whatever other disasters crop up."

"Great idea," I said. "If she'll do it." Mrs. Kendall was a law unto herself. She might not be willing to accept an extra job. But it certainly wouldn't hurt to ask.

Not getting the attention he wanted from Laurel, Khat turned to me. I picked him up, scratched his ears, and began to survey the shop, which (unlike my house) was beautifully decorated for Christmas, with wooden bowls of clove-studded pomanders and potpourri, a tiny Christmas tree decorated with gingerbread cookies and popcorn-and-cranberry chains, and fresh green branches of rosemary everywhere.

But I wasn't admiring the Christmassy effect, I was checking to see what required special attention. Thyme and Seasons is small, which makes it easy to see at a glance what items we need to restock or reorder. Wooden shelves hold books, essential oils, and jars of bulk herbs, as well as the herb products I buy from local crafters: jellies, vinegars, seasoning blends, potpourris, soaps, and cosmetics. Baskets of dried strawflowers, poppy pods, statice, artemisia, and baby's breath fill the corners, along with pots and buckets of Christmas herbs: rosemary, ivy, holly, lavender, thyme, mistletoe. The stone walls and cypress-beamed ceiling are hung with garlic braids, red-pepper ristras, wreaths, and—

I frowned as a large bare space caught my eye. One entire wall—and the ceiling as well—should have been hung with holiday wreaths, our best-selling Christmas item.

"Hey, Laurel, we're sold out of wreaths again," I said. Just a day or so ago, when I'd checked, there'd been plenty. We buy from several local crafters, but the most popular holiday wreaths, garlands, and swags come from two sisters, Donna and Terry Fletcher, who use herbs and flowers gathered from the fields of their flower farm and dried in their barn.

Laurel nodded. "The Fletchers were supposed to bring in two dozen twenty-four-inch grapevine wreaths and a dozen swags yesterday, but Donna called to say they'd be late with the order." Laurel tied on her Thyme and Seasons apron and reached for the broom. "Things have been pretty hectic at the farm, apparently. Something's wrong with their van, and their dog got his leg caught in a trap."

"Oh no, not Max!" I exclaimed. Max is classic Border collie, intelligent, confident, and totally in charge of everything. "He's not—"

Laurel shook her head. "He'll be okay. The leg was pretty badly mangled, but Donna said the vet managed to save it. Apparently Aunt Velda is taking it worse than Max." She chuckled. "She's convinced that the Little Green Men set the trap in order to capture him. She thinks they want her back, too."

This is one of those things that shouldn't be funny, but it is. Aunt Velda was abducted by aliens two years ago, and she hasn't been the same since they sent her home on furlough. I don't know how Donna and Terry find the patience to deal with her various weirdnesses, but their aunt is their only living relative and they refuse to pack her off to a nursing home until it is absolutely necessary. It may be a while before that happens. Aunt Velda is pushing seventy-five, but she's as strong as she was at sixty and twice as stubborn. In spite of having been abducted by aliens and given the grand tour of the galaxy, there isn't much wrong with her.

"Why don't you give the farm a call and tell them I'll pick up the order," I suggested. Khat squirmed and I put him on the floor, where he stalked off in search of his catnip mouse. "I'm taking Brian to spend the night with his grandparents, near Seguin. It's not much out of my way." I glanced around. "We've sold almost all of the mistletoe, too, I see."

At Christmas, mistletoe is our best-selling herb, hands down. I buy it wholesale from a local supplier and Laurel and I package it in plastic bags tied with festive holiday ribbons. During the holiday season, we process hundreds of mail and telephone and E-mail orders for the plant, which grows in basketball-sized clumps on the hackberry and pecan trees in the wooded hills to the west of Pecan Springs. Once you've seen those fresh yellow-green leaves and translucent berries, glowing like huge pearls, you can understand why our mistletoe is so popular—especially when you compare it to the cello-wrapped, dried-out bundles of twigs and scrawny berries you find at the grocery store. Texas Hill Country mistletoe has a special charm, too. When you've been kissed under a sprig of it, you know you've been kissed.

"The mistletoe man was supposed to bring in three bags last week," Laurel said, "but he didn't show up." She wrinkled her nose. "Not a surprise, I guess. He's not very dependable."

Finding reliable suppliers is a challenge in any business, but especially when it comes to herbs. The weather is always a problem, of course. The growers who supply me with live plants and dried herbs have to cope with drought, flooding rains, and blazing sun. But some herbs—mistletoe, for instance—aren't cultivated, they're gathered from the wild. My mistletoe supplier is a guy named Carl Swenson, who brings in two or three garbage bags full of the stuff every week, starting in early November and continuing through the end of the holiday season. During this six-week period, we sell enough mistletoe to decorate every door from here to Dallas.

"Maybe we ought to give Swenson a call," I said.

"Good idea," Laurel replied, "except that we don't have his phone number. For all I know, he doesn't have a phone."

That wouldn't be a surprise. Swenson is a sour-faced man with a straggly beard and an Army private's burr haircut. He doesn't have a regular job and turns a blind eye to friendly gestures. I couldn't imagine that he had enough buddies, or even acquaintances, to warrant subscribing to Five Cent Sundays. I didn't know much about him except that he lived alone about twenty miles outside of town, and that he only came to Pecan Springs to get supplies. The Hill Country attracts people like that—people who value their privacy, elect a simple life, and try to make it without a regular job. Of course, it's not easy to live off the land, and I know only a few people who actually manage it. The Fletcher sisters, for instance, who earn a modest living from their flower farm. And Swenson, who makes some money selling mistletoe and a little more selling goats. They won't get rich, and maybe they're not even happy. But they're doing what they choose, and that's got to be worth something.

I glanced at my watch. "Oops. Ruby's waiting for me." We were supposed to go over the tearoom books together this morning and come up with a projection for the next couple of months' expenditures and income.

Laurel gave me an inquiring look. "What's been going on with Ruby the last couple of days? She seems, well . . . different. Distracted."

I shrugged. "You know Ruby. She's always distracted by one thing or another. Remember when she started doing past-life regression? She walked around in a trance for weeks. I never knew whether she had decided to live in this century, or was just here on a visit."

"I know, but this is different," Laurel said. "She isn't sick, is she?"

"Are you kidding?" I shook my head. "Ruby takes every vitamin and antioxidant known to humankind, plus she's got a positive attitude that won't quit. Her immune system must be totally germ-proof."

"Well, then, maybe she and Hark are planning something," Laurel replied. "She's acting like she has a secret."

"If she and Hark are up to something, she hasn't told me," I said. Hark Hibler is the editor of the Pecan Springs *Enterprise*. He and Ruby have been seeing one another off and on for five or six months, and I had been wondering if their relationship might be getting serious. But the paper keeps Hark pretty busy, and Ruby has been working overtime to get the new tearoom into operation.

"Then I must be imagining things," Laurel said. "If anything momentous was happening in Ruby's life—an engagement to Hark, for instance—you'd be the first to hear it."

"I don't know about that," I said, more soberly. "Ruby's been, well, distant lately, but I don't think it has anything to do with her private life." I shook my head. "Let me give you a piece of advice, Laurel. Don't go into business with your best friend—not if you value the friendship, that is. It's pretty hard to be easy and casual with somebody when both of you are nervous about the bottom line."

"I agree that Ruby hasn't been herself for the past week or so," Laurel said thoughtfully, "but I don't know that it has anything to do with your partnership. Both of you seem to be handling the business end of things pretty well, especially now that Mrs. K's in the kitchen. Maybe it's McQuaid."

"McQuaid?" I gave her a blank look.

"Yeah. When Ben and I got married, my best friend decided that there wasn't room for two significant others in my life and excused herself. I had a hard time convincing her that I could love both of them."

Laurel might have a point. Ruby had been in my life for a year or two before McQuaid came along and she'd never seemed jealous of the time I spent with him. In fact, she started encouraging me to make a commitment long before I was ready to think about it for myself. But it was certainly possible that she felt left out, now that I'd actually taken her advice and gotten married. I had to admit that we didn't get together as we used to, and when we did manage to steal an afternoon or an evening for ourselves, we usually spent it talking business—not exactly the best way to nurture a friendship.

Laurel was watching my face. "Why don't you just come right out and ask her what's wrong? It certainly can't hurt, and maybe she'll tell you what's on her mind."

Another one of Laurel's sound, practical ideas. "Thanks," I said. I headed for the door that connects my shop to the Crystal Cave. "Yell if you need me for anything."

The first thing you notice when you step into Ruby's shop is the scent. She burns a different incense every day, and the fragrances mix and mingle in an indescribable aroma that clings to the books and other items even after you've taken them home, a lingering reminder of your visit to the Crystal Cave. She also plays a different kind of music every day—Native American one day, whale songs another. Today it was Celtic, and the haunting melancholy of harp and flute filled the scented air.

Ruby doesn't open until ten, and early morning is a good time to catch her doing her housekeeping: restocking bookshelves, straightening merchandise, dusting the crystals and wind chimes, bringing her account books up to date. Today, I found her at the back of the shop, near the curtained dressing-room alcove where she hangs the hand-painted tops, gauze skirts, scarves, and crazy hats that her customers love. She was dressed in one of her usual eye-catching outfits—a slim, shapely ankle-length black silk skirt and a loose, cowl-necked velveteen top, painted with galaxies of glittering stars—and was standing in front of the full-length mirror, admiring her reflection. Since Ruby is six feet tall in her sandals, there's a lot of reflection to admire, especially when she puts on high heels and frizzes her orangey-red hair, adding several more inches to her already Ruby-esque stature.

I stood and watched, unobserved, while she turned in front of the mirror, running her hands over her breasts and down her hips, smoothing the velvety fabric against her body. As I watched, she did it again, and then again, the gesture of a woman who takes a healthy pleasure in the shape and feel of her body. But there was nothing sensuous or sexy or even graceful about the way Ruby was touching herself. Her movements were jerky and nervous, and in the mirror her face wore an odd, lost look, vulnerable and apprehensive. It was unnerving to see Ruby when she wasn't charging around like a dynamo, fueled by her usual self-confidence and whiz-bang kinetic energy.

"Hi," I said tentatively.

Ruby gave a startled yelp and whirled around. "China! I . . . I didn't see you." Her voice was scratchy and she blinked rapidly.

"You were busy seeing yourself," I said. "That's a very nice outfit." I stepped closer and stroked her velveteen sleeve. "Touchable, too."

Ruby jerked away as if my fingers were hot.

I dropped my hand. "Sorry."

The bright red in her cheeks contrasted oddly with her gingery freckles. "I thought I could have a little privacy," she muttered testily. "I didn't expect somebody to just walk in on me."

Privacy? That was *my* issue, not hers. And I had never thought I was just an ordinary "somebody" in her life.

"Maybe I'd better back up and start again," I said, stung. "This time I'll knock." I took two steps backward, thinking that maybe we should go back even further, to the point before we became partners. If Ruby was going to be annoyed by a little thing like my coming into the shop unannounced—

"No, that's okay," Ruby said. She took a deep breath and pasted on an artificial smile. "So what did you want to ask me about, China?"

"Excuse me," I said. "I thought we had planned to get together this morning and talk about money. You know— the green stuff that pays the bills and keeps the tearoom going. We were going to make some projections."

Ruby's phony smile slipped, and I saw the lost, vulnerable look again. "Oh, right. Money." She straightened her shoulders, repaired her smile, and became suddenly businesslike. "Well, then, come on. Let's get to it."

People may think Ruby is a flake, but one of the things I've learned since we became partners is that she has a hidden talent for organization. I followed her to her mini-office, which is tucked compactly behind a bookcase. She sat down at the small table she uses for a desk, and I perched on a stool, watching her. She took out the ledger and the checkbook and put them on the desk, and I saw to my surprise that her hands were trembling.

"Ruby," I said, "what's wrong?"

"Wrong?" She hesitated, then looked up at me, widening her eyes and offering that counterfeit smile. "Why does something have to be wrong? Can't a person take a good look at herself in the mirror without somebody giving her the third degree?"

"The third degree?" I gave a short laugh. "Is that what you think this is?" I worked as a criminal defense attorney before I moved to Pecan Springs, and I was pretty good at interrogating reluctant witnesses: The more disinclined they were to tell me what they knew, the more determined I was to get them to cough up their secrets—one way or another. Faced with the challenge of Ruby's denial, I could feel some of the old instincts kick in. Anyway, Laurel had encouraged me to find out what her problem was.

"Come on, Ruby," I coaxed. "I'm your partner, remember. And your friend. Something is gnawing at your insides and making you very upset. You know what you always tell me—if you don't let it out, it'll just grow bigger and bigger until it consumes you."

A look of something like fear crossed her face and she sucked in a deep breath as if I'd hit her. For a minute I thought she was going to fall apart; then she stiffened. "You have no right to cross-examine me," she snapped. "I'm not under oath. I don't have to bare my soul to you."

"I just hate to see you so disturbed about something you're not willing to share," I said truthfully. Ruby may be volatile, but she doesn't usually stew about things, or bury them deep inside her. When something's bothering her, she talks about it. And talks and talks and talks. I have never known her to keep a secret—especially her own—for more than about thirty seconds.

Ruby's mouth tightened and her green eyes blazed. She banged her fist on her desk. "So now this is all my fault!"

"Of course not," I said, trying to defuse her anger. "It's nobody's fault. It's just—" I stopped. I didn't like the way this conversation was going. It might be better to walk away and come back to it later. But if we didn't confront the problem now, the eventual eruption might be even worse.

"It has something to do with us, doesn't it?" I said quietly. "You're upset with me because I don't spend enough time with you now that McQuaid and I are married. And you wish we hadn't gone into business together."

She hesitated, biting her lip. I leaned forward, hoping that she was deciding to be honest with me. Instead, she crossed her arms over her chest and said, "If it had anything to do with our partnership, I'd let you know, wouldn't I?"

"That's a non-denial denial," I said. I was no longer coaxing or cajoling, I was commanding. "Be straight, Ruby. Tell me what's going on."

She rubbed her arms as though she were trying to get her circulation going. "You don't have to be confrontational. That's no way for a friend to act."

"I'm not being confrontational. But there's no use trying to deny it or sweep it under the rug. Something is on your mind, and it's affecting the way you act. Why, even Laurel has noticed."

"Laurel?" Her voice rose. "What business does *she* have poking around in my affairs?"

"Forget Laurel," I said. "Directly or indirectly, this thing has to do with *us*. I need to know what's going on."

Ruby uncrossed her arms and took a deep breath, drawing herself up with great dignity. "Do you really want to know what's going on?" She didn't give me time to answer. "What's going on is that you're pissed off. You're mad at me because for once, I won't let you intrude into my private life." She balled her hand into a fist and thumped the ledger. "I'm telling you, China, *back off*!" And with that, she burst into hot, angry tears.

Instinctively, I reached forward to put my arms around her, but she turned away, shaking her head hard, rejecting me. The back of her neck where the hair curled looked fragile and vulnerable, and I longed to comfort her. But all I could do was sit there, stunned by the violence of her weeping, by her fierce dismissal. It was hard not to be angry with her for behaving so irrationally.

After a moment, though, I began to calm down. Although I had no idea what Ruby's problem was, I could certainly understand her insistence on keeping it to herself. After all, personal privacy has always been important to me, and I have my own ways of fending off assaults on my personal space, of defending myself when circumstances seem to close in around me and threaten my security, even my identity. Right now, I could only respect Ruby's way of dealing with whatever was bothering her. The best thing I could do was leave.

Still, if I had known what was eating away at Ruby—if I could have reached past her anger and her fear to the dark and secret thing that was hidden deep within her—I would have folded her in my arms and held her until there were no more tears. And then I would have held her even harder, and never let her go. Never, ever. For the thought of life without Ruby is . . . well, unthinkable.

Chapter Two

In Norse mythology, the sun god Balder had become invulnerable because of the powerful spells of his mother, the goddess Freya. But Balder's vengeful enemy, Loki, discovered that Freya had neglected to protect her son from the mistletoe. He crafted a dart from the wood and gave it to the blind god, Heder, to use in a game. Heder threw the dart, missed the mark, and Balder was killed, an invincible hero slain by an insignificant twig thrown by a blind man.

China Bayles
"Mistletoe Magic"

Goldthwaite, a small town in Mills County in West Central Texas, is "the mistletoe capital of the world" because more than a million packages of mistletoe are sent out each Christmas season to cities all over North America.

V. M. Bryant, Jr.
"Why We Kiss Under the Mistletoe at Christmas,"
1991

Brian leaned over and turned up the heater of McQuaid's old blue pickup. "Are we there yet, Mom?"

"In a minute," I said, and turned a sharp corner from the blacktop highway onto a rocky road. I pointed to a sign that read Mistletoe Creek Flower Farm. "See that? It's not far now."

When McQuaid and I were married, Brian decided, without any prompting from his dad or me, to call me Mom—and I'm still new enough at this business of mothering to feel touched and a little surprised when he says the word. (Surprised, as in "Is he talking to me?") Brian's real mother, Sally, lives in New Orleans and occasionally sends inappropriate gifts, but that's the extent of her mothering. I'm mostly it for Brian, and he's definitely it for me. At forty-five, with the big hand of my biological clock approaching the witching hour, a child of my own is out of the question.

"Mistletoe Creek Flower Farm," Brian read out loud, peering out the window at the cheerful red-and-green painted sign, surrounded by yuccas and prickly pear cactus. He wiped the steamy window with his sleeve and peered at the sign through the light drizzle—a cold drizzle, since the temperature wasn't much above freezing. "What do they do in the winter when the flowers don't grow?"

"They make wreaths and things out of flowers they gathered in the summer," I replied. "And they take care of their greenhouses and fields. There's always a lot of work, even in the off-season." There are only a half-dozen houses along Comanche Road, which traces a twenty-mile loop off the main highway south of Pecan Springs, and there's so little traffic that the county doesn't bother to maintain it. We hadn't seen another vehicle since we pulled off Route 12.

The Texas Hill Country is a beautiful place in three seasons of the year—spring, summer, and fall. By early winter, though, the colors and textures of the landscape have subtly altered, and the Edwards Plateau, rising westward from I-35 and the lip of the Balcones Escarpment, can seem bleak and unwelcoming, especially on a rainy afternoon. The cedars keep their rich bronze-green color all year and the live oaks clutch their foliage possessively until March, but the early-winter pecans and hackberries and mesquite are only skeletal reminders of their luxuriant August selves, and the last ragged leaves on the post and shinnery oaks have already turned the color of mud. The witch grass and Indian grasses are brown and sere and even the all-weather prickly pear seems shriveled and naked among the chunks of limestone that litter the hills and ridges. Look close, and you might see a white-tailed deer among the willows along a creek; look closer and you can glimpse the wild turkeys stalking like elusive brown phantoms through the brush. But since this is hunting season, you'd better be on the lookout for the hunters, too. They shoot first and ask questions later, even if your name isn't Bambi and you're wearing Day-Glo orange. A significant proportion of the males in this area must be color-blind, judging from the number of accidental shootings reported during hunting season.

About two miles from the corner, on the left, we passed a rusty mailbox on which the name Swenson had once been painted. Nearby, along the old barbed wire fence that edged the road, stood a row of hackberry trees heavy with berry-laden mistletoe clumps. The plant grows from seeds that stick to the feet or beaks of birds. Under natural conditions, mistletoe germinates almost anywhere, but the parasite is successful only if the germinating seed can penetrate thin, tender bark. Its roots, or haustoria, eventually insinuate themselves into the tissue of the tree and suck out its nutrients. Mistletoe loves hackberry because the bark is rough and loose, and the seeds find a good purchase until they have grown securely into the tree. If Brian and I hadn't been pushed for time, I would have hopped out and harvested a couple of buckets of the stuff. As it was, I made a mental note. If Swenson didn't bring the promised order to the shop, Laurel and I would come out here to gather it. The land behind the fence might be his, but the right-of-way is public property, and these hackberry trees were fair game.

The Fletcher sisters' flower farm is located on a small patch of arable land along both sides of Mistletoe Creek, which eventually flows into the Pecan River west of New Braunfels. The soil in this bottomland is relatively deep, a silty loam that has to be amended with lots of organic matter before most flowering plants—other than our Texas natives—can tolerate its alkalinity. Decades ago, some optimistic farmer had aimed his mule and walking plow up and across the hillside, probably hoping to expand his precious few acres of arable land to plant cotton, the chief cash crop in those days. But cotton is long gone from Adams County, and the soil that was plowed along those rocky terraces quickly washed downhill. In the little valley along the creek, the Fletcher sisters are left with just space for their wood-frame house, a red barn, a couple of greenhouses and a long row of cold frames, and two narrow five-acre fields.

That's room enough, though, to produce a glorious three-season harvest of cut flowers—snapdragon, larkspur, delphiniums, phlox, sweet William, dianthus, painted daisies, sunflowers—which the sisters sell to the florist trade in Austin and San Antonio. Terry, Donna, Aunt Velda, and the two or three local teens who come to pick during the busiest month of the growing season have been known to pack and ship a thousand mixed bouquets in a week, hanging what doesn't sell in the barn to dry for the wreaths the sisters make during the autumn and winter. It's hot, hard, demanding work, but when the flowers are blooming, the customers are waiting, and you have bills to pay, the work is welcome. The Fletcher sisters have been doing it for six or seven years, since they bought the land from Carl Swenson, and they seem to be making a success out of a high-risk, long-odds venture. Personally, I admire their courage and stubbornness. You have to be gutsy to grow flowers for a living in Central Texas, where summer sizzles for six months and winter temperatures dive below zero just long enough to wipe out your best cash crop while scarcely inconveniencing the weeds.

We crossed the wooden bridge over Mistletoe Creek, and I pulled the truck to a stop in front of the house. As Brian and I climbed out, we were greeted by Max, who came bouncing down the path on a bandaged right front leg. The black-and-white Border collie was followed by a sturdy-looking woman in jeans, sweatshirt, and green down vest, a muffler around her neck and a yellow baseball cap pulled over her taffy-colored hair. Donna, the younger and more likable of the two sisters, is pushing thirty-five. She manages the sales and deals with the public while Terry handles production, but there's enough work on both sides so that they occasionally have to swap off. And after Aunt Velda came back from her tour around the galaxy and required more supervision, Donna has taken care of her, as well. She has her hands full.

"Hey, Max," I said, as Brian got down on his knees to pet the dog. "I heard you'd been eaten by a possum trap. What are you doing out and about?"

"Border collies don't know the meaning of the word bed-rest," Donna said. Her nose was red with the cold, and she swiped it on her sleeve. "Sorry you had to drive out all this way just to pick up those wreaths." She nodded ruefully at the brown van parked beside the barn, its innards spread over the ground and covered by a tarp. "Looks like we won't be driving Lizzie until Terry gets her repaired. We can use Aunt Velda's old Ford truck around the place, but we can't drive it on the highway. It doesn't have a current license plate."

I understood. Around here, people with big ranches hang onto their junky old pickups and use them to check on the cows, monitor fences, and haul hay and firewood. "No problem," I said. "Brian is spending the weekend with his grandparents in Seguin, and this stop was on our way."

Brian turned to me. "Is it okay if me 'n' Max go down to the creek and look for frogs?" He looked up at the sky, anticipating my objection. "It's stopped raining—almost."

"The creek's only a trickle along here," Donna said. "It's not deep enough for him to get into any trouble."

"Okay—but your grandmother won't be very happy if you show up at her house with wet shoes," I told Brian. "Stay out of the water." I watched as boy and dog trotted off toward the creek, thinking that it's a funny thing about boys. If you put a rake in their hands and shove them outdoors on a cold, drizzly day, they'll howl as if you're engaging in child abuse. But put them within fifty yards of a creek and they'll want to be in the water, no matter how cold it is.

"The wreaths are in the barn, boxed and ready to go," Donna said as we started up the path. "I'm sorry Terry isn't here. She borrowed a friend's car and went to San Antonio for parts for Lizzie. But there's coffee and pecan pie—

pecans from our very own trees. We had a great crop this year." She gave me a sidelong glance. "I hope you've got time for a slice before we load your truck."

"Pecan pie?" I said warmly. "You bet! I don't have to get Brian to his grandparents' until six."

The Fletchers' house is a small, tin-roofed Texas cottage, its board-and-batten wood siding painted gray, the window frames and trim a cheerful red. In the summer the walls are covered with moonflowers and morning glories and cardinal climber, but the first frost had killed the vines and nothing was left but a sinister brown tangle. We followed the gravel path around the corner of the house, sending three or four Rhode Island Reds scrambling out from under a waist-high rosemary bush. Lavender and sage grew along the wall, and the path was bordered by bright green curly parsley, which survives all but our hardest freezes. From the ragged look of the foliage, though, I guessed that it might not survive the chickens. I wondered if they were laying eggs with chlorophyll-colored yolks.

Donna opened the door and we went into the kitchen. A gas stove, sink, and refrigerator were arranged along one wall, and the room was heated by a cast-iron woodstove, which radiated a welcoming warmth. A gray tabby was curled on a blue braided rug beside the woodbox, which was piled high with split cedar. A pot of soup simmered on the back of the woodstove—pea soup with ham, judging from the rich, savory fragrance. Somebody had put out a few holiday decorations: a dried-flower swag over one doorway; a ribbon-tied bunch of mistletoe over another; a bowl of oranges, apples, and pine cones in the middle of the table, garnished with sprigs of fresh green rosemary.

"It's *cold* out there," Donna said, closing the door

against the chill wind and unwinding her muffler. "Bet it'll drop into the twenties tonight."

Of course, cold is relative. To a Yankee, today might seem like Indian summer. But our average December temperature is 50 degrees and we seldom have more than a couple of dozen days below freezing. In this part of Texas, that's cold enough—especially for those who have to keep their greenhouses warm.

I shrugged out of my denim jacket and Donna hung it on a peg beside her down vest and yellow cap. "Cream or sugar?" she asked.

"Both, please." I glanced around the room while Donna poured coffee and cut two generous slices of pie. The windows were curtained in red-checked gingham, there was a red-painted rocking chair beside the woodstove, and several of Donna's watercolors—she's a talented artist, among other things—hung on one wall.

I sat down at the table and Donna brought the coffee and pie. "Hey, this is super," I said, when I had tasted it.

The supreme test of a Texas cook is her pecan pie, and we all have a favorite recipe that we swear by. But the real secret is the nuts themselves, the fruit of the state tree of Texas. Fossilized remains of pecan trees have been found in lower Cretaceous formations to the north of Adams County, so it's safe to say that the trees and their nuts have been around for a lot longer than people. Indians gathered and ground them into a seasoning flour for their gruel and bread, or fermented them as a ceremonial intoxicant called *powcohicoria*. With an eye to future celebrations, they planted pecan groves around their campsites along creeks and rivers and near springs. By the late 1800's, pecans were worth five times as much as cotton, and after modern breeding techniques began to improve the size and quality of the nuts, they became a cash crop worth cultivating.

I savored the first bites of pie, then said, "Are you growing pecans for sale?" If they were, it could be a lucrative
sideline business.

"We're not, but from the size of this year's harvest, we
think we could," Donna said. "These nuts came from the
trees above Mistletoe Spring." She pulled out a chair and
sat down across from me. "The trees must be sixty or seventy years old, but you'd never believe how many nuts they
produce. A couple of hundred pounds a tree."

Now that she was sitting at the table, under the overhead
lamp, I could see that her tanned skin had a sallow cast and
her brown eyes were shadowed.

"Is everything going okay?" I asked casually.

Donna looked relieved, as if she were glad that I had
opened a difficult subject. "The business is going well," she
said, "but we've got a problem we don't know how to
handle." She shifted uncomfortably. "I wish Terry were
here, because she's the one who—" She stopped. "But I
guess I'd better ask you about it. With the holiday coming
up, there might not be another chance."

"Ask me what?"

"Terry and I need some legal advice. The problem is
getting out of hand. Every new day brings a—"

"I keep tellin' you," said a cracked voice, "it ain't our
problem. It's Carlos's."

With those words, Aunt Velda stumped into the room
and lowered herself into a chair at the table. She was wearing the same thing she'd had on the last time I was at the
Fletchers': patched Army pants and an old field jacket with
corporal's stripes on the sleeve. But today she had added a
rainbow-hued crocheted shawl and a green-and-purple knit
cap, pulled down to her ears so that her straggly gray

hair hung down beneath it like a dirty floor mop. A purple plastic badge was pinned to the cap, with *I Am a Klingon* emblazoned on it in silver letters.

"Hello, Aunt Velda," I said.

"What you doin' out today, China?" the old lady asked. "Colder'n a witch's tit out there." She fished in several pockets and pulled out a crumpled brown-paper cigarette, hand-rolled. She lit it and peered at me through the smoke. "You ain't seen Carlos hangin' around, have you?"

"His name isn't Carlos, Aunt Velda," Donna said patiently. "It's Carl. Carl Swenson. And I wish you wouldn't smoke in the kitchen." She got up and poured a cup of black coffee for her aunt.

"Pie, too," the old lady said imperiously, ignoring Donna's request. "Cut me a piece o' that pie, girl. Tastes better to me, remember'n' how mad Carlos got over them pecans." While Donna was cutting another piece, Aunt Velda leaned toward me and giggled, like a teenager sharing secrets. "Shoulda seen him, stompin' around an' wavin' his arms and yellin' 'bout them pecans. Boy howdy, that was funny! Made me bust out laughin' right to his face." She narrowed her pale blue eyes, blew out a stream of smoke, and sat back. "But that boy ain't long for this earth. I beamed his vectors up to the ship and they're fixin' to set a trap for him, like they did for Max. Only Carlos ain't as smart as Max. He won't git away. Where's that ashtray, Donna?"

"It wasn't the pecans he was yelling about, exactly," Donna said to me. With a resigned look, she put a metal ashtray in front of her aunt and sat down. "It was the land where the trees are located. Which is what Terry and I wanted to talk to you about."

"Too bad," I replied. "Nothing makes for hard feelings

like a land dispute." I sipped my coffee, thinking that Carl Swenson wasn't someone I'd like to provoke. He had a taut, tense look, like a man riding a nasty, reined-in temper. "How did the misunderstanding come about?"

Donna didn't answer right away, and Aunt Velda spoke up. "Reason Carlos has gotta go," she said grumpily, "is that he poisoned poor old Lizzie. Like this." She dumped three heaping spoonfuls of sugar into her cup and began to stir it with a violent motion, slopping the coffee onto the tablecloth.

"Carl Swenson put sugar in your gas tank?" I wasn't exactly surprised. There was something furtive about Swenson. He struck me as the kind of man who'd prefer to come at your back, rather than take you on face to face.

Donna put her hand over the old lady's. "We don't know for sure Carl did that," she said quickly. "We have no evidence."

"They saw him," Aunt Velda replied, still stirring, still slopping. "From the ship. When they re'lized how much trouble he wuz causin' down here, they decided to take him up there." She glanced pointedly toward the ceiling, chuckling slyly. "They got uses for dimwits like Carlos Swinberg, y'see. They put 'em to work scrubbin' decks and washin' dishes, stuff like that. Them big ships, they take a lot of housekeepin', which Klingons don't much cotton to."

"Aunt Velda," Donna said, "please don't—"

"Hey, China," the old lady said. "Did I ever tell you 'bout my trip across the galaxy? Eight years, two months, and sixteen days I wuz gone, and when I got back I wasn't one second older'n when I left. Didn't do no dishes, neither. They treated me like I wuz a queen. Had a window seat the whole trip, champagne, movies, even a pair of them little felt booties to keep m' tootsies warm."

Donna gave up trying to reason with her aunt and turned to me. "To answer your question, the disagreement came about because we didn't have the money for a land survey when we first bought this place from Carl."

"Had he owned it for a long time?"

"It was part of his family's ranch. This house used to be the ranch manager's house. We bought it and two hundred acres, on a contract of sale. Only a small part of the land is arable, though."

"Two hundred acres?" I was surprised. Their farm was bigger than I had thought. "How much did that leave Swenson?"

"Oh, five or six hundred acres, I guess. The way I understand it, the land had been in his family since before the First World War. They used to run cows, but that was a long while ago. Carl doesn't do any ranching. Just those goats."

"Goats." Aunt Velda made a rude noise. "All them goats is good for is to—"

"At the time we bought," Donna said, "we didn't have a lot of money. Terry had just—" She stopped, coloring, and looked away. "Aunt Velda loaned us the down payment. But there wasn't enough for the survey. We put it off until we could afford it."

I nodded. In a settled area, where every foot counts, the first thing a potential home buyer does is to get a professional survey to check out the boundary markers. It's not that formal in the country, where surveying is expensive. People tend to go by landmarks and old fences, and spend the money on a survey only when it becomes a problem.

"But we did really well last year, financially speaking," Donna went on. "We added anemones and *Ranunculus* as a winter cash crop, and that brought us some new accounts—a couple of big florists in San Antonio. We also tried painted daisies and scabiosa and *Ammi bisnaga*, which got to be over six feet tall, with really pretty lacy green foliage which is perfect for bouquets. We got the idea from Pamela and Frank Arnosky at Texas Specialty Cut Flowers, over in Blanco. They've been a big help, even though we're competitors." She stopped, and brought herself back to her subject. "Anyway, we did well enough to be able to pay off the note in a few months." She smiled dryly. "That was a big surprise for Carl. He probably figured all along we'd go broke and quit."

"Which would leave him with everything you'd already paid on the note, and the land to boot," I said. It was an old trick. Sell a few acres of marginal land to an unpromising buyer; then, when he fails to make the payments, call the note and take back the land. It doesn't happen so much anymore because banks and other lending institutions have gotten into the act, but there are parcels of land around Pecan Springs that have been sold a half-dozen times and still belong to the same guy. Swenson had probably needed money, and when the Fletcher sisters came along with their goofy idea of growing and selling flowers, he'd seen an easy mark.

Donna stirred her coffee. "But what jolted him even more was what happened when we got the property surveyed, three months ago. When we bought the place, he told us that the boundary line was twenty yards below Mistletoe Spring, along the old fence. Well, it turns out to be forty yards *above* the spring, which takes in the whole top of the ridge, including the pecan grove. Of course, he didn't believe it, so he hired his own surveyor, who put the line in the same place." She bit her lip, remembering his reaction. "He was really mad about it. He swore he was going to get the whole farm back—which of course he can't do, as long as we're making our payments."

Aunt Velda cackled. "Mad? You bet yer boobies he was mad! Why, he came roarin' over here like a bull that's had his nuts cut." Donna shook her head at her aunt's language, but the old lady paid no attention. "That don't matter none, though," she added, patting Donna's hand comfortingly. "He'll forget all about it when they hoist his ass up to the ship and put him to work."

"I suppose the spring is valuable," I hazarded, beginning to see why Swenson might have been angry. In Texas, a source of water can be worth a great deal of money, and conflicts over water can be as fierce as those over oil.

"It's even more valuable now that we've cleaned it out," Donna replied. "Some years back, one of the Swensons apparently decided to plug Mistletoe Spring in order to increase the flow to a spring on the other side of the ridge, closer to their house. They used that spring for their main water supply, and Carl uses it to water his goats."

"Goats," Aunt Velda remarked disgustedly. "Filthy, smelly critters. Look at all the damage they caused. Ask me, ain't good for nothin' but cabrito."

"Damage?" I asked.

"Swenson's goats have been getting through the fence and onto our property lately," Donna said. "And you know how goats are—they'll eat anything. Fruit trees, flowers, even the laundry on the line."

Aunt Velda brightened. "Hey, I'll bet they ain't never tasted cabrito up there on the ship. I could show 'em how my husband Louie used ta fix it. He'd git him a young white kid—the white ones wuz best, he allus said—and take it out under the tree and cut its throat, and when the blood all drained out, he'd take his knife and—"

"Thank you, Aunt Velda," Donna said firmly. "We can imagine the rest." To me, she said, "Anyway, somebody had dumped a big load of rocks and dirt down the spring to choke off the flow, then piled on a ton of junk—an old air conditioner, a washing machine, a mile of broken plastic pipe, some wooden pallets, stuff like that. Terry and I pulled it all out and hauled the debris to a gully we've been wanting to fill in."

"I drove," Aunt Velda said proudly. "Drove my old Ford truck and left the totin' and haulin' to the young ones." She picked up her cup and sipped her coffee reminiscently. "I like to drive. Don't git the chance much lately, though, since I got back from the ship." She frowned at Donna. "The girls don't let me out much. They don't keep up the license on my truck, neither."

Donna went on with her story. "When we got the spring cleaned out, a lot more water started flowing into Mistletoe Creek. In fact, there's so much water that we're using the creek to irrigate. Which means we can put another five acres under cultivation next spring, maybe more." She paused. "Oh, and there are the arrowheads, too."

"Arrowheads?"

"When we were cleaning out the spring, we found a cache of over a hundred Indian arrowheads."

"*I* found it," Aunt Velda said. "Tell it like it is, girl. What's more, I aim to git back up there and find me some more, quick as I can. I aim to find that cave again, too. There wuz lots more arrowheads in the cave."

Donna nodded. "Aunt Velda's the one who found the arrowheads. Terry says they might be really valuable."

Terry was right. Collectors pay hundreds of dollars for certain well-made arrowheads. And the find signaled the possibility that Mistletoe Spring was an archeological site, which could make it a treasure trove of ancient artifacts. The Fletcher property could prove very valuable—another reason for Swenson to lose his temper.

But something else had occurred to me. "What happened to the spring on the other side of the ridge when you un-plugged Mistletoe Spring?" I asked.

Donna sighed. "I'm afraid that's the real problem. The other spring more or less stopped flowing. There's enough for the house, but—"

"But Bozo's goats ain't got no water," the old woman said cheerily. She took a small wooden box from the pocket of her jacket and put it on the table. "D'ja ever meet Louie?" Louie had been Velda's brother.

"Not now, Aunt Velda," Donna said hastily, but it was too late. The old lady lifted the lid and the box began to play the first few bars of "The Eyes of Texas Are Upon You."

Aunt Velda gazed fondly into the box. "There he is," she said. "Ain't he fine?" She sifted the gray grit through her fingers. "O' course, there wuz more of him once, but I left some here and there. On Mars and Jupiter. Venus too. He allus liked Venus."

"I'm sure," I said, smiling. "Thank you for letting me have a look."

Satisfied, Aunt Velda put the lid back on Louie's box and the tune stopped abruptly.

"If Swenson needs the water for his livestock," I said to Donna, "you could sell him some."

"We told him we'd be glad to let him run a pipe from Mistletoe Spring to his stock tank. All we wanted was a nominal fee—a dollar a year, say—that would acknowl-edge our ownership. But that only seemed to make him angrier." Donna made a face. "Anyway, the water isn't the only issue. It's the pecan trees, too. Apparently, his father grafted those pecans back in the twenties, with some sort of special stock. And of course, he's always gathered the mistletoe there. I guess he figures we're going to cut it and sell it ourselves."

"You bet we are," Aunt Velda said with satisfaction. She gave me a commanding look. "Next year, you're gonna buy ever' last bit of your mistletoe from us, y'hear?"

"Sounds like a complicated situation," I said. "I wonder how Swenson managed to misplace the boundary line."

"The surveyor said it was because the land is so broken and hilly along that ridge," Donna replied. "I wish we could negotiate some sort of deal," she added unhappily, "but Carl won't listen to reason. He swore he was going to make our lives so miserable that we'd be glad to turn the place back over to him. And now we think he's resorting to vandalism. First there were the goats, which practically destroyed our new peach trees, and the possum trap that Max got into, which was set on our property. Then there was the sugar in Lizzie's gas tank, which has caused no end of trouble. And last week, somebody slashed the plastic covering on the small greenhouse, where we had some plug trays filled with campanula seedlings. We can repair the greenhouse, but it's way too late in the year to reseed those plants. They were a big investment—the seed isn't cheap." She rubbed her forehead with her fingers. "Terry and I have been standing watch at night, but we can't keep that up forever. You're a lawyer, China—we were hoping that you could tell us how to put an end to this."

It's true that I'm still a lawyer. I've been careful to keep my options open by maintaining my membership in the Texas Bar. But I haven't been in a courtroom since I came to Pecan Springs, and I'm not ready to start now. Still, I could see that the Fletcher sisters had a problem and I wanted to help them if I could. I admire women for whom the impossible is all in a day's work.

Aunt Velda leaned over and stroked Donna's blue-jeaned thigh. "I keep tellin' you, dear," she said comfortingly, "Carlos Swansong is history. You'll see—they're gonna take care of him. Next thing he knows, he'll be up there cleaning out them Klingon latrines."

"It doesn't sound as if you have the evidence to get Swenson charged with vandalism," I said, "but you might be able to make a stalking charge stick. You'd have to testify that on at least one occasion he threatened, either by his actions or his words, to inflict injury on you, your family, or your property. Were there any witnesses to his temper tantrum?"

"Just Aunt Velda and me," Donna said. She hesitated. "Would Aunt Velda have to testify in court?"

I frowned. The case would stand a better chance if the old lady could testify, but she'd make a terrible witness. Anyway, stalking was only a Class B misdemeanor, which at best would get Swenson a two-thousand-dollar fine, maybe a few weeks in jail. Or maybe not, depending on the judge.

"How about an alarm system?" I asked. "Or maybe you could hire somebody to keep an eye on the place at night."

"We've already thought of an alarm," Donna said, "but we don't have that kind of money. And both of us agree that even if we could afford a security guard, we don't want one. We value our privacy. And who wants to live in an armed camp?"

I could understand that. "Well, my best advice is to document everything," I said. "Every event that happens, every word he says to you. Take your flash camera when you stand watch at night. If you could get a picture of him doing his dirty work, he could be charged with criminal mischief. That could be a first-degree felony, depending on the amount of the damage. It would put him out of circulation for a while."

Donna looked crestfallen, and I knew she hoped I'd come up with something more sure-fire. "I'll talk it over with Sheriff Blackwell," I added. "He's a good friend of my husband's, and it happens that he's coming over for dinner tonight." *My husband.* Like "Mom," the words had the power to jolt me into the sudden awareness that my life had radically changed.

"Is Mike still the Pecan Springs police chief?" Donna asked.

I shook my head. "He was just filling in until the City Council hired a new chief." McQuaid had left Houston Homicide some years before, earned a Ph.D., and joined the CTSU faculty. He was a natural for the job of interim police chief, and had been the Council's first choice for the permanent position. But he took himself out of the running when our friend Sheila Dawson applied for the job, and was as glad as I was when she got it—or at least, that's what he told me. "Chief Dawson will be there tonight too," I added. McQuaid and I tried to get together with Sheila and Blackie at least one Saturday night a month. "Maybe the four of us will be able to come up with an answer to your problem."

"I keep tellin' you," Aunt Velda said jovially. She had taken off her Klingon badge and was polishing it on her sleeve. "Carlos ain't no problem. My friends upstairs'll take care of him."

CHAPTER THREE

The ancient Italian opinion that mistletoe extinguishes fire appears to be shared by Swedish peasants, who hang up bunches of oak-mistletoe on the ceilings of their rooms as a protection against harm in general and conflagration in particular.

Sir James George Frazer
The Golden Bough

Sitting under the mistletoe
(Pale green, fairy mistletoe)
One last candle burning low,
All the sleepy dancers gone,
Just one candle burning on.
Shadows lurking everywhere:
Someone came and kissed me there.

Walter de la Mare

Twilight was falling and Donna and I had just finished loading the wreath boxes into the truck when Terry drove in. She climbed out of the borrowed car and came toward us.

"Hello, China," she said, hardly smiling.

If you didn't already know, you'd never guess that Donna and Terry are sisters. Donna is slender and decorative, while Terry looks as if she'd be more at home behind the wheel of a tractor-trailer rig. If this had been summer, the blue heart tattoo on her right bicep would've been visible, but she was wearing a corduroy jacket zipped to her chin, and a black cowboy hat, cocked at a combative angle. She has a tough face, and she doesn't smile easily. She's not a woman you'd want to cross.

"Donna told me that you've got a problem with Lizzie," I said, gesturing toward the old brown van, which was parked alongside a red Ford pickup that sagged in the right rear. The truck's passenger-side door was slightly concave and the broken window was covered with a taped-on piece of cardboard.

Terry's strong mouth tightened. "Yeah. Swenson dumped sugar in the tank, and it gummed up everything. Looks like I'll have to pull the head and replace the valves. Maybe the carburetor, too. We'd get a new van if we weren't trying to pay off the note on this place."

"We don't *know* it was Swenson," Donna said in a nervous tone.

"Don't be a fool, Donna," Terry said sharply. "Who else would it be? Auntie's Klingons?" She slanted a glance at me. "Donna give you a rundown on the situation?"

I nodded. "I suggested taking a flash camera with you when you go on watch at night. You might get enough evidence to stick him with felony criminal mischief. Another alternative is to try for a restraining order. That way, if he comes around you can call—"

"Call who?" Terry asked curtly. "The county mounties don't cruise out here. By the time the sheriff shows up, the damage will be done. Anyway, we don't want people messing around. This is our place, and it's private." She grinned mirthlessly. "But I've got a shotgun. That'll take care of the bastard, and we won't have to wait for the law to get around to it."

Donna gave me an anxious glance. "She doesn't mean that," she said, in a half-whisper. "She's just talking big. She does that when she gets angry."

"The hell I don't!" Terry exploded angrily. "Crissakes, Donna, wake up and face facts! Swenson wants us off the place, and he's willing to do whatever it takes to make that happen. If we let him get away with this, we're in for a lot worse. How would you like to wake up one night and find the barn on fire? Or the house? If that bastard comes on our land and starts damaging our property, I've got a right to shoot him. Isn't that so, China?"

"Under certain conditions," I said carefully, wishing she hadn't put me on the spot. When it comes to using deadly force to protect yourself and your property, Texas is more permissive than most other states, and juries often give defendants the benefit of the doubt. I cleared my throat. "If Swenson came into your house with the intent of harming you or vandalizing your property, the court would probably hold that you were justified in shooting him, especially if he were armed." I gave her a warning glance. "But if you shoot an unarmed trespasser who presents no threat—"

"Oh, he presents a threat, all right," Terry growled. She shook her head. "You can forget that camera shit. I'll take care of Carl Swenson."

And with that, she turned on her heel and strode off.

"So what did you say after she said that?" McQuaid asked, leaning his elbows on the kitchen table. He held out his dessert plate. "I'll have another piece of your great cheese-cake."

I pushed back my chair and stood up. "It's not my cheesecake," I said. "Mrs. Kendall made it. We didn't sell all of it today, so I brought home what was left. Pretty good, huh?"

"Don't change the subject, China," Blackie Blackwell said. "I want to hear what an officer of the court said when this jolly green giant threatened to use her shotgun on Carl Swenson."

"Terry isn't a giant," I retorted, going to the kitchen counter. "She's just . . . well, strong. And full of righteous indignation."

"I guess I'm not surprised to hear that they're having trouble with Carl Swenson," Sheila Dawson said. "He's a weirdo. I ran into him at Bean's a couple of weeks ago, where he was selling some goats to Bob." Bob Godwin, the owner of Bean's Bar & Grill, raises goats for a hobby. "He and Bob got into a major disagreement over who owed what, and Bob ordered him out of the place. Swenson almost slammed the door off the hinges." She looked up at me. "If you're cutting more cheesecake, I'll take a slice."

"While you're up, I'll have some too," Blackie said. "That cook of yours can make cheesecake for me any day of the week."

"Swenson's not all that weird," McQuaid said, as I handed out second helpings. "The Hill Country is full of loners like him. They build themselves a cabin or get a little house trailer, buy a few goats and a four-wheel drive, and come to town when they're low on supplies."

"Or crave female company," Blackie said.

Sheila made a face. "That might not be easy for Swenson. He smells. Essence of goat."

"There you go, Sheriff," McQuaid said. "You've got nothing to worry about."

We all laughed comfortably. Sheila and Blackie, who are both in law enforcement, seem to be a perfect match. Blackie is a third-generation lawman—a square-shouldered, square-jawed, laconic man with a lot of savvy, the kind of guy you wouldn't mind having around if you found yourself in a jam. Sheila spent several years as a street cop before she took the job of chief of security at CTSU. Now she's the chief of police for Pecan Springs, a job she took over from McQuaid a couple of months ago, after she solved Edgar Coleman's murder (with a little help from Ruby and me). Sheila—her friends call her Smart Cookie—has got to be the most striking police chief in the entire United States. She's tall and blond, with a delicate, willowy grace that would make her look at home in an evening gown at the Junior League Ball. But looks are deceiving. She's tough and she don't take no sass, as we say around here.

"I'm afraid you guys aren't taking this very seriously," I said, going back to the subject. I looked across the table at McQuaid and Blackie. "We're talking about two women and their elderly aunt being harassed by a man who told them he intends to run them off their land. You don't want Terry to ventilate Swenson's backside with a load of double-O buckshot, do you?"

"I suppose you advised them to document all their interactions with this guy," McQuaid said.

"You bet," I said emphatically.

"How about an alarm system?" Sheila suggested. She frowned. "Although that won't work if they've got livestock. Any movement triggers the alarm."

"Do they have a dog?" Blackie asked.

"Didn't I tell you about that?" I replied. "Somebody set a trap that nearly took off his leg. On *their* property."

"Burglar's rule number one," Sheila said. "Disable the dog."

"Tell them they need to file for a peace bond," McQuaid advised. "They might not get it, but it'll put the situation on record. Then all they have to do is get evidence that Swenson is behind the vandalism."

"Easier said than done," I replied. "I just hope the first piece of evidence isn't a dead body."

While the guys did the dishes and cleaned up the kitchen, Sheila and I went into the living room to settle down in front of the fire with a glass of apple brandy, Fannie Couch's annual holiday gift to all her friends. Fannie starts making it in October, as soon as she can find Granny Smith apples at the grocery, and by Christmas, it's tasty and mildly alcoholic.

"You don't think Terry would actually shoot Swenson, do you?" Sheila asked. She sat down on the sofa and propped her boots up on the old pine carpenter's chest we use for a coffee table. Not just any boots, either, but trim suede boots that were the perfect complement to her fawn-colored stirrup pants and matching bulky knit sweater.

"I doubt it," I said, poking the fire. "But they've been harassed for weeks, they're probably not getting enough sleep, and their nerves are raw. You can't tell what might happen in a situation like that, especially if Swenson goes poking around there after dark." I took a split oak log out of the copper wash boiler that serves as our woodbox and put it on the fire. "It's too bad the law can't intervene before something happens, rather than waiting until somebody turns up dead. If you ask me, Blackie has probable cause to talk to Swenson about the vandalism at the farm."

"What about evidence?" Sheila asked dryly.

I straightened. "What about articulable suspicion?"

Sheila arched both eyebrows. "China, I'm surprised at you. You're the one who's always talking about the need to preserve privacy and to keep the government out of people's business."

I sat down in McQuaid's big leather chair and took a sip of brandy. "I know," I said, "but—"

"But what? You really don't want Blackie to bang on Swenson's door and order him to stay away from the farm—which he still owns, by the way, until the sisters pay off the note. And you certainly don't want him to send one of his deputies out there to confiscate Terry's shotgun. You'd be the first to start yelling police harassment." She grinned. "Why, you'd probably be standing in line to offer your legal services in a lawsuit against the sheriff's office."

"That's the old me," I said. "I'm a little more mellow these days. But you're right—I don't like the idea of the cops interfering. And Terry isn't keen on getting the law involved either." I paused. "It strikes me that this is a lot like a stalking case, Smart Cookie. As a law-enforcement officer, what do you do when a woman comes to you and accuses her former boyfriend of harassing her? You know, the usual little things." I gave her an ironic look. "Cutting her phone line, slashing her tires, entering her house when she's at work. Do you tell her to be cool, be calm, and come back to see you after he's taken a shot at her? Or do you tell her to go out and get herself a hungry rottweiler and a 9mm handgun?"

"Well . . ." Sheila shifted uncomfortably. "It's a problem. You may see something coming but you don't always have the power to stop it. The ex-boyfriend is innocent until he's proven guilty. The Fletcher sisters don't have any proof that Swenson is their vandal. And everybody's got a right to privacy."

"Seems like privacy is the issue of the week." I laughed shortly. "Ruby brought it up this morning when I tried to get her to tell me what was on her mind."

Sheila drained her glass and put it down on the end table, her brow furrowed. "I'm glad you mentioned that, China. I'm really worried about Ruby. We were supposed to have lunch together last Monday, but she didn't show up. I called her, but she wasn't at home or at the shop."

"She's closed on Mondays," I said.

"Right. It turned out that she'd gone to Austin and forgotten all about our lunch. We rescheduled for a couple of days later, but she called and canceled. And then, when I went over to the shop this afternoon to ask her if she'd like to spend Christmas Eve together, she said she wasn't making any plans for the holiday. She said she might not be here."

I sat up straight. "Might not be here? But Christmas is her favorite holiday!" Ruby usually hosts an early December tree-decorating party for her friends, organizes a carolsing for the kids on her block, and roasts a couple of Christmas Day turkeys for her entire family (two grownup daughters, three sisters, mother, and a startling assortment of aunts, uncles, nieces, nephews, and cousins). "I've been at her house when she cooked for twenty-seven people and we had to eat in shifts," I added. "She may be a flake who reads the stars and consults the spirits, but she's passionate about the holidays. She looks forward to Christmas all year long. There's no way she'd miss it."

Sheila nodded. "That's what I thought. I pushed her a

little, but her last word on the subject was 'Bug off,' so I did. She seemed awfully jittery, as if she was under a lot of stress." Sheila chewed on her upper lip. "Which isn't like Ruby at all, you know. She's usually very laid-back."

"I know," I said. "It's a big mystery. But thanks for telling me. Now I know it isn't something I've done."

"She's been acting weird to you, too?" Sheila asked, surprised.

"Very. I thought it might have something to do with the partnership, or maybe it was McQuaid and me." I sighed. "I certainly don't intend for her to feel left out, but with the shop and the tearoom and Brian and McQuaid, there hasn't been much time left over. I thought maybe she was feeling neglected."

"I know how that is," Sheila said ruefully. "The chief's job is so demanding that I'm ready to crawl into bed at nine o'clock. You and Ruby are the only friends I have left—and I don't see you often enough." She paused. "Maybe Ruby's feeling overworked and wants to take some time off. Are things going okay with the new tearoom?"

"I think so. The remodeling took longer and cost more than we thought. And we had to experiment a good deal in the first month or so, trying to get the menus right and the costs down. But then Mrs. Kendall showed up, just when we needed an experienced cook, and she had a bushel of great ideas. When she took over the kitchen, everything clicked into place." I lifted the brandy bottle inquiringly, and Sheila held out her glass for a refill.

"I've been wondering if Ruby might be upset about Hark," Sheila said, while I poured.

"That occurred to me, too," I said. "But I don't know what the problem could be. They seem to get along together—which has sort of surprised me. They're not at all alike."

"I can hazard a guess at the problem," Sheila said. "Hark's been seeing Lynn Hughes lately."

"Lynn Hughes!" I squawked. "Why, she's hardly out of puberty!" Lynn works in Charlie Lipman's law office. She's a sweet young thing, with the accent on "young." She just finished her senior year at CTSU in June.

"Well, she's a little older than that," Sheila said with a smile. "She's smart, as well as pretty. And since Hark lost all that weight, he's very nice-looking. I can see the attraction."

I poured another glass for myself. "How do you know they're dating?"

"I've run into them at lunch twice, and last weekend, Blackie and I saw them at Crandall's. They were, shall we say, tête à tête? Very cozy."

"Crandall's," I muttered. It's a fancy new restaurant with an elegant ambiance and a big-ticket menu, the kind of place you take someone you want to impress. "Poor Ruby."

"So you think that's Ruby's problem?" Sheila asked worriedly. "She and Hark have broken up, and she's eating her heart out?"

"It makes sense. She's dated Hark longer than anybody else since her divorce." I frowned. "But why hasn't she told us? Why is she making such a big deal about keeping it secret?"

"Maybe her pride is hurt," Sheila said. "Lynn is . . . well, young. Even if Ruby's not that upset about losing Hark, it might be a real blow to her self-esteem."

"You'd think the guy would have better sense." I shook my head sadly. "Poor Ruby," I said again. "She's always worked so hard to keep her own balance and not let outside forces send her into a tailspin."

"She must love Hark more than we guessed," Sheila said. "She probably sees his interest in Lynn as a terrible betrayal. I can understand that."

I nodded, agreeing. Yes, I could understand that feeling, too. I'd been there myself.

McQuaid, clad only in T-shirt and jockey shorts, rinsed toothpaste out of his mouth and glanced at me in the bathroom mirror. "What does Hark see in Lynn Hughes?" He repeated my question with an amused smile and an arch of one black brow. "I should think that would be obvious."

"But Hark is old enough to be her father," I said, around my toothbrush.

He dried his hands on a towel. "So what? Lots of older guys get their heads turned by young women." He colored slightly and looked away.

Almost a year ago now, McQuaid had had a brief affair with a younger woman, a Texas Ranger. It caused me enormous pain at the time, but after all the trauma of the months following the affair—McQuaid's getting shot, his difficult recovery, the unhappy accident in a barn that laid me up for a couple of months—it has assumed a place of minor significance in our relationship. You don't linger on something like that. You accept it and get on with your life, and after a while you look up and see that what was once a vast and ugly crater in the green landscape of your experience isn't even visible any longer. Ruby would find that to be true, too—but in the meantime, there was still the hurt.

McQuaid put a still-wet hand on my shoulder. "What I

mean is," he said in an explanatory tone, "that maybe Ruby isn't . . . well, paying enough attention to him. After all, she's been pretty busy with the new tearoom."

I rolled my eyes, not believing what I'd just heard. "That's it," I said disgustedly. "Blame the victim." I rinsed out my mouth and made a face at him in the mirror. "Are you going to talk to Hark?"

McQuaid stepped back and leaned against the door, playing dumb. "Talk to Hark? What about?" He had stripped off his shirt, and I could see the jagged scars, reminders of the shooting.

"What about!" I whirled. "About Ruby, that's what! She's so upset that she can't even share her feelings with her best friend. Hark needs to know how much pain and suffering he's causing."

McQuaid shook his head. "It's none of our business, China," he said quietly. "Whatever's going on, it's a private matter. Stay out of it."

"But she's my best friend!"

"Ruby's an adult. She's a strong woman. She can handle whatever comes her way."

"You haven't seen her," I said grimly. "You don't know."

"I just know that it's not our business. Anyway, Hark may not be the problem." McQuaid paused. "Ruby could be upset about Wade coming back to Pecan Springs."

"Wade? Wade Wilcox?" He was Ruby's ex, whom she divorced nearly ten years ago. It had been an acrimonious divorce, full of bitter arguments about money and property. The last I'd heard, Wade was living it up in Denver with the young woman for whom he'd left Ruby. That memory brought me up short. Hark Hibler wasn't the first man who had betrayed Ruby for a younger woman—she had been there before, too. "What's he doing back here?"

"Starting a new business."

I frowned suspiciously. "What kind of business?" I've only met Wade Wilcox once or twice, but I've got him pegged as a troublemaker. Maybe he'd heard about Ruby's lottery win and thought he could get some money out of her. Maybe he was trying to drag her into one of his shady deals, like the old days, when he'd tangled her up in thousands of dollars of debt. Maybe—

"How should I know what kind of business Wade's in?" McQuaid asked. "He's not exactly my kind of guy." He turned and limped into the bedroom.

I watched him as he went, my suspicions of Wade Wilcox submerged in the sweet relief and deep gratitude I always feel when I see McQuaid walk without his canes. Given the uncertainty of the doctors' prognosis, his steady recovery has seemed almost miraculous, as if we are the special beneficiaries of some unimaginable grace. But while I don't discount miracles, I doubt that the doctors took McQuaid's willpower and determination into account when they said that it wasn't likely he'd ever walk again. They didn't take into account the fact that he had spent three grueling years working for the quarterback slot at the University of Texas, or that the white scar that runs diagonally across his forehead was left by a crack-crazy doper who slashed him with a knife during an arrest. He'd heard the doctors' gloomy prognosis as a challenge, and while there were setbacks—times when he was so despondent that he could only sit and stare out the window—the challenge fired his determination. He's regained his strength to the point where he can do almost everything he did before, almost as well. Some things, I think, he does even better, but I may be prejudiced.

He was stretched out in our brass bed, the sheet pulled up to his chin. His T-shirt and jockey shorts were on the floor beside the bed, as usual. I went to my dresser, got my hairbrush, and began brushing my hair in front of the round antique mirror his parents gave us for a wedding present. A hundred strokes will probably never do much for the wide streak of gray at my temple, but it's a bedtime ritual I can't do without. Then I found my night lotion—some creamy, light herbal stuff a friend made for me—and began smoothing it onto my face. Then—

"Aren't you coming to bed?" McQuaid asked.

I put the cap on the lotion. "What? Are we in a hurry?" I opened the top drawer of the dresser, took out my orange Hook 'Em Horns nightshirt, and started to pull it over my head.

"You won't need that," McQuaid said. He gave me a sly look and pointed over his head. "See?" There was something thumbtacked to the ceiling. A little knot of shriveled green leaves sporting one or two white berries, tied with a droopy red ribbon.

I squinted. "It must be mistletoe," I said. Of course, that was just a guess. It was clearly not Texas mistletoe, or if it was, it wasn't fresh. But it's the thought that counts, right?

"I saw it in the grocery store when I bought the wine for dinner, all done up in a little plastic box." McQuaid was clearly pleased with himself. "I figured you'd like it." He threw back the blanket with a lecherous grin. "Come on, China, climb in. I'm going to kiss you all over."

"Yum," I said, and dropped the nightshirt.

One thing quickly led to another, and kissing wasn't the only thing we did. My husband's hands moved over my body, and I found myself eager for his touch, his hard mouth, his urgent hunger. My breath deepened with his energy, my heart quickened with his kiss. Shifting slightly, we found the movements we needed to fit each other's rhythms in a way that was deep and perfect and fulfilling, as if we had been practicing this lovemaking all our lives.

A little later, McQuaid stirred. "If I'd known marriage could be like this," he said sleepily, "we'd have done it a long time ago. Remind me—why did we put it off?"

"One of us was silly and stubborn," I said.

"Yeah, right." He nuzzled me. "We won't name any names. 'Night, babe."

I shifted so that I could see his face. His lashes were long and dark against his tanned cheek. Gently, I traced the curve of his mouth, set in a face that was at once familiar and yet strange. The face of my husband.

"Good night." I looked up at the scrawny little clump of dried leaves, his gift to me. "Thank you for thinking of the mistletoe," I added. "It's sweet."

"I knew it would turn you on," he said, and flung his arm across me.

The moon came out from under a cloud and bathed the mistletoe in a silvery glow, making it look almost pretty. "In Sweden, they used to hang mistletoe from the ceiling to protect against fires caused by lightning," I said. "They had the idea that mistletoe was produced by lightning, because it grows in trees and never touches the ground. *Ergo*, it could serve as a lightning-conductor. If a bolt of lightning hit the house, it would strike the mistletoe and the house itself would be protected." I smiled, appreciating this odd bit of folk-logic and glad to be able to share it. "Isn't that fascinating?"

I was answered by a gentle snore. McQuaid was sound asleep.

CHAPTER FOUR

In the Victorian language of flowers, mistletoe symbolized "I overcome everything"; "I surmount difficulties"; "I rise above all."

Kathleen Gips
Flora's Dictionary

In Northern Italy, mistletoe is thought to grow where a tree has been struck by lightning. It can be destroyed by neither fire nor water, and it communicates its indestructibility to the oak on which it grows.

Italian folklore

When McQuaid and I were married, I decided to stop opening the shop on Sunday afternoons, to give myself a little more free time. Since we're not open on Mondays either, I now have two full days to get more or less caught up on the necessities of life: sleeping, shopping, and the laundry. On this particular Sunday, I also had to begin decorating for the Christmas Tour, an event which was looming like a black cloud over the weekend ahead.

Our rambling old five-bedroom Victorian has a wide veranda, a large fireplace, and a dignified staircase. I could keep people from going up to the second floor by putting a red rope across the stairway. I could put the large Christmas tree in the corner by the living-room fireplace, where we had it last year, and a tabletop tree in the dining room, along with a bowl of glass ornaments and holiday cookies and a three-tiered silver epagier piled with fruit and pine cones. I could put potted poinsettias on the floor, swags on the banister, a couple of rosemary topiaries in the hallway, and wreaths in all the windows. Of course! Wreaths and swags—and I had plenty of those, still in boxes in the back of the truck. I could hang them here until after the tour, then take them to the shop to sell. Now, if I just had somebody to help with all this. Not McQuaid, though. His idea of a Christmas decoration is a poster-board picture of Santa tacked on the front door. Anyway, McQuaid had gone to pick up Brian and visit with his folks.

And then I thought of Ruby. Since she apparently wasn't planning a big Christmas at her house, she would probably be willing to help with mine, and a little holiday cheer might raise her spirits. It was nearly two in the afternoon. I'd call and invite her over, and while we were working, we could have some good old-fashioned, soul-baring girl talk.

I went to the phone and punched in Ruby's number. There was no answer—and no answering machine, either, which struck me as strange. Ruby loves to be in touch. Her answering machine is always on. While I was at the phone, I called Mrs. Kendall, thinking that I'd better pin her down about helping with the food for the Tour. She answered on the second ring. In reply to my question, she said, reassuringly, "Of course I'll help. Tell me what you'd like to serve and I'll bring it over on Sunday morning."

"That's wonderful," I said enthusiastically. "Thank you. You've saved my life."

Mrs. Kendall had become such a fixture in our lives that it was hard to believe that neither Ruby nor I had ever met her before that October morning, almost two months ago, when she appeared unannounced in the tearoom. She introduced herself and said that she'd heard we might be seeking help in the kitchen.

"You'll find me a rather good cook, if I do say so myself," she remarked confidently. She spoke in one of those clipped, precise British accents that always sound so cultured in contrast to our sloppy, folksy Texas drawls. She looked to be in her late forties, with brown hair twisted into a loose knot at the back of her head, piercing blue eyes behind gold-rimmed glasses, a beige sweater set and brown tweed skirt, sensible brown shoes. I could see her hiking long distances over the open moors or putting a corgie through its paces at a dog show. She was a bit dowdy and rather heavy of movement, but commanding all the same. The sort of woman who inspires confidence.

Ruby and I exchanged startled glances. The tearoom had gotten off to a strong start because Ruby's friend Janet, an experienced cook, had helped us out in the kitchen. Two weeks after the opening, however, Janet had to go to Dallas to help settle her mother's estate. She'd only been gone a few days when we saw that, where the kitchen was concerned, we had definitely bitten off more than we could chew. Not that our menus were terribly complicated. We were open only for afternoon tea, which is pretty simple— scones, an assortment of sandwiches, a few cakes, some jam, and tea, of course. Lots of teas, herbal, black, green, flavored, you name it. Ruby and I knew we couldn't turn much of a profit with the limited hours and we were afraid that our customers would soon get tired of the restricted fare. But we rationalized the decision by reminding ourselves that we were just getting started. There was time to add a lunch menu when we had a bit more experience under our belts, when we gained a little more confidence in what we were doing. When we found a good cook to replace Janet.

"Exactly how good are you, Ms. Kendall?" Ruby asked.

"One doesn't wish to boast, of course," the woman said modestly, "but until quite recently, I worked in a splendid tearoom in Sussex called The Royal George. A lovely little place, right in the village High Street, owned by two very dear women. I did enjoy working for them. They were so very kind and attentive. Should you see fit to employ me, I'm sure you would find my work quite satisfactory." She paused and then added, "Although, as I said, one doesn't like to boast."

"Oh, quite," Ruby said hastily. "Quite, indeed. Rather."

Mrs. Kendall made a judicious survey of our newly renovated, newly decorated tearoom, with its stone walls, green wainscoting, chintz chair cushions and place mats, the baskets of ivy and philodendron hung from old cypress ceiling beams. Through the open doorway, she could see the sparkling, fully equipped kitchen installed at the behest of the Texas Department of Public Health. But from her look, it was clear that she was comparing Thyme for Tea with The Royal George and finding it wanting on several important counts. She sighed.

"Well," she said matter-of-factly, "one has to begin somewhere, doesn't one? I've no doubt that we could work up a menu quite similar to the one we had at The Royal George, which enjoyed a brisk luncheon trade."

I frowned. "I'm not sure a British menu would go over very well here. After all, this is Texas."

"Just because one lives in Texas," Mrs. Kendall said

loftily, "one is not required to behave like a barbarian. I'm sure that even Texans must enjoy a bit of civilized dining now and then, given the opportunity."

Stung, I opened my mouth to retort, but Ruby interrupted. "Why don't we ask Mrs. Kendall to make some suggestions about the menu," she said tactfully. "We can study them and decide whether we think they'd work." Her reproving look told me to stop behaving like a barbarian.

"Whatever you want," I said, shrugging. I glanced at the woman. "You've got references, I suppose."

"To be sure," Mrs. Kendall replied graciously. "But I expect you'd rather sample my culinary skills than read my recommendations. I should be delighted to prepare luncheon for you. At no charge, of course."

"Luncheon!" Ruby exclaimed. "What a perfectly delightful idea." She looked at me. "Isn't it, China?"

"Well, sure," I said. I waved my hand carelessly. "Be our guest. Show us your stuff."

"My . . . stuff?" The woman frowned.

"China means that we would love to sample your dishes," Ruby explained.

"Well, then, I'll just have a look around." Mrs. Kendall turned and went into the kitchen, and we could hear the sound of doors opening and pots rattling. In a few moments, she was back. "It seems that you have most of the necessary equipment. I'll pop round to the market and pick up a few things. And if you have a moment, you might just step out to that lovely little garden and pick a few fresh herbs—basil and dill, please, and a bit of lemon thyme and parsley would be splendid." A watch was pinned to her sweater and she took it off for a look, exactly as Mary Poppins might have done. I almost expected her to click her heels and twirl an umbrella. "You may expect luncheon in . . . shall we say, ninety minutes." She turned and marched out the door.

"A spoonful of sugar makes the medicine go down," I said.

Ruby rolled her eyes. "Pinch me. I think I'm dreaming."

I grinned. "If she can't cook, maybe Sheila could use her on the police force."

"She certainly has a managerial personality," Ruby agreed. "She'd take a bit of getting used to. But we need somebody experienced in the kitchen. If she can cook, she'd be the answer to our prayers. An angel from heaven, so to speak."

"Rather," I said dryly.

Exactly an hour and a half later, Ruby and I were sitting at a table in our tearoom, our lunches arranged attractively before us. I tucked into a savory sausage roll, creamy to-mato soup with basil, and a dilled-cucumber salad. Ruby had soup and a garden salad, plus a shepherd's pie, made with ground beef, onions, and vegetables and topped with garlic mashed potatoes. We hardly spoke except to trade remarks like "Delicious" and "Superb" and (once, surrepti-tiously) "Supercalifragilisticexpialidocious." When we were finished, Mrs. Kendall, wearing a neat green apron over her tweed skirt, brought in a plate of cheese and fruit and three cups of Earl Grey tea. She sat down and spread two sheets of paper, neatly lettered, on the table in front of us.

"For luncheon," she said, "I propose that we begin by offering Shepherd's Pie, served with soup and salad and crusty bread. We might also offer a sausage roll, also with soup and salad and bread. After a few weeks, I recommend the addition of a Quiche of the Day, smoked salmon on a roll, and a Ploughman's Lunch. Your kitchen is a bit small and will limit the menu, but these dishes are quite within its capabilities."

"A Ploughman's Lunch?" Ruby asked. "What's that?"

Over the tops of her gold-rimmed glasses, Mrs. Kendall gave Ruby a pitying look. "A Ploughman's Lunch traditionally consists of a hot roll, three slices of a good Stilton, mustard, a pickle, a pickled onion, and a salad."

"I don't know about the pickled onion," Ruby muttered, but I could tell she was blown away by the woman's skill and experience. I was too.

"And what about afternoon tea?" I asked, trying not to show how impressed I was.

Mrs. Kendall referred to the other sheet of paper. "At tea," she said, "one can be quite creative without risking a great many resources. You're already serving the staples— tea sandwiches, scones and jam, cakes, and so forth. I propose to reorganize these same items around several traditional teatime themes. For instance, one might offer a Savory Tea—sandwiches and cheeses—or a Sweet Tea, which is miniature pastries with a fruit garnish. Both very simple but elegant. And for the youngsters, one might include a Mad Hatter's Tea." She folded her hands. "Alice, you know."

"It's very British," I said to Ruby, *sotto voce*. "I don't know how it'll go over here in Pecan Springs."

"But it's unique and different," Ruby said, also in a low tone. "I think our customers will love it. And they don't all come from Pecan Springs, of course." This was true. Tourism is the Hill Country's biggest business, attracting people from all over the world.

"If you would like to talk it over privately," Mrs. Kendall said tactfully, "I should of course be glad to—"

"No, no," Ruby replied. "We love your ideas. And your

food." She gave me a meaningful look. "Don't we, China?"

We hired her on the spot, of course. She had the required green card, so there was no problem with her papers. As an employee, however, Mrs. Kendall was a challenge, because she preferred to give orders rather than take them. What's more, she took only the suggestions she wanted to take, when she felt like it. But we had to admit that for all her highhanded ways, she was an eminently fair and reasonable person who did the right thing, at least as she saw it.

And as a cook, she was indisputably without peer. She produced one tasty dish after another with aplomb, and she never looked ruffled or harried. In fact, her manner was so aristocratic and imperious that Ruby and I took to calling her the Duchess—behind her back, of course. To her face, the only familiarity we were allowed was "Mrs. K." We knew from her employment application that her first name was Victoria, that she was forty-seven, and that she had been in the United States for four months. But that and her address (a small apartment a few blocks away) were the only facts we could ascertain about her personal life. Ruby had once joked that maybe she de-materialized when she left the kitchen and materialized again the minute she put on her neat green apron.

But who cared what the Duchess did in her off-hours? She was exactly what we needed. We couldn't imagine what we had done before she showed up. We couldn't imagine what we'd do without her. Now, feeling grateful to her for agreeing to help me meet my obligations to the Christmas Tour, I asked about her holiday plans.

"I have no plans," she said. "I have no family left, you see, and no one with whom to celebrate. I'm entirely alone in the world." She sighed heavily. "My husband is gone.

My parents died when my sister Amanda and I were very young, and Amanda herself died ten years ago. I still miss her quite dreadfully." Another long sigh. "I brought her up, you know, after Mother and Father died."

I could hear the sadness in her voice, and something else, as well. The Duchess, usually so crisp and precise, was uncharacteristically rambling, her words slightly slurred. Had she been nipping at the sherry, at two o'clock on a Sunday afternoon?

"I'm sorry," I said, not knowing exactly what to say.

She hiccupped so delicately that I almost didn't hear it, and I pictured her taking another sip of sherry. "My sister was so beautiful, and such a loving and generous person." Mrs. Kendall's voice became bitter. "Her death was an unspeakable tragedy."

"I'm so sorry," I said again, with more feeling. I had a sudden vision of the Duchess sitting all alone in a drab, cheerless apartment, with nothing to do but sip sherry and mourn her sister's death a full decade ago. It was pathetic.

I heard a sudden sharp intake of breath, as if Mrs. Kendall was trying to get hold of herself. "I apologize for having imposed my sadness and anger on you, Ms. Bayles." Her voice took on some of its customary briskness, and I could almost see her squaring her shoulders and putting on a stiff upper lip. "I'm afraid I must ring off now. I have an important engagement this afternoon."

We said goodbye and I put down the phone with the feeling that Mrs. Kendall's afternoon engagement was with the bottle at her elbow. It must be terrible to lose a sister and even worse to live with feelings of grief and desperate longing for the rest of your life.

•　•　•

I tried calling Ruby again, but there was still no answer. So I spent Sunday afternoon doing the Christmas decorating in my usual haphazard, uninspired way, hanging wreaths and swags, arranging candles in trays covered with rosemary branches sprayed with fake snow, putting up a small artificial tree on the hutch in the dining room. I stood back to survey my handiwork, feeling that it all seemed— well, rather ordinary and unremarkable, hardly something you'd go out of your way to look at. I could imagine the Christmas Tourists shaking their heads and muttering critically to one another, and Rowena Riddle, frowning in disappointment. I sighed. Where was Ruby when I needed her? Where was Martha Stewart?

Finally, in an act of desperation, I dragged in a pot of prickly pear cactus from the patio and looped it with miniature white lights. Then, on a whim, I put my cowboy boots—the ones I wear when McQuaid and I go dancing at the Broken Spoke—beside the fireplace and filled them with rosemary branches and some bright red chile peppers. When I stepped back to admire the boots and the cactus, I realized I'd accidentally discovered my theme. I took the pine-bough garland off the mantel and substituted a red-pepper *ristra* and a garlic braid from the kitchen, hung with a few ornaments. Voila! A Texas Country Christmas. A few miniature Texas flags, a ceramic armadillo wearing a Santa hat, Brian's toy gun and lariat looped around a grapevine wreath and hung with holly, and the picture would be complete. To go with the theme, I'd persuade Mrs. Kendall to try her hand at some Texas party foods—tiny tacos, red and green salsa, Fiesta pie, and tortilla snacks.

When McQuaid and Brian got home, we put up the tree we'd picked out the week before and decorated it with the hodgepodge of ornaments we've independently collected over the years, half of which are broken and none of which match. When you marry a man, you marry his Christmas ornaments as well.

And his dog. In the middle of the tree-trimming festivities, Howard Cosell, McQuaid's grumpy old basset, stumped in, sniffed happily all around the cactus pot, then lifted his leg. Of course, Howard has probably used that pot as a fire hydrant several times a day for as long as we've lived here, and nobody has ever said a cross word to him about it. But the cactus was under new management and Howard would have to do his doggy business elsewhere until the Tourists had come and gone. Explaining this to him wasn't easy, for while Howard responds with tail-wagging and eye-rolling enthusiasm to complicated sentences such as "Would you like to go for a ride in the truck?" and "It must be almost time for Howard's dinner," his vocabulary does not include the word *no*.

But Howard Cosell's affinity for the cactus pot was a minor glitch in an otherwise merry Christmas-tree-decorating party, our first as a family. McQuaid and Brian and I ate popcorn and drank mulled cider as we worked, and told stories of Christmases past. When we were finished, Brian was given the honor of switching on the tree lights in the darkened room. "Awesome," he said when the tree was lit, and McQuaid and I, our arms around each other, had to agree. Everything was perfect—the cowboy boots, the lariat wreath, Howard's cactus, the Christmas tree. Even the ceramic armadillo looked right at home.

"Good job, Mrs. McQuaid," my husband said, and kissed me. To the rest of the world I am still and always China Bayles, but McQuaid can call me Mrs. McQuaid whenever he likes and I won't complain.

Just because my house was decorated didn't mean it was

clean, however—especially after we'd dragged out the boxes of ornaments, tracked popcorn and tinsel across the carpet, and sprayed messy drifts of artificial snow on the windows. At eight on Monday morning, Brian went to school and McQuaid disappeared into his study to work on the book he's writing, a history of the Texas Rangers. At least that's what he's supposed to be doing with his sabbatical semester, although he's only produced about thirty pages of it. It's shaping up to be a controversial book, McQuaid tells me, and a great deal more difficult to write than he had originally thought. The only other important history of the Rangers is Walter Prescott Webb's 1935 book, *The Texas Rangers*, which J. Frank Dobie called "The beginning, middle, and end of the subject." Except that Webb's vision of his subject was colored by his admiration for these guys in white hats. He was a Ranger fan. He made them look good even when they were bad, even when their exploits included the murders of unarmed men and assaults against innocent citizens. If McQuaid actually finishes this revisionist history, he might be in for some serious flak from his law enforcement buddies.

I tackled the vacuuming and dusting and straightening with enthusiasm. While I was working, I thought briefly about the bad old days, when I was still at the law firm. On Monday morning, I'd slap on my makeup, squeeze myself into a dress-for-success uniform, and tackle the Houston freeway system with all the aggressiveness of the Oilers right offense. At the office, still juiced from battling I-10, I'd bully the secretary into typing my brief ahead of anybody else's, then charge off for the rest of the day's confrontations before the bench or behind the desk. At the end of twelve hours, I'd still be at max warp. I rarely wound down, even on weekends. But I don't recall those litigious times with any nostalgia, believe me. I am physically and psychologically healthier now that I no longer have to torque myself up for my job as if I were heading into Desert Storm. I'd much prefer to be running the vacuum in stained yellow sweats and dirty sneakers than standing up before a jury in a power suit and high heels to defend a client who was probably guilty as sin. Household dirt is a whole lot cleaner than the other kind.

After the downstairs was as respectable as it was going to get, I took the vacuum and worked my way up the stairs and down the upstairs hallway. But when I got as far as Brian's bathroom, I found something that needed doing more than the carpet. There were at least three loads of laundry heaped on the floor, including (my nose told me) several moldy towels and maybe a dozen filthy socks. Take it from me—when you marry a man with a thirteen-year-old boy, the deal had better include a reliable washer and dryer and an ample supply of detergent and hot water.

I was starting the second load when the phone rang. I went into the bedroom, picked up the cordless, and started back to the laundry room.

"Mornin', China," Blackie said. "I've got a problem."

"Haven't we all?" I asked, thinking that when I finished Brian's laundry, I'd better go over to Ruby's house. There was still no answer to my persistent calls, and I was getting a little worried.

There was a click on the line. "Hello," my husband said cheerfully. "McQuaid here."

"Ah, both of you," Blackie said. "That's good."

"Excuse me, China," McQuaid said. "I didn't know you'd picked up the phone."

"That's okay," I said, cradling the phone with my shoulder as I dredged one of Brian's muddy towels out of the laundry basket. "I'll get off the line and let you guys talk. I'm pretty busy just now." I shook out the towel and discovered one of Brian's large lizards. "Yikes!" I said, startled, and then, "Damn," because the silly thing had dived into the washing machine, which was half full of dirty clothes and soapy water. And then "Damn" again, louder this time, because there wasn't just one lizard, there were two, and the second was paddling around with his buddy in the soapsuds.

"Excuse me?" Blackie asked.

"What's going on?" McQuaid asked.

"I'm doing the laundry, that's what's going on," I said disgustedly. I hit the washer's Off button and began to fish around in the water. "And Brian is going to lose his Internet privileges if he doesn't keep better tabs on his lizards. Last week, I found one curled up inside my bath mitt. Now there's a pair going for a swim in the washer."

"Better fish them out," McQuaid said urgently. "They're not amphibians. They'll drown."

"Serve 'em right," I gritted. I grabbed one by the tail and tossed it into the laundry sink.

"I realize that you two have other things on your mind," Blackie said mildly, "but I need China's help. This is an official problem."

I retrieved the second lizard and sent it after the first. "You'll have to get in line," I said. "After I've finished the laundry and the vacuuming, I have to go check on Ruby." "Then there's the grocery shopping. Then—"

"The mail carrier found Carl Swenson in the ditch in front of his place about an hour ago," Blackie said. "Dead."

"Dead!" McQuaid blew out his breath.

I said, cautiously, "I don't suppose the sheriff would be involved if Swenson had died of natural causes. A heart attack, say." I thought of Terry's shotgun, and shivered.

"Right the first time," Blackie replied. "I'm at the scene now."

"So how *did* he die?" McQuaid asked.

"Hit and run," Blackie replied.

I felt an intense relief. Not a shotgun, after all. And the last time I'd seen the Fletcher sisters' van, the engine had been in pieces all over the ground.

"When did it happen?" I asked. In the laundry sink, the two lizards were scrabbling over one another, trying to climb up the slick sides.

"Sometime yesterday," Blackie replied. "It rained about ten o'clock last night. Swenson's clothes are wet. The ground under him is dry."

"What do you want China for?" McQuaid asked.

Blackie grunted. "Isn't it obvious? The Fletcher sisters live less than a mile away. They had a couple of dozen good reasons to want this guy dead. I need to hear their story, and I thought the conversation might be more comfortable for them if China was there. If she can spare the time from her laundry." His voice became dry. "And her lizards."

"Wait a minute," I said. "I hope you're not asking me because I'm a member of the bar." But that didn't make sense. A sheriff doesn't take a lawyer with him to question a suspect. It's up to the suspect to get a lawyer.

"Lord help us," Blackie said. "No. I'm asking you because you're their friend, and they've already talked to you about their problems with Swenson."

I was silent for a moment, thinking. I've never known Blackie to lie, but I couldn't help thinking there was more to it than that. "Do you have any particular reason to suspect that Donna and Terry are involved in Swenson's death?" I asked warily.

"Other than your graphic description of Terry and her shotgun?" Blackie countered. "And the fact that they're the nearest neighbors?"

"They're not the nearest neighbors," I retorted. "Somebody named Tuttle lives on the other side of the road, around the curve. I've seen the name on the mailbox. And there's a house trailer just past the Tuttle place, on the other side of the road. The Fletcher farm is further on. Anyway, their van isn't drivable, remember? Somebody put sugar in the gas tank."

"Yeah, I remember," Blackie said. "And thanks for the information about the neighbors. We'll check out these other folks." He paused. "But I really would like you to be there when I talk to the ladies, China. It'd be easier for them, and for me. What do you say?"

"She says yes," McQuaid put in promptly. "Right, hon? You don't have much to do this morning, do you?"

I gritted my teeth. Being called "hon" is my biggest peeve, next to lizards in the laundry, having words put into my mouth, and hearing that I don't have much to do. But the Fletcher sisters were my friends, or at least Donna was. She'd probably feel better if the sheriff showed up in my company. Anyway, who was I trying to kid? I wanted to know what had happened to Swenson and I wasn't going to learn it hanging out here, chasing lizards and waiting for bulletins from the sheriff's office.

And there was an added incentive, albeit a trivial one that I am slightly embarrassed to mention in the face of death. It was obvious that Carl Swenson wouldn't be delivering any more mistletoe. If I wanted some for the shop,

I was going to have to harvest it myself—and there was a very nice batch of it growing along the right-of-way not far from where the man had been killed.

"Okay," I said. "I'll be there as soon as I can, Blackie."

"Thanks," Blackie said. "I appreciate this, China."

"I don't have anything very important to do this morning," McQuaid said promptly. "I'll drive you, China."

"If you've got some time, that would be great, Mike," Blackie said. "I'm short a deputy today. You can lend a pair of hands."

"Another pair of eyes never hurts, either," McQuaid said. To me, he added: "I hope you got those lizards out of the wash."

"They're in the sink," I said. I leaned over to look in. One lizard was in the sink. The other was missing, and so was the drain cover. The absent lizard had probably gone down the drain.

CHAPTER FIVE

In Wales, a sprig of mistletoe gathered on Midsummer Eve is placed under the pillow to induce prophetic dreams.

Welsh folklore

European mistletoe has long been known as "all-heal," a plant with many medicinal applications. It has a long tradition of use as a remedy for epilepsy and other convulsive disorders, and as a heart tonic, in place of foxglove (digitalis). American mistletoe was used by Indians to treat toothache, measles, and dog bites.

China Bayles
"Mistletoe Magic"

When we got to the crime scene a half-hour later, Swenson's body still lay on the ground, probably because the local Justice of the Peace had arrived only a few minutes before we did. In Texas, when death by foul play is suspected, a JP is supposed to inspect the scene and file a report—an archaic requirement that sometimes causes a fair amount of confusion and delay. This particular JP was a man named Bull Arnold, who is not known for his high intellectual achievements or his skills in diplomacy. He's coming up for reelection next year, and there's going to be some stiff competition for the post. I know that Blackie, for one, will be just as glad if Bull loses.

Bull is a loud-talking, barrel-chested man who moves as slow as molasses on a cold December morning. This morning was plenty cold too, with the temperature hovering around 35 degrees and a chill drizzle misting through the air. Blackie and his deputy, who was holding a camera, were standing beside the sheriff's car, talking to Bull. They were wearing hooded yellow slickers, and McQuaid and I pulled on our own slickers as we got out of the truck. McQuaid left his cane in the truck. Macho pride, I thought. But I was glad to see him getting around without it.

Bull squinted at us through rain-spotted glasses. He took the damp cigar out of his mouth. "Well, if it ain't McQuaid," he bellowed. "Thought they booted you outta the chief's job a coupla months ago and put that goldanged woman in your place. What the hail you doin' out here?"

McQuaid smiled. "Oh, just keeping my hand in. Don't want to get rusty, you know." He turned to Blackie. "How's that goldanged woman of yours, Sheriff?"

"The chief? Hey, she's doing great." Blackie's eyes lightened. He shot a sidelong glance at Bull. "She stopped a guy for running a light yesterday and found a quarter-pound of crack stashed in his trunk."

"Sheila's one tough cookie," McQuaid said. He looked directly at Bull, who colored. "Smart, too. Got the makings of a goldanged good chief." He turned toward Swenson's body, which was covered with a yellow tarp.

Bull jammed his cigar back in his mouth. "Seems like it was a hit and run," he barked importantly, to show that this was his precinct and he was still boss. "That's how I'm gonna write it up. Somebody came along, accidently clipped him a good 'un, and got scairt. Fled the scene."

"Any idea what time it happened?" I asked.

Bull gave me a look which suggested that I shouldn't have been allowed to leave my laundry. "Sometime 'fore dark yestiddy," he said, gesturing toward an aluminum ladder that was leaning against a hackberry tree. "It looks like he wuz out here trimmin' trees. Which don't make a hail of a lotta sense." He frowned, and I could see him wondering why anybody would go to the trouble of trimming hackberries along a county road.

Blackie pursed his lips. "Hey, Bull, I sure hate for you to stand around out here all morning and get wet. Why don't you go on back to your office? We'll wrap it up here, and you can fax me your paperwork."

An EMS ambulance came around the corner and pulled onto the grass. They weren't running the siren, and they didn't seem in a big hurry. They'd probably been told that their patient wasn't going to suffer a relapse.

"Reckon I will," Bull said, deciding that the trees weren't something he ought to worry about. "I got me plenty o'thangs to do." He lowered his head and shook it, and I could see where he got his name. "Ask me, wimmin don't got no bidness in law enforcement," he muttered. "Who's gonna stay home and mind the kids?"

Blackie hooked his thumbs in his belt and smiled a long, lazy smile. "Why, Bull, I just might do that, if the chief and I ever decide to have any. Sure beats rounding up hit-and-run drivers."

Without a word, Bull stalked off, climbed into his Jeep Cherokee and spun his wheels, splashing mud over us.

"Sonofabitch," McQuaid muttered.

The deputy looked down at his mud-spattered slicker.

"That's why we signed on to be cops," he said. "So we'd get some respect."

A grin cracked Blackie's face. "Hail," he said, "I thought we done it to harass the local JayPees. You got all the photos you want, Pete?"

"I'll get a couple more long shots," the deputy said.

Blackie glanced from McQuaid to me. "Want to take a look at the body?"

The ditch was full of chunks of limestone rock. Swenson was face down, arms flung out, legs at odd angles. His blond hair was rain-slicked, his denim jacket and jeans soaked through. One boot was missing, one leg clearly broken, and there was a puddle of blood under his mouth. In life, he hadn't been much to look at, but death had brutally altered him, twisting his face in a mask of anguish and pain and rendering him vulnerable, helpless. I thought of the ugliness of violent death, and the sadness of dying alone, and swallowed hard.

"Looks like he died of a skull fracture," Blackie remarked matter-of-factly. "Left side's caved in." He sighed. "But I don't think he died fast."

I didn't think so either. In his last agonized moments, Swenson had clawed at the dirt, trying to pull himself out of the ditch. He had died clutching fistfuls of dry, dead grass.

"Any sign of paint flecks on the clothing?" McQuaid asked.

"Didn't see any," Blackie replied, signaling to the EMS team. "But we've located some glass—headlight glass, probably—at the point of impact. Everything will go to Travis for analysis." Adams County is too small to have its own crime lab, so anything that might turn out to be evidence in a criminal case is sent to either the Travis or Bexar County labs.

"Where's the glass?" I asked.

We left Swenson to the tender mercies of the EMS crew and Blackie led us up the road about five yards, past a leather cowboy boot, its location marked with a flag of yellow tape. We stopped beside a scattering of glass shards along the gravel shoulder, also flagged. Nearby, a portable metal frame had been set up—around a tire print, I assumed—and a plaster cast was hardening, shielded from the rain by a square of plastic.

"Is the print a clear one?" I asked.

Blackie tilted his hand to show that it was maybe good, maybe not so good. "It won't help us locate the vehicle, but it might help identify it."

McQuaid knelt down to peer at the glass. After a minute he looked up. "Got a collecting kit? There are a few paint flecks here too. Red, looks like."

"No kidding?" Blackie looked pleased. "Yeah. I'll get you a kit."

I turned to look along the fence line. A few yards away was the ladder. On the ground next to it was a five-gallon plastic bucket. I went over to look. The bucket was half full of mistletoe. A pair of loppers lay beside it.

"Well, we know what he was doing when he was killed," I said.

"Clearing that stuff out of the trees?" Blackie asked, coming up beside me. "But hackberries are just trash trees, and these aren't even on his property. So why was he bothering?"

"Because he was getting paid for it," I said. "That bucket of mistletoe, full, would be worth twenty dollars wholesale. He supplied my shop, and he had quite a few other customers." I looked twenty yards further up the road, where a new green Dodge pickup, was parked near a mailbox. In it, I spotted a half-dozen or more filled garbage bags. The rest of the harvest, waiting for Swenson to truck it off to market.

Blackie put his hand on my shoulder. "How about it, China? You ready to go see the Fletcher sisters?"

"I guess," I said. "But I don't see the point. Their van's out of commission. They couldn't have—"

"Fine," Blackie said. "It'll be just a friendly visit. Come on. We'll take my car."

I shook my head. "Let's take McQuaid's truck," I said. "As long as this is just a friendly visit." I paused. "But before we leave, there's something you can do for me."

"Yeah? What?"

"Let me pull those bags of mistletoe out of Swenson's truck. It's already cut and there's no sense in letting it go to waste." Whatever else the man might have been, he was certainly industrious. And he must have had some other source of income, besides mistletoe. You don't make the payments on a twenty-thousand-dollar truck out of pocket change.

"Let's take a look," Blackie said. We walked to the truck, where he peered into each of the bags. "Well, that clears up one mystery," he said.

I grinned. "So what did you think it was, Sheriff Blackwell? Marijuana?"

He returned my grin. "I never saw marijuana with little white berries on it. Take what you want and let's go."

The rain had slowed to a chill drizzle when I drove up in front of the Fletcher house and leaned on the horn. The racket brought a still-bandaged Max bouncing out of the barn and Donna, more slowly, out of the greenhouse. Terry was nowhere in sight. I took a quick look and saw, to my surprise and dismay, that the brown panel truck was gone from its parking place beside the barn.

"Hi," Donna said, coming up to greet us. She pushed her taffy-colored hair out of her eyes with a nervous gesture. "Didn't expect to see you again so soon, China." Her eyes flicked to Blackie. She took in his uniform with barely disguised dismay, then focused on me again. "Did you want more wreaths? If you do, I'm afraid we'll need a little more time. Everything's piling up, what with the work of repairing the greenhouse and the van and all. We're pretty swamped just now and—"

I raised my hand to stem the babble, not liking the apprehension and anxiety I heard in Donna's voice. Did she know about Swenson? "We'll probably need some more wreaths before Christmas," I said, "but not right away." I turned. "Donna, this is Sheriff Blackwell. There's been an accident up the road and—"

"An accident?" Donna asked, her eyes widening. She thrust her hands into the pockets of her green down vest. "Oh, gosh, I hope nobody was hurt."

"Somebody was killed, Ms. Fletcher," Blackie said soberly. "A neighbor of yours. Carl Swenson."

Donna's hand flew out of her pocket and went to her mouth in a gesture of surprise and dismay so faked that it wouldn't have fooled a five-year-old. "Oh, dear!" she cried shrilly. "Oh, I'm so sorry to hear that! When did it happen? This morning?"

"We're not quite sure yet," Blackie said. "Why don't we go inside? I have a few questions I'd like to ask you, and it's pretty wet out here."

"But I don't know anything about the accident," Donna protested, shaking her head emphatically. "We're at the end of the road, and I didn't see or hear a thing. Not a single thing." She stopped talking but kept on shaking her head.

"Donna," I said quietly, "let's go inside. The sheriff has been out in the rain for the last hour, and a hot cup of coffee would help take the chill off."

Donna drew in her breath as if to protest again, but changed her mind. "Oh, of course," she said in a tinny voice. "By all means, do come in and get warm, both of you."

On the way up the walk, she turned to me and said, "I would have asked you in right away, but I didn't want to bother Aunt Velda. Today isn't one of her better days, and strangers really set her off. She always thinks they're from—well, you know." She glanced at the sheriff and added, "Our elderly aunt lives with us. She isn't . . . well, she's not exactly right, mentally. Alzheimer's, they think. The social worker says we ought to put her in a nursing home, but we want to keep her with us as long as possible."

I was a little surprised to hear this. Aunt Velda had some strange ideas, but I hadn't heard that she might be suffering from Alzheimer's.

"We won't disturb your aunt," Blackie said in a kindly voice, and Donna seemed to relax a little.

The kitchen was warm and the coffee was hot, but neither helped to get the conversation off to a comfortable start. Blackie took off his gray felt Stetson and put it on the table, while Donna fidgeted with coffee cups. In a moment, she had poured the coffee and was sitting down across from us.

"Mr. Swenson was struck by a vehicle and killed," Blackie said, "near his home. The driver didn't stop. Since you're his neighbor, I wondered whether you or your sister might have seen anything out of the ordinary." He looked straight at her. "Something you'd like to tell me about."

"No," Donna said quickly. "As I told you, I don't know anything about it. I didn't go out at all yesterday." She laughed shakily. "Well, of course I was *outside*. In the barn and the greenhouse, I mean. But not on the road. I didn't go out on the road at all. So I can't help you, I'm afraid."

"What about your sister?" Blackie asked. He looked around. "Is she here?"

Again that emphatic shake of the head. "She's in San Antonio. She left early this morning. Really early, when it was still dark. A friend has loaned us a car to use until our car is fixed. That's what she drove. She—"

"Thank you." Blackie took out a pen and a small notebook and flipped it open. "What vehicles do you own?"

"Vehicles?" The color came and went in Donna's face. "Our van, of course. But it's out of commission. Somebody put sugar in the—" She stopped. "We've been having a lot of trouble with it lately."

"Where is the van?" I asked.

"It's in the barn," Donna said. "Terry didn't want to work on it in the rain."

"It was parked beside the shed when I saw it on Saturday," I said. "Did Terry get it running enough to drive it into the barn?"

Donna shook her head. "We towed it in with the tractor." I relaxed a little, but Donna didn't. "What are all these questions about?" she asked, her voice rising. Her eyes went from me to Blackie. "You can't possibly think that we had something to do with—" She stopped. "You can't possibly, that's all."

"It's just routine," Blackie said. "We'll be talking with all the neighbors." He didn't look at me. "However, China told me you've been having some trouble out here, and that you suspected Swenson might have something to do with it. Is that true?"

Donna threw me a glance that was at once angry and pleading, but she didn't have a chance to speak.

"Damn right we been havin' trouble," said a shrill, parrotlike voice. "But if you're here to settle ol' Carlos Swenbug's hash, you're a day late and a dollar short. That boy got took yestiddy. Them folks up there don't mess around."

I pulled in my breath sharply. *Got took*?

Donna stood. "I thought Terry told you to stay in your room," she said tightly. She took the old woman's arm and began to tug. "Come on, Auntie. You're not well."

Blackie had risen too. He smiled invitingly and pulled out the chair beside his. "From all I hear," he said to Aunt Velda, "Mr. Swenson was a hard man to deal with. He gave you a bad time, did he, ma'am?"

"A bad time?" Aunt Velda hooted. She shook off Donna's restraining hand and sidled, crabwise, toward the table. She seemed to be limping badly, and I saw that she was wearing one black sneaker and one crocheted bootie. "Hear that, Donna? This good-lookin' young feller wants to know did Carlos Swinster give us a bad time?" With a sarcastic cackle, she sat down in the chair and wrapped her red, white, and blue shawl (this one was knitted in the design of the American flag) around the shoulders of her field jacket. "You wanna know the truth, sonny, he screwed us six ways from Sunday. He deserves to be cleanin' latrines fer as long as them Klingons'll have him."

"Aunt Velda," Donna said desperately, "please watch your language. This is Sheriff Blackwell." She leaned closer, trying to command her aunt's attention. "He's come to tell us that Mr. Swenson is—"

"They got ol' Carlos, that's all I care about," Aunt Velda said in a celebratory tone. "Bully for them, is whut I say!" She banged her fist on the table. "Where's my coffee, girl? How come I ain't got no coffee?"

Wordlessly, her face as white as the tablecloth, Donna got up to pour another cup of coffee. It was clear that she had wanted to get Swenson's death on the record before the old lady had a chance to say something she shouldn't. But Aunt Velda had beaten her to the punch.

Blackie leaned forward, intent. "*They* got ol' Carlos?" he repeated.

The old lady clapped her gnarled hands. "See there!" she crowed. "This feller's a smart'un. He knows all about 'em."

She hoisted her bootied foot, which seemed to have been injured, onto a chair. "While you're up, girl, why don't you cut us a piece of that chocolate cake? You cain't make pie worth a durn, but your cakes ain't bad."

"*They* are the Klingons," I said quietly to Blackie, and pointed to the plastic badge on Aunt Velda's knit cap. "Their spaceship is parked upstairs. They've been waiting to snatch Carlos—er, Carl Swenson. Aunt Velda knows about this because she has been a guest on the ship herself. They took her on an extended intergalactic voyage."

Blackie nodded, and I could see him processing the information. When he leaned forward again, his voice was casual, interested. "How do you know the Klingons got Mr. Swenson?" he asked. "Did you see it happen?"

Aunt Velda shut her eyes. "Well, not quite. But they borrowed the truck and—"

There was a loud crash and a cry. Donna had dropped

the coffeepot into the sink, splashing hot coffee over her right forearm from wrist to elbow. Blackie jumped up, turned on the tap, and held her arm under the cold water. She resisted at first, but then stood quietly, biting her lip.

"That's a bad burn," he said, after several minutes. He turned off the tap. "You'd better get medical attention."

Donna shook her head and reached for the aloe plant on the windowsill. "I'll put some of this on it," she said, and broke off a fat, succulent leaf. "It'll hurt for a while, but it'll be okay."

I took the leaf from her, stripped off the tough outer skin, and smeared the gel on the burn. I worked as gently as I could, but she still winced at the touch, and made a little sound. The burn wasn't as bad or as extensive as it had seemed from her reaction, I thought.

Blackie had gone back to his chair. "I was asking whether you had seen them take Mr. Swenson," he said to Aunt Velda, "and you were saying—"

But the old woman had closed her eyes; her chin had dropped onto her chest, and she was snoring, her bootied foot still propped on the chair.

"She falls asleep like that all the time," Donna said, sitting down at the table again. Her tone was at once relieved and embarrassed. "You can't tell when she'll wake up, or what she'll say when she does." She looked straight at Blackie. "You can't believe a word she tells you, about Carl Swenson or anything else. She's crazy."

"What is your aunt's name?" Blackie asked, picking up his pen.

"Velda Fletcher."

"Her age?"

"Seventy-five. Before she came to live with us she left her apartment and wandered around lost for several days.

She couldn't be trusted to live alone any longer, so we take care of her."

"When was the last time she was out of the house?"

"The last time?" Donna said quickly. "Oh, it must have been a couple of months ago. That was to go to the doctor." Her smile was small and tight. "We can't allow her to go out, Sheriff. We have to watch her all the time to keep her from wandering off and getting hurt. You can see for yourself that she's not mentally competent."

I looked up quickly. Aunt Velda was a couple of bricks shy of a load, as we say here in Texas, but I didn't believe she was as disabled as Donna made her appear. On Saturday, the old girl had been eager to claim the credit for discovering the arrowhead cache up at the spring and was proud of herself for helping her nieces haul out the debris in the farm truck.

The farm truck. I pulled in my breath. Aunt Velda's old red Ford that couldn't be driven on the highway because it didn't have current plates. But the old lady was allowed to drive it around the farm, to make her feel she was doing something useful. Had she driven it yesterday?

"What is her social worker's name?" Blackie was asking.

"I'll get her card," Donna said. Cradling her burned arm, she got up and opened a cabinet drawer, fished for a moment, then came back to the table. "Here it is," she said. "Shirley Cowan. You ask her, Sheriff, she'll tell you that Aunt Velda is delusional. A couple of years ago, she got up one morning claiming that she'd been abducted by the Klingons. Since then, she sees an alien behind every bush." She laughed a little, sadly. "She even sees them watching her through the windows and stealing her underwear. She's convinced that they set a trap for our dog, and she thinks they intend to capture Mr. Swenson." She appealed to me for confirmation. "You heard her talking about that just a couple of days ago, didn't you, China?"

"When I was here on Saturday," I said slowly. If I was going to say something about that damn truck, now was the time.

Blackie finished copying the information from the card into his notebook. "So your aunt didn't leave the house yesterday?"

"Oh, no, sir," Donna said. "Absolutely not."

"And your sister?" Blackie asked.

"We were all three right here together, all day and evening. If you don't believe me, you can ask Terry." She laughed a little. "In fact, we can't go anywhere until she gets the van working again. Our friend was nice enough to loan us her little white Geo. We don't want to abuse the privilege."

I wanted to believe her but I was finding it difficult—and of course, if we asked Terry to confirm, we'd get the same story, true or false. Belatedly, I opened my mouth to ask about the farm truck, but Blackie was closing his notebook and standing up.

"Thank you, Miss Fletcher," he said. "I think that's all the questions I have for you at the moment." He glanced at Aunt Velda, snoozing comfortably in her chair. I knew he'd like to wake her up and ask her what she had seen. But it was clear that he wasn't going to get any more information out of her just now, and if he did, it wouldn't be reliable. She might know something, but it would take a lot of perseverance—and luck—to dig it out of her confused memory.

"Oh, there is one more thing," Blackie added, as if it

were an afterthought. "Do you mind if I take a look at your van?"

"Of course," Donna said, with so much alacrity that I knew we wouldn't see anything out of the ordinary. She shrugged into her down vest, clearly anxious to get us out of the house before Aunt Velda woke up.

"What about that burn?" Blackie asked. "Shouldn't you bandage it?"

Donna gave him a brave smile. "It'll be all right," she said. "That aloe works wonders."

Leaving the old woman snoring at the table, we went back outdoors and down the path to the barn. I looked for the red Ford pickup, hoping it would be parked where I had last seen it, beside the van. The space was empty. Both vehicles were gone.

But the van was in the barn, just as Donna had said, its essential parts spread out on a canvas tarp on the dirt floor, both headlights intact. A couple of Rhode Island Reds were roosting on the roof of the van and Max crawled out from under it, wagging his tail, happy to have company. Donna lifted the lid off a metal garbage can and took out a handful of corn for the chickens, while Blackie walked around the van, inspecting it. I scanned the barn for Aunt Velda's truck, but it wasn't there.

Blackie came around the van. "Thank you, Miss Fletcher," he said, putting out his hand to Donna. "Please tell your sister that I may have some questions for her. If I need any more help, I'll call."

And that was it. We said our goodbyes, climbed into McQuaid's truck, and drove off.

I had swung out of the lane and was headed back down the gravel road toward Swenson's place when Blackie put his hand on the wheel. "Pull over," he said.

When the sheriff speaks to you in that tone of voice, you pull over, immediately. "What's up?" I asked.

"You tell me," Blackie said. "Cough it up, China."

I sat for a moment, wrestling with my conscience. On the one hand, I liked and admired the Fletcher sisters for their guts and determination. They had put their hearts into their flower farm and I wanted them to succeed. I was also glad that Carl Swenson was no longer going to make their lives difficult, although I would have preferred him to back off voluntarily. I liked Aunt Velda too. She wasn't a whole lot nuttier than the thousands of Trekkies who show up at the Star Trek conventions outfitted in bizarre galactic masks and costumes.

On the other hand, I liked and admired Blackie. And not for nothing had I been educated and trained to respect the law. In this case, Blackie was The Law, and I had an obligation to tell him what I knew. I also had an obligation to the truth, whatever that meant.

"They own another vehicle," I said. "A beat-up old red Ford pickup with the right side smashed in. It's not tagged or inspected, so they don't take it off the place. They let Aunt Velda drive it around." I made a face, not liking to give him this information. "In fact, she drove it when they were cleaning out the spring, not very long ago."

He took that in, obviously measuring it against Donna's statement that the old woman hadn't been out of the house for a couple of months. "Where is this truck? Have you seen it?"

"When I was out here on Saturday, it was parked beside the barn, next to the van. It's not there now, though. I looked. It's not in the barn, either."

"The old girl is a half-quart low," Blackie said musingly,

"but she might have seen something yesterday. Or done something."

"You think she might have been involved in Swenson's death?"

"*That boy got took yestiddy*," Blackie quoted.

I frowned. "That doesn't necessarily mean—"

"Come on, China." Blackie gave me an impatient look. "You know what it means as well as I do. The old woman knew Swenson was dead. And what's more, her niece knew it too. Before we got there. That oh-dear-I'm-so-shocked act didn't fool me. Neither did that little business with the coffeepot."

I had to agree. Donna's imitation of surprise hadn't been very convincing. "So what do you think happened yesterday?"

Blackie slid down in the seat and tipped his Stetson over his eyes. "Could've been an accident. Say the old lady hops in her Ford and goes out for an illicit Sunday-afternoon spin. Say that Swenson is standing beside the road when she comes around the curve and she knocks him a good wallop. What happens next?"

I squeezed my eyes shut, not wanting to think about it. After a moment I opened my eyes and said, unhappily: "I suppose she goes home and tells Terry and Donna what she's done." I frowned. "No, I don't think so. I think maybe she tells them that their problems are over, that the Klingons have beamed Carlos Swenson up into their spaceship. That she saw him being snatched, just the way she predicted." I remembered something else Aunt Velda had said. "Or that the Klingons borrowed the truck and ran him down."

"Whatever. Doesn't matter."

"Of course it matters," I said sharply. "It goes to com-

petence. If Aunt Velda struck him with the truck but be-
lieves that he was abducted by aliens, she's incompetent.
She can't be charged with his death."

The brim of Blackie's hat was riding on the tip of his
nose. "You lawyers make it so damn difficult to get a con-
viction," he growled.

"That's the way it's supposed to work. It's not called an
adversarial system for nothing."

"Don't include me in that adversarial shit. All I have to
do is get the evidence. The rest of it's up to the district
attorney and the grand jury." He pushed up his hat with his
thumb and turned to look at me. "But I'm afraid there's
more here than just a hit-and-run, China. Say the old girl
comes home with her story—accident, little green men,
whatever. The nieces check out the truck, discover the broken headlight, and come looking. They find Swenson dead.
Obviously, there aren't any witnesses, or it would have
been reported. In fact, they're positive that nobody else has
even seen the body. So they go back home and hide the
truck somewhere on their property and try to get the old
lady to keep her mouth shut."

I couldn't fault Blackie's logic. I'd been harboring
something of the same idea since Donna's clumsy perfor-
mance in the kitchen. I just hadn't wanted to put words
to it.

"So you think Donna and Terry are shielding their aunt,"
I said reluctantly. If this was true, they were both in serious
trouble—more trouble, probably, than their aunt, who was
clearly certifiable. Once the judge read the psychiatric eval-
uation, Aunt Velda would never see the inside of a jail,
although she might think that being confined to a nursing
home wasn't a very attractive alternative. But if Donna and
Terry had done what Blackie was suggesting, they could

be charged with hindering apprehension—usually known as obstructing justice. It's a Class A misdemeanor, with a fine of up to four thousand dollars, a year's jail time, or both. A high price to pay for protecting their aunt.

"I don't know about Terry, but Donna is sure as hell covering up for somebody," Blackie said. He shook his head. "She was nervous as a mail-order bride. She didn't want us in the house where her aunt might pop in on us, and when the old lady showed up, she did everything but stuff a dishrag in her mouth to keep her quiet. Even dropped the coffeepot to distract us."

"I can't argue with you," I conceded. "So what are you going to do?"

Blackie sat up and stared out the windshield. "Need to find that truck," he muttered. "Can't prove anything without it."

"I suppose you could get a warrant and search the place," I said.

"How many acres did you say they've got?"

"Two hundred, I replied. "And most of it's pretty rough. Might be hard to locate that truck, unless you use a helicopter."

"A helicopter?" Blackie snorted derisively. "Hell, I'm lucky if I can buy gas for the squad cars. This isn't Bexar County, you know. If you don't count the jailer, I've only got two deputies and a half-dozen patrol officers. *Helicopter.*" He snorted again. "Even if I had one, I wouldn't have anybody to fly it. And if I had somebody to fly it, I wouldn't have anything to pay him with."

"It was just a thought," I said. "Guess you'll have to haul Donna and Terry in and put them through the third degree. Or you might try questioning Aunt Velda again, and see how far you get."

"I've got a better idea." Blackie looked at his watch. "I need to interview the other neighbors. How would you feel about going back to the farm by yourself and talking to those Fletcher women? Both sisters, I mean, and the aunt. You could let them know the downside to what they've done and encourage them to come clean. If they've done it," he added hastily. "Innocent until proven guilty."

"Thanks, Sheriff," I said dryly. In my experience, most police (and this includes even the good guys, like Blackie) see it the other way around.

"Well, I mean it," he said, frowning. "Except for the fact that Donna withheld information about the existence of the truck and lied about her aunt's not having left the house in the past few months, there's no evidence to suggest that their truck was involved." He paused. "Not yet. But you know damn well what's going to happen when we get the report back on that glass. And on any paint flecks on Swenson's clothing."

I knew. Somewhere in the bowels of the FBI there is a computerized database that provides profiles for the paint of every vehicle manufactured in the United States in the last couple of decades. If it turned out that a red Ford truck was involved, the sheriff would be out at the flower farm with a search warrant faster than forked lightning. It would go a lot easier for Donna and Terry if they came forward voluntarily and confessed the cover-up—if they had anything to confess. But something else—my curiosity—was urging me to do what Blackie asked. I wanted to know what Aunt Velda had done or seen. I wanted to know what Donna was hiding. And where did Terry fit into all of this?

I squirmed uncomfortably. Sure, I wanted to know. On the other hand—

Blackie gave me an inquiring glance. "What are you thinking?"

"That I don't like to corner my friends."

"Look at it this way. If they've committed a criminal act, you're the best thing that could happen to them."

"I'm not a criminal lawyer. Not anymore."

"You could help them find one."

"I'm not your deputy, either. And I won't pull any funny stuff."

"Like what?"

"Like an illegal search, that's what. And I can't go back until this afternoon. I've got to check on Ruby this morning. Something's going on with her and I don't know what it is."

"This afternoon is fine. Gives them a little time to think about it." Blackie rubbed the side of his face. There was a nick on his jaw where he must have cut himself shaving that morning. "And I'm not asking you to do a search. All I want you to do is encourage those women to tell the truth. In the long run, that's the best thing they can do, and you know it."

I sighed heavily. "All right, I'll do it. On one condition." I turned the key in the ignition and started the truck.

"What's that?"

"That I come straight out and tell them it was your idea." I wasn't going back there under false pretenses. These were women whose hard work and dedication I admired. "I'd also like access to any information you dig up, and I want to be part of the team. Unofficially, of course." I grinned. "Which means you don't have to pay me. I'm cheaper than a helicopter."

Blackie thought for a minute, figuring out just how much this deal might cost him. He eyed me. "You're sure you're not going to take on their case?" Translated, this meant, *You promise not to give them anything you get from me?*

"I can guarantee you that I will not become their lawyer," I said without hesitation. "The prosecutor will have to hand over all the exculpatory evidence, anyway, whoever is charged."

"You're on," Blackie said. "But let's keep this arrangement between ourselves. It's a little irregular."

"I don't know what you're talking about," I said. "You're the sheriff. This is your county. You can do whatever you want to do, right?"

"Yeah, sure," he said. "I just don't advertise."

So that was how we left it. When we arrived back at the crime scene, the EMS guys had taken Swenson away, McQuaid had bagged up the glass, and he and the deputy were on their knees, making an inch-by-inch search. The rain had started falling again.

"I knew we should have brought two vehicles," I said to McQuaid. "I need to go back to town and make a bank deposit. I have to check on Ruby, too."

McQuaid got painfully to his feet. "Why don't you take the truck and go on, China? When everything's wrapped up here, I'll catch a ride with Blackie or Pete."

"You sure?" I asked. "It's wet out here." And cold, too. The wind had started blowing, which meant that the chill factor was 10 or 15 degrees below freezing. I pulled my sheepskin-lined jacket tighter around me.

"Yeah," he said. Water was dripping off his nose and his shoulders were hunched against the wind, but he was grinning. "It's fine, really. You go on back." He rubbed his thigh. "You could leave my cane, though. And there's a pair of gloves under the seat."

I shook my head. "I'm not believing this. It's raining,

the thermometer's heading south, and you're having a great time."

McQuaid grinned a little sheepishly. "Well, it's a change. I get tired of sitting in front of the computer."

I sighed. Once a lawman, always a lawman. Oh, well. At least nobody was shooting at him. And if I was going to agree to do a little investigatory work for Blackie, how could I begrudge McQuaid the exquisite pleasure of crawling around a crime scene in the rain?

CHAPTER SIX

In northern Europe, mistletoe is thought to act as a master-key, for it is said to open all locks.

Sir James George Frazer
The Golden Bough

From the centre of the ceiling of this kitchen, old Wardle had just suspended with his own hands a huge branch of mistletoe, and this same branch of mistletoe instantaneously gave rise to a scene of general and most delightful struggling and confusion; in the midst of which Mr. Pickwick, with a gallantry that would have done honour to a descendant of Lady Tollimglower herself, took the old lady by the hand, led her beneath the mystic branch, and saluted her in all courtesy and decorum.

Charles Dickens
The Pickwick Papers

Ruby's house is almost as flamboyant as she is. Shaded by huge old live oaks and surrounded by composed, commonplace houses, it's a staid old Victorian with original gingerbread trim and shutters, radically rejuvenated by sensational combinations of gray, green, fuschia, and plum paint. The front porch is filled with white wicker furniture and hung with baskets of asparagus fern, which keeps its cheerful green color all winter long. I know why Ruby's Painted Lady makes her neighbors uncomfortable. It is as if your grandmother has suddenly taken to wearing fire-engine-red lipstick and mauve eyeshadow and going out dancing in the middle of the week.

There was no response to my loud knocking at both the front and back doors. I checked the garage to see if Ruby's red Toyota was there, and frowned when I saw it—her bicycle, too. We don't have public transportation in Pecan Springs, unless you count the Greyhound bus that goes to Austin and San Antonio, and Tippit's Taxi, which takes senior citizens to the grocery store. I couldn't imagine where Ruby might have gone without her car. I went back to the truck, retrieved the cell phone from under the seat, and called Ruby's number again. No answer.

I stood for a moment, hesitating. Fictional sleuths do it all the time, but I am not fond of breaking and entering. It is an easy way to lose your bar privileges, which I have gone to some effort to retain over the years. It was a good thing Ruby kept a spare key hidden under the second brick to the right in the path that led to the kitchen door. She left it there, she always said, so that I could come in and make myself at home if she happened to be out—which covered this situation exactly.

Except that when I looked for it, the key was gone. I straightened up with a sigh. Well, there are certain circumstances under which breaking and entering are justified, such as when you are worried about the psychological stability and physical health of your best friend. Her car was in the garage, wasn't it? This gave me probable cause to believe that she might be in the house, in need of aid and assistance, didn't it? I went to the garage, located a screwdriver, and jimmied a window. I climbed through and found myself on the table in Ruby's breakfast nook. So far so good, except that I knocked a bowl onto the floor as I was climbing off the table.

Guiltily, I picked up the broken pieces of china and put them in the garbage. Then I stood still and looked around. Inside this gorgeous Painted Lady, Ruby has stripped the woodwork and floors to the original light oak and papered and painted the walls—but not in their original fusty old tints. Ruby is fond of oranges, yellows, and reds, charged with occasional stripes and checks and colorful patterns. The kitchen, wallpapered in red and white, with a watermelon border around the wainscoting and red-painted table and chairs, is particularly zingy. When you first come in, it takes a while to get used to the decor, and to the New Age music and incense that wafts gently on the air.

But not today. Today, nothing wafted, not a sound, not a scent. I raised my voice and shouted Ruby's name. Nothing. The house was quiet as a tomb—and about as cold as one, too. The heat wasn't turned on. Looking around, I noticed something else strange. The kitchen was absolutely immaculate, the counters shining, the towels folded on the racks, the stove gleaming. And when I walked through the dining room and into the living room, I saw that these rooms were spotless too—and not just dusted and vacuumed, but neat. It was an altogether unnerving sight.

I'm afraid this sounds terribly tacky, but it isn't meant to, believe me. Ruby is an artistic person who thrives on creative chaos. She is happiest when she is totally surrounded with clutter. Her sewing machine sits for weeks on the dining room table, there are untidy heaps of book-marked magazines beside her reading chair, and dust bunnies lurk in the corners while last night's dinner dishes marinate in the dishpan.

Today, however, the sink was empty and shining, the dining room table was cleared, and there wasn't a dust bunny or a dirty dish to be seen. The house was picture-perfect, as if it were awaiting a photographer from *Better Homes and Gardens*, or a convention of real estate salesmen. But without Ruby's wonderful messes, the rooms seemed empty and vacant. It was as if the real Ruby had abandoned ship, moved out, gone somewhere else, leaving only her memory behind.

I went to the foot of the stairs, intending to go up and check to make sure that something terrible hadn't happened. But when I put my foot on the first tread, I hesitated, not because I was afraid of what I might find (I really did have the sense that the house was empty) but because I was suddenly and uncomfortably aware that I was violating my friend's privacy. If she had wanted me to know she was going away, she would have told me. If she had wanted me to know where she was going, she would have told me that. And here I was, breaking into her house, poking my nose into a part of her life that she obviously intended to keep from me. Who did I think I was? What kind of arrogant, disrespectful person would intrude where she wasn't wanted?

And yet—

And yet, Ruby was my friend and my partner, and what concerned her concerned me. Maybe she was feeling bad about Hark, or was trying to escape from Wade. Maybe she was in some kind of trouble and needed me. Maybe she didn't even *know* she needed me, so she couldn't ask for my help. But I knew, and I wasn't going to let her down. I took a deep breath, pocketed my apprehensions, and started up the stairs, calling her name. The weight of the silence told me that there would be no answer.

In Ruby's bathroom, the towels hung pristinely from the racks, the fixtures polished and shining. The bedroom, which was usually as cluttered as a teenager's with clothes, makeup, and books, was as uncharacteristically neat as the downstairs had been, the bed made with the gorgeous blue comforter she'd bought a couple of months before, the bed-side tables tidied. I went to the closet to check for her suitcase, which always sits in the corner behind her coat. It was gone.

I was standing there, trying to think what I should do next, when the brash jangle of the telephone shattered the silence. I hesitated a moment, then picked it up. The caller might have a clue to Ruby's whereabouts.

It was Wade Wilcox. "I need to talk to Ruby, China," he said, after I had identified myself. There was an urgent edge to his voice. "Where is she?"

"I don't know," I said truthfully. But even if I had known where Ruby had gone, I wouldn't have told Wade. Ruby had married him when she was a college sophomore and divorced him after seventeen years, a daughter named Shannon, and a big house just off the country club's ninth green. Shannon was out of college now and working for a computer company in Austin, the big house had been sold to pay off the big bills, and Ruby had built a successful business and a new life. Her ex-husband had no right to think he could just waltz back in and claim her attention.

Wade cleared his throat. "Something serious is going on with her and I want to know what it is," he said, sounding genuinely concerned. "I tried calling all day yesterday, but she wasn't home. And the answering machine is turned off. That's not like Ruby. Where is she, China?"

"I'm telling you, Wade, I don't know. I'm as much in the dark as you are." I paused. The only Wade I know is the handsome, charming, sexy jerk who hurt Ruby so deeply that it's taken her years to recover—if she has. Given the fact that she's never maintained a romantic relationship for more than a few months, I've occasionally wondered whether she was still carrying a torch for him. But I hadn't seen him for a long while. Maybe he'd grown out of his jerky phase. Maybe he'd cleaned up his act. "What do you think is going on?" I asked cautiously.

"I can't even hazard a guess," he said. "We had dinner on Friday evening and she seemed—I don't know. Angry, maybe. Resentful. Certainly very upset. But she wouldn't give me a clue. She kept saying that this—whatever it was—was something she had to deal with herself."

I frowned. Ruby had gone out to dinner with Wade? Why hadn't she mentioned it to me? But after our argument on Saturday morning, she probably hadn't been in the mood for girlish confidences about old lovers.

"I was afraid maybe it had something to do with Shannon," Wade was saying. "That she was sick or in trouble or something. But Ruby's always been straight with me where Shannon's concerned, so I don't think it's that." He sighed heavily. "Maybe it's just me. I guess I couldn't blame her if she was a little ticked off about the way I've treated her. I haven't exactly been Prince Charming."

I wasn't going to argue with that. Prince Charming doesn't run off with a young woman barely out of her teens, or put his wife through an agonizing divorce. But Wade had brought up something I hadn't thought about. Maybe Ruby's strange behavior had something to do with Shannon. Or with Amy, the daughter she had borne out of wedlock before she married Wade and who had re-entered

Ruby's life a couple of years ago. I doubted whether Wade knew about Amy, so I wasn't going to mention her name. But it was something I could check into. Amy lives and works in Pecan Springs.

"My husband told me you were back in town," I said evenly. "You're going into business here?"

"I'm planning to open a financial consulting office," Wade said. "You know, advice on stocks, bonds, mutual funds, insurance—that sort of thing." His voice got slick, smiling, and I could picture him sitting back, putting his feet up, sticking a cigar in his mouth. The big man. The high roller. "Maybe we could get together and talk about your financial future, China. Every business owner ought to have a retirement plan."

"Thanks," I said dryly, thinking that Wade Wilcox, with his affinity for the baccarat tables at Vegas, was hardly the man I'd choose to help me with my investments. "But I'm afraid my funds are tied up just now."

"Yeah, Ruby told me that you and she had gone into business together. Some sort of lunchroom, something like that?"

"A *tea*room," I said emphatically.

"I thought everybody in this town drank Lone Star. You sure you gals know what you're doing?"

"You bet we do," I growled.

"Well, you don't need to bite my head off," he said, offended. He was silent for a minute, then his voice changed again, became softer, more personal. "Listen, China. I know you're Ruby's best friend, so I don't mind telling you what's on my mind. I've been hoping that maybe she and I could . . . well, you know." He laughed awkwardly. "Second time around."

Second time around! I nearly snorted. If you asked me, the only reason Wade Wilcox was interested in Ruby was because he'd heard that she'd won the lottery and he hoped he could get a piece of the action. The guy had some nerve. If he'd handed her that line of bull, I wasn't surprised that she'd seemed angry and resentful.

"I've always cared for her, you know," he went on. His voice had taken on a velvety sound, like a forties' crooner singing his favorite song. "I always respected her right to do what she chose, to make her own decisions, even when I felt that she was making a mistake. And deep in my heart of hearts, I've never stopped loving her. We were good together once, I know we could make it happen again. And now that we're a little older, a little wiser, I bet it'll be better than ever. I've talked to Shannon about this and she thinks it would be wonderful."

Talked to Shannon! I was indignant. What business did Wade have dragging her into this? And what daughter wouldn't want her parents to get back together again? If Shannon had called her mother and pressured her to go back to Wade, I wasn't surprised that Ruby had packed up and fled.

Wade was warming to his subject. "China, I'll bet you could help. How about if you talk to Ruby? She always listens to you. You could tell her how much I—"

Horsefeathers. "Wade," I said, interrupting, "I can't help you. Ruby hasn't confided in me. I don't know what her feelings are, and I feel uncomfortable talking like this behind her back." On her phone. In her bedroom. In her absence. I looked around at the neat, quiet room, feeling a sudden panic. Where the hell *was* she?

"Well, I can certainly understand how you feel." Wade made one more effort to sound like the concerned ex-husband. "But I tell you, China, I'm worried about her. If you find out what's going on, will you let me know?"

"Probably not," I said fiercely, and hung up the phone. I hadn't accomplished a single thing by coming here, except to get trapped in an unwelcome, thoroughly unpleasant conversation. I might as well leave—through the door, this time.

But before I went, maybe it would be a good idea to look for Shannon's and Amy's phone numbers. I could call them and ask if they had any idea what was going on with their mother. There was a small writing desk by the window, overlooking the bleak and wintry garden at the back of the house. On the desk was a telephone and a Rolodex. I flipped to Wilcox—nothing but a phone number for Wade, with a Denver area code. I went back to the beginning and began to leaf through all the cards. I found the numbers I wanted filed under *G*—for girls, probably. I'd call them this evening. But I wouldn't tell them that I had gotten their numbers by breaking into their mother's house.

When I got back to the truck, I realized that my surreptitious activities had made me hungry. I put the truck in gear and drove to the Nueces Street Diner, thinking that it was a good day for a hot meatloaf plate. And since it wasn't quite noon yet, my chances were good. If you get to the Diner at the tail end of the lunch hour rush, you can't count on the meatloaf.

The Nueces Street Diner ("Best Down-Home Cookin' in Texas!") belongs to Lila Jennings and her daughter Docia, who take turns cooking and waiting the counter. A few years back, Lila and her husband, Ralph, bought an old Missouri and Pacific dining car and hauled it to the vacant lot kitty-cornered across from the bank. Ralph always said that he parked it there so the bank could see what he was doing with its money. He died before the note was paid off, but Lila and Docia have soldiered on, with the help of Docia's daughter Lucy. They've done well enough to add a larger kitchen on the back and an entryway on the front and spiff up the old diner with a red Formica counter and fifties-style chrome-and-red tables and chairs. The walls are covered with Texas memorabilia. (My favorite is the framed clipping from the *Dallas Morning News* announcing that three women lawyers had just been appointed to a special Texas Supreme Court—the first all-women high court in the United States. It is dated January 1, 1925, the same month that Ma Ferguson, Texas's first woman governor, was inaugurated.)

There were three or four regulars at the long counter, but the tables were still mostly empty when I walked in and hung my coat on the peg by the door. Somebody had put up a miniature artificial tree and a lifesize cardboard cutout of Santa Claus, and "I'm Dreaming of a White Christmas" was playing over the loudspeaker. A large clump of mistletoe, one of the prettiest I'd seen, hung over the swinging door that led to the kitchen, and red and green paper streamers were draped around the glass pie shelves. Lila and Docia had gone in for Christmas in a big way.

Lila was waitressing today, which meant that either Docia or Lucy was cooking. According to the menu, which is posted on a blackboard behind the counter, I had my choice of meatloaf plate, fried catfish, or chicken and dumplings. Today's sides were mustard greens, deep-fried corn on the cob, and black-eyed peas, and either lemon or coconut pie for dessert. I contemplated this list happily. Out of regard for my cholesterol count, I have lunch here only once every couple of weeks, but when I do, I go whole hog.

I sat down at a table by the front window and Lila came

over, pulling her order book out of the pocket of her pale green nylon uniform. A perky little white hat was perched on her bleached blond hair, which she rolls under like one of the Andrews Sisters. In that getup, she looks right at home among the fifties fixtures.

"Where's yer better half today?" she asked, taking a pencil out of her hair.

"He's doing a little work for the sheriff," I said incautiously. "Have you got plenty of meatloaf?"

"Enough fer you," Lila said, and scrawled a big ML on the order pad. She tilted her head, her eyes bright. "I'll bet they're out investigatin' poor Carl's accident."

I sighed, wishing I'd had the sense to keep my mouth shut. But Lila had no doubt already heard the news. In Pecan Springs, gossip is like a deadly virus, so communicable that nothing will stop it.

Lila pulled down the corners of her lipsticked mouth. "Carl was Lucy's boyfriend, y'know."

"He was?" I said, in some surprise. Carl Swenson was a loner, and Sheila's comment about essence of goat had been on the mark. The idea that the man might have been romantically involved with someone had never crossed my mind. But now that I thought about it, they seemed to be a pretty good match: a pair of misfits who might have found consolation in each other. Lila's granddaughter is not particularly attractive—tall, skinny, and graceless, with dark, stringy hair and a half-furtive, hangdog look about her. She might be prettier (and happier) if she'd pay some attention to herself, but she didn't seem to think it was worth the trouble.

Lila nodded. "They been seein' each fer, oh, near a month now. Lucy was 'spectin' a proposal." She jerked her head in the direction of the mistletoe. "He brung that, you know. Gave her a big kiss under it, too."

"Give Lucy my condolences," I said. I tried to conjure up a mental picture of Carl Swenson and Lucy sharing a kiss under the mistletoe, but it wouldn't come.

Lila's eyes darkened. "Yeah, the little gal's really grievin'. She's back there in the kitchen right now, cryin' so's she can hardly cook. First batch of meatloaf, she left out the tomato sauce." She made a small grimace. "Came out lookin' real funny an' gray. Don't taste half-bad, though, if you put catsup on it. Or salsa." She picked up the salsa jar and inspected it to make sure it was full. "Or you can wait fer the next batch. Ten minutes, mebbe."

I don't care much for gray meatloaf, and I'm leery of Lila's salsa. It'll burn holes in your tongue. I didn't want to wait, either. "Guess I don't feel much like meatloaf today," I said. "Think I'll go with the chicken and dumplings."

Lila leaned over, nearly overpowering me with the scent of her Evening in Paris. "And it weren't no ak-se-dent, neither," she whispered. "Carl was kilt on purpose."

No accident? I felt the hair on my neck prickle. "Who says?"

"Lucy says, that's who," Lila said. She straightened, her eyes slitted suspiciously. "There was somethin' about that man made me nervous. Somethin' strange goin' on there. No job, no vis'ble means o'support, 'cept fer mistletoe and goats, and whut's that amount to?" She made a scornful noise, and answered her own question. "A hill o' beans, that's whut. I told her she didn't have no bidness with him, that he'd use her up and toss her out, but she wudn't listen." Lila made a scornful noise. "Romance. That's all the girls think about these days. Show 'em a good, solid man, such as Orville Pennyman, who works at the Fina station and brings a good paycheck home to his mama ever' week, an' whut do they do? They go runnin' after the nearest rat."

We were getting off the subject. "Lucy thinks that Carl Swenson had enemies?"

"A passel," Lila said with relish. "People who'd love to see him done in. Leastways, that's what Lucy told her mom. Her 'n' Docia both live with me now, you know. Saves money that way. Lot cheaper than for all three of us to be payin' rent."

A man at a window table, a regular, lifted his coffee cup and Lila gave him a curt nod. He put the cup down with a complaining sigh, but he knew the rules. When Lila gets involved in a conversation with one of her customers, the others have to wait. I know—it's happened to me.

"I don't suppose Lucy mentioned who they were," I remarked. "Swenson's enemies, I mean."

Lila tapped her pencil against her teeth. "Well, fer starters, there's that neighbor of his, that Tuttle woman. Lucy says she threatened to give him a good dose o' buckshot next time she saw him, on accounta them goats. Maybe she figered it'ud be safer to hit him a good clip with that old maroon Mercury she drives. Safer fer her, I mean. That way, he couldn't shoot back."

A maroon Mercury, huh? I made a mental note to ask Blackie whether he had taken a look at Mrs. Tuttle's car. "That's interesting," I said encouragingly. "Who else?"

Lila frowned. "Well, there's Bob Godwin, just a fer instance, though you don't need to go tellin' him I said so. Him and Carl got into a fight over some money Bob claimed was owed him. Wouldn't put it past Bob to try and collect. And you know what a temper that man has." She shook her head with a disapproving *tch-tch*.

"Now, Lila," I said. I didn't put much stock in this charge, since Bean's Bar and Grill, which Bob owns, is one of Lila's chief competitors. She's always finding some way to run him down.

"Whut d'ya mean, 'Now, Lila'?" she asked haughtily. "You ain't seen Bob when he's got his back up about something? He's hell on wheels, believe you me. Didn't you read in the paper last week about him gettin' into that fist fight with Harley Moses? He ain't got red hair for nothin'." The outside door opened and she looked up. "Well, if it ain't Mr. Hotshot Hibler, the editoor of our very fine newspaper, who printed that story his very own self."

Hark peeled off his windbreaker, pulled out the chair next to me and sat down, brushing raindrops out of his dark hair. "Hello, Lila," he said in a mild tone. "Kinda damp out there, isn't it? Hi, China."

I frowned, recalling what Sheila had said about Hark and Lynn Hughes. It was entirely possible that Wade's return had nothing to do with Ruby's recent behavior, and that her weirdness was due to her problems with Hark. But the guy is my boss—I edit the weekly Home and Garden section for the *Enterprise*—and we've been friends for a couple of years, so I wasn't going to jump down his throat. I intended to find out what was going on, however.

"Hello, Hark," I said. "How's life?"

Hark began rolling up the sleeves of his shirt. "Not too shabby," he replied. "You doin' okay?"

Pointedly ignoring Hark, Lila scratched out ML on her order book and wrote down CD instead. "What'd'ya want with yer chicken and dumplin's?"

"Mustard greens," I said. "And deep-fried corn on the cob." I smiled in anticipation. "And coconut pie."

She stuck the pencil into her hair. "Be right out," she said, and turned to walk away.

"Hey, Lila," Hark said, raising his voice. "I'll have the meatloaf plate."

"Lucy left out the tomato sauce," I said in a warning tone. "She's grieving for Carl Swenson."

Hark's dark eyebrows went up. "Lucy was a friend of Swenson's?"

Lila wheeled around. "And whut's wrong with that?" She put her fists on her hips. "Mebbe you think it's a crime fer two people to fall in love and get married and practice fam'ly values, Mr. Newspaper Editoor. Mebbe you'd ruther print dirt about dope and preverts an' such, so's you can sell more papers."

"Carl Swenson and Lucy were *married*?" Hark asked, even more surprised. "How the hell did I miss that?"

"Lila says Lucy was expecting a proposal," I said quickly, forestalling one of Lila's snappish replies. I don't understand why Hark eats at the Diner, given the way Lila criticizes him. She thinks that the *Enterprise* pays too much attention to crime, which Arnold Seidensticker, the newspaper's former owner, swept under the rug. Arnold saw the *Enterprise* as a family newspaper, so he printed stories that Dad could read aloud to his wife and children at the dinner table every Wednesday, when the paper came out.

But Hark bought the newspaper from the Seidensticker family in the fall, and things have changed. To Hark's way of thinking, his readers have a right to the truth, however disagreeable. Moreover, the *Enterprise* is now a daily. As a result, Pecan Springs is waking from its self-satisfied trance to the startled realization that it is not the squeaky clean village it thought it was. It is just like every other small town, populated by people who make mistakes, accidentally go wrong, or are intentionally corrupt. These imperfect people probably don't outnumber the rest of the populace, of course—it's just that errors, accidents, and corruption naturally seem to demand a certain amount of press attention, and Hark is happy to oblige.

Not everybody is pleased by this new journalistic realism, of course. Those who object write letters to the editor, threatening to cancel their subscription so they won't have to read that the mayor was forced to resign because of a sex scandal or that the town's favorite dentist had abducted his granddaughter. (Both events made headlines in September.) But Hark says that it pays to tell the truth, even when it doesn't taste good in your mouth. And he must be right. For every cancellation, there are two new subscribers.

Lila pushed her lips in and out, considering. There was a calculating gleam in her eye. "I reckon you'll put the story on the front page," she said judiciously. "Poor Carl bein' hit an' run an' all."

Hark nodded. "I suppose you'd rather we didn't cover it at all, but—"

"You can have Lucy's high school grad-u-ashun photo," Lila said. "It's got a gold frame on it, though, an' glass, so you got to be careful. I don't want it broke."

Hark blinked. "Lucy's . . . photo?"

"Well," Lila said, "I just thought that since she's the grievin' fee-an-say, you'd want to put her picture in the paper, alongside his. Human int'rest, y'know." She smiled, showing her gold tooth. "Be sure and put in that she works at the Diner, 'longside her mother and grandmother. It won't hurt fer us to get a little publicity."

"Oh, right," Hark said. "A little publicity." Then, capitalizing on Lila's change of attitude, he added quickly,

"While you're here, I'll have what China's having, except I'll take black-eyed peas. And lemon pie."

"You got it, Mr. Editoor," Lila said cheerfully, and sashayed off, ignoring the man at the window table, feebly hoisting his coffee cup.

"Breaking news," I said, grinning.

"Sheesh," Hark muttered. "I don't believe Swenson was involved with Lucy. She's not—well, not his type."

"You can't believe everything you hear," I said, and segued neatly into the subject at the top of my mind. "I just heard about Lynn Hughes, for instance." I gave him a meaningful look.

Hark looked confused. "What's Lynn Hughes got to do with Swenson and Lucy?"

"Nothing. I heard that you took her out to dinner. At Crandall's. And that you two were exceedingly cozy."

Hark shook his head disgustedly. "Was it Sheila who told you that? I saw her and Blackie come in. She gave me the evil eye."

"I was just wondering," I continued, "whether Ruby knows about Lynn."

Hark frowned. "Ruby? Sure she knows. The restaurant was her idea."

"Excuse me?"

"I'd been courting Lynn for a couple of weeks," Hark said patiently. "When she finally said yes, Ruby suggested that Crandall's would be a great place to celebrate. She was going to join us, but at the last minute she had to go to San Antonio."

I shook my head. "I can't believe this, Hark," I said numbly. "Lynn Hughes? When's the big day?"

"Not until the first of the year. Lynn's got to stay on until Charlie finds a replacement."

"You mean she's leaving Charlie?" He'd be madder than steamed jackrabbit. He'd put a lot of effort into training that girl, and he'd bragged over and over about how great she was. And now she was quitting to get married.

Hark gave me a strange look. "Well, of course she's leaving Charlie. How else could she come to work for me?"

My mouth dropped open. "*Work* for you?"

"What in hell did you think she was going to do for me? Sign on as my mistress? She's going to be my assistant." Hark grinned triumphantly. "Charlie-boy is so mad, he could spit nails. But I did it fair and square. I made her an offer, took her to lunch a time or two to explain what's involved with the job, and told her to discuss it with Charlie. I thought maybe he'd up her salary to where I couldn't compete. But she's got a journalism degree, and even ol' Charlie has to agree that it's a natural fit, so he let her go." He grinned widely. "And now she's all mine."

"I see," I said, feeling abashed. "So Ruby doesn't have any reason to be upset with you." It was more a statement than a question.

"Why should she?" Hark asked. "Which doesn't mean she isn't." He leaned back in his chair, frowning. There was a coffee stain on his loosely knotted green tie and he was missing a button on his shirt. Otherwise, he looked good. Hark is no movie star, but he's lost forty pounds over the last year, including two spare chins and a roll of flab around his waist.

I sighed. "You too, huh? Join the club."

He raised one eyebrow. "But you're her best friend. You mean, she's been acting weird with you?"

"Weird to the max, as Brian says. I've been trying to call her all weekend, with no success. So this morning I stopped at her house. The place was locked up and her suitcase is gone. The house is neat and tidy and so clean you could eat off the floors. She—"

"Clean?" Hark asked in amazement. "Neat and tidy?" Both eyebrows shot up. "I don't want to sound judgmental, but those are not adjectives that I'd use to describe our Ruby's living quarters—under normal circumstances, anyway. She's wonderfully creative, but a housekeeper she ain't."

"I know," I said sadly. "The place looks empty and lonesome. However, while I was there, Wade Wilcox called."

Lila appeared with a tray and began to shuffle plates across the table. "Lucy says she don't want you to have her grad-u-ashun picture," she said grimly. "She says she don't want her private life splashed all over the newspaper."

Good for Lucy, I thought. Maybe there was hope for her after all.

Hark looked down at his plate, then over at mine. "I thought we were getting chicken and dumplings."

Lila was grim-faced. "Lucy's grievin' so much that she forgot to put the bakin' powder into the dumplin's. But them biscuits 're just as good, even if they are left over from breakfast. Spoon a little chicken gravy over 'em, and yer mouth won't know the difference."

"I knew I should have gone to Bean's for chicken-fried," Hark said with a long-suffering look.

"Then you wouldn't of got the scoop on Carl and Lucy," Lila snapped, "even if you can't have her picture for yer dirty old rag." She stalked away.

Hark picked up his fork. "So Wilcox called, huh? What did he want?"

"He wanted to talk to Ruby, but he settled for me. He says he's worried about her too. He'd like to patch things up." I was less tentative about saying this now that I knew that Hark wasn't the source of Ruby's heartache.

Hark began peppering his chicken. "Yeah, sure," he said sarcastically. "What Wilcox really wants is to get his greasy hands on Ruby's lottery winnings. You know what he told her? That she should tell the lottery people to change her payment schedule. Instead of getting it monthly, like she does now, she should get it all in one lump sum and give it to him to invest. The guy's got a lotta nerve." He paused, frowning. "You say her suitcase is gone?"

I looked straight at him. "Do you know where she is?"

He met my eyes. "I wish I did," he said quietly. "I wish she trusted me enough to tell me what's bothering her. I wish—" He swallowed painfully, and his mouth twisted. "Lord, China, I *love* that woman. I want to marry her, take care of her. I want to make things good for her."

"Have you told her this?"

"Told her!" Hark exploded angrily. "Hell, yes, I've told her. Over and over again. For a while, I thought she might be on the verge of saying yes, but now she says we should stop seeing one another. She won't give me an explanation, either."

"It's not Wade, is it?" I asked.

"I don't think so," Hark said. "She's made two or three trips to Austin and San Antonio lately, one of them an overnight." He poked at his biscuit with a fork. "If you ask me, she's seeing somebody else. A doctor, maybe. I walked in on her when she was leaving a message for him to call her."

Hark is a great guy and I like him, although I've never believed that he and Ruby are a perfect match. She loves to party, and he'd rather stay home and watch CNN. Still, hearing this spontaneous confession of unrequited love, I felt a wave of sympathy for the man.

"I love her too," I said. "But I guess there's a limit to how much we can pry. She doesn't have to tell us everything that goes on in her life."

"Yeah," Hark said. "She's entitled to her privacy. Damn it."

We ate our chicken and leftover biscuits in a gloomy silence.

CHAPTER SEVEN

Many cultures were awed by the fact that mistletoe berries ripened in late autumn and persisted through the winter. In some countries, the plant was worshipped as the fertilizing dew of the supreme spirit and the berries were thought to be drops of the gods' semen. As such, they were believed to have extraordinary powers, and used to enhance fertility.

China Bayles
"Mistletoe Magic"

When I got back to the truck, I checked the cell phone and found a message from Blackie, letting me know that he had interviewed Mrs. Tuttle, who said she'd been indoors all Sunday and couldn't provide any information. He'd also drawn a blank at the house trailer, where there was no one at home. He added that the crime scene work was finished. He was heading back to town and would drop McQuaid off at the house. "And don't forget that you agreed to talk to the Fletcher sisters again," he said. "I sure would like to be able to get a look at that truck."

"Okay, okay," I muttered, stowing the phone. "But first the deposit." I was carrying around several days' worth of checks and cash receipts from the shop and getting them to the bank would only take a minute. I pulled the blue plastic deposit bag out from under the truck seat and ran across the street, dodging the raindrops.

When you visit Pecan Springs, Ranchers State Bank is one attraction you won't want to miss. It isn't just that the building is a fine old example of Main Street architecture (although it is), or that the fixtures—pressed-tin ceilings, glass-topped oak tables with green-shaded lamps, pink marble counters and polished brass tellers' cages—are original and in beautiful condition. No, the bank has other claims to historical fame. One muggy July day in 1878, famous Texas outlaw Sam Bass sauntered in, glanced around, and spotted the sheriff leaning against one of the tellers' cages. The sheriff looked up and recognized him, and Sam beat an unceremonious retreat to his horse. Outdistancing pursuit, he rode fifty miles north, intending to rob the bank in Round Rock. Instead, he ran into seven armed lawmen and a hailstorm of bullets. So it was Round Rock and not Pecan Springs that went into the history books as the site of the death of the notorious Sam Bass.

The bank was not quite so lucky one winter weekend in the early twenties, when the three Newton boys—Willis, Joe, and Jess—came to town, fresh from robbing the San Marcos and New Braunfels banks. They blew the door off the safe with nitroglycerin and vamoosed with fifty thousand dollars in gold, more or less. According to local legend, the boys went in different directions after the heist, Willis and Joe heading south for a rendezvous on the other side of the border. But Jess, who was carrying the stolen money, stopped to see a girlfriend in New Braunfels. He got to drinking, rode out into the Hill Country, and stashed the gold under a rock. When he sobered up, he discovered that one rock looked pretty much like another, and he couldn't remember where he'd hid it. Like most bank-robber tales, this one probably isn't true. Or if it is, Willis and Joe never told it, although they didn't keep much to themselves. Jess died early, but his two brothers lived to be nearly ninety, cashing in on their outlaw reputations by giving occasional interviews. They even appeared on the Johnny Carson show in 1980.

I like all of the bank's tellers, but my favorite is Bonnie Roth, who is a member of the Myra Merryweather Herb Guild and a frequent customer at the shop. She was wearing a sprig of holly tucked behind her name tag and a pair of Rudolph the Red-Nosed Reindeer earrings. I unzipped the deposit bag, took out the cash and the checks, and slid them over to her.

I let her count the cash in silence, then asked, "What's new?" as she put a rubber thimble on her left thumb and began running a tape on the checks.

"Well, I suppose you're terribly busy decorating for the Christmas Tour," she said, the fingers of her right hand flying over the calculator keys. "Rowena is thrilled that you've allowed your house to be included." She lifted her head and smiled at me. "You're quite a celebrity in this town, you know."

"Oh, come now," I said modestly, wondering which of my talents was being singled out. My expertise in herbs? My acute business sense? Or was it my role in helping to solve the murder of a local real estate developer?

"Don't try to deny it, silly," Bonnie said with a bright little laugh. Her fingers paused for a moment. "You're married to our former acting chief of police, aren't you? Everybody thinks Mike McQuaid is just the sweetest guy. You're awfully lucky." While I was biting my tongue, she added,

"I can't wait to see your decorations, China. I'm sure they'll be spectacular."

I took a deep breath and said in an offhand tone, "Actually, I'm not doing anything special for the Tour. It's just our usual Texas-style Christmas."

Still clicking the calculator, Bonnie smiled. "Well, whatever it is, I'm sure it will be terribly creative. I'm lucky just to get the tree to stand up straight." She missed a check, peered at the tape, added it in and went on. "Speaking of Christmas, you buy your mistletoe from Carl Swenson, don't you? Did you know he got killed yesterday? Somebody ran him down."

"My stars," I said, feigning amazement. "Where'd you hear that?"

"Mrs. Tuttle was in here just a minute ago," Bonnie replied, her fingers still zipping over the keys. "She was at Cindy Sue's window, though, and I was busy with Mr. Dooley's deposit and didn't get to hear all the details. Just that he got hit, and the driver didn't stop. Mrs. Tuttle lives across the road, which is how she knew about it, I guess." She shook her head. "It's really too bad."

"Did you know him?"

"No, but my husband did. They were in the same class at Pecan Springs High."

"Swenson grew up here, then?" Somehow I'd assumed that he was a recent arrival.

"That's right. On that place where he lives now. But he left after high school and was gone for quite a while. Somebody told me he'd been in prison."

I was taken aback. "In prison!"

Bonnie nodded. "Surprised me, too. But of course, you can't always believe what people tell you." She tapped the checks into a neat stack and deftly clipped them together.

"It's too bad about the accident," I said. "People drive too fast, and they don't pay attention." I paused. "Did Ms. Tuttle say whether she saw it happen?"

Bonnie initialed my deposit slip. "Gosh, I don't know. All she said was, the sheriff had talked to her about it." She filled out the bank's deposit receipt and pushed it through the window. "If you want to ask, you can probably catch her at the pharmacy. She said she needed to get a prescription filled."

"I'm not sure I know Ms. Tuttle," I said. "At least, not to recognize her."

"Of course you do," Bonnie replied. "Don't you remember? Corinne Tuttle. She's the one who always brings that awful lamb casserole to the October herb cookoff."

"Oh, right," I said. "Corinne. I guess I just didn't remember her last name." But I remembered her lamb casserole, that's for sure. Two years ago, I was one of the judges. A dish like that you never forget.

Bonnie put the checks in her drawer and pushed it shut. "She never gets a prize, poor thing," she said. "Maybe the judges don't like lamb. You'd think she'd take the hint and try something else."

Every Christmas, Mr. Hobbs, the pharmacist, invites the local elementary-school artists to paint his front window, and today was the day. All the drugstore items had been moved out of the window and a half-dozen kids were noisily creating an eight by ten picture of Santa's workshop, staffed with elves working under the supervision of a beaming Mrs. Claus. They weren't gifted artists, but they were having fun.

In the back of the store, Mr. Hobbs was handing a white

paper sack to a heavyset woman in black slacks and a green coat with a fake fur collar, carrying a furled black umbrella.

"One every four hours," he said cheerily. "Should take care of your nerves."

"Oh, I hope so," the woman said. "I need to get a good-night's sleep."

"Corinne!" I said, when the woman turned around. "So nice to see you again." When she looked puzzled, I added, "Maybe you don't remember. I'm China Bayles."

"Of course," she said, not very cordially. "You were one of the judges at the herb cookoff a couple of years ago."

"That's right," I said. "That lamb casserole of yours missed by that much." I held up my thumb and forefinger to show how close the casserole had come to—something. Being tossed out, maybe?

"It did?" Her smile was surprised. "How nice of you to remember. It's my favorite recipe—and original, too, if I do say so myself. Not something I clipped out of a magazine."

"I could never forget that casserole," I said truthfully. I glanced down at the sack. "I couldn't help overhearing. Have you tried kava for your nerves?"

"Kava?" She looked doubtful. "What's that?"

"It's an herbal remedy that reduces anxiety and stress. And St. John's Wort is good for depression. Neither are addictive, like the chemical alternatives."

Corinne frowned. "Thanks for the suggestion, but I called Dr. Nichols and he thought I ought to have this." She was clutching her bag as if it were a life preserver. "I need something that *works*. My nephew Marvin has been staying with me since August. He had a job but he quit, and he hangs around the house all the time. He's driving me crazy. My nerves are a wreck, and I'm not getting enough sleep."

I nodded sympathetically. "Kids are like that." I paused. "I understand you've had some trouble out your way."

"You've heard about Carl Swenson, then," Corinne said nervously.

"How did it happen?"

She shifted from one foot to the other. "All I know is that he was out cutting mistletoe along the road and somebody hit him."

"How awful," I said. "Did you see it happen?"

"Oh, no, of *course* not," she said quickly. There was a nervous tic at the corner of her eye and her face had a grayish tinge. "It was drizzly yesterday and I was feeling very low. I didn't go out the whole day. In fact, I didn't know a thing about it until the sheriff stopped this morning and told me. It was quite a shock to my nerves. I'm not a complainer, but I just don't know how much more I can take."

"I'm sure it's very hard," I said, wondering if Corinne had happened to mention Marvin to the sheriff. "With a hit-and-run, they may never find out who did it unless they can find a witness. Somebody who saw the vehicle."

Up front, where the painting party was going on, one of the kids squealed, "I'm going to tell on you!" Corinne gave a startled yelp. Her hand went to her heart and she began to breathe quickly.

I put my hand on her arm. "Maybe you ought to sit down, Corinne. Just to catch your breath."

She shook off my hand and edged toward the door. "No, no, I can't sit. I'm in a hurry. I have to see about my car."

"I'll walk with you," I said, following her. Outside, she put up her umbrella, made a right turn, and quick-stepped along. I pulled up the sheepskin collar on my jacket and lengthened my stride. "The thing is that you have so little traffic out there," I went on, taking up where we'd left off. "So the person who hit Carl Swenson probably lives on that road, don't you think?" Some instinct made me add, "Or is visiting somebody."

"I *never* have visitors," she replied, with a quick, dismissive emphasis, and walked faster. She was holding her umbrella directly over her head, not offering to share it. The water was dripping onto my shoulder.

"What about your nephew?"

"Oh, but he's not visiting, he's family. My sister's son." She frowned. "The man who lives in that trashy old house trailer, Clyde McNabb? I hate to say it, but he's terribly reckless. He drinks, too, and he's got a nasty temper. Last year, he got drunk and hit two of Swenson's goats. They had a big argument over it. I don't suppose it would be a surprise if—" She broke off and gave me a quick sideways glance to make sure that I was paying attention. "I wish I'd thought to mention this to the sheriff. Although of course, I don't for a minute mean to suggest that Clyde did it."

Of course she had meant to suggest it. Which suggested to me that she was hiding something, maybe something to do with her nephew—the one who wasn't a visitor, but family. The one who got on her nerves so badly.

Corinne made a sharp right at the corner and I stayed with her. "I understand that the Swenson family has owned that land for quite a while," I said. "But somebody told me that Carl moved away after high school."

"Moved away, joined the Army, got himself into trouble, and ended up in prison." Corinne sniffed. "His father died just about the time he got out, so he came back here and took over the ranch. Not that he does what you'd call ranching. Just a few hundred goats. They're always getting out through the fence. They got in my garden this summer and ate all my sweet corn."

"I wonder why he went to prison."

"I never heard." She seemed more willing to talk now that the conversation had shifted to Swenson. "He didn't have a job, you know. But he didn't appear to need one. He sold two hundred acres to those two women who turned it into a flower farm, so he must have been getting regular payments from them. Every month or so, he'd drive off with a load of goats. And there was the mistletoe."

"It's amazing how little money some people can get by on," I remarked.

"He didn't seem to want for anything, though," Corinne went on, half to herself. "I overheard Marvin telling somebody on the phone that he'd just finished building a greenhouse. I guess Swenson saw how well those women were doing and decided he'd go into the flower business."

I frowned, remembering Donna's story about the argument over the ownership of Mistletoe Spring. Maybe Swenson had counted on his own spring for irrigation. And maybe, after the sisters took possession of Mistletoe Spring and cleaned it out, he'd decided to force them off the land and take over their established fields.

Corinne stopped. "This is as far as I go."

I looked up. We were in front of Gus's Body and Paint Shop. "Oh," I said. "Having some work done on your car?"

"An estimate." She gave a nervous little laugh. "Marvin hit a deer last week and smashed the fender."

"Just the fender?" I pushed my hands into my pockets. "You're lucky. I know a guy who totaled his brand new SUV when he ran into a big buck."

"The fender is bad enough," she said with a sigh. "I'm

afraid it will cost more than I can afford." She managed a
shaky smile. "I've enjoyed talking to you, China. Come out
sometime and I'll cook that lamb casserole you like so
much."

"That would be wonderful," I lied.

What in the world did we do before the cell phone was
invented? Now there's no more standing out in the rain to
use a pay phone, or darting into a convenience store and
yelling over the noise of video games. Back at the truck, I
turned on the ignition, flipped the heater to high, and called
the sheriff's office to give Blackie the information about
the smashed fender on Corinne Tuttle's maroon Mercury,
which seemed to me to be top priority—and urgent. Gus
often had a backlog and couldn't get to a repair job for a
couple of days. On the other hand, if the customer slipped
him a little something extra to go to the top of the list, he
could be agreeable. But when the dispatcher said that
Blackie couldn't be reached, I elected to call home rather
than leave a message. McQuaid picked up the phone on the
first ring.

"McQuaid here," he growled. "Who is it?"

"Uh-oh," I said. "Writer's block?"

"How'd you guess?" He sighed. "I never should have
started this damn book. If I tell the truth, none of my
Ranger buddies will ever speak to me again. If I don't tell
the truth—"

"—there's no point in writing the book."

"Exactly." McQuaid sighed again. "Hell's bells. I'd a
whole lot rather crawl around that crime scene than face
this stuff."

"Did you guys turn up anything useful?"

"The usual roadside litter. Nothing that really stood out, other than the paint chips and glass fragments. If you're on your way home, bring a six-pack. When Hemingway hit a dry spot, he'd tie one on."

"You'll have to get it yourself, Ernest. I'm headed for the flower farm. Blackie wants me to see if I can get any more information out of Donna and Terry."

"I'll go with you," McQuaid offered quickly.

"I'm afraid this is a girl thing. They're more likely to be straight if they're talking just to me. But there's another angle you could check out, if you don't have anything better to do."

"Oh, yeah?" He sounded eager. "What's that?"

"I ran into Corinne Tuttle at the pharmacy a little while ago."

"Who? Tuttle? Oh, yeah. The neighbor. Blackie's already interviewed her. She didn't see anything."

"Right," I said dryly. "Well, it turns out that she's taken her car—a maroon Mercury—to Gus's Body Shop. Her story is that her nephew Marvin hit a deer."

"A deer, huh?" McQuaid gave a low whistle. "And Tuttle told Blackie that she lived alone. She didn't say anything about a nephew."

"I wonder why."

"Yeah, me too. You know, I've been meaning to ask Gus to take a look at the back bumper on the van. It's been rattling something fierce."

"It might be a good idea to do that pretty quick, before he does any work on the Tuttle vehicle." I didn't say "before he destroys any potential evidence," but McQuaid got the point.

"I'm on my way." He paused. "But there's something I

was supposed to—Oh, yeah. Amy called. She wants you to call her at work."

"Amy!" Ruby's older daughter. Maybe she was calling with a message from her mother. "Did she leave a number?" The one I'd copied from the Rolodex was her home phone.

"Yeah. Here it is." He gave it to me and I jotted it down on the corner of an advertising flyer. "I'll call when I've finished at Gus's," he added, sounding much happier than he had at the beginning of our conversation. "Have I told you today that I love you?"

"Yes," I said. "Early this morning. Before we got out of bed." I smiled. "But I don't think we're limited to once a day."

"I hope not. I love you. Consider yourself kissed in all the right places."

I grinned. "I'll bet you're just saying that because I told you about Corinne Tuttle's car being in the shop."

"How'd you know?" I could hear the answering grin in his voice. "Hey. I'll do anything to get away from this damn book for a couple of hours."

CHAPTER EIGHT

It is laid down as a rule in various parts of Europe that mistletoe may not be cut in the ordinary way, but must be shot or knocked down from the tree with stones. Thus, in the Swiss canton of Aargau, the peasants procure it in the following manner. "When the sun is in Sagittarius and the moon is on the wane, on the first, third, or fourth day before the new moon [late November-early December], one ought to shoot down with an arrow the mistletoe of an oak and to catch it with the left hand as it falls."

Sir James George Frazer
The Golden Bough

Amy is doing an internship at the Hill Country Animal Clinic as part of her graduate studies in veterinary medicine at Texas A & M. And since the clinic was on my way out of town, I decided it would be better to talk to her in person, rather than on the phone.

I know the inside of this clinic quite well, since it's the place Howard Cosell and Khat go for their regular check-ups. The waiting room held the usual assortment of animals and their human companions. I gave my name and asked for Amy, and there was a short wait while somebody went to find her. Behind the desk, the clinic's resident parrot, Poirot, was giving the weather forecast. "No rain today!" he screeched. "Hot and dry! Hot and dry."

The door opened and I saw Amy, dressed in her white lab tunic and pants. "China!" she exclaimed. "I'm so glad you came!"

Amy has grown up a great deal since the day she walked into the Crystal Cave in search of the birth mother who gave her up for adoption in the first week of her life. Over the intervening few years, Amy and Ruby have sorted out their relationship and what they mean to one another. After some initial uncertainty about her life's direction, Amy has included both her birth mother and her adoptive mother in it. And me, too. As Ruby's best friend, I have a special status with her daughter, something like an aunt or an older sister. Amy listens to my advice, then does exactly as she pleases.

"It's raining, it's pouring," the parrot remarked. "Hot and dry!"

"Let's go in here," Amy said, drawing me into one of the treatment rooms. "That parrot drives everybody crazy."

She shut the door, turning to lean on it. Like Ruby, Amy is tall and thin, with the same coppery hair, gingery freckles, and intense hazel eyes. When I look at this spirited, energetic young woman, I imagine I am seeing Ruby twenty-five years ago.

"When was the last time you talked to Mother?" she asked without preamble.

"Saturday, at the shop," I said. "I've been calling her house, but the answering machine is turned off. I stopped by this morning. She's not home, and her suitcase is gone. Do you know where she is?"

Amy shook her head unhappily. "I wish I did. She hasn't

been herself for a couple of weeks. I'm getting awfully worried about her, China."

"She hasn't given you any idea about what's bothering her?"

"No. What has she said to you?"

"Not a word. In fact, I thought maybe I'd done something to make her upset with me." I sighed ruefully. "I don't seem to have as much time for friends as I did before McQuaid and I got married."

"I don't think that's the problem." Amy crossed her arms over her chest. "We had dinner together last Wednesday, and she seemed—I don't know, really weird. Spacy. Like, she wasn't there. I mean, she carried on a conversation and everything, but her mind wasn't on it. A couple of times she didn't even seem to hear what I said to her, and even when she heard, she just sort of half responded." She stopped, cleared her throat, started again. "When I got ready to go, she gave me an enormous hug. You know, the way you do if you're going away somewhere and won't be back for a while. A long while."

Both of us thought about the implications of that for a moment, not saying anything. The treatment room had an antiseptic smell, like a hospital. It was chilly, and I shivered inside my coat.

"I'm sorry," Amy said finally, uncrossing her arms. "I'm probably overdramatizing this. Mother doesn't . . . I mean, she isn't—" Her smile was crooked. "She may dress like an exotic dancer out for a night in Paris, but inside, she's still a mom. If she was planning something really crazy, she'd tell me. Or Shannon."

I nodded, agreeing. "Speaking of Shannon, has she told you that her father has come back to Pecan Springs? Or did Ruby mention it to you?"

"No!" Amy's eyes widened. "Do you think that has anything to do with the way Mother is acting?"

"It might," I said. "I thought maybe—" I left the sentence unfinished. "But he called while I was there this morning and claimed to be as much in the dark as we are. I also talked to Hark Hibler. Hark says he thinks Ruby might be seeing somebody new."

Amy pulled her coppery eyebrows together. "A new boyfriend?"

"Yes," I said shortly, nettled at her tone. She sounded disapproving, as if she thought that her mother was getting too old for a new romance. Old, hell! Ruby is a year younger than I am.

There was a long pause. Amy pursed her lips, considering. "Well," she said slowly, "I suppose that explains the negligee."

"The *negligee*?"

"Gown and robe. Ivory satin trimmed in heavy lace. Very sexy, like something Garbo might have worn. I don't think Mother intended for me to see it. I was using the upstairs bathroom, and it was in a box on her bed, packed in tissue paper. I couldn't resist peeking."

I frowned. A nightgown? Ruby has always claimed that it's healthier and more fun to sleep in the buff. And a sexy satin negligee isn't her style. It was beginning to look like Hark was right, and Ruby had fallen in love with someone—we didn't know. Someone out of town. But why was she hiding the truth? Why wasn't she telling us?

Amy clasped her hands behind her and began to pace. "There's something else, too. I didn't think much about it at the time, but the phone rang while I was at her house last week. I don't know who Mother was talking to, but whoever it was, she seemed almost furtive. I overheard her saying that she'd be ready on Saturday evening after work. So she must be spending the weekend with somebody."

"Shannon, maybe?" I hazarded.

Amy reached the end of the room and turned. "Uh-uh. Shannon and I talked on the phone this morning. She and Mother had dinner together on Tuesday night, and she had the same feeling about it that I did. Mother didn't pay attention and seemed to barely listen. Shannon has no idea what's going on, and she's worried too." Amy looked at me and shook her head, frowning. "I don't like this, you know. Peeking and prying into Mother's private life, talking about her behind her back, trying to dope out what she's up to. I don't feel right about it."

"I don't either," I said, guiltily recalling my invasion of Ruby's house. "She's entitled to her privacy."

Amy stood still. "Yeah, sure. Everybody's entitled." Her voice grew angry. "But there's a flip side, damn it. Doesn't she have a responsibility to us? We're her *family*, for Pete's sake! Shannon and me and you. She's not being fair to us, treating us this way! Where's she gone? What's she up to? And why all the mystery?"

I didn't have any answers. "I guess we'll just have to wait until she gets around to telling us," I said.

"Well, I wish to hell she'd hurry," Amy muttered.

The crime-scene tape was still strung along the edge of the gravel road when I drove past the spot where Carl Swenson had died. The body was gone, of course, bundled off to the morgue by the EMS crew. The ladder was gone and the truck too, probably to the county impound yard. Other than the tape, there was no sign that somebody had died at this spot. I wondered if Swenson's relatives, if he had any, would put up a cross here, the way people sometimes do in Texas, decorated with plastic flowers and a little inscription: "Gone to God" or "With the Angels." But maybe he didn't have any relatives. Maybe there was no one to honor the place where he'd died, or even remember that he had lived or what he had done with his life. It was a sad thought.

Fifty yards further along, past the curve and on the right, I saw Corinne Tuttle's mailbox and her house, a white-painted, metal-roofed farmhouse that stood well back from the road. I slowed the truck and pulled off to the side to get a good look. In the summer, the house would be screened by low-hanging branches and an unruly mass of yaupon holly and roughleaf dogwood. Now, most of the leaves were gone and I could see through the tangled brush to the graveled area in front of the house. A red Camaro was parked there, a recent model with spoilers on the rear end and a cutesy leather bra across the front. Corinne had said she didn't have visitors, so I could only assume it was Marvin's car.

Which posed several interesting questions. I didn't keep up on the price of sports cars, but it was a good guess that this one had cost the buyer upwards of thirty thousand dollars, depending on the extras. And Marvin had no job, according to Corinne. Where did he get the money? And if he could afford a Camaro, why the hell was he hanging out here? Why wasn't he chasing girls in Austin or San Antonio?

I downshifted and was pushing the accelerator when I saw a slim, angular young man in jeans and a leather jacket open the screen door. He paused to say something over his shoulder, then ran to the Camaro and jumped in. I turned in the seat to watch him back out of the driveway, fast, spinning his tires on the loose gravel. I couldn't see the front end—anyway, it was covered with leather—but as the Camaro swung onto the road and raced off in the opposite direction, I managed to catch the first three letters on the license plate: HOT. It figured. I watched the car until it was out of sight, then jotted down the letters on a scrap of paper, thinking that Blackie might be interested. An unemployed kid who could afford a pricey car and vanity plates was worth a hard look.

I pulled back on the road again. Another fifty yards further on and also on the right, I saw the small house trailer that belonged to Clyde McNabb, the man Corinne Tuttle had accused of reckless driving. I slowed again, giving it a once-over. The trailer was propped up on concrete blocks and a crooked tin flue pipe stuck through a broken window. The yard was littered with trash, beer cans, and piles of rusted junk. A surly looking brown dog, chained to a pecan tree, had retreated into a fifty-gallon oil drum turned on its side to serve as a doghouse. In the pasture adjacent to the house, a flock of goats browsed among a half-dozen abandoned cars and trucks. There was no vehicle parked out front, though. It didn't look like Clyde was at home. I made a mental note to pass along Corinne's hints and innuendoes to Blackie, so he'd have them in mind when he interviewed the man.

But Clyde, Corinne, and Marvin were Blackie's problems, not mine. I was here to talk to the Fletcher sisters and Aunt Velda. I put the truck into gear and drove on.

This time it was Terry who came out of the house in response to Max's barking. As I got out of the truck, she strode down the path to meet me, wearing a heavy corduroy jacket and jeans stuffed into scuffed leather boots. A black knit cap was pulled down over her ears.

"Donna said you were here this morning," she said shortly. She shoved her hands into her pockets. "With the sheriff."

"That's right," I said. I smiled, being nice. "Maybe you and I could talk for a few minutes."

She didn't smile back. "What about?"

We weren't going to be nice. "About Carl Swenson's death," I said.

"If you're here to take up a collection for flowers, you can forget it." She wiped her nose on the sleeve of her jacket. "We're not in the mood to contribute."

"And about that red Ford truck I saw here on Saturday," I said quietly. "When the sheriff and I were here this morning, it was gone." I glanced around. "Looks like it's still gone. I wonder what happened to it."

Terry's tongue came out and she ran it over her lips, already chapped from the cold and wind. Her eyes were fierce. "Now you look here, China Bayles. You don't have any right to come onto our property and accuse—"

I raised my hands. "I'm not accusing anybody of anything. And I'm not the one you should be worried about."

"What's that supposed to mean?"

"It's the sheriff who's breathing down your neck, not me. He wants to know what happened to that truck."

Her jaw jutted belligerently. "Yeah, but you're the one who brought him out here. You told him about that truck. And now you're back to harass—"

I sighed. "Look, Terry, I'm your friend."

"Oh, yeah?" Her voice dripped scorn, her eyes were accusing. "Some lousy friend. Bringing the damn sheriff out here, pestering a poor old lady—"

I went on as if I hadn't heard her. "I want to be sure you know what you're doing. If you've hidden that truck, the legal consequences could be pretty serious."

Terry's gaze slipped away from mine. "I don't know what you're talking about," she muttered.

"I think you do," I said evenly. "Look, if you're not going to invite me into the house to talk, how about the barn? It's damn cold out here."

Terry hesitated, then wheeled suddenly and stalked off down the path, Max hobbling at her heels. The barn wasn't any warmer, but at least we were out of the wind. The innards of the brown van were still spread on the floor, and the chickens were still strutting and preening on its roof. When they saw us coming, they clucked an alarm and scattered into the shadows. Max slipped under a sawhorse and settled into a nest he had made in a pile of loose hay.

Terry turned to face me, her eyes dark, her mouth set. "You wanted to talk," she said fiercely. "So talk. And make it fast. I've got things to do."

"The sheriff is looking for the vehicle that hit Swenson," I said. "He'd like to examine your red truck."

"He's out of luck. The truck isn't here."

"Where is it?"

"I have no idea," she said stonily. "Neither does Donna. End of story."

I didn't believe her. "Let's talk hypothetically for a minute," I said. "Let's say your aunt was out for a Sunday afternoon drive—"

"You can forget that shit! Donna told you that Aunt Velda's not allowed to touch that truck."

"Let's say she took her eyes off the road for a minute," I continued, "and accidently hit Carl Swenson. If she turns herself in and tells the sheriff what she did, she'll be charged with failure to stop and render assistance. Given her mental condition, though, it's not very likely that she'll be convicted or serve any time."

Terry was silent for a minute. "If she says she did it, they'll put her in an institution," she said finally, her voice flat. "It would kill her. It would kill Donna, too. Aunt Velda is the closest thing to a mother we have." The tongue came out again, took another swipe at her cracked lips. "Don't get me wrong, China. I'm not saying she's guilty. I'm just saying—"

"It's not a certainty that she'd be institutionalized," I said. "Your aunt is an old, sick woman. Any psychiatrist who examines her will find her incompetent. Under the circumstances, the court might remand her into your custody, with supervision by the appropriate authority. I'd be glad to help make that happen, if I can." I stopped to let the offer sink in, then hardened my voice.

"But there's more to this hypothetical. Let's say that Aunt Velda came back home and told you what happened. You went outside, took a look at the truck, and saw that the right front headlight was broken and the fender damaged. At that point, you—meaning you or Donna or both of you—decided to conceal the truck, hoping to keep your aunt out of trouble."

"That's not the way it happened," Terry said passionately. Her jaw was working. "I swear to God, China!"

I shook my head. "Let's also say that the sheriff runs an FBI check on the paint flecks found at the scene and comes up with a match for a red Ford truck. He brings out a team of deputies, searches your two hundred acres, and eventually finds the truck. After the work and expense of beating the bushes for a couple of days, everybody is mean and short-tempered and nobody feels much like being lenient. The district attorney upgrades the charge to manslaughter, and also charges you and Donna with hindering apprehension and prosecution. Aunt Velda will still be declared incompent. You and Donna could pay a fine and go to jail."

Terry made a noise deep in her throat.

"Yeah, right. It's a tough world." I gave her a hard, straight look. "If I were you, I'd hand the truck over and concentrate on getting the best deal you can for your aunt. You'll have help. You won't have to do it alone."

Terry ducked her head. "We're not protecting her," she said in a muffled voice.

"Where's the truck?"

"I don't know."

"Does Donna?"

Her head came up. "Neither of us has a clue. Aunt Velda drove it out of here sometime yesterday afternoon and walked back about six o'clock. Donna thought she was with me in the barn, working on the van. I thought she was with Donna in the workroom, making wreaths. We didn't even miss her until Donna put supper on the table. That's when she came in from outside, wet and cold. She'd hurt her foot, too." Her voice thinned, and I heard a note of panic. "It's God's truth, China. Honest!"

Maybe, maybe not. But I had the feeling we were getting closer. "What did she say about where she'd been?"

"Her usual crazy stuff. That the Klingons had taken Swenson to the ship, and she was afraid they were after the truck too. So she parked it where they wouldn't think to look for it." She made a little grimace. "It was already dark by that time, no point in going out to look for the damn truck then. Anyway, we didn't figure it was urgent. Why should we? We had no idea that Swenson was dead."

"When did you find out?"

She took a breath. "This morning, a little after seven.

Jane Wilson has loaned us her Geo until I get the van fixed, and I was on my way to San Antonio for more parts. I saw Swenson lying beside the road. But the body was stone cold by that time. There wasn't a damn thing I could do. I came back here and told Donna, and we decided to act like we didn't know anything about it." She gave me a sullen look. "Anyway, we don't. Our loony old aunt says she parked the truck somewhere, and can't or won't say where. That's all we know."

"You can stick to that story," I said, "but in all fairness, I have to tell you that there's a problem with it."

Her glance was apprehensive. "A problem?"

"Yeah. Your prints are all over that truck. Yours and Donna's. Right?"

"Well, sure. I mean, I guess they are. We drive it around the place all the time, hauling plants and tools and stuff."

"Okay. When the truck is located—and it will be, believe me—the sheriff will pull every print he can find, and they'll all be used as evidence. If that Ford was the vehicle that killed Swenson, you could find yourself in some pretty serious trouble. I know this district attorney, a guy named Dutch Doran. He's a grandstander. He just might decide that you and Donna are lying when you say your aunt was driving that truck."

She frowned. "Lying? Why would we lie?"

"Come off it, Terry." I gave a dry chuckle. "That old lady is conviction-proof. You'd be a fool not to shift the blame to her. What's more, once the D.A. starts toying with the idea that you or Donna hit Swenson, he might figure that it maybe wasn't an accident. He might think Swenson was run down on purpose. After all, the guy was causing you a lot of grief."

"Shit," Terry said feelingly.

"Yeah," I replied. "Big time." I added, with emphasis: "The best thing to do is turn that truck over to the sheriff voluntarily, before he gets a search warrant and comes looking." I paused. "Mind if I talk to your aunt and see if I can get any more out of her?"

Terry closed her eyes and pressed her lips together. Then she took a couple of deep breaths, opened her eyes and said, flatly, "Hell, yes, I mind. But I guess I don't have any choice."

We found Donna in the small workroom off the kitchen, perched on a stool in front of a wooden easel that supported a large wreath, almost finished. Buckets of dried artemisia, strawflowers, baby's breath, golden yarrow, rosemary, and holly were arranged within reaching distance, and scissors, tweezers, floral pins, wire, and a glue gun lay on a table beside her. A woodstove in the corner radiated heat.

"Go get Aunt Velda," Terry said brusquely. "We need to have a talk. About the truck."

Donna's eyes widened. "But I thought you said she wouldn't have to—" She glanced nervously from her sister to me and back again. "I mean, I thought we agreed not to bother her about it, Terry."

Terry's mouth was set and she wore a poker face. "China says we could get into serious trouble about this. If Aunt Velda hit Swenson and the D.A. thinks we concealed the truck to protect her, he might charge us as accessories. He might even—" She gave Donna a hooded look, as if she were signaling something, and a silent communication seemed to pass between them. "China says he might even try to prove that one of us was driving it when Swenson was killed."

"One of *us!*" Donna exclaimed. "But that's impossible," she said, very fast. "We were both here, together. All afternoon. How could we—"

"Go get Aunt Velda," Terry said tersely. Her eyes slid to me to see if Donna's assertion had registered. "I'll fix us some coffee."

Terry was filling coffee mugs when the old lady limped into the kitchen, followed by Donna. She wore a man's dirty brown corduroy bathrobe over yellow sweatpants and a purple sweatshirt, and ragged moccasins on her feet. Her Klingon badge was pinned to the lapel of her bathrobe. She sat down and reached for her Mister Spock coffee mug.

"Where's the cookies?" she asked in a whiny voice. "Donna, be a dearie and get me my cookies. My foot's sore."

From the cupboard, Donna produced a plastic tub of chocolate chip cookies. Aunt Velda pried off the top and popped one into her mouth.

"I was wondering," I said, "if you'd tell us what happened when the Klingons came after Carl Swenson yesterday afternoon."

"Yer cookies is better'n yer cake," Aunt Velda said to Donna, taking two more.

Donna's smile was tremulous. "Thank you. What about yesterday, Aunt Velda? Tell China what you told us." She gave the old lady a pleading look. "What we talked about, remember?"

Fastidiously, the old lady brushed the crumbs from the front of her yellow sweatshirt. "Yestiddy? Yestiddy? That wuz a long time ago." She darted a bright glance at me.

"Where's that nice feller you wuz here with this morning, China? A looker, he wuz."

"I'll tell him you said that," I replied. "What about yesterday, Aunt Velda?"

"Yestiddy, today, they're all the same," she said philosophically. "Get to be my age, one day ain't no diff'rent than another. 'Less you're goin' fer a ride around the galaxy, o'course." Her smile was reminiscent. "Now, *them* days is really diff'rent, b'lieve you me. Lots o' stars to look at, black holes, quasars, stuff like that. And them Klingon ships—they're a real trip." She circled her mug with her hands and hunched over to drink out of it, her chin almost on the table.

"I understand that the Klingons took Carl Swenson, and that you hid the truck to keep them from taking it too," I said.

Aunt Velda's eyes opened wide. "Is that right?" she asked in amazement. "I'll be durned." She sighed heavily. "Well, that's whut happens when y'git old. You gals think y'er so smart now, but y'all just wait, it'll be yer turn afore too many more years. Yer mem'ry'll be the first t'go, then yer sex drive." She leered at me. "But you just trot that nice young man back here and see if my sex drive ain't still chuggin' right along. Nothin' wrong with me in that compartment. Not yit, anyhoo."

I smiled. "If you can't tell me anything about the truck, Aunt Velda, what *can* you tell me about what went on yesterday afternoon?"

The old lady pulled down her brows in a ferocious scowl, signifying deep thought. After a moment, she said, "Well, this is gonna get me in a passel o' trouble. But I guess if I gotta tell the truth, I gotta."

"Please, Aunt." Donna made an anxious sound. "Tell

China what you told us. What we talked about. Remember?"

Aunt Velda put two cookies in her mouth and munched for a moment. She swallowed. "I remember lookin' fer the cave."

"The cave!" Terry exclaimed. "But that isn't—"

"Oh, Aunt!" Donna cried. "How could you? You were very, very bad!"

"Whut'd I tell you?" Aunt Velda said pathetically. "Now they're gonna yell at me."

"You're damn right we're going to yell at you!" Terry shouted. "It's dangerous for you to go climbing around these ravines. You're too old."

"Anyway," Donna said, "there isn't any cave. We've looked and looked. If there were a cave, we'd have found it."

"Well, the Indians sure enough found it," Aunt Velda retorted in a petulant tone, " 'cause there's plenty of arrowheads and skulls and stuff layin' around." Her chin jutted out and she added, with a toss of her head: "I found it once, and I aim to find it again, soon as I remember how."

"But you don't remember what happened to Carl Swenson?" I asked. "You don't remember hiding the truck, and telling Terry and Donna about it when you came home for supper?"

The old lady rolled her eyes in exasperation. "Truck, truck, truck," she said. "Is that all you care about?" She yawned. "I think I'll just catch me twenty winks." Her eyelids drooped. A moment later, there was a loud snore.

CHAPTER NINE

Folklore had it that one mistletoe berry down the gullet of a curious child meant almost certain death. But a recent study done by three Denver physicians suggests that mistletoe may have been getting a bad rap. The doctors found that 14 children who ingested mistletoe suffered no serious toxicity. They also analyzed 318 cases of mistletoe ingestion reported to the Food and Drug Administration and found no toxic symptoms or reported deaths.

D. Eicher
"Mistletoe Tale Deflated"
Denver Post Dec. 15, 1986

•

Back on the road again, I had plenty to think about. Before I left the flower farm, Donna and Terry had put the old lady in her room and locked the door. They were going out, they said, to check the three or four places they thought Aunt Velda might have hidden the truck, all of them within a mile or so of the house—close enough that she could have walked back home. I could come with them if I wanted to, or they'd call me as soon as they found it.

More to the point, I told them, they should call Sheriff Blackwell. I'd done my job. I'd advised them of the legal difficulties they might face if they had helped to conceal the truck. The rest was up to them, and to the sheriff. I completed my obligation by calling Blackie on the cell phone. I didn't have any better luck than I'd had earlier, but this time I left a message, saying that I'd talked to the sisters and they had agreed to look for the truck. I'd be glad to give him my report in person, when he had time to listen. And that was that. I had other things to do, and it was time I did them.

But still, the conversation stayed in my mind, and as I drove, I puzzled over the major ambiguities. Knowing something about the old lady's erratic behavior, I might be able to buy the goofy idea that she'd hidden the truck and forgotten where it was. But if she had really told that story to Terry and Donna, why wasn't she able, or willing, to repeat it to me? Was it sheer orneriness, or a stubborn and knowing refusal to participate in a lie that her nieces had constructed for her? And if it was a lie, what was the ugly truth it was designed to conceal?

I was equally troubled by the sisters' contradictory alibis. Terry claimed that she and Donna hadn't missed their aunt because each thought the old woman was with the other, but Donna asserted that she and Terry had been together all afternoon. Terry herself had caught that contradiction, and was worried that I might have heard it too. Of course I had. Obviously, one of them was lying. Which one? Why? I didn't envy Blackie the job of sorting the truth out of the tangle of conflicting stories.

Heading north on Comanche Road, I passed Clyde's disreputable house trailer. A couple of goats had gotten through the fence and were browsing the cedars beside the road. The surly dog was still lying in his oil-drum doghouse, waiting for his master. Nothing else was changed.

At Corinne's house, the Camaro had not reappeared and the gravel drive was empty. There was a light at the back of the house, and if I'd had more time, I would have been tempted to stop and find out more about Marvin's connection to Carl Swenson. But Brian would be home from school soon, and it was my week to cook. I had to start thinking about dinner.

I *was* tempted, however, to learn more about Swenson. I slowed as I passed the place where he'd been killed. His mailbox was about twenty yards ahead on the right, next to a gravel lane that presumably led to his house. A gate was closed across the lane, but while there was a chain and a padlock on the gate, the lock hung open. If it hadn't been so close to dinnertime, I would have opted for a trip down the lane and a look around his place. As it was, I opted for the mailbox.

Stealing mail is a federal crime, and I've never liked dealing with the feds, who tend not to listen very well. But I wasn't going to steal anything. I only wanted to take a look. I slid over to the passenger side, rolled down the window, and opened the mailbox.

It wasn't a big haul. Just a single nine-by twelve-inch glossy envelope, a high-class, expensive mailing piece. But the stamps caught my eye—Brazilian—and the return address: Rio de Janeiro. I turned the envelope over. From the photograph and the information printed on the back, it looked like somebody had sent Carl Swenson a brochure for a posh high-rise condominium called the Pousada do Gramado, overlooking Guanabara Bay. I turned the envelope over again and saw that it was addressed to Mr. Charles Seymour, 921 Comanche Road. I glanced at Swenson's rusty mailbox. It bore the ragged numerals 921.

Charles Seymour, Carl Swenson. The initials were the same. Coincidence or design?

I stared at the envelope for a moment, now sorely tempted to break my rule and steal a piece of mail. After all, it was only an advertisement, and it wasn't even addressed to the owner of the mailbox—who wouldn't be going to Rio anytime soon and could hardly file a complaint, in any event. I'm sure that Kinsey Milhone or Sharon McCone would have stuck the envelope in her bag and driven off without a second thought. But I am basically a law-abiding person, which under some circumstances is a curse. I found an old credit card receipt under the car seat, located a pen, and jotted down the address of the Pousada do Gramado and the name Charles Seymour. Then I put the envelope back in the mailbox, slid back under the wheel, and put the truck into first gear. A hot, hearty soup would be nice on this chilly day, with garlic bread and a salad.

Portuguese sausage soup, maybe. Don't they speak Portuguese in Brazil?

Dinnertime is Brian's time, when McQuaid and I catch up on our son's daily doings—school, friends, hobbies, pets, and so on. Usually, we restrict the conversation to pleasant topics, since it is my theory that the human body handles digestion better when it isn't stressed. But tonight it was my sad duty to tell Brian that a pair of his lizards had gone for a swim in the washing machine, and that one of them had made a dive down the laundry sink drain.

"And if there are any more loose lizards," I added sternly, "we are going to have to make some changes in the zoological accommodations." I picked up the ladle. When we're not having company, I put the soup pot on the table and serve directly out of it. "Who's ready for seconds?"

Beside McQuaid's chair, Howard Cosell thumped the floor urgently with his tail, reminding us that he hadn't had firsts yet.

Brian frowned. "It went down the *drain*? Why didn't you stop it?"

"I'll take some more," McQuaid said, handing me his bowl.

I smiled at McQuaid and frowned at Brian. "Give me a break, kid. I was trying to rescue lizard number two from drowning in soap suds. I wasn't keeping tabs on lizard number one." I filled McQuaid's bowl and passed it back to him. "Anyway, those lizards should have been in their lizard hotel, not lurking in a towel on your bathroom floor."

"Was it the horny toads or the green anoles?" Brian asked.

"Not the horny toads," I said. "But they weren't green, either. Tannish brown, sort of. We didn't introduce ourselves." My favorite among Brian's animals is a fat and lazy tarantula named Ivan the Hairible, who fits neatly into the palm of one's hand—not *my* hand, though. I admire Ivan from a distance.

"The green anoles change color," Brian said. "Like chameleons. Their real name is *Anoles carolinensis*, if you want to know. They were probably in the bathroom hunting for crickets."

"It's a little late in the year for crickets," I said. "I'm sorry about the drain, Brian, but if they'd been where they were supposed to be, it wouldn't have happened."

"We could take the pipe apart," Brian said to his father. "Like we did that time your girlfriend lost her diamond earring in the bathroom sink. He's probably still in that elbow thing."

"What girlfriend?" I asked. "What diamond earring?"

"That was a long time ago," McQuaid said. "Before you and I got serious." He looked at Brian. "If the lizard went down the drain, he probably drowned. The elbow is full of water."

"Drowned!" Brian pushed back his chair. "Can I go look? Maybe he climbed out of the sink and is hiding somewhere."

Howard Cosell clambered expectantly to his feet, hoping that Brian was going to put his soup bowl on the floor for a lick.

"Don't beg, Howard," I said. "Okay, Brian, you can go look, but don't get your hopes up." I raised my voice as Brian dashed out of the room. "And put the other one in the terrarium, where he belongs."

McQuaid glanced up from his bowl. "Good soup," he said. "What's in it?"

"Sausage. A couple of onions, lots of garlic, a can of chopped tomatoes, etcetera." I didn't tell him that it also included two cleverly camouflaged zucchini. McQuaid will not eat squash of any description. "Why would Carl Swenson be getting mail under the name of Charles Seymour?"

"I'll have some more of that garlic bread," McQuaid said. "How do you know what names he's getting mail under?"

"Because I looked in his mailbox." I handed him the bread basket, which contained only three more slices. Garlic bread goes fast at our table. "The only thing in it was an expensive advertising brochure."

"Junk mail," McQuaid said dismissively. He tore off a chunk of the bread and dropped it on the floor. Howard

Cosell put his paw on it to keep it from getting away, then began to lick it. Garlic is one of his favorite herbs, or maybe it's the butter he likes. "It could have been sent to the wrong address. Or maybe this Seymour guy used to live there."

"It was the right address," I said. "And it wasn't junk mail. It looked more like a real estate sales solicitation. From an expensive condominium unit in Rio de Janeiro. With a view of Guanabara Bay."

That got McQuaid's attention. "Rio de Janeiro?"

"Yeah. Charles Seymour, Carl Swenson. Same initials. I don't think it's a coincidence. I'd bet—"

There was a loud crash upstairs. "Brian!" McQuaid and I yelled in one voice.

"It's okay," Brian called. "I caught him!"

"I'd better go see what that noise was," I said, standing up.

"Brazil, huh?" McQuaid remarked thoughtfully. "No extradition."

"No problem," Brian called again. "Don't bother to come upstairs."

Hearing no more noises, I sat back down. "It looked like a *very* expensive place," I said. "I'll bet you couldn't buy a condo in that unit for less than a quarter-million dollars."

"Maybe Swenson was thinking of renting," McQuaid said with a straight face.

"A couple of thou a week, easy," I said. "More, with maid service. You don't pick up money like that selling a few goats. I wonder—"

Brian loped triumphantly into the kitchen, a lizard in each hand. "See? I found *both* of them! They were in the laundry hamper."

"Wonderful," I said with enthusiasm, relieved to know

that I hadn't drowned my son's favorite lizard. "What was that crash?"

Brian looked puzzled. "Crash? I didn't hear any—"

"Brian," McQuaid said.

"Oh, *that* crash," Brian said. "Oh, no problem. I'll sweep it up." He found a bowl and put the lizards in it.

I frowned. "Sweep what up?"

"The soap." Brian put a glass lid on the bowl, put the bowl beside his plate and sat down. "It was the shelf over the dryer that fell down. Bleach and stuff. But nothing broke," he added hurriedly. "Just a bunch of soap spilled on the floor." He looked at me. "What's for dessert, Mom?"

McQuaid sighed. "Take those lizards upstairs and put them where they belong. Then get the broom and sweep up the soap. *Then* we might consider dessert."

"Cookies and ice cream," I said.

Brian frowned. "Store-bought cookies? Or did you bring home some from the tea room?"

"Brian!" McQuaid said sternly.

"Okay, okay," Brian said, pushing his chair back. "Don't get your dandruff up." He picked up the bowl of lizards and departed hastily.

"Dandruff," McQuaid said, rubbing his temples. "Good Lord, that makes me feel old. I used to say that to my old man when I was his age."

I leaned my elbows on the table. "So what did you find out about Corinne's car when you went to Gus's?"

McQuaid looked up. "Nothing. It wasn't there."

I stared at him. "But she said Gus was giving her an estimate."

"Just one spoonful, please." McQuaid held out his bowl. "She didn't give him the chance. She told him she'd changed her mind and decided it wasn't worth spending money on an old Mercury that didn't run very well. She'd already driven it away before I got there. I've told Blackie," he added, taking the bowl from me. "He said he'd go out to her place and take a look. He asked me to tell you thanks for your heads-up. It was a lucky thing you happened to bump into her." He set the bowl on the floor and Howard Cosell began to work on it, tail wagging ecstatically. He gets plenty of dog food, but it isn't the same as the people-food that comes from the table.

"That wasn't luck, it was superior detective work," I said. "I followed her from the bank to the pharmacy, and then to Gus's." I made a face. "Wish I'd followed her into the body shop."

But I wouldn't have been any the wiser, even if I'd got a look at the car. Only an expert could tell whether the Mercury had hit a human or a deer, and that, after testing the blood spatters. Still, Corinne had certainly acted suspicious, pulling her car out of the shop immediately after our conversation. And I hadn't seen it in the driveway at her house. Where was it?

"Maybe all that stuff about Aunt Velda's truck is totally irrelevant," I said. "Maybe it was Corinne who hit Swenson. Or Marvin. By the way, he drives a red Camaro—an expensive vehicle for an unemployed kid. I saw the car, but the front end had one of those leather thingies on it and I couldn't tell whether there was any damage. I'll tell Blackie to check it out, too."

"Speaking of the old woman," McQuaid said, "what did you learn when you went out to the flower farm?"

I summarized as well as I could. "The bottom line," I concluded, "is that the sisters claim that Aunt Velda drove the truck away yesterday afternoon. But she came home on foot, and Terry and Donna insist they don't know what she did with the vehicle."

McQuaid looked skeptical. "Sounds pretty far-fetched to me. You sure one of the nieces wasn't driving?"

"I'm not sure of anything at this point," I said. "I've left a message for Blackie," I added. "When he phones, I'll update him."

McQuaid sat back in his chair. "What did you find when you stopped at Ruby's?"

"Absolutely nothing," I said sadly. "She's gone, her suitcase is gone, and her house is so clean, you'd think she was expecting a potential buyer." I stopped, and a horrible thought hit me. "Omigosh," I exclaimed. "You don't suppose Ruby's putting her house up for sale!"

"Not without telling you, surely," McQuaid said with a frown. "After all, you're partners."

"Yes, but she's been acting so strange lately—maybe she's decided she wants out of the partnership." The thought made my stomach tighten. What would I do without her? I didn't mean that just in terms of our joint business arrangement, either. Ruby's my dearest friend. I *love* her.

McQuaid frowned. "How about her daughters? Did you connect with Amy? What did she have to say?"

"I stopped at the clinic. Amy doesn't have a clue, and she says Shannon doesn't either. I fielded a phone call from Wade while I was at Ruby's. He says he loves her and wants her back—"

"After six or seven years?" McQuaid asked incredulously. "Maybe he just found out about the lottery."

"Whatever, he claims not to know what's going on with her, and I believed him on that score. I also had a talk with Hark."

McQuaid frowned. "I hope you didn't give the guy a hard time about Lynn Hughes."

I made a wry face. "Sheila and I were wrong about that. He was hiring Lynn, not seducing her."

"Oh, yeah?" McQuaid shot me a triumphant look. "Maybe next time you won't be so quick to accuse a guy."

I ignored that. "Hark's theory is that Ruby's seeing somebody new. Amy agrees, and thinks maybe she went away for the weekend with her new lover. That seems to be the best guess, but it's just a guess. We don't have anything to go on."

"Ruby's an adult," McQuaid said reasonably. "She's certainly entitled to a little R and R every now and then. And there's no law that says she has to tell her kids or her business partner every little detail of her life." He stood up. "I'll check on Brian, then I'm going to the university. There's a book in the library I need, and some notes I've left in my office. I may be late. Can I help with the dishes before I go?"

I shook my head. "That's okay." At our house, the cook usually does the dishes—that way, he or she isn't tempted to dirty every pan in the cupboard. "Is the writing going any better?"

McQuaid shrugged. "I'm into the section about Bill Sterling, the Ranger commander who was tried for murder in 1915. He put a bullet in the back of an unarmed South Texas rancher. It's ugly, but the facts are undisputed. What's more, nobody can accuse me of making it up. It's in the archives—along with the story about Tom Horn, the guy who captured Geronimo. He was hanged for murder in 1903."

"Police brutality," I said.

"It was a brutal era," McQuaid replied. "Not even the

ordinary citizen had any respect for the law."

"How can citizens respect the law when law enforcement officers behave like hooligans?" I shot back.

McQuaid grinned. "You'll have to read the chapter when I've finished it, Counselor. I think you'll approve." He came around the table and bent to kiss me. "Thanks for the dinner. Sorry about the lizards and the soap. The kid is getting out of hand."

"The kid is fine," I said, and grinned. "Especially considering that most of his friends wear earrings and nose rings and are hard-wired for rap. Compared to that, a few lizards and tarantulas are a picnic."

"Yeah. Come to think of it, he's not so bad." He kissed me again and left.

I cleared the table and was rinsing the plates when Blackie called. I told him what I'd found in Swenson's mailbox and gave him a quick report, conveying as much as I could of the flavor of the conversation at the flower farm—admittedly a difficult task.

"I told them to call you if they find the truck," I concluded. "I don't think there's much more I can do, at least at this point. The sisters' stories don't jibe, and Aunt Velda can't or won't confirm that she concealed the truck. Maybe you should talk to them again and see if you can sort it out."

"I'll give it until midmorning," Blackie said. "Could be that they'll come up with the truck before then. I plan to be out that way first thing tomorrow, anyway. I'm going to drop in on Corinne Tuttle. I want to take a look at her car and talk to that nephew of hers." He paused. "Thanks for the lead, China. Tuttle sure didn't give me any indication that she was hiding a damaged vehicle. Or an unemployed nephew with an expensive red car."

"You probably scared her," I said. "Maybe it was the uniform. Are you going to follow up on the brochure in Swenson's mailbox?"

"I'm not sure what bearing it has on the hit-and-run," he replied.

"I'm not sure, either. Maybe I've just got a case of idle curiosity."

Blackie chuckled dryly. "Yeah, well, I've got a couple of other investigations going on right now. I don't have time for anything idle—curiosity or otherwise."

We said good night and I went back to my work. I was loading the plates into the dishwasher when Howard Cosell raised his head and gave a low, throaty growl. Basset hounds aren't much good as watchdogs, but Howard is fiercely possessive about what he regards as his personal property. When he hears a step on the path outside, he lets you know that there's an invader out there, and that he is preparing to take matters into his own hands. He hopes, however, that you will stand by with the broom, just in case the marauder is larger and more aggressive than expected. Howard is not as brave as he would like you to think.

I went to the kitchen door, turned on the porch light, and looked out. It had started to rain again, and the slanting drops shone silver in the light. Someone was standing on the steps, shoulders hunched under a heavy wool cape. Raindrops were shimmering in her red hair.

I flung the door open. "Ruby!" I exclaimed, astonished and delighted. "Come in!"

"Is it okay?" she asked in a small voice. "I don't want to interrupt your dinner. I know I should have called first, but—"

"Of course it's okay, silly," I said happily, pulling her

into the kitchen. "I'm so glad to see you! Where have you been, for heaven's sake? I've been calling and calling, but your answering machine was turned off."

"I've been . . . away," she said, and shrugged out of her cape. I hung it on the peg by the door and turned. She was wearing jeans and an old green sweatshirt, and she looked haggard and weary. There were dark circles under her eyes, and her gingery freckles stood out against her pale skin. She clasped her arms around herself, shivering.

I frowned. Something was definitely wrong here. Ruby was in some sort of serious trouble. "You need a cup of hot coffee. Have you eaten dinner?"

She collapsed into a chair. "Dinner? I don't think I—" She frowned, as if she were trying to remember when she had eaten last. "I'm not hungry, China. Let's just talk, if you've got a few minutes."

"I have all evening," I said briskly. "And yes, you *are* hungry. You're having a bowl of sausage soup." I ladled some of the still-hot soup into a bowl, added the last two pieces of garlic bread, and put it in front of her.

Rubbing her forehead, Ruby looked down at the bowl. "Honestly, China, I don't think I can—"

"Eat," I commanded sternly, pouring coffee. "No excuses. What's more, you're not allowed to say a single word until it's all gone. Every drop, down the hatch. Now."

She gave me a small, tight smile. "Is that the tone of voice you use to Brian?"

I grinned. "You bet. When I talk tough, the kid knows he'd better toe the line. You too. No back talk. Just *eat*."

Ruby heaved a dramatic sigh to show that she was acting under duress and picked up her spoon—very slowly, to show that she couldn't possibly manage more than a single mouthful.

But she did. I tidied the counter, scrubbed the sink, and turned on the dishwasher, noticing that the more Ruby ate, the more eagerly she went about it. By the time I was finished, her bowl was empty and the garlic bread had disappeared. I put a plate of cookies on the table, poured myself a cup of coffee, and sat down across from her.

"That was very good," I said approvingly. "Now we can talk."

"Thank you," she said. Her color was better and she seemed more relaxed. But her eyes were still dark and the hand that held her coffee cup trembled a little. "I came to say I'm sorry, China. I know I've been behaving very badly the past couple of weeks." She took a deep breath. "But maybe you haven't noticed. You've been pretty busy."

"I've noticed," I said. "I thought maybe you were mad at me for being so busy. I wouldn't blame you," I added.

She sighed heavily. "I wish that was it. It'd be a lot easier to tell you what's going on."

I swallowed hard. What was it? Was she getting married? Was she moving to another city? Had she killed somebody?

"So?" I said. "What the hell is it?"

"It's hell, all right." She put down her cup and looked straight at me. "I have breast cancer, China."

CHAPTER TEN

ML-1, the galactoside-specific lectin found in mistletoe, has been used by German researchers in controlled medical experiments with cancer patients who were undergoing other conventional treatments, such as chemotherapy. These studies suggest that ML-1 used as a complementary treatment enhances the activity of most immune parameters and improves the quality of life.

summarized from Ralph W. Moss
Herbs Against Cancer
Chapter 9, Mistletoes and Medicine

I felt as if all the breath had been sucked out of me. As if the solid Texas limestone under my feet had just gaped open. As if I were sliding down the tilted deck of the *Titanic* into a sea as cold as death.

"Breast cancer!" I whispered. "Oh, Ruby! Oh, no!"

"Oh, yes," Ruby said. She managed a crooked grin. "Weird, huh? I mean, I've done everything right. Light on the red meat, heavy on fish and chicken, five-a-day fruits and veggies, plenty of exercise, safe sex, no cigarettes, hours of meditation, tons of positive attitude." Her voice broke, and I could hear tears in it. "I have enough positive attitude to make the world go round. And when I bought that new life insurance policy last summer, I got their top rating. I could live to be a hundred. I could be immortal. I can't have breast cancer. It's impossible." She closed her eyes, sighed, and opened them again. She gave weight to each word. "But it's true."

I stared at her bewildered, only half-comprehending. "But what . . . where . . . how. . . ." I thought of her absence over the past few days, and my glance went to her breasts, full and round and beautifully shaped under her green sweatshirt. Breasts I had envied, had coveted, flat-chested as I am. "I mean, you haven't. . . ."

"Haven't got my boob amputated yet?" Ruby asked wryly. "Later. I mean, soon. Soon enough. But not yet."

"Then where . . ." I couldn't seem to finish my sentences, couldn't string enough words together to ask what I needed to know. But it didn't matter. Ruby read my mind again.

"Where have I been? I decided I was going to go crazy if I didn't get away. Maggie picked me up on Saturday evening. I've been staying in a cottage at St. Theresa's, trying to get my head straight."

Of course. St. Theresa's is a monastery in the Hill Country west of Pecan Springs. Sister Margaret Mary—our friend Maggie Garrett, who used to own the restaurant across the street from our shops—is one of the Sisters of the Holy Heart. They live at the monastery and support themselves by growing the best garlic in Texas. They also offer their guest cottages for personal retreats. I've been there before, and so has Ruby. St. T's is a good place to go when you've got something on your mind and you need to be quiet and alone with it.

Something like . . . breast cancer. I suddenly felt desolate and deserted, as if Ruby had started off on a long, dangerous journey and had left me behind in a place that was safe and comfortable but cold and terribly, terribly lonely. I thought of all the things we had done together over the years of our friendship, the shared pleasures, the shared pain. I thought of all the lessons Ruby had taught me about being partners, about being sisters, and my chilly desolation suddenly flared into a hot and bitter anger. When it came to something really important, she hadn't cared enough to share it with me. She hadn't given me a chance to help.

"I would have been glad to go to St. Theresa's with you," I said. The resentful tears began to run down my cheeks. "Why did you leave me out? For Pete's sake, Ruby—why didn't you *tell* me?"

Ruby gave me a look of startled compassion, intent and somber. "I'm sorry if you feel left out," she said. Her voice seemed to be coming from a great distance.

I was almost blinded by tears. "Well, then, why—"

"Because I needed to live with this thing alone for a while, by myself. I had to think about what it means, and what I ought to do. I have some big decisions to make, and I didn't want anybody else—not even you—to bear the burden of making them."

"But I would have been glad—"

"You're the first to know, China," she said quietly. "I haven't told Shannon or Amy, or even my mother. I came to you first."

I stared at her, suddenly realizing that my tears were the self-pitying tears of a little girl who is crying because she has to sit on the sidelines during the crucial inning of the big game. At the same time, they were the frightened tears of an adult woman who is terrified that she might be dragged into a game she can't win. If Ruby could have cancer, so could I. It was my own desperate fear and vulnerability that had brought me to tears, and I felt immediately ashamed.

I gulped. "I'm sorry," I said. The words were so slight, so meager, that I wished I hadn't said them. "I'm terribly sorry," I said, but that wasn't any better. I reached across the table and took both of her hands. "What can I do?"

"Nothing, for now," Ruby said. "Just hold my hands."

The old schoolhouse clock over the refrigerator ticked somberly. The water heater in the closet gave a hissing burp as the gas came on. Howard Cosell lifted his head, sighed, and put it down again. Ruby's hands were colder than mine.

"I'm scared," I said finally. "Are you?"

"I'm so terrified I can hardly think," Ruby said thinly. "I wake up in the morning in a cold sweat. During the day, I can't concentrate. When I go to bed at night, it's hours before I fall asleep. And I'm angry, too." Her voice rose and she gripped my hands passionately. "This isn't fair, damn it! Everything was so wonderful! I won the lottery, we've just opened the tearoom, my daughters have grown into lovely women. And now this!"

I wanted to say that fate isn't fair, that good fortune is just that—fortunate, arbitrary, capricious—and we don't always get to choose all the circumstances of our lives. But the words seemed so silly that I swallowed them. Ruby didn't need to hear my moralizing. What *could* I say?

We sat for a while, she in her anger and fear, me in mine, desperately holding each other's hands as if we were clinging to a life raft in an icy sea, as if there were no life raft and all we had was each other. After a while, the questions started rising inside me. At first I held my breath and pushed them down, not wanting to give them voice, not wanting to hear the answers, as if the weight of the words might swamp our fragile raft. But pushing them down made my chest hurt so much that I couldn't breathe, and at last my need to know overcame my fear of the truth, and they came bursting out all at once.

"Which breast? What kind of cancer is it? Did you find a lump? What are they going to do? When?"

"It's in my right breast, but there's no lump," Ruby said. "You can't feel a thing. You can only see it on the mammogram, and only if you know what you're looking for. It looks like a bunch of teensy white specks—dead cancer cells. The cancer is called ductal cancer in situ. DCIS."

I frowned. *In situ* was a phrase I knew from legal Latin. "Inside the milk duct?" I guessed.

"Right. They won't know for sure until the surgery, but they think the cancer is preinvasive, which means they've caught it before it's had a chance to grow through the duct and get into the breast tissue." She gave me a lopsided grin. "While I was at St. Theresa's, I read a couple of books. If you've got to have breast cancer, DCIS seems like the best kind to have."

My chest suddenly didn't feel so tight. "That's wonderful!" I exclaimed. I frowned. What was I saying? "I don't mean wonderful," I said, biting my lip. "I mean—"

"That's okay." Ruby squeezed my hand. "I know what you mean. It's all relative."

I swallowed, trying to think what I'd read about breast cancer treatment. "So what's next? A lumpectomy, then radiation? Then chemo?"

Ruby pulled her hands away. "No," she said. There was a tiny white line around her mouth. "What's next is a mastectomy."

"A mastectomy!" I gasped. "You're not serious."

Ruby leaned forward, her eyes holding mine. "That's

why I went to St. Theresa's, China. To think about this, and figure out what to do. I've seen two oncologists. They both say that with a cancer like mine, the surgeon would have to take a pretty big slice out of my breast to be sure to get it all. And even with a big slice, it's not a sure thing. There'd have to be radiation to kill any cancer cells the surgery missed."

I started to say something, but she held up her hand. "But even with surgery and radiation—even with all that, there's a risk of recurrence. Only one in ten, they say, pretty good odds. But it's still a risk. On the other hand, if I have a mastectomy and there are no problems with the lymph nodes, I won't have to worry. With a mastectomy, the cure rate is essentially a hundred percent."

"But your . . . breast!" For an instant, I remembered seeing Ruby turned sideways before the mirror at her shop, gazing at her reflection. She must have been imagining, at that very moment, what it would be like to lose a breast. What it would look like, what it would feel like. How much she would miss it.

. Ruby gave me an ironic grin. "Yeah, my breast. Well, it's true that I'm kind of attached to it. I've always considered my breasts rather sexy, and it's nice that they come in pairs." She looked down, cupped her hands under her breasts, and lifted them. Then she dropped her hands and gave a little shrug. "But I can live without a breast. And I'm definitely not going to keep a part of my breast if I can trade the whole damn thing for better odds."

"But to let them take your breast—" I stopped, helpless. "It's so . . . so barbaric! Like something out of the Dark Ages."

Her mouth tightened. "Cancer is barbaric. I vote that we stop lobbing satellites at Mars and spend the money on breast cancer research." Then she lifted her chin defiantly. "But you're wrong, China—I'm not letting them take it, I'm *telling* them to take it. I have a choice, and I choose mastectomy." She grinned suddenly and raised her clenched fist in a salute. "Off with the boob! On with the rest of my life!"

God, I admired her courage. And it was great to hear that determined tone in her voice, and see that flash of self-assertion and boldness and humor that I love so much. To see the old Ruby prevail, when she might so easily have been swept away by anger and despair.

I forced an answering grin and said, flippantly, "Well, they do wonders with reconstruction these days. Implants, I mean—saline, not silicone. And I saw on TV that they can take a flap of tissue from your own body to create a new breast. The Bionic Boob. You probably won't even miss the old one."

Ruby dropped her arm and sat silent for a moment, as if she wanted to tell me something but couldn't quite make up her mind to say it—not for her sake, but for mine, because she wasn't sure how I'd take it. Finally, she said: "To tell the truth, China, I'm feeling pretty negative about reconstruction. I don't think I want somebody to stick a foreign object into my body, even if it is filled with saltwater instead of Silly Putty. And I don't like the idea of slicing off a piece of me to patch another piece, especially when I can't be sure how it will turn out. What if they don't get it right? What if one side is bigger than the other, or harder, or higher, or lower?" She shrugged. "I'm not saying reconstruction is wrong. I'm sure it's right for lots of other women. But not for me."

"But won't you—" I put my hand on my breast, trying to imagine going through life without it. It suddenly felt very precious. "I mean, won't it seem a little—"

"Weird? Yeah, maybe. It's a double-breasted world, and there are plenty of Barbie dolls around to remind me, if I forget. But if I feel the need to be symmetrical, I can always wear a prosthesis." There was that grin again. "A falsie. You buy a bra with a pocket where you slip it in. Some falsies even have nipples. They're made out of silicone and they jiggle, like the real thing. Isn't that a hoot?"

I was abashed by Ruby's bravery. If I had to give up a breast, what would I do? Would I endure the pain and uncertainty of the additional surgery to get a new one, or would I learn to live without it? "I'm sorry," I said, past the painful lump in my throat. "You're right."

Her face darkened. "I don't know about being right. I just have to get through this, one step at a time. First the surgery, then—" She frowned. "No, *first* I have to tell Shannon and Amy and Mom—and it's Christmas. The timing sucks, doesn't it?"

"We can all chip in and buy you a nightie for the hospital," I said, and then bit my lip. We didn't have to buy her a nightie. She already had one, a negligee that made her feel like Garbo. And that doctor Hark had mentioned— probably one of the oncologists she had consulted. Our suspicions, our theories, all wrong. Dead wrong.

I forced myself to smile. "What about Hark? Are you going to tell him? He's convinced himself that you've fallen in love with a doctor."

"Oh, God," Ruby sighed. "Why does life have to be so damn complicated?"

"He says he loves you. He wants to marry you."

She closed her eyes, opened them again. "Poor Hark. He's a really sweet guy. He deserves some gal who'll put him at the center of her world. Before this happened, I thought that might be me, if I worked at it. Your getting married reminded me how nice it is to have somebody you can count on when things get rough."

"You don't think you can count on Hark?"

Ruby sighed heavily. "I'm sure he'd jump at the chance to be a hero. But I've got enough to do just to take care of myself. I don't want to be responsible for him. That may not be fair, but who said any of this is fair?"

I nodded. I could understand her worry about being responsible. It was almost as if Ruby and I had traded places. "When is your surgery?"

"Two days after Christmas, in San Antonio."

I was aghast. "But that's almost three weeks! Why do you have to wait so long? Why can't you just have it done—like, tomorrow?"

"It's the holidays, I guess—although this kind of surgery isn't considered to be an emergency. But it's still a bitch. It's like there's this giant surgical knife poised over my head and I have to wait three weeks for it to fall."

I grinned. "We'll have to make sure you keep busy."

"Right." She sat up straighter. "I'm not going to sit around and let myself get depressed. I've decided to start weightlifting. And maybe I'll borrow Amy's in-line skates."

I blinked. That wasn't exactly what I had in mind. "But shouldn't you get some rest? I mean—"

Ruby slammed her fist on the table. "I'm not *sick*, damn it! I don't need rest. Rest is depressing. And I don't need to read any more books about cancer, either. What I need is distraction."

Ruby was right. She is a person of spirit and energy, but she has an unfortunate tendency to obsess. Ruby needed something to think about besides her cancer.

"Well, then," I said, "before you get involved with lifting weights and zipping around on Amy's skates, maybe you could try a little mental exercise. Put your mind to a case of hit-and-run."

She frowned. "Hit-and-run?"

"Yeah. Somebody ran over Carl Swenson yesterday afternoon."

"Carl Swenson?" She stared at me, suddenly sober. "The mistletoe man?"

"Right. He was cutting mistletoe on Comanche Road, not very far from his house. Somebody hit him and kept right on going." I sighed. "Unfortunately, that somebody might have been the Fletcher sisters' aunt. You met her when you and Betsy Williams and I went out there to pick flowers for my wedding. Remember?"

"Who could forget?" Ruby shook her head. "She's the one who's convinced that the Klingons are parked overhead with their warp drive engines on idle, waiting to take her to a galaxy far, far away."

"That's her," I said. "Only now she says they've taken Carl Swenson instead, to wash dishes and clean latrines." Then I told Ruby the whole long tale—from the discovery of Swenson's body early that morning down to my discovery of the Brazilian real estate brochure in Carl Swenson's mailbox just before dinner.

"Rio!" Ruby stared at me, her eyes big. "That's where all the drug dealers go to hide out, isn't it?"

I nodded. "Of course, that doesn't mean that Carl Swenson is a drug dealer. Anyway, it might have been a mistake. The brochure wasn't even addressed to the right person."

"Maybe, maybe not," Ruby replied. "But assuming it was sent to him, it certainly is suspicious. Where would a guy like Swenson get the money for a plane ticket to South

America, let alone a condo on the beach in one of the most expensive cities in the world?" She wrinkled her nose. "He didn't make it raising goats or cutting mistletoe. He must have been growing something else. Or selling it."

"It's certainly a mystery," I said, eyeing her. She was animated now, and interested, and the weariness had disappeared from her face. I thought of something else—something I'd forgotten to mention to either McQuaid or Blackie. "Corinne Tuttle told me that Swenson built a greenhouse. She overheard her nephew telling somebody about it on the phone." I frowned, wondering for the first time why that particular piece of information had been important enough for Marvin to pass along—and to whom.

"A greenhouse!" Ruby sounded awed, and even a little bit scared. "China, I'll bet that guy was growing marijuana. And Corinne Tuttle's nephew Marvin was helping him. Or maybe Marvin was selling it for Swenson. Or something. I'll bet they were in cahoots." She scooted forward to the edge of her chair. "And didn't you say that Marvin's red Camaro was wearing one of those leather whatchacallits? Maybe Marvin put it on to hide the fact that the front end was damaged. Maybe the two guys had a fight over money or dope or something and Marvin ran him down."

In the past, I've had to warn Ruby about jumping to imaginative conclusions on little or no evidence. But I was so glad to see that this cloak-and-dagger stuff was distracting her from her problems that I was willing to go along with anything she might come up with, no matter how weird or off-the-wall.

"You might have something there, Ruby," I said encouragingly. "Anyway, it's an interesting speculation."

"That's the understatement of the year, China." Ruby was almost breathless with excitement. "Who knows where Swenson's pot has ended up, or how many kids have been hooked on it? And maybe it's more than pot. Why, he and Marvin could've been manufacturing all kinds of illegal stuff out there, and nobody would ever be the wiser." She pursed her lips, concentrating. "Do you know if Blackie searched Swenson's place?"

"I don't think so," I said. "He'd probably have mentioned it if he had. As a matter of fact," I added, "the sheriff doesn't seem to be paying any attention to Swenson. He's fixated on finding the vehicle and the driver—which is probably the right approach, given his assumption that this was an accident."

"Yeah, well, he's still thinking inside the box," Ruby said critically. She frowned. "Maybe it wasn't Marvin after all. Maybe Swenson got crosswise of the drug lords." She caught the quizzical look on my face and added, "Don't be so negative, China. And don't say it can't happen here. Remember that big shootout in Brownsville last spring? And just a couple of weeks ago there was a bust near Kerrville. The guys who were growing it got away, as usual, but the narcotics people confiscated some money and a hundred pounds of marijuana."

"I am not negative," I replied defensively. "I'm thinking."

Until this minute, I hadn't seriously considered the possibility that Swenson's death might be anything other than what it looked like: a tragic accident that had been criminalized by the driver's failure to accept responsibility. I'd been focused on a scenario involving crazy old Aunt Velda and her two nieces—which was just about as far-fetched, now that I thought about it, as Ruby's idea about drugs.

I hesitated. The sensible, responsible thing would be for me to call Blackie and suggest that when he went out to talk to Corinne Tuttle the next morning, he should drive up Swenson's lane and take a quick look in that greenhouse, just to make sure that the guy hadn't been in the pot business. But sitting across the table from me was Ruby, who needed a distraction to keep her mind off her problem. And here was the perfect distraction. I rose to the occasion.

"What would you think about going out to Swenson's place?" I asked. "We could take a look at that greenhouse. If there's anything suspicious about it, we can report it to Blackie." As far as I was concerned, this was a low-risk venture. Chances were that we wouldn't find anything more suspicious out there than a few resentful goats.

Ruby stood up, went to the door, and opened it. "It's pouring rain," she said, coming back to the table, "and it's pitch-dark. We'll need ponchos and flashlights. And I'll have to borrow a pair of boots." She held out one sneakered foot. "It's too wet to go hiking around in these."

Now, *this* was the old Ruby. "I didn't mean right this minute. Let's get some sleep and head out there when it's light. With an early start, we can be back by the time we have to open the shops. Anyway, Laurel will be there, if we're a few minutes late. And Mrs. K has the tearoom under control. She can manage without us until noon."

"That's a good plan, China," Ruby said. She frowned. "But I think we ought to be prepared. If Swenson's been running a major drug operation out there, he hasn't been doing it single-handed. We might run into some of his friends—or enemies. The situation could get dicey. I know how you feel about your gun, but I think we ought to be armed."

I frowned. I do have a gun, a 9mm Beretta. I am trained to use it and I am licensed for concealed carry, now that the Texas voters have decided that it's kosher to hide a gun in your boot as long as you have the blessings of the Department of Public Safety. But I have always maintained that unless I am fully committed to using a weapon for its designated purpose—to kill or maim someone who menaces my person or the persons of those I love—I am better off leaving it in a locked drawer. On the other hand, it looked as if Ruby was getting into this in a big way. I could always leave the bullets at home. That way, there'd be no chance of an accident.

"Ruby," I said with feigned enthusiasm, "you're right. I'll bring my gun. We'll feel better knowing we can defend ourselves if we have to."

"Absolutely," Ruby said. "And I'll bring my chile-pepper spray. That stuff'll knock the socks off a grizzly bear. If somebody jumps us, he'll be sorry." The lines were disappearing from Ruby's face, and she looked lively and eager. My harebrained diversionary scheme was working.

"What time do you want me to pick you up?" I asked.

"How about five-thirty?"

I blinked. "Why don't we make it a little later? It's pretty cold at five-thirty in the morning. And very, very dark. The sun doesn't come up before seven, you know."

"I say five-thirty. We want to be there before any of Swenson's cronies show up to clean the place out—if they haven't done it already. We probably should have gone out there tonight, instead of sitting here talking about it." Ruby looked at her watch. "Gosh, China, it's after ten. I'd better get home and get some stuff together." She gave me a grin. "Hey, you know, I haven't thought about my boob for a whole fifteen minutes?" Her grin went crooked. "Until just now, that is."

"That's okay, Ruby," I said. "This expedition will be so exciting that you'll forget about your boob for hours at a stretch."

Little did I know.

CHAPTER ELEVEN

It is not a new opinion that the Golden Bough [that Aeneas carried into the underworld] was the mistletoe. True, Virgil does not identify but only compares it with mistletoe. But this may be only a poetical device to cast a mystic glamour over the humble plant. Or, more probably, his description was based on a popular superstition that at certain times the mistletoe blazed out into a supernatural golden glory.

Sir James George Frazer
The Golden Bough

I didn't intend to go dashing off to Swenson's place before dawn on that Tuesday morning without letting my husband know, but I'm afraid that's what happened. McQuaid must have gotten involved with his research, because he didn't get in until late—what time, I'm not sure, because I was already sound asleep. When I tried to rouse him at quarter to five, all I got was a muttered "Whazzat? Whozzit?" and a resonant snore.

What the heck, I decided. Let him sleep. If I woke him up to tell him where I was going, I'd have to tell him why, which would mean telling him about Ruby's cancer. The news would hit him as hard as it had me. It could wait until this evening, when we'd have time to talk it through.

I pulled on thermal underwear, a flannel shirt, and jeans, and took my unloaded gun out of the locked drawer. I hefted it, frowning. In the years since my father gave me the Beretta, I have developed an attitude about it. It's not the gun's fault, of course—guns are neutral. As Sheila frequently points out, I'd probably feel better about it if I'd shoot it more often, although somehow I haven't quite gotten around to that. As I stood there, thinking these unproductive thoughts, it occurred to me that Ruby might ask how much ammunition I'd brought, and that I'd feel more guilty about lying than I would about carrying the ammo. I took six rounds and went downstairs for coffee. If I couldn't wake McQuaid to tell him where I was going, I could leave a note.

But I gave it up after a couple of tries. How could I say, in twenty-five straight-faced words or less, that Ruby and I were playing a predawn game of cops and robbers out in the Hill Country? I scrawled, "I'll be in the shop between ten and noon," and pinned the note to the door of the fridge with a rooster magnet. I gulped down my coffee and shrugged into my jacket, the Beretta in one pocket and the ammunition in the other. I grabbed my shoulder bag, gloves, a wool cap, and a muffler and let myself quietly out the door.

The Pecan Springs Chamber of Commerce probably wants me to tell you a different story, but the truth is that December can get pretty damn cold around here. My Datsun turned over reluctantly a couple of times before she gave an out-of-sorts hiccup and started. I didn't blame her, poor old thing. It was five-fifteen in the morning and the temperature was probably close to fifteen degrees when the wind-chill was factored in. If I wasn't out of sorts myself, it was only because I was warmed by the feeling that I was undertaking this uncomfortable mission on behalf of a very important person: my friend Ruby, who is definitely worth the effort.

At Ruby's house, I didn't even have to honk. Dressed in jeans, cowboy boots, and a dark wool coat, cap, and scarf, Ruby was waiting on the front porch. When she saw me pull up at the curb, she ran down the walk and jumped in.

"You're late," she said breathlessly, dropping her canvas tote bag onto the floor, where it landed with a clunk.

I turned on the overhead light and looked at my watch. "Three minutes. The car didn't want to start." I peered at the tote bag, which looked heavy. "What did you bring?"

"Oh, *loads* of stuff," Ruby said. She opened the bag and began taking things out. "A Thermos of hot chocolate, granola bars, and some raisins."

"Ah," I said. "The well-provisioned sleuth."

"Plastic zipper-top bags, pepper spray, some bolt cutters, a lock-pick kit, a—"

"Wait a minute," I said. The bolt cutters and lock-pick kit I understood, although it wouldn't have occurred to me to bring them. "We won't need the bolt cutters—there's a padlock on the gate but it's hanging open. What are the bags for?"

Ruby gave me a look that suggested that I should be able to figure this out for myself if I'd take the time to think about it. "The bags are for any evidence we want to collect for Blackie. And even if the gate is open, we might need to get into one of the buildings."

"I see," I said.

"I've also brought some money, some powdered sugar, and a few joints." With a flourish, she displayed a thick roll of greenbacks, a plastic bag filled with some suspicious-looking white stuff, and a couple of hand-rolled brown-paper cigarettes.

"Excuse me, Ruby," I said. I tried to keep my voice low and even, but it rose in spite of me. "I know I shouldn't pry into your private affairs, but WHERE IN THE HELL DID YOU GET THAT MARIJUANA?"

"In my kitchen cabinet," Ruby said. "But it's not what you—"

I wasn't listening. "I don't care where you got it," I said sternly, "we are getting rid of it this instant. I am not about to get my ass busted for possession, thank you very much."

Ruby gave me a look of great forbearance. "It's not marijuana, it's oregano," she said. "Here. Smell."

I sniffed at the joint she held out. By damn, it *was* oregano. "But why—" I sputtered. "What could you possibly—"

I stopped suddenly. Wait a minute. I was acting as if this trip we were making was for real, but it wasn't. Blackie was an excellent lawman. If there'd been anything worth investigating at Swenson's place, he would have been out there a couple of days ago. This expedition that Ruby and I were making was a diversion, pure and simple, like one of those murder mystery weekends where people go hunting for planted clues and stumble over live dead bodies and generally make fools of themselves, all in the name of the game. If Ruby was taking it seriously, well and good, but it *was* only a distraction. And I was here to play along. All the way.

I put on a humble look. "I think I'm missing the point, Sherlock. Please tell me why we are carrying a wad of money, a bag of powdered sugar, and a couple of oregano joints."

Ruby put the powdered sugar and the joints back into her bag. "When people practice espionage, they have a cover story. This is our cover. We don't have any idea who we might run into out there, so you and I have our own little stash of cocaine and grass. Just-pretend, of course."

Oh boy. "That's not just-pretend money," I said. "Jeez, Ruby, that's enough to bankroll the next City Council election."

"It only *looks* like a lot," Ruby said, putting the money into her pocket. "Actually, it's just a couple of fifties rolled around a big bunch of ones." She patted my arm with a smile. "It'll be fine, China. Trust me."

Over the years, I've learned that when Ruby gets enthused about something, I might as well quit arguing and go along for the ride. Anyway, in this instance, there wasn't any particular harm in acting like a pair of idiots, because we weren't going to have an audience. The only live critter we were likely to encounter would have four feet and horns and smell like a goat.

I turned off the overhead light and started the Datsun. "Buckle up, babe," I said, in my best Bogart. "We're outta here."

The sky overhead was still as dark as the inside of a cow when we reached the turnoff to Swenson's house thirty minutes later. I pulled over to the far left as we approached the mailbox. "Let's take another look at that envelope," I said. "Maybe you'll see something I missed."

I rolled down my window, letting in the chill, cedar-scented air. But when I opened the mailbox and reached inside, it was empty. Frowning, I rolled up the window. "I guess the sheriff took it already," I said. Which was odd. When I'd talked to Blackie the night before, he hadn't seemed in any great hurry to send somebody to pick up the brochure.

"He must have decided that it was a clue to the man's intentions." Ruby said. "I hope he hasn't beaten us to it."

I was still thinking about the empty mailbox. "Beaten us to what?"

"To the greenhouse, what else?" Ruby replied. She peered through the windshield. "I thought you said the gate was unlocked."

"It is. The padlock is hanging open."

"It isn't," she said. "I can see from here. But it's no problem." She reached into her canvas bag and pulled out the bolt cutters. "I told you these would come in handy." She hopped out, slammed the door, and began attacking the rusty chain that fastened the gate.

Up to this point, Ruby would have to bear her share of blame for what happened that morning. But from here on out, in all fairness, I have to say that it was my fault. If I had jumped out, snatched those bolt cutters, dragged her back to the car, and driven to the Diner for jelly doughnuts and fresh hot coffee, none of the other events would have happened. But I wasn't paying the right kind of attention to what Ruby was doing. Instead, I was trying to puzzle out the significance of the locked gate.

It had been unlocked when I stopped at the mailbox yesterday evening.

Who had locked it?

Why?

Was there any connection between the locked gate and the missing brochure?

What was going on here?

I was still puzzling when the door opened and Ruby slid into the car, triumphantly brandishing her bolt cutters. "I've done it!" she said. "Now we can drive through."

I blinked. "Do what?"

"Drive, China," Ruby said, with exaggerated patience. "Make a left turn through the gate and onto that lane. Go, girl!"

With a sinking feeling in my stomach, I went. But I was no longer so cheery about our little adventure. Driving onto private property through an unlocked gate is one thing. You can always argue that you took a wrong turn. But cutting a chain in order to enter private property is something else altogether. It is spelled t-r-e-s-p-a-s-s. In Texas, this is taken very seriously, and has on more than one occasion been used as the basis of a justifiable-homicide defense.

Ruby, however, was plagued by none of these sobering thoughts. She was thoroughly preoccupied with the game, and that was worth a great deal. I swallowed my apprehensions and began paying attention to the road.

Most people who live in the Hill Country locate their houses within easy reach of a highway, to cut down on the cost of building and maintaining a road. But not Swenson. The pot-holed trail we were following—two gravel tracks with a strip of brown weeds down the middle—looped through a rock-strewn meadow, followed a limestone ridge for about a mile, then dipped down the lip of a cedar-filled ravine, at something like a 15-degree grade. The Datsun gasped and so did I, and Ruby grabbed for the door handle with a muttered "Whup!" But after a moment we straightened out, more or less, climbed the other side of the ravine, and emerged onto another meadow. I let out the breath I'd been holding and Ruby let go of the door handle.

"I'm dying to find out what Swenson has been up to in

this godforsaken place," she said. "Drugs may not be the half of it, China. For all we know, there's a bunch of dead bodies buried out here. You know, like serial murders. Or maybe buried treasure."

The Datsun dropped its left front wheel into a hole the size of Canyon Lake and I nearly bit my tongue in two. "Serial murders?" I muttered.

"Well, that's probably an exaggeration, but you've got to admit that it's the perfect spot for skullduggery. You could get lost out here and nobody would find you for weeks and weeks. Maybe months." She shuddered. "Maybe years."

The sky was turning shell-pink in the east and there was enough light to see that the day was not going to be one of Texas's finest. Angry gray clouds scudded overhead on a stiff north breeze. The rugged, rocky landscape was barricaded by fierce-looking prickly pear cactus and fortified by sentinels of Western red cedar, standing at attention in the pale dawn light. This was deserted country, starkly and severely beautiful, deceptive and treacherous and full of unpleasant surprises. If we had an accident or car trouble, it'd be a long hike back to the road. Surreptitiously, I reached under the driver's seat to make sure the cell phone was there, and came up empty-handed. *Damn.* It was still in the truck. The one piece of equipment we really needed, and I'd forgotten to bring it along. But I wouldn't mention it to Ruby. It might jar her faith in me.

We drove another half mile in silence. Just when I was ready to quit and turn back, the lane dipped and rose again and crossed a small open meadow. We had found Carl Swenson's house.

I stopped a little distance from the house and turned off the ignition. In the gray predawn light, we could see that there was no sign of a car, and the graveled area between the outbuildings and the house was empty. The house itself was a large, well-kept, two-story affair with a cedar-shingled roof and a wide porch across the front. A neatly mowed lawn extended around the house, and the whole area was landscaped with native shrubs, yaupon and agarito and cenizo. The place had a prosperous look.

"Interesting," Ruby said softly. "Swenson didn't pay for this with his mistletoe money."

"It's been here for a while," I said. "Swenson inherited the land from his family." Still, I was surprised. I had expected something more along the lines of Clyde's hovel, with surly dogs lounging in the dooryard and goats and pigs eating garbage out back. This place had three or four bedrooms plus a couple of living areas and had been recently renovated—or so I guessed—with skylights and glass gables. Sited as it was, almost at the top of a ridge, it commanded a sweeping view of hills and trees.

I thought again about the locked gate. "Do you still want to have a look around?" I asked nervously. "Maybe we just ought to bag it and go home."

"What do you mean, bag it?" Ruby was indignant. "We came to take a look and we're taking a look. Let's go."

With a sigh, I started the car again, drove into the parking area, and stopped. Ruby fished in her bag, retrieved her pepper spray, and pocketed it. Then she stripped off her wool cap and yanked a black ski mask over her face.

"Is that really necessary?" I asked doubtfully.

"Yep," Ruby said, pulling her cap back on. The black mask muffled her voice and gave her a malevolent, sinister look, like something out of *The Texas Chainsaw Massacre*. "Here's one for you." She thrust a red wool mask into my hand. "Don't argue, China. Just put it on." She began tugging a pair of black leather gloves on her hands.

"I hate these things," I muttered, pulling the mask over my head. "They make me feel like an Egyptian mummy."

Ruby picked up her canvas bag and slung it over her shoulder. "I'm ready. Are you?"

I opened the door and got out, swiveling my head to check for loose rottweilers. If I lived this far out in the country, I'd keep at least two. Maybe a half dozen. If I were really paranoid, I'd probably arrange a few booby traps in convenient places. As I was wondering how paranoid Carl Swenson had been, a gust of icy wind lifted dust from the parking area and flung it into my face, and I realized that the ski mask hadn't been such a bad idea after all. It limited visibility to what was directly in front of me, but I was glad for its protection.

"I wonder where the greenhouse is," Ruby said, her voice low.

I glanced around, getting my bearings. The house was on a grassy knoll and the outbuildings—a double garage; a tin-roofed shed that sheltered a tractor, an old truck, and some farm equipment; and a substantial gray metal building, maybe thirty by sixty, with twelve-foot double doors— were off to the east, fifty yards or so away. All the buildings except for the house looked as if they'd been constructed in the last couple of years. Well-constructed, too, not a tumbledown shanty among them.

I turned back, squinting, my attention belatedly caught by the truck in the tractor shed. It was dark under the tin roof and difficult to tell at a glance, but I was getting that twitchy feeling that tells me I'm onto something important. I strode toward the shed, Ruby running to catch up.

"I said, I don't see the greenhouse," she repeated. "Where do you think it is?"

We reached the shed. The truck was wedged, nose in, between the tractor and a couple of pieces of farm equipment, both new. The truck wasn't new. It was red, it sagged in the right rear, and the right-side window was covered with ratty-looking cardboard. It was a Ford.

"By damn," I said softly. "We've found Aunt Velda's truck."

"The truck?" Ruby made an excited noise. "But what's it doing here? Who put it here? What—"

"I have no idea," I said. "Stay put. There's only room for one person in there."

I squeezed between the truck and the tractor, stepped around the front, and took a look. What I saw sobered me. The right front headlight was broken and there were spatters of something that looked like blood on the grille. I walked back around to the passenger side, stood on tiptoe, and peered through the window. The key was still in the ignition.

I rejoined Ruby. She'd wrapped her arms around herself and was jiggling up and down, trying to keep warm.

"Well?" she asked. "Is it what you thought?"

"It is," I said grimly. "There's blood on the grille and the right front headlight is broken." I was wishing like hell for my cell phone. Some smart investigators we were. We'd brought props and costumes—and no means of communication. I glanced toward the house. There had to be a phone inside. "This changes everything, Ruby. We're not playing a game. We need to get Blackie out here. Right away."

"I don't get it, China," Ruby said, puzzled. "Why would Aunt Velda have hidden the truck here? You'd think it's the last place she'd put it."

"Because she's completely loony, that's why," I replied crossly. "Because the Klingons told her to do it. Because—"

I stopped. "Because it's the last place anybody would think to look," I said softly. Which was not so loony, after all.

"Do you really think that old lady could have driven it here and then walked all the way back to the flower farm? It's an awfully long way back to the mailbox, and from there, it must be three or four miles to the farm."

I glanced up, assessing where we were. "I'll bet it's not as far as that. We drove quite a distance to the south, but Comanche Road loops back, and the flower farm is on this side of it. For all we know, the Fletcher place is just over the next hill."

That made sense, actually. Donna had said that their house used to belong to the ranch manager. Surely the manager wouldn't live a couple of hours' horseback ride from the main house. Still, Ruby had a point. The terrain was pretty rugged, not easy for an old lady to hike across.

"But maybe Aunt Velda didn't actually do it," Ruby said, thinking out loud. "Maybe somebody took her truck, ran Swenson down, and then drove it here. Somebody like, well, Marvin."

"If he did, his prints will be on it." I turned toward the house. "Come on. Let's see if we can find a phone. We need to get Blackie out here."

Ruby grabbed my arm. "Before you go calling the cops, I think we ought to check out that big metal building over there." She pointed. "If it was me growing grass, I'd put my greenhouse indoors, under lights and a metal roof. That way, nobody could see what I was up to." She headed off in the direction of the metal building.

I have to give it to Ruby. When she gets an idea, she sticks with it. And for all I knew, she was right. I've cultivated a lot of herbs in my life, but *Cannabis sativa* is not one of them. While I am not one of those who condemn the plant outright—after all, it enjoyed a long and honorable history as a fiber and medicinal plant long before we criminalized it—my distaste for spending time in jail has overcome my desire to have a plant or two in my own personal collection. And even though my previous job required me to defend my share of users and dealers, I don't keep up on recent advances in commercial pot culture.

Anyway, there was a certain logic to Ruby's idea, and I went after her. Aunt Velda's red Ford truck had been parked in Swenson's tractor shed since Sunday afternoon—it could sit there a few hours longer. Aunt Velda wasn't going anywhere. And if there was something illegal in that barn, we could alert Blackie to the fact, so he would come prepared.

Ruby and I stood together in front of the building. I assumed that the double doors—sliding doors, hung from a track at the top—would be locked, and wondered whether it was time to use Ruby's handy-dandy lock-picking kit. But the right-hand door hung open a couple of inches. Ruby pushed it to the side until the opening was just wide enough to slip through.

"Wait, Ruby," I said cautiously. "Somebody might be in there."

"If anybody's in there, they're in the dark," Ruby retorted.

"We'll be in the dark, too. Did you bring your flashlight?"

"No, but I brought this." She reached into her canvas bag and took out the can of pepper spray. "Are you coming or do I go by myself?" And with that, she stepped through the door. I had no choice but to follow her.

It was pitch-black inside, but my nose told me that

something—pot or not—was growing in this building. The smell of rich, damp earth and green leaves was unmistakable, and the air was warm, 50 degrees or so.

"Smell it?" Ruby asked excitedly. "He's growing stuff!"

"Maybe it's orchids," I whispered.

"If I were a light switch," Ruby said, "where would I be? To the right, just inside the door?"

"Wait, Ruby!" I exclaimed. But it was too late. She'd found the switch and flipped it on. A string of bulbs suspended overhead came on, not very bright, but bright enough to show us what we'd come all this way to see.

Swenson's greenhouse. Not your everyday glassed-in variety, but a large, open growing area in the middle of a dirt floor. This rectangular space, covered with several inches of pine-bark mulch, was home to forty or so rows of robust, flourishing green plants. Some, in three-gallon pots, were head-high and obviously mature; others were waist-high; still others, in gallon pots, were knee-high. Along the right, on wooden tables, were flats of tiny green seedlings. Banks of fluorescent tubes, not operating at the moment, were suspended over the growing area, along with a complex web of what looked like sprayers or misters. With a metallic grunt and a whistle, a blower came on and the leaves began to stir slightly in the mechanical breeze.

We moved forward and to the right for a better look. As we stood there, taking all this in like a pair of open-mouthed tourists on the South Rim of the Grand Canyon, we heard a loud click. The fluorescent tubes blinked and brightened, flooding the growing area with an intense, full-spectrum light that made the leaves look intensely, potently green. Seconds later, the misters came on, spraying clouds of sparkling droplets. The system was obviously regulated by electronic timers which measured out just the right amount of sun, wind, and rain. The result was an extremely lucrative harvest of green plants that were almost literally worth their weight in gold.

I blinked against the bright light. Ruby sucked in her breath and let it out again in a long hiss. "Wow," she whispered. "I thought we might find a few plants, but this is— It's—" She gave up trying to find words. "The mind boggles," she said, and fell silent.

"Yeah," I agreed, and did a rapid-fire calculation. There were maybe eight hundred to a thousand plants in front of us. What was the street value? A million dollars? Two million? My stomach lurched. My lower lip was hung up between my teeth. No wonder Swenson could afford to shop for a Rio condo. Hell, if he'd been doing this for a while, he could probably buy the whole damn condo complex. With pocket change.

Beside me, Ruby was taking very deep breaths. "Do you know what this means, China?" she asked in a threadlike voice. "It means that—"

I put my hand on her shoulder. "It means that you were right. It also means that we'd better get to that phone, on the double. Blackie is going to have one hell of a drug bust on his hands, and he'll want—"

The lights went out. *All* the lights. The dark was immediate and stifling, a thick, warm, earthy blanket. I froze in place. It was hard to hear anything over the sudden pounding of my heart. I didn't have time to guess who, or why, or what was going to happen next—I was too busy kicking myself for letting us get into this mess.

"Don't panic, Ruby," I whispered. "We'll let our eyes get accustomed to the dark, then we'll turn around and walk toward the double doors." We had left them open, so there'd be a strip of light down one side. "Then we'll get in the car and drive like hell to Corinne's. We can borrow her phone."

It was a reasonable plan, under the circumstances. But before we could put it into operation, we were assaulted by a brilliant spotlight, as sharp and penetrating as a dagger, that pinned us to the spot where we stood.

I threw up my arm, shielding my eyes against the blinding light. Beside me, Ruby was suddenly and violently wrenched away. Then I heard the sharp *hssst* of Ruby's pepper spray, and then somebody—a man—howling in furious pain. Then there was the sound of a scuffle, and sharp pantings and gaspings, and a shrill, despairing cry. "Help, China!"

But I couldn't help her. I couldn't even help myself. At the instant Ruby sprayed her attacker, somebody had thrown a burly arm tight around my neck and thrust the business end of a gun against my neck, just behind my ear.

CHAPTER TWELVE

In Sweden mistletoe is diligently sought after on St. John's Eve, the people believing it to be, in a high degree, possessed of mystic qualities; and if a sprig of it be attached to the ceiling of the dwelling-house, the horse's stall or the cow's crib, the Troll will then be powerless to injure either man or beast.

Sir James George Frazer
The Golden Bough

The man who was holding me was a head taller and had a wrestler's grip. He smelled of old sweat and wet wool and strong tobacco. "One wrong move," he rasped in an ugly tone, "and I'll blow your stupid head off."

"I'm not moving," I choked, pulling at his arm. "Loosen up. I . . . can't breathe." I was struggling to break the stranglehold, but his arm was clamped tight across my windpipe. "Please, loosen up!"

"Shut up and stand still," Ugly Voice said, but he relaxed his grip just enough for me to take a breath, compensating for his generosity by shoving the gun even harder against my neck.

Somewhere nearby, the man Ruby had sprayed was choking and hacking, still moaning in pain. I could hear

Ruby whimpering, a hurt little-girl whimper, then more scuffles, a sharp curse, and a muttered, incredulous, "The goddamn bitch *bit* me!" There was a sharp slap, and another whimper.

"Ruby!" I cried. But I couldn't get enough air to make the word audible. I tried to turn my head to see what was happening to her, but my ski mask was twisted across my face, cutting off my vision.

"Stop fuckin' around, you guys," another man yelled. "Hit the lights!"

I felt, rather than saw, the spotlight go off. I made another effort to call to Ruby, but all I could manage was a mouselike squeak.

"Shut up, I said," Ugly Voice snarled. "Come on."

He tightened his hold again, yanking me against his chest, pulling me off my feet, half-carrying, half-dragging me across the floor. I hung onto his arm with both hands, trying to take some of the pressure off my windpipe. My insides had turned to a quivering, cowardly, self-reproachful jelly. We'd been so stupid! We'd blundered into the biggest pot farm in Texas and gotten ourselves nabbed by Swenson's nefarious cronies. And not a single soul on earth—not McQuaid, not Blackie, *nobody*—knew where we were. These guys could kill us and bury our bodies somewhere in this desolate stretch of Hill Country, and we'd never be found.

Ugly Voice dumped me onto the floor like a sack of garbage. On my knees, I sucked in air in huge gulps. My nose was running. I couldn't swallow and the saliva pooled in my mouth. I was going to throw up. Somebody reached into my pocket and pulled out my gun, then yanked off my ski mask, getting a handful of my hair in the bargain.

"Shit," Ugly Voice said, full of surprised disgust. "Who the bloody hell is *she*?" He was standing in front of me. In the light of the overhead bulbs I could see his black running shoes and the blue knees of his coveralls. I managed to lift my head and saw him holstering his gun, a wicked-looking magnum .357. Over the coveralls, he was wearing a dark blue jacket, zipped. He was brown-skinned, with a droopy Zapata mustache and a couple days' worth of patchy black beard. On his head was a dark blue baseball cap with the bill turned backward. "Somebody go see if Marvin needs any help," he said. "The other one sprayed him good."

I was sweating and shivering at the same time. So Marvin was in on this, after all. Well, it figured. You don't pay for a Camaro out of your aunt's cookie jar. But it didn't explain Aunt Velda's truck.

Ugly Voice kicked my knee with his foot, and I gasped at the pain. "Who the fuck are you?" he demanded. "What are you doing here?"

"We'll find out soon enough," somebody else said, behind me, clipping the words. He was firm, authoritative, in command. "Take her to the kitchen, Jose. Zacho, you take the other one. Search them both. I'll interrogate them when we've got the area secured."

I was still doing deep breathing, trying to keep from throwing up, but that got my attention. *Interrogate them? Got the area secured?* Who the devil *were* these guys anyway?

"Yessir, Cap'n," Jose growled, and yanked me roughly to my feet. He shoved the gun into my ribs with an enthusiastic zeal and pushed me forward. "Don't try anything, babe. It'd be real easy for my finger to slip."

"Be cool," I said. I lifted my arms. "I'm just wondering who you are, that's all."

"Forget it," Jose said. "You're the one who's gonna be answerin' the questions, not me."

But at that moment, another man—also wearing blue coveralls and jacket—crossed my field of vision. As he turned, I caught sight of the red letters on the back of his jacket.

South Texas Regional Narcotics Unit.

When Zacho brought Ruby into the kitchen, she looked sick and scared, and there was a bloody scratch down one side of her face. Her eyes were red and her nose was dripping, but she was trying not to cry. "I'm sorry, China," she said dejectedly. "This was a lousy idea."

"Who could've guessed we'd walk into the middle of a drug bust?" I said. "Have you seen Marvin? Wonder what he looks like."

If these were feds, then Marvin must be a narc. I hoped he wasn't hurt too badly. I couldn't remember the penalty for assaulting a federal agent, but it was probably something on the order of ten years at hard labor.

Zacho left. Jose brandished his gun and instructed us to line up facing the kitchen wall, legs splayed, arms braced against the wall over our heads. He took his time patting us down, familiarly and ungently, then shoved us onto chairs and cuffed our hands in front of us. I could have protested against being searched by a male, but under the circumstances, it seemed politic not to. Especially when, going through Ruby's canvas tote, he found the bag of white powder, the two joints, the wad of money, and the rest of Ruby's stage props. At that point I offered to explain, but he was too busy gloating to listen. He told me to shut up.

A few minutes later, Zacho came back into the kitchen with Ruby's bolt cutters, my shoulder bag, and the black plastic garbage sack full of leafy stuff that he'd found in my trunk—Swenson's mistletoe, which I'd stashed in the car the night before, planning to take it to the shop. The bag was securely tied. It rustled.

Jose's eyes widened at the sight of the bag. "Man, these chicks don't mess around. They got enough stuff to supply half the kids in San Antonio."

Ruby coughed. "Honestly, it's not—"

"Shut your face," Jose said sternly. "Marvin okay?"

Zacho dropped the bag on the floor and everything else on the kitchen counter. "Burned the shit out of his eyes," he said gruffly. "He's still blind as a bat and in a lot of pain. Must've been allergic to whatever was in that can." He glared at Ruby and went out again.

"If you'll take these handcuffs off," Ruby said after a few minutes, "I'll make you some coffee."

Stroking his black mustache, Jose considered this suggestion more carefully than my offer of an explanation. But in the end he refused it too, although his "Shut up" was a bit more regretful.

Not having anything better to do, I looked around. The kitchen was nicely arranged, flooded with natural light, and furnished with new appliances. Through an open door, I could see a large pine-paneled dining area and a living area with a massive stone fireplace in one wall, plush rugs on polished oak floors, and expensive-looking leather furniture. The house might be sixty or seventy years old, but it was well maintained and Swenson had put a substantial amount of money into it fairly recently. I could guess where the money had come from.

We sat for a while in silence while I considered various

options for action or negotiation, none of which seemed very satisfactory. I no longer feared that Ruby and I would be dismembered and our body parts distributed among the prickly pear but it was clear that we were in for a long and tedious round of embarrassing explanations which would probably culminate in my losing my law license. The Ethics Committee of the Texas State Bar would not be amused by our oregano joints and confectioners' sugar cocaine.

At last, Ruby began to squirm. "I have to go to the bathroom," she said.

Jose frowned. "Hold it," he ordered.

Five minutes later, Ruby made a whimpering noise. "I really have to go, sir. It hurts."

Jose was about to say "Hold it" again when I spoke up. "You'd better let her go pee, Jose. She's got cancer. She could get really sick."

"Cancer!"

I gave Ruby a look that said, *I'm sorry.* She gave me back a tiny smile.

"I'm scheduled for surgery two days after Christmas," she said to Jose. "If you don't believe me, I'll give you my doctor's number and you can call him."

Jose's nostrils flared and he gave his head an I'm-not-believing-this shake. After a moment of sour deliberation, he stood up, holding the gun on us.

"Okay," he said curtly. "Both of you, down the hall. No funny business."

We stood up and he pushed us ahead of him. When we got to the bathroom at the end of the hall, he made us face the wall. With one eye on us, his gun held shoulder-high, he opened the bathroom door and glanced in—checking, I supposed, for a means of escape. Satisfied, he motioned with his head.

"Okay, you," he said to Ruby. "Pee fast." To me, he said, "Face the wall."

Ruby held up her cuffs. "Can you take these off, please?" she asked humbly.

Jose shook his head. "You can pee with 'em on."

"But I can't get my pants down!" Ruby wailed. "They're too tight."

"Pee through your pants," Jose growled.

"I'll help you get your pants down, Ruby," I offered over my shoulder.

"I said, face the wall," Jose snapped. To Ruby, he said, "Go pee, for crissake. And don't take all day."

Ruby went in and shut the door. I took the opportunity to say, in a conversational tone, "This isn't what you think, you know. Those joints are only—"

"Face the wall," Jose said.

"—oregano."

"Yeah." He barked a laugh. "That's what they all say. I suppose that white stuff is powdered sugar."

"Right. Taste it if you don't believe me. And the stuff in the garbage bag is mistletoe."

"Mistletoe! You two are something else, you know that?" He smirked. "I suppose the gun is a cap pistol, right?"

"No," I said. "Any fool can see it's a Beretta."

"Shut up," Jose said. He frowned at the door. "She's taking a helluva long time."

"Women have bigger bladders than men. And she's got those clumsy cuffs on, so it takes longer. You ever try to get your pants down when you're cuffed?" I turned half-around and added, cordially, "You guys are a little out of your territory, aren't you? What brings you up here from South Texas?" I paused, thinking that Blackie had been conspiciously absent from this bust. "Does the sheriff know you're here?"

Jose's eyes became flintlike. He started to say something, then shut his mouth.

I leaned my shoulder against the wall and cocked my head to one side. "So how long has Marvin been on the case? Was that how you got the lead on Swenson?"

"Marvin?" He fixed his eyes on me and his jaw began to work. "What d'you know about Marvin?"

My lips twitched. I gave him a look that said I knew a lot, but he wasn't going to hear any of it.

"Face the wall," he growled. "I don't want any more shit outta you."

There was the sound of a toilet flushing, then water running. The bathroom door opened and Ruby stepped out.

"Next," she said politely. "But I'm afraid I used the last of the toilet paper."

"That's okay." I took a step toward the bathroom. "I can drip dry."

Jose grabbed my shoulder and jerked me back. "Forget it, smartass. You ain't got cancer, you can hold it. Back to the kitchen, both of you."

We'd been sitting for about twenty minutes when another man in coveralls came in, the one with the clipped, authoritative voice, whom Jose had addressed as "Cap'n." He was short and sallow and without expression. He wore his blue cap with the bill forward. His eyes were icy blue.

Ruby and I sat in silence as Jose pointed out, with an unmistakable relish, the various items he and Zacho had confiscated, evidence of our criminal connections to the drug world. My gun was there, too. When I saw him looking at it, I said, "I'm licensed for concealed carry."

The captain turned for a disdainful look at me, then went

back to the loot. He and Jose held a muttered consultation, during which I heard the whispered word "Marvin." The captain took my billfold out of my purse, studied my driver's license, and put it back. He jerked his head at me.

"You," he said. "Into the dining room."

We left Ruby under Jose's supervision, and took seats at the dining room table, where the captain recited my rights, fast. Then he leaned back in his chair and folded his arms, regarding me. He gave me about fifteen seconds of flinty-eyed silence.

"All right, Ms. Bayles," he said at last. "I want to know who the hell you are and what you're doing here, and I want it straight."

"Excuse me," I said, "but who the hell are you?"

He leaned toward me, narrowing the space between us just enough to be threatening. His eyes got icier. "I am Captain Ron Talbot, South Texas Narcotics Unit."

"I need to see your identification," I said.

He made a low growl.

I smiled. "Identification, please."

Angrily, he stood, unzipped his jacket, unsnapped his coveralls, and went deep inside for his badge. Pulling it out, he flashed it at me, very fast.

"Excuse me," I said. "I'd like to see the number."

With another growl, he shoved it forward, about three inches from my nose. I pulled my head back and read off the digits, mouthing them as if I were memorizing them. "Thank you," I said.

He reversed the unsnappings and unzippings and sat back down. "I don't want any more crap out of you," he said. "Now, *talk*."

I'd already determined that there wasn't any point in trying to avoid the embarrassing truth, so Talbot got the full story, or most of it. I left out Blackie's request to drop in on the Fletcher sisters and the bit about Corinne Tuttle and her nephew, and the discovery of Aunt Velda's truck in Swenson's tractor shed. I also explained, briefly, that the white substance in the Baggie was sugar, the joints were oregano, and the stuff in the large plastic bag was mistletoe. I didn't try to tell him why or how we had happened to come equipped with these things.

"You can get the sugar and the oregano tested," I concluded. "You can tell what the mistletoe is by looking at it. You can call my husband, who will be glad to ID me. You can also check me out with Sheriff Blackwell." I paused, and with a knowing emphasis, added, "And just where *is* Sheriff Blackwell? This is his county. Why isn't he in on this bust?"

Talbot regarded me with angry contempt. "What makes you think I'd answer those questions?" he demanded. "And just who the hell do you think is running this show, anyway? It sure as shit ain't some half-assed county sheriff who can't find his—"

But that was the end of the captain's tirade. The front door burst open with a bang to reveal Sheriff Blackwell himself, jaw set, mouth tight, eyes blazing.

"Hello, China," he said tautly.

Oh, rats, I thought to myself, *now I'm in for it,* and mentally ducked.

But I wasn't Blackie's target. He strode to the table, put both hands flat on it, lowered his head and snarled, "What the devil are you doin' here, Talbot?"

Talbot, suddenly deflated, made an ineffectual effort to speak.

Blackie pushed his face closer and overrode the man. "I thought I made it clear the last time this happened. You

come into my county to do a bust, you notify me. No no-
tification, no cooperation, no bust. Is that clear?"

Talbot said nothing.

Blackie snatched at the bill of Talbot's cap and yanked
it down over his nose. "Is that clear?" he roared. "Or do
you want me to file another goddamn complaint? How's
that gonna look on your record after that mess down in
Kerrville last month?"

Slowly, with an attempt at dignity, Talbot raised the bill
of his cap. "It's clear," he said, through clenched teeth. "But
I thought we had the lid nailed on."

Blackie snorted sarcastically.

"Where was the leak?" Talbot persisted. "Was it Marvin? He's not one of mine."

"You don't want to know."

"Like hell!" Talbot's nostrils flared. "That goddamn
Marvin, that's who it was."

"It wasn't Marvin." Blackie gave him a malicious grin.
"One of your prisoners called me on the phone."

There was a moment's silence. "On the *phone*?" Talbot
asked incredulously.

Blackie's grin got wider. "She called the dispatcher and
left a message. I was out this way on another matter, so I
thought I'd join the party." He stopped grinning. "Especially since I should've gotten an invitation in the first
place."

Talbot's eyes darted to me. "Was it you?" he snarled.

"Me?" I lifted my shoulders, let them fall, completely
innocent. "Not me. I left my cell phone at home. Must've
been Ruby."

"But . . . but where?" Talbot sputtered. "How?"

"From the bathroom, maybe," I offered helpfully. It was
the only time Ruby had been out of my sight. "Jose's got

a soft spot in his heart for ladies in distress. He let her pee."
I grinned. "She must've leaked."

"Aw, jeez." Talbot slapped his forehead with the heel
of his hand and turned away in disgust.

Blackie put his hand on my shoulder. "This turkey been
giving you a hard time, China?"

"Moderately," I said. "He might've figured he was entitled, though. We crashed his bust." I looked at Talbot.
"Sorry about that, Captain. It wasn't intentional, believe
me. I hope none of the bad guys got away."

Blackie gave an unkind laugh.

Talbot's eyes slitted. "Don't tell me she's one of yours,"
he said to Blackie. "If she is, you've got one hell of a
problem in your shop. She is the most untrained, unprofes-
sional, amateurish—"

"Not one of mine," Blackie said. "What are you going
to do with her?"

Talbot pulled himself up and stood looking down his
nose. After a moment, he said: "Just to show you my generous intentions, I hereby remand this prisoner into your
custody. The redhead, too. Good riddance."

Blackie held up his hands, looking alarmed. "Oh, no,
Talbot. You're not foisting them off on me. They're dangerous. If I were you, I'd turn 'em loose, fast. Both of 'em.
The redhead is weird as hell, and this one is very bad news.
Her husband is a former Houston homicide dick and a re-
tired police chief. She's a defense attorney. She'll sue your
ass, and he'll kick it from here to Dallas."

"Aw, hell," Talbot said disgustedly.

I held out my hands. "Now that we've cleared that up,
how about getting these cuffs off?"

Without a word, Talbot got up and went to the kitchen.
In a moment, Jose came in, patting his pockets for the key.

I was rubbing my wrists when Talbot returned to the room, Beretta in one hand and ammunition in the other. With a disdainful flourish, he dropped both on the dining room table.

"Thanks," I said.

"Yeah." He looked at me, nostrils flaring. "Next time you decide to do a drug bust, you oughta ask the sheriff to show you how to load."

"All right, you two," Blackie said sternly, when we got outside. "I want to hear the whole story, start to finish. Straight and fast, just the way it happened. And don't try to make it pretty."

Ruby shivered. "Let's do it in the car," she said plaintively. "It's cold out here."

We got into the sheriff's car, Blackie and I up front, Ruby in the back, behind the wire screen that separates the front of the car from the rear. I told my part first. Since it was my second telling in less than an hour, I got through it quickly. This time, I left out Ruby's cancer. Blackie was Ruby's friend, and I wanted her to tell him in her own way. I did, however, report our finding of the truck.

"It's here?" Blackie exclaimed incredulously. "The red Ford we've been looking for?"

"In that shed," Ruby said, pointing out the window. "Beside the tractor."

Blackie craned his neck for a look. "The right front headlight is smashed," I said, "and there's blood on the grille. The key is in the ignition. Looks like the vehicle that killed Swenson."

Blackie was silent for a moment. "So what do you think?" he asked finally. "The old lady drove it here and parked it and walked back home?" He frowned. "It'd be quite a hike, wouldn't it?"

"I'd have to look at a county map," I said. "You got one?"

He did, under the seat. With Ruby peering through the wire screen, we located Comanche Road and the lane leading to Swenson's place, then traced Comanche as it looped around to the flower farm. On the map, we could see that the distance between this house and the Fletcher sisters' house was just over a mile. Between the two was Mistletoe Spring, clearly designated on the map.

"Looks to me like the old lady could've walked it," the sheriff said, studying the map. "It's not that far."

"I'm not sure," I replied. "I think she could make that distance by road. But this terrain is really rugged. I don't know whether she could manage a cross-country hike." On the other hand, Aunt Velda had said that she'd been looking for a cave. Maybe the old lady was more nimble than I thought.

"But if she didn't park the truck in the shed," Ruby said, "who did? Terry? Donna?"

Blackie was reaching for his radio. "I'll get somebody out here to print and impound that truck. And then we need to have another talk with the old lady."

"You could ask Talbot to do the printing," I suggested with a grin.

"Hell, no." Blackie gave a scornful snort. "He'd screw it up. That jerk has blown three busts in the last six months and hasn't made a single arrest. He's got the worst reputation in the whole damn narcotics division."

"It's a thankless job," I said with a grin. "Give the guy a break." I turned around in the seat. "Ruby, you saved our butts by phoning the sheriff's office. Talbot was ready to haul us off to South Texas. I'm sure he'd've turned us loose eventually, but not before we had an arrest record and a day or two in the Brownsville jail." I shuddered. "I interviewed a client there once. It's way down on my list of South Texas tourist attractions."

"Thank you," Ruby said modestly. "The odds weren't in our favor, and I could tell that those guys would have a hard time believing our story. I thought we needed help, so I called the cops."

Blackie swiveled. "Is it true that you phoned from the bathroom?"

"Yeah." Ruby leaned back in the seat. "There was a phone on the wall."

"A phone!" I stared at her. "But Jose checked before he let you in. How come he didn't see it?"

"Because somebody used it for a hook, to hang up a towel," Ruby replied. "When I went to use the toilet, the towel fell down, and there was the phone."

Blackie shook his head. "Like I said, you two are dangerous." With a chuckle, he clicked on his mike.

CHAPTER THIRTEEN

If mistletoe was hung in the dwelling as a protection
against ailments and the terrors of an unseen world,
woe betide those who left the charm hanging there
too long! Herrick gives fair warning to all who would
venture to do so after Candlemas Eve (February 1),
for he wrote:

> *Down with Bays and Mistletoe,*
> *Down with Holly, Ivy, all*
> *Wherewith ye deck the Christmas hall*
> *That so the superstitious find*
> *No one least branch there left behind.*
> *For look! how many leaves there be*
> *Neglected then (Maids, trust to me)*
> *So many Goblins you shall see.*

H. H. Warner
"Mistletoe," 1931

A couple of hours later, the old Ford truck was on a flatbed
tow truck, headed for the sheriff's impound yard. Ruby was
on her way back to town in my Datsun, to check in with
Laurel at the shops and make sure that everything was okay
in the tearoom. And Blackie and I were in the sheriff's car,

on our way to the flower farm. I hadn't wanted to go, but Blackie persuaded me that I might be able to help.

"I still don't understand what you two thought you were doing at Swenson's place," Blackie said as we drove. "It seems like a dumb stunt."

"Yeah, maybe," I replied uncomfortably. "But I was curious about Swenson. When Ruby and I got to talking about what he might've been growing in that greenhouse . . . Well, it seemed like a good idea to take a look. The way things turned out, though," I added ruefully, "I wish we'd stayed home. I had no idea that Marvin was a narc. I hope he wasn't injured. And I'm really sorry if we caused you or Talbot any trouble."

"The bust would have gone down the way it did with or without you," Blackie said evenly. "And Marvin was a snitch, not a narc. He was Swenson's hired help. When he found out that Swenson was dead, he figured the hit was drug-related. He panicked and called the Regional Office. Talbot decided to buzz on up here and seize the plants, without even thinking about the rest of the investigation. He must have had fantasies of bagging a couple of hundred pounds of weed to shore up his sorry batting average. When you and Ruby walked into the middle of things, he thought he'd really scored. He figured you were part of Swenson's distribution system."

"Maybe they'll find his little black book," I said. "Or the equivalent. Swenson had to have had some way to keep in touch with his distributors."

"You can bet they're looking for it. Talbot's men were searching the house and the captain was logging onto Swenson's computer when we left." He shot me a look. "I hate to say it, but I'm glad you went out there, China. I was treating Swenson's death like an ordinary hit-and-run.

I doubt that I would've bothered getting a warrant to search his place, especially since I'm short-handed. It could've been a week or more before Talbot got around to informing me of the bust. In the meantime, he has the authority to impound every piece of equipment on the place. That Ford truck might've ended up on a lot in Brownsville, and we'd never have known it was there."

"Yeah," I said glumly. "Now we've got the evidence. We can arrest Aunt Velda. Whoopee."

"Maybe," Blackie said. "It would have been real tough for that old lady to hike over that hill. Which leaves us with the sisters."

"Yeah," I growled. "Which leaves us with the sisters."

When we got to the Mistletoe Creek Flower Farm, it was shortly after noon. The clouds still scudded low over the hills and the wind was chill. Donna and Aunt Velda were in the kitchen. Aunt Velda, in her rocking chair, was wrapped in a purple afghan and crocheting what looked like a red and green wool cap. Donna was clearing the table after a soup-and-sandwich lunch.

"Would you like a cheese sandwich?" Donna asked after she'd invited us in. "There's some tomato soup left, too."

I glanced at her and then back again, startled. Her face was a dull, grayish color, and her eyes were hollowed.

"No, thank you," Blackie said, hat in hand. With a glance at Aunt Velda, he said in a low voice, "I'm afraid this is an official visit, Ms. Fletcher. We've located your aunt's truck. From the physical evidence, there's reason to believe that it was the vehicle that killed Carl Swenson."

Donna gave a muffled gasp and a low, protesting "Oh, no." She sank into a chair as if her legs wouldn't hold her. I had the feeling that this response, like the one on the previous day, was not entirely genuine. She was anguished—but not surprised.

Rocking vigorously, Aunt Velda looked up. "Well, it's about time you found it," she said. To Donna, she added, "I told you it'ud turn up sometime or other. Them Klingons is trickier than slicky dickens, but they ain't all that smart." She grinned flirtatiously at Blackie. "Sure is nice o' you to come and tell us, young man. Didja bring it back?"

"I'm afraid not," Blackie said. He turned to Donna. "I need to take your aunt to Pecan Springs for questioning. Please get her coat and whatever she'll need for an overnight stay."

"Hooboy," Aunt Velda said, delighted. She tossed her crocheting into a basket and sat forward in her chair. "Yer takin' me to town, huh? Donna, git my stuff. I'm ready!"

Donna made an inarticulate sound.

"You can come too," Blackie said in a sympathetic tone, "although I'm afraid I can't allow you to be present during the interrogation. I'll arrange for her social worker to be there, of course. And you'll want to contact a lawyer."

Donna had gone completely white. She sat staring at Blackie, her hands twisted tightly together. She seemed to be having trouble breathing. But after a moment she said, in an unexpectedly clear, distinct voice, "That won't be necessary, Sheriff. I'm the one you want."

I drew in my breath, startled. This wasn't what I had expected. Not Donna, surely!

Blackie's mouth tightened. "Are you saying that you were the driver of the truck that killed Carl Swenson?"

I found my voice. "Sheriff!" I said sharply.

Blackie nodded. "Ms. Fletcher, I must tell you that you have the right to remain silent. If you do not remain silent, anything you do say can and will be used against you in a court of law."

"I don't want to remain silent." Donna stood up, steadying herself with a hand on the table. "I just want to get this over with." She took a deep breath and squared her shoulders. "Yes, I was driving the truck."

"Don't, Donna," I said emphatically. "You need to talk to a lawyer before you make a statement."

She ignored me. "It was an accident. I didn't mean to kill him. But when I saw that the truck was damaged, I panicked. I drove it to Swenson's place because I was afraid to bring it back here and I couldn't think of anywhere else to hide it." She threw a small smile in my direction. "And I don't need a lawyer, China. I intend to plead guilty. There's no use spending a lot of money on an attorney when I know I did it."

Blackie's jaw muscles were tight. "You'll have to come with me, Ms. Fletcher. Is there someone who can stay with your aunt?"

Aunt Velda was scowling. "Reckon this means I don't git to go to town after all," she said crankily. "Means I gotta stay here."

Donna went to the old woman and bent down close to her, smoothing the tangled gray hair tenderly. "Terry will be back in twenty minutes, Aunt Velda."

"Maybe it would be better if we waited," Blackie said.

"No, no," Donna said quickly. I had the impression that she didn't want to see Terry, to explain what she was doing. Or maybe she didn't want *us* to encounter Terry. To Aunt Velda, she continued, "I want you to promise to stay indoors and not mess with the stove."

Aunt Velda put on a ferocious pout. "You 'n' Terry git all the fun." She leaned over to look past Donna to

Blackie, then gave a gusty sigh. "Sure wish I wuz goin' with you. He's sexier 'n' Bruce Willis."

Blackie smiled. "Tell you what," he said. "How would you like to give me your fingerprints? I promise it won't hurt—just a little ink, that's all."

"Sure thing," the old lady said with a grin. She held out her gnarled hands. "Come and get 'em, sweetie. Anything I got is yours."

Donna bent over again and kissed the old lady's cheek. "Tell Terry I'll talk to her when I can."

While Blackie fingerprinted Aunt Velda, I went with Donna to get her jacket. As she took it off the hook in the hall, I gave her a long, straight look.

"If you make an untruthful statement to the police, you can be charged with obstruction of justice. And if you lie under oath, you're committing perjury. If you want to protect your aunt from prosecution, Donna, this is *not* the way to do it."

Without answering, Donna pulled her crocheted wool cap over her ears. From the jumble of stitches and the rainbow of mismatched colors, I could guess that Aunt Velda had made it for her.

It was a long, silent ride back to town.

"Donna killed Swenson!" Ruby exclaimed, startled. "You're kidding!" She was sitting in the empty tearoom, the cash drawer and her calculator on the table in front of her. She had traded her early morning Indiana Jones outfit for a denim dress with a sunflower-print vest.

"That's what she says," I replied grimly. "She claims she hid the truck in the shed, too. Blackie's got her at the county jail right now. He's agreed to hold off on the formal questioning until she has a lawyer—which she doesn't want."

I sat down across from Ruby. Laurel, who helps Mrs. Kendall with the tables and the register, had swept the floor and set the tables for the next day's lunch, and the place looked wonderful. I'd been skeptical about the color scheme Ruby had suggested—hunter green trim and wainscoting, green-painted tables and chairs with floral chintz chair pads and napkins. But I had to admit now that it was perfect, as were the dozens of stylish touches Ruby had added: terra-cotta pots of rosemary and thyme on the tables, floral paintings, hanging pots of ivy. I'd been reluctant to become her partner in this enterprise, but now I couldn't imagine the tearoom—or my life—without her. I thought of her upcoming surgery and swallowed the sudden cold fear.

"How'd we do today?" I paused and added, as casually as I could, "Are you feeling okay?"

"I'm fine, but this place has been a three-ring circus," Ruby said, deftly rolling the cash register tape and securing it with a paper clip. "I got here just as sixteen ladies of the Library Book Club were starting their lunch. When they left, a big group of tourists strolled in. Mrs. K was terribly out of sorts about something—I never figured out what— and things were pretty chaotic for a while. But we rang up over four hundred dollars on the tearoom register alone, which is pretty amazing for a cold and rainy Tuesday."

"That's terrific," I said, impressed. I reached for a stack of freshly washed green napkins and began to fold them. They'd go into the water glasses at each place.

Ruby nodded. "We're doing great. But we probably need to hire somebody to help Mrs. K in the kitchen. Today was almost more than she could handle by herself."

I finished the first napkin and laid it aside. "Oh, by the way, I meant to tell you that I talked to her on Sunday afternoon, to ask if she'd do the refreshments for the Christmas Tour. I think she'd been tippling."

"Tippling? The Duchess?" Ruby's eyes opened wide. "I would have thought that lemonade would be her absolute limit."

"It was the anniversary of her sister's death. She seemed pretty depressed." I took another napkin and began folding.

"That's a shame," Ruby said sympathetically, clipping the checks and putting them into a bank bag. "Maybe that explains the way she was acting today. We were busy, sure, but that didn't seem to be her problem—at least not entirely." She pulled the cash drawer toward her and took out the twenties. "She left early, without even saying goodbye. Laurel and I were talking about Carl Swenson, and when I looked up, the back door was closing behind her. She and her sister must have been very close. I wonder how she died." As she counted the twenties, a shadow crossed her face. I hoped she wasn't thinking of cancer.

"I don't know," I said. "Speaking of sisters, I need to call Terry and let her know where Donna is."

"I hope you're also going to call Justine." Ruby entered the twenties total into her calculator. "Donna may not want a lawyer, but she needs one. And Justine is the best." She picked up the tens and began to count.

Justine is Justine Wyzinski, known to her friends as the Whiz. She and I were in law school together at the University of Texas. She practices in San Antonio—family law, usually, but she helped out when Dottie Riddle was arrested for her neighbor's murder. If anybody could get Donna out of this jam, the Whiz could.

"I put a call in to Justine from the jail," I said. "She's

in Austin, so I left a message asking her to stop by the jail and have a chat with Donna on her way back to San Antonio." I leaned my chin on my hands. "Something is bothering me about this thing, Ruby." I reported Donna's reaction when Blackie told her that the truck had been found, and summarized my misgivings. "It's hard for me to imagine Donna doing such a thing. Terry, yes, and even Aunt Velda. But if I'd had to put those three women on a suspect list, Donna would have been at the bottom."

Ruby counted the fives and entered the number into her calculator. "Do you think she's covering for Aunt Velda?" She picked up the stack of ones.

I frowned. "Or her sister." I wasn't sure why I said that, exactly. Maybe it was the way Terry had acted the day before, when I talked to her in the barn. Or the silent communication that had passed between the two women a little later, or the clumsy way Donna had tried to alibi Terry, contradicting what her sister had already told me.

Ruby counted the ones. "I can understand Donna taking the blame for that poor old woman. But why would she cover for her sister?" She entered her count and began adding up the total. "It doesn't make any more sense than hiding the truck in Swenson's tractor shed. That was just plain stupid."

"I'm not sure I agree," I said slowly. "If you think about it, hiding the truck in the victim's shed isn't such a goofy idea, after all. They couldn't leave it beside the road or out in the middle of a field, and they sure didn't want it at the flower farm. When you come right down to it, Swenson's shed is the last place anybody would think to look. Even if somebody did happen to spot the truck, they'd figure it belonged to Swenson. And unless they were just looking for front-end damage, they'd never see it, the way that truck was parked." I paused. "But I have absolutely no idea why Donna would take the blame for her sister—if that's what she's doing. It's a mystery to me."

Ruby didn't seem to be listening. She was frowning at the total on the tape. "Something's wrong, China. We're two hundred dollars short."

"Did you count the checks and the credit cards?"

"Of course I did," she said with a withering look. "I always count the checks and the credit cards before I start on the cash." She pushed back her chair and stood up. "I need to call a customer about a special order. Why don't you run the tally over again and see if you can find my error."

But I didn't have any better luck. "I'm afraid you're right," I said, when she came back a little later. "We're two hundred dollars short, to the penny."

We looked at one another, open-mouthed. In addition to Ruby and me, only two people have access to the tearoom's cash register during the day: Laurel and Mrs. Kendall. Laurel has worked for me for almost five years and we've been friends longer than that. It was inconceivable that she would take anything out of the register. Which left—

"Mrs. K," Ruby and I said in astonished unison. There was a moment's silence while we tried to digest this information.

"It can't be," Ruby said at last. "There must be another explanation. Goblins or something. Let's think for a minute. Maybe it'll come to us."

We stared at the tape. It stared silently back. Nothing came to us.

"Well," I said finally, "We know for sure that it isn't you or me, and neither of us is willing to believe that Laurel did it. That leaves Mrs. K."

"I would never have thought it," Ruby said sadly. "She's such a fine person—so trustworthy, so competent, so full of wonderful ideas."

"I'm afraid we've got a problem, Ruby," I said regretfully. "We can't make any accusations we can't prove. But we can't afford to have a thief working for us. Even if we watched Mrs. K like hawks, we'd always know we couldn't trust her. We'd be miserable."

"But we *need* her!" Ruby cried distractedly. "What in the world would we do without her?"

"We'd be in deep, serious trouble," I said, meaning it.

"And we've got to remember that I'll be out of commission after my surgery," Ruby said. "I don't know how long, but at least a couple of weeks."

"We can't have you rushing it." I picked up the cash drawer and stood up. "I'll phone Terry and bring her up to date on Donna's situation. Then I think you and I should pay a visit to Mrs. K."

Ruby bit her lip. "But if we don't have proof, what can we do?"

"We can lay all our cards on the table. We can tell her about the shortage and ask her if she knows anything about it. Maybe she'll admit the theft and return the money." I thought about Mrs. Kendall's deft handling of culinary complexities and her tasty shepherd's pie. "In which case I'd be inclined to give her a second chance."

"And if she doesn't admit it?"

"She may get huffy and quit, and if not, we'll have to fire her. We don't have an employment contract and she's only been here a couple of months—well within the term of a probationary period. We don't have to give a reason for letting her go."

"Spoken like a lawyer," Ruby said. She looked at me,

her eyes wide. "But what will we *do*, China? We have to have somebody in the kitchen. And Mrs. K is—was—perfect." She gave a longing sigh. "Her tomato-and-cheese soup is fabulous. Everybody at lunch today raved about it."

"Don't worry," I said comfortingly. "I can make tomato-and-cheese soup, too. If worst comes to worst, I'll cook."

Ruby made a wry face. "I was afraid you'd say that."

"What's this 'afraid' stuff?" I was indignant. "I'm not a bad cook. And now that we've got the menu straightened out—"

Ruby put out her hand. "You're a *great* cook, China," she said in a placating tone. "You'd do just fine. I just meant that—" She shifted uncomfortably. "Well, you're not exactly long on patience. I can just imagine you in the kitchen and sixteen women from the Library Book Club in the tearoom, all wanting sausage rolls and shepherd's pies at the same time. You'd start yelling."

Ruby knows me better than I know myself. "You're right," I conceded. "I don't have the patience to be a chef. I wouldn't just yell, I'd probably throw eggs or something. But don't worry. We'll figure it out."

"Who's worrying?" Ruby tossed her head. "It's all relative, China. In the grand scheme of things, losing a cook is pretty insignificant." She grinned. "Compared to losing a boob."

I forced an answering grin. "I won't argue with you there."

CHAPTER FOURTEEN

*The real reason why the Druids worshipped a
mistletoe-bearing oak above all other trees of the for-
est was a belief that every such oak had not only been
struck by lightning but bore among its branches a
visible emanation of the celestial fire; so that in cutting the mistletoe with mystic rites they were securing
for themselves all the magical properties of a thun-
derbolt.*

Sir James George Frazer
The Golden Bough

Terry didn't seem surprised when I told her that Donna was
being held in the county jail.

"How soon can I see her?" she asked gruffly.

"Tomorrow morning, I'd guess," I said. "You can phone
the jail and find out about visiting hours. I've put in a call
to a friend of mine—a lawyer—who might be able to take
your sister's case. If she can't, she'll be able to recommend
somebody."

There was a silence, then Terry replied: "Donna doesn't
want a lawyer."

"Donna doesn't know what's good for her," I said

shortly. "If she doesn't get a lawyer, the judge will appoint somebody to defend her."

"She doesn't want a defense. She thinks she'll get off easier if she pleads guilty."

I narrowed my eyes. It sounded as if Donna had told her sister what she intended to do. More likely, she and Terry had cooked this thing up between them. The thought made me steam.

"Whose side are you on?" I demanded angrily. "Have you forgotten what I told you yesterday? The district attorney is going to be taking a close look at this case. If there's any evidence—anything at all—that might indicate that Swenson's death was something other than an accident, Doran will charge your sister with vehicular homicide." I paused to let that sink in, and added, slowly and emphatically: "Donna needs a lawyer. A good one."

Another silence. "Yeah, sure," Terry said. "I didn't mean—" She cleared her throat. "Tell that lawyer friend of yours that we want her to take the case. Whatever it costs, we'll come up with the money." More throat-clearing. "You don't think I can see Donna tonight?"

"Call and ask," I said. "They might let you if there's a compelling reason." I thought for a second and came up with one. "Like finding out about your aunt's medications."

"Yeah, right." Terry sounded relieved. "Aunt Velda's medicine. That's what I'll tell them."

"Look, Terry," I said grimly, "I'm going to level with you. I have my doubts that Donna was the one who drove that truck, and I'm pretty sure the sheriff shares that feeling. Taking the rap for somebody else is a stupid thing for her to do. And if you're letting her do it, you're stupid, too."

There was a silence. "You think that's what she's doing?" Terry asked uneasily.

"I'd bet on it. Who's she covering for? You or your aunt?"

For a moment, I could hear Terry's uneven breathing. Then there was a click. She had hung up.

The address Mrs. Kendall had given us—3437-B Pecos Street—was that of a garage apartment behind a large Victorian house in the older part of Pecan Springs. For years, the residents of this neighborhood have put up elaborate Christmas decorations, vying with one another for the honor of being named Christmas House of the Week on the front page of the *Enterprise*. As we drove through the early dark, we saw a fantasy wonderland, tiny white lights like ribbons of stars draping the houses and topiary reindeer glittering on the lawns, while Christmas carols rang out from hidden loudspeakers. There was no snow, of course—in fact, a chill drizzle was misting through the air—but it was beginning to look a lot like Christmas.

Ruby pointed out the number we were searching for, and we pulled into the drive that led around behind the big house. We saw a large double garage next to the alley, and above it, an apartment—but we didn't see Mrs. Kendall's white Plymouth. We parked, got out, and went around to the stairs at the side, where a light illuminated the apartment number and under it, on the mailbox, a card bearing the name Victoria R. Kendall. We climbed the stairs and knocked. No answer. The windows were all dark and the door, when I turned the knob and pushed, was locked.

"Maybe she's out buying Christmas presents," Ruby suggested.

"Yeah," I growled. "With our two hundred dollars."

The drizzle was turning into something that felt suspiciously like sleet. Ruby pulled her coat closer. "What do we do now?" she asked with a shiver.

I pushed back my sleeve and peered at my watch. It was after five-thirty. "We do dinner now," I said. "Brian's eating with a friend tonight, but McQuaid's expecting to be fed. Let's go to my house and cook a pot of spaghetti. We can come back in a couple of hours. With any luck, Mrs. K. will be home by then."

"Sounds like a plan." Ruby raised a hopeful face to the dark sky. "You don't suppose it could snow, do you?"

My idea of a quick and scrumptious dinner is a pot of *al dente* spaghetti dressed lightly with chopped fresh parsley and a full-bodied olive oil and served with tomato sauce and Parmesan cheese, hot herb bread, and a tossed salad—a meal which takes all of about fifteen minutes to throw together. By the time the pasta pot was boiling, the home-canned sauce was bubbling on my old Home Comfort gas range and the air was rich with the summer fragrance of tomatoes, basil and garlic. Exactly eight minutes later, I was draining the pasta while Ruby put the finishing touches on a garden salad and took the foil-wrapped bread out of the oven. McQuaid came in from his workshop, letting a blast of cold air into the kitchen, and the three of us took our places, McQuaid at the end of the scarred pine table, Ruby and I across from each other.

While the food was going around and Ruby and Mc-Quaid were speculating about how bad the weather might get before it got any better, I sat, quietly observing. McQuaid and Ruby are the two people I am closest to and I love them both—love them with a fierceness that almost surprises me. As a young woman, schooled in the feminist movement and eager to carve out a career for myself in a male-dominated world, I thought that the way to success was to be independent, unconnected, uncommitted—to keep other people at arm's length, so that their messy emotions didn't spill into my life and complicate it. Over the past half-dozen years, though, I've learned that we can't live that way, not if we expect to live fully and deeply. Now I know that you have to love, even when your lover betrays you. You have to embrace intimacy, even though you fear to lose your closest and dearest friend. Ten months ago, I had to come to terms with the realization that I might lose McQuaid. Now, I was sick with worry about Ruby. I loved them both all the more because I know how fragile we humans are, and how much we mean to one another— which made me think of Carl Swenson, and wonder whether he had been loved, and how deeply, and by whom. He had been hated, too—had that been the reason for his death?

McQuaid forked spaghetti onto his plate. "Blackie tells me," he said conversationally, "that the two of you created some excitement out at the Swenson place this morning."

Ruby's glance said, *You're married to him. You handle this.*

"A cheap thrill," I replied with an elaborate shrug. "Nothing we couldn't handle."

McQuaid grunted. "Almost got yourselves arrested for possession, I hear." He didn't look up as he spooned tomato sauce onto his spaghetti and passed the bowl to Ruby.

"Possession of what? A garbage sack full of mistletoe?" I gave a short, casual laugh. "But while we were poking around, we just happened to find the truck that killed Carl Swenson. If we hadn't been there, Captain Talbot might have towed it to Brownsville."

"Yeah. Heard that, too. Congratulations." He looked up, his pale eyes glinting with amusement. "Also heard that when you two got through with Talbot, he was mad enough to eat a duck."

"Yeah," Ruby said gleefully. "And spit feathers."

McQuaid laughed out loud. "Couldn't happen to a nicer guy," he said. "I gotta hand it to you. You were on the right track about Swenson." He looked at me. "Was it the Rio condo brochure?"

"That, and Corinne Tuttle's remark about a new greenhouse," I said. "And Ruby's intuition."

"A lucky guess," Ruby said modestly.

McQuaid frowned. "Of course, Swenson's pot-growing operation complicates the investigation. It opens up a whole new series of questions."

"Not really," I said with a sigh. "At least not yet. The Fletcher sisters are still front and center, I'm afraid."

"Donna's confessed," Ruby said.

"No kidding," McQuaid said. "With pot in the picture, my money was on one of Swenson's confederates. Tell me about the Fletcher woman."

I had just finished giving him the details of Donna's confession when Howard Cosell, who had been patiently waiting for his chance at the sauce bowl, got up and went to the door, growling low in his throat.

"Company, Howard?" I asked.

"On a night like this?" McQuaid said, surprised.

Howard's rumbling growl was drowned out by a heavy-knuckled rap-rap-rap at the kitchen door. Before I could push back my chair, it came again, louder and more impatient.

"It's the Whiz," Ruby said.

McQuaid raised his eyebrows. "Another intuition?"

"Nope," I said. "There's only one person in the entire world who knocks like that."

It was indeed the Whiz, standing on the back porch with an umbrella and a bottle of red wine, waiting impatiently for me to open the door.

"When you get to heaven," I said, letting her in, "you'd better knock with a little more finesse. You might find yourself locked out." I closed the door against the sleety rain and relieved her of the dripping umbrella, the wine, and her coat.

"Who's going to heaven?" Justine said, running her hands through her damp hair. "Not me, that's for sure." She nodded at Ruby. "Hey, Ruby. How ya doin'?" Without waiting for an answer, she went on. "I'd get bored sitting around with a harp all day. I need action." She smacked her fist against her palm. "Gotta keep the blood pumping, the body moving. Gotta outrun Father Time."

"Have you tried aerobics?" McQuaid wanted to know.

"Ha ha," the Whiz said. She rubbed her hands together, eyeing the table with pleasure. "Just in time for dinner, I see. Hey, look at that spaghetti! Good thing I brought burgundy."

When Justine Wyzinsky and I were in law school together, she whipped the pants off all the competition—including me—to get to the top of the class. Now, twenty-odd years later, she's still just as competitive and a lot more experienced. But Justine is still every bit as untidy as she was in her student days. She's short and stout, with broad hips and shoulders to match, and her clothes always look like she's just returned from a cross-continental trip on the Trans-Siberian railway. Tonight, there was a coffee stain on the lapel of her wrinkled gray jacket, a splash of mud on the hem of her crooked skirt, and if she'd combed her brown hair and put on lipstick since she got up this morning, there was no sign of it.

I set another plate at the table and handed McQuaid the wine and a corkscrew. "You got my message, I assume," I said, getting out the wineglasses. "Have you seen Donna yet?"

"Yes to the message and yes to the client." Justine sat down and used her napkin to polish the water off her plastic-rimmed eyeglasses. "Although I must say that she didn't seem overly enthusiastic when I offered my services. I got the impression she'd just as soon hang out in her cell as talk to me, and that she intended to plead guilty and go straight to prison without the formality of a trial. In fact, she as much as told me she didn't want to be bailed." The Whiz put her glasses back on, pushed them up on her nose, and pursed her lips. "Odd, wouldn't you say? Most people facing arraignment are delighted when somebody shows up with a key." She looked at me. "Makes me think there's something going on here."

"There is," I said, as McQuaid poured the wine. I took a sip. The burgundy was robust, a perfect foil to the spaghetti sauce. "Very nice wine, Justine. Thanks." I put down my glass. "I think she's covering for somebody."

"Probably her sister," Ruby put in.

"Her sister?" McQuaid asked, surprised. "Yesterday, Blackie seemed to think it was the old lady."

"That was before we located the vehicle," I said. "It's possible that Aunt Velda was driving the truck, but not likely that she hid it. It's only a mile across the ridge between Swenson's place and the flower farm, but the terrain is up and down, mostly up. Aunt Velda is spry enough to walk a mile on level ground, but it would've been hard for her to cross that rocky ridge."

Justine helped herself to spaghetti. "Pardon moi, but none of this makes a dime's worth of sense. I need the whole story, start to finish. What you know and what you surmise."

It took a few minutes to sketch out the situation, starting from the time Swenson's body was discovered, ending with Donna's trip to the jail, and including a heavily edited sketch of the drug bust at Swenson's place. While I talked, Justine dispatched one helping of spaghetti and started on another.

"Let's see if I've got this straight," she said, wiping spaghetti sauce off her chin with her napkin. "Initially, both sisters claim that the old lady drove off with the truck and came back without it. They deny any knowledge of the hit-and-run or the whereabouts of the truck. When the vehicle is discovered in the victim's shed, Donna abruptly changes her story. She says she accidentally hit Swenson, then hid the truck at his place." She paused, frowning. "What does Terry say?"

"She'll say whatever Donna says," I replied wryly. "If there's a cover, she's in on it."

"Maybe they're all three guilty," Ruby ventured. "Maybe Aunt Velda drove the truck, and both of the sisters hid it."

Justine made a face. "What a can of worms," she said disgustedly. "I hate cases like this. There's no good hook to hang a defense on. The jury will be cross-eyed." She brightened. "But we're only talking accidental death. At the worst, failure to lend assistance, maybe obstruction. If Donna's willing to plead, we can bargain. I can probably get her off with two years, and she'll be out in half that time."

"It might not be as easy as that," I said. "Swenson and

the sisters had a disagreement over property. They were convinced that he was behind some vandalism at their place, and Terry was sitting up nights with her shotgun, all set to blow him away. Dutch Doran may not let Donna plead to the lesser charge. He might try to bump this up to vehicular homicide."

"Your district attorney is an idiot," the Whiz snapped. Justine and Dutch have been acquainted for years, since they both worked in the San Antonio D.A.'s office. "He doesn't have the brains to spit downwind."

"And there's the pot-farm angle," McQuaid put in. "Dutch ran for office on a get-tough-on-pot platform. He'll be on it like a hound on a ham bone—and he won't let go."

"But there's no way he can connect the flower farm and Swenson's operation," Ruby protested.

I nodded. "Not even Dutch would be dumb enough to try that."

"Dumb is Doran's middle name," Justine said. She frowned. "But you're sure there's no connection?"

"Good question," McQuaid said, looking at me. "How do you know the sisters aren't growing marijuana in one of their greenhouses? Maybe that story they gave you about the survey boundaries was just a bunch of cock and bull. Maybe they've been growing pot and Swenson decided to muscle in on their business."

"That's nonsense," I said sharply. "Whatever those women are up to, marijuana has nothing to do with it."

McQuaid gave me a skeptical look. "Oh, yeah? How do you know?"

Slowly, thoughtfully, Justine took another helping of spaghetti. "How long have these women lived here?"

"Six or seven years," I said.

"Where were they before?"

I shook my head. I'd never bothered to ask.

"California," Ruby said. "That's what Donna told me, anyway."

Justine wound spaghetti around her fork. "Has either of them been in trouble with the law? Possession, maybe? Or dealing?"

"Not that I know of," I said. I frowned. "What are you getting at, Justine?"

Justine rolled her eyes. "Come on, China. You can figure it out for yourself."

And then I saw it. "Of course," I said, and made a face. "Why didn't I think of that?"

"Because you're too close to the situation," Justine said. "These people are friends of yours, or at least friendly acquaintances. You'd like to believe that they are who they say they are." She regarded me thoughtfully. "Which is hardly ever the case—as you'll recall if you'll cast your mind back to your legal career. People are almost never who they pretend to be. They always have something to hide."

Ruby put down her glass with a thump. "What are they hiding?" She frowned. "What are you two talking about?"

"A possible motive for Donna to protect her sister," McQuaid explained.

Justine reached for her wine and leaned back. "If the defendant has a record of prior prosecutions, a court is likely to assess a higher penalty than it would in the event the defendant had never before been charged with a crime."

Ruby blinked.

"In other words," I said, "somebody who's clean gets off easier than somebody with a criminal record. Justine is suggesting that Terry has been arrested before, and that this is a possible motive for Donna to take the rap."

"Oh, dear," Ruby said sadly.

"A *possible* motive," I repeated, with a glance at Justine. "We don't know that's what happened."

McQuaid pushed back his chair and stood up. "I'll put in a call to Blackie. He would've automatically run a check on Donna, but he probably won't think to see if the other sister's got a record." He gave Justine an inquiring look. "Got any problem with that, Counselor?"

Justine shook her head. "Absolutely not," she said emphatically. "If my client is innocent, let's get her the hell out of jail."

When Justine had gone, Ruby and I put the dishes in the dishwasher, got back in the Datsun, and navigated through the icy rain to Mrs. Kendall's apartment. This time I drove through the alley, thinking that there might be a light in the back of the apartment. There was a second stair that looked like it might lead to the kitchen, but no light, and no sign of the Plymouth.

"Maybe she's skipped town," Ruby said glumly.

"Maybe it's time we talked to her landlord," I said.

We drove around to the street, parked, and knocked at the Victorian house at the front of the lot. The door was opened by a thirty-something man wearing jeans and a flannel shirt and holding a paintbrush in one hand. Behind him, through the open door, we could see that he was painting the hallway, with the help of a little girl who looked to be about four years old. She was happily smearing yellow paint on the wall he was about to cover. Upstairs, a baby was crying.

"I understand that you have a garage apartment," I said.

He nodded. "It's rented right now, but our tenant just gave notice. Are you looking for a place?" He glanced from me to Ruby. "It's kind of small for two people."

I started to speak, but Ruby interrupted me. "We know somebody who is," she said. "When is your tenant moving out?"

"Daddy," the little girl said, "look at the flower I painted."

"Early next week," the man said. "I'll need a day or so after she's out—got to fix the hot water heater and replace the bathroom faucet." He cocked his head. "I might even knock a little off the first month's rent, since I wouldn't have to go to the expense of advertising."

"Daddy!"

The man turned. "I'll look at it in a minute, Taffy. I'm talking to these people right now."

"What's the rent?" Ruby asked.

The man turned back to us. "Four-seventy-five a month. All bills paid. We let our current tenant go month-to-month because she wasn't sure how long she'd be in the United States. But we'd rather have a lease." He grinned. "You know how it is in a college town."

"Sounds great," Ruby said enthusiastically. "What's your phone number?" He told her, and she jotted it down on a piece of paper from her handbag. "Thanks," she said. "If things work out, I'll be in touch in the next day or two."

We thanked the man and went back to the car. "So Mrs. K is leaving town!" Ruby exclaimed, climbing in.

"I guess that settles it," I said. "I suppose she needed the two hundred dollars for travel expenses."

Ruby wrapped her arms around herself, shivering. "Are we going to stake the place out and wait until she comes home?"

"On a night like this?" I put the key in the ignition and started the car. "Anyway, we were up at five this morning, and it's been a long, hard day. I'd rather go home and make myself a hot toddy and fall into a bubble bath."

"But what about Mrs. K—and our two hundred dollars?"

"I'm sure we'll never see her again, or the money, either. I vote that we write her a termination letter first thing in the morning and send it by registered mail."

Ruby sighed. "Sounds like a good idea. Anyway, I need to call Shannon and Amy. I'm going to have both of them over for dinner later this week and tell them about my surgery." She didn't sound as if she was looking forward to it.

I put the car in gear. "What was all that stuff about renting the apartment?" I asked with a frown. "The landlord seemed like a nice guy who's trying to make his mortgage by renting out the rooms over the garage. It wasn't very nice to mislead him."

"I wasn't misleading him," Ruby replied. "Amy's been looking for a place to live. I'm going to tell her about this one. It's a nice neighborhood, and the rent is less than she's paying now." She pushed her hands into her pockets. "Except that I forgot to ask about pets. Amy has cats. I'd better call him back and check before I get her hopes up."

"Good luck," I said, and turned the corner onto Nueces. I thought of Mrs. K and sighed. "Unfortunately, Justine was right. People aren't always who they pretend to be. Who would have guessed that the Duchess would stoop to stealing money?"

Ruby turned to look at me. "With Mrs. K gone, we'll have to make some immediate plans. Which of us is cooking tomorrow?"

I stopped at the light at Nueces and Rio Grande and

reached into my coat pocket. "We'll flip for it," I said, handing her a quarter. "Heads you cook, tails I cook."

Ruby flipped the coin and caught it on the back of her hand. She peered at it. "It's tails," she announced.

"Oh, goody," I said. "Guess I'll go in early and make sure I know what I'm doing. Do you think we have enough supplies? Do you suppose Mrs. K wrote down her recipes? Maybe we should change the menu. I'm really good at spaghetti."

Ruby looked at me. "Maybe we should put an ad in the paper right away."

CHAPTER FIFTEEN

On Midsummer Eve people in Sweden make divining rods of mistletoe, or of four different kinds of wood, one of which must be mistletoe. The treasure-seeker places the rod on the ground after sundown, and when it rests directly over treasure, the rod begins to move as if it were alive.

Sir James George Frazer
The Golden Bough

I parked the car in front of the Diner and got out, shivering in the cold, crisp morning air. The temperature was just below freezing, which was worrisome. The weather forecast for the day—Wednesday—included precipitation. That might mean rain, which isn't much of a problem, or it might mean ice, which nobody in the Hill Country likes to think about. We can handle 100-degree days, two-year droughts, and six-inch gully-washers, but a half-inch of ice can bring down century-old oaks, knock out all the utilities, and glaze every road in the county. When there's ice, all we can do is shut down for the duration.

It was almost seven, and the Diner was empty except for a couple of construction workers sitting at the booth in the far corner, tucking into heaping plates of eggs and ba-

con with grits and gravy. Docia was in the kitchen and
Lucy was out front, which was just fine with me. If Lucy
was still grieving for Carl Swenson, there was no telling
what she might do to the biscuits.

Anyway, I wanted to talk to her. Belatedly, I had remembered Lila's cryptic remark that Swenson's death
hadn't been an accident and that Lucy knew something
about it. The conversation was probably a waste of time—
without a doubt, it was the old Ford that had killed Swenson, and the vehicle belonged to the Fletcher sisters. But I
wanted to tidy up all the loose ends, and Lucy was a loose
end. Unlike her grandmother, though, she's usually re-
served and uncommunicative. I didn't think I'd get much
out of her.

"Mornin', China," she said in her laconic voice, as I sat
down at the counter. Under her white bibbed apron, she
was wearing jeans and a navy shirt that made her olive
complexion look even more sallow. "Coffee?"

"Please. And I'd like scrambled eggs, a small bowl of
grits and gravy, and orange juice."

Lucy wrote this down, pushed the order through the
wide pass-through to her mother, and turned back with the
pot to pour my coffee. Her lank, stringy hair was tied back
in a ponytail. It needed a wash.

"Your grandmother said yesterday that you and Carl
Swenson were close," I remarked. "I'm sorry about his
death. It must have been a shock to you."

Lucy bit her lip. "Yeah." She pushed the cup toward me
and went to the juice machine. She put a glass under it and
pulled the handle. The juice foamed over the rim of the
glass. She wasn't looking at me.

"I understand from your grandmother that you don't
think his death was an accident," I said quietly.

Lucy's head jerked up and she looked directly at me,

startled out of her reserve. "Gramma told you *that*?"

I added cream and sugar and stirred my coffee. "If it's true, I'd like to hear about it."

She put the juice in front of me, her dark eyebrows pulled together in a frown. There was a pimple on her chin. "Is this about . . . I mean, is your husband . . ." The frown became a scowl. "But he's not the chief now. So how come you're asking?"

I kept wishing that Lucy would meet my eyes. "I'm asking because Donna Fletcher has been arrested for running him down. I want to help her, if I can. If there's any reason to believe that somebody else wanted Carl Swenson dead—"

Lucy's head came up. "Donna's been arrested?" she asked, disbelieving. She was looking straight at me, her dark eyes wide. *"Donna?"*

"Lucy," Docia called sharply. "Them eggs is sittin' out here gittin' cold. Come and git 'em."

With a visible start, Lucy turned, took the plate of scrambled eggs and a small bowl of grits and gravy, and put them in front of me. Her head was down again. I couldn't see her eyes. "I can't believe they've arrested Donna," she muttered. "She's really nice. Such a hard worker out there on that farm, and taking care of her aunt and all. She's the last person in the world you'd think would—" She stopped.

I leaned forward. "Do you know whether anybody threatened Swenson? Did he get any phone calls or letters? What about his business associates? Did he mention any problems with them?"

She stood for a moment, thinking. Her glance went to the left and the right, as if she were making sure we weren't overheard. There were red blotches in her sallow cheeks.

She leaned forward and licked her lips. "Not exactly," she said, "but—"

Docia banged a plate on the counter of the pass-through. "Lucy!" she barked. "Y'er slow as cold drippin's this mornin'. That second coffee urn needs fillin' an' you got customers waitin' for their tickets."

"Yeah, Mama," Lucy said over her shoulder. "I'll take care of it." But she didn't make a move toward the coffee urn. For the space of ten seconds or so, she stood in front of me, her lips pursed, as if she were thinking what to say.

Docia raised her voice. "Well, then, hop to it, girl! And stop that moonin' over Carl. Talkin' about him ain't gonna bring him back from the dead, you know. Not that you'd want to. You oughta start thinkin' 'bout your future. Orville Pennyman came in for supper last night, after you went home. Said he'd sure like to take you to a movie Friday night."

Lucy made a sarcastic face. "Yeah, right, Mama." But she turned away.

I picked up my fork. Lucy needed to get out from under the twin thumbs of her mother and grandmother, who seemed to dictate everything she thought or said. Anyway, it was clear that I wasn't going to get any information out of her here, where her mother could interrupt us every two minutes—and maybe not at all. But I gave it one last shot.

"I'll be at Thyme and Seasons all day and at home this evening," I said with a smile. "If you'd like to talk, just give me a call."

I've got to hand it to Mrs. Kendall—she wasn't just a great cook, she was a terrific organizer as well. I arrived at the tearoom well before eight and went into the kitchen with a cold feeling in the pit of my stomach, wondering what I was going to find when I opened the cupboard doors. But the menus were posted on the wall, every pot and pan was in its place, and the pantry and freezer were full of everything we would need to feed our customers. There was even a loose-leaf binder on the counter, filled with recipes inserted neatly into plastic sleeves. I went through it, locating all the recipes I would need for the day and thinking sadly that no matter how hard we looked, we'd never be able to find anybody as good as Mrs. Kendall.

I was setting out the ingredients for vegetable quiche when Laurel blew in through the back door, pulling off her knit cap and mittens and blowing on her fingers to warm them. She looked surprised when she saw me.

"What're you doing in the kitchen?" She pulled off her coat and hung it in the back entry. "Where's Mrs. K?"

"The tearoom register was short two hundred dollars yesterday," I said. I took down a canister of flour and a bottle of canola oil. I don't think oil pastry is as tender as pastry made with shortening, but it's a lot easier to stir together and roll out, especially when you're in a hurry. "When Ruby and I went to Mrs. K's apartment to confront her about the missing money, we found out that she'd already given notice to her landlord." I reached for a large bowl. "It looks like she won't be with us any longer. Ruby and I will be taking turns in the kitchen until we find a replacement."

Laurel looked stunned. "But Mrs. K didn't take that money," she cried. "*I* did! And what's more, I left you a note telling you what I'd done."

I whirled around, horrified. *"You!"*

"I'm not believing this," Laurel moaned, dropping her face into her hands. "Oh, poor Mrs. K! She must have been terribly hurt when you accused her. Didn't she tell you that she's innocent?"

"She didn't tell us anything because she wasn't there." I put my hands on my hips and regarded her incredulously. "You're saying that *you* stole that money? And what's this about a note? Ruby and I didn't find any note."

"I didn't steal the money," Laurel said, her brown eyes snapping. "That's not the way it was. If you'd just give me a chance to explain—"

"Then explain already," I said. "Let's get to the bottom of this."

Laurel flipped her heavy brown braid back over her shoulder. "The Thyme and Seasons register was short of change yesterday, and I was too busy to run to the bank. So I took two hundred dollars in tens, fives, and ones out of the tearoom register. When I closed last night, you and Ruby were closeted in here, having some sort of serious discussion. It was late and I didn't want to bother you, so I just put the extra money into an envelope and left it with a note in the cash drawer. I figured you'd find the extra two hundred when you cleared the register last night."

"I didn't clear that register," I muttered, feeling awkward and foolish. "I had to talk to Terry about getting a lawyer for her sister, and then Ruby and I drove over to talk to Mrs. K. I left the register for this morning, and then it turned out that I had to cook today and—"

I stopped. Laurel's revelation changed everything. Since Mrs. Kendall hadn't taken the money, she'd be coming in to cook today as usual, and I'd be off the hook. On the other hand, we knew for a fact that she'd given her notice at the apartment, which indicated that she was planning to leave. But maybe she'd just found a different apartment. Maybe—

Laurel was staring at me. "A lawyer for Donna? Donna Fletcher? Why does she need a lawyer?"

"She's being held at the county jail," I said. "She's confessed to running down Carl Swenson and concealing the truck." I frowned. "Did Mrs. K say anything to you about looking for another apartment?"

"Uh-uh." Laurel shook her head distractedly. "It's news to me."

"Or leaving town?"

"No. You know how she is—we don't talk about personal stuff." Laurel was gnawing her lip. "Gosh, China, Donna's such a compassionate person. If she accidentally hit Swenson, I can't believe she'd drive off and leave him lying beside the road. If you'd said it was her sister, I might buy that. Terry has always seemed . . . well, kind of cold and deliberate. And she doesn't like Swenson. She might—"

"Good morning, everyone!"

Laurel and I whirled at the sound of the brisk greeting. It was Mrs. Kendall. She twirled her umbrella outside the door to shake off the drops, propped it against the wall, and took off her coat. "My goodness," she said, "it's cold out there. Do you suppose it will snow?"

"I doubt it," I said feebly. "It almost never snows here."

"Well, there's a first time for everything, I always say." Mrs. Kendall rolled up her sleeves. "Where Mother Nature is concerned, one never quite knows what to expect, does one? Perhaps there'll be a white Christmas." She came into the kitchen and stopped short, staring at the things I'd put out on the counter. Her eyebrows went up. She gave me a questioning look.

"I was just . . . I mean, I—" I took a breath and tried again. "I came in early to try my hand at that vegetable quiche that you make so well." I managed a smile. "One shouldn't let oneself get out of practice, should one?" Hastily, I put the flour and the oil back on the shelf. "But now that you're here, I'll get out of your way and let you get to work. I can make the quiche another time."

"Excuse me," Laurel said in a small voice, edging toward the door to the shop. "I've got a few things to do before we open."

"Actually, I'm glad to have this chance for a private chat," Mrs. Kendall said when Laurel had gone. She reached for her apron and tied it around her waist, and I noticed that her usual cheerfulness seemed dimmed. "I've enjoyed helping you and Ms. Wilcox find your feet, but I'm afraid I must give in my notice."

"You're planning to leave Pecan Springs?" I made an effort to appear surprised, but I didn't have to try to sound disappointed. Now that we'd cleared up the mystery of the money, I'd give anything to have her stay.

She took down a large soup kettle and put it on the stove. "Friday will be my last day. My elderly aunt is quite ill, you see, and I feel that I should be with her." She took several onions out of a bin.

"But I thought—" I began. She dropped one of the onions and I bent to pick it up for her.

"I'm afraid it will be difficult for you," she went on regretfully, "but I'm sure you understand." She poured a dollop of oil into the soup kettle and turned on the burner. "I've also given notice to my landlord, who has been very kind to me. He's a lovely man, quite helpful. I'm so sorry to be leaving Pecan Springs, but family matters have to take a high priority, don't they?" She pushed back her graying hair and I saw that her eyes were weary. Her cheerful manner was a façade.

"Of course," I said slowly.

She took out a knife and a chopping board and went to work on the onions, slicing and dicing expertly. "I see that you've already discovered my reference guide," she added, with a nod toward the loose-leaf binder that was lying on the counter. "I've put all the recipes into it, with detailed instructions for various quantities and a complete shopping list. I've also included some suggestions for future menus, and several recipes for the Christmas Tour. And I'll be glad to go through everything to make sure that you won't have any major difficulties." She gave me a regretful glance. "I do so hate to leave you in the lurch, just at the holiday season. But I'm afraid it can't be helped. I'm so sorry."

"We're sorry too," I said. "You've gotten us off to a great start. We appreciate all the work you've done and—"

The back door opened for a third time, and Ruby came in. "Whew," she said. "It's really nasty out there." She began to unwrap her wool scarf. "I don't think we need to worry about having a big lunchtime crowd today, China. They're already starting to put sand on the overpasses and—" She turned and saw Mrs. Kendall and her mouth dropped open. "Mrs. K? What are you doing here? I thought—"

"Mrs. K has just given us her resignation," I interrupted quickly, before Ruby could say anything about the missing money. "She has a family problem and has to leave us. Friday will be her last day."

"I see." Ruby took off her coat, her eyes narrowing suspiciously. "I'm sorry to hear that you're leaving us, Mrs. K." She turned to me. "But what about the—"

"About the kitchen?" I held up the binder. "She's written down all her recipes, with detailed instructions, even a shopping list. If we study it, it should tide us over until we find a replacement." I gave her a significant look. "And you'll be glad to know that last night's little mystery has been solved. It turns out that we really didn't have a problem. We completely misjudged the situation."

Ruby blinked. "Solved? Misjudged it? But how—"

"Come on," I said, picking up the reference guide and pushing Ruby toward the door to the shop. "Let's leave Mrs. Kendall to her work. Laurel and I will tell you what happened."

Ruby was right about the weather. Only a few hardy customers braved the sleety rain. After we got the awkward business with the cash register straightened out, Ruby went to her shop and Laurel and I spent the day catching up on all kinds of necessary business—restocking the shelves, calling customers about special orders, even making a batch of kissing balls out of the bag of mistletoe I'd been carrying in the trunk of my car. At lunch, we were the only diners in the tearoom, so Mrs. Kendall went home early to pack and get ready for her trip. At three o'clock, when we hadn't had any customers for an hour or so, I sent Laurel home too.

I had just settled down at the desk in my cubby-hole office to figure up the payroll tax deposit—one of my least-favorite jobs—when the phone rang at my elbow. It was Blackie.

"The lab report on the truck came in about ten minutes ago," he said. "It's the vehicle that struck Swenson, all right. The blood on the grille is his ABO type. The DNA test results won't be available for a while, but there's no doubt in my mind that we've found the right vehicle."

"Damn," I said, under my breath. I sat back in my chair.

The information wasn't really news, but it had a note of finality.

"Yeah," Blackie said. I could hear the suppressed excitement in his voice. "But where the prints are concerned, we came up with something unexpected, China. The only ones we found on the steering wheel and the gearshift were Terry's."

I frowned. "The *only* ones?"

"Well, not quite. There were three unidentified prints on the inside of the driver's-side door, as if somebody had put a hand through the window to pull the door open. But that was it. Terry was the last person to drive that truck."

My frown deepened. "You didn't find any of Donna's prints? Or Aunt Velda's?"

"Oh, you bet. All over the dash, on the plastic seat, on the passenger-side door. But not on the steering wheel or the gearshift—where you'd expect, if either of those women had been driving that vehicle recently." He paused, then said grimly: "Donna is covering for her sister, China. And I know why, thanks to McQuaid's phone call last night."

"You found a criminal record?"

"More than that. I've just learned that Terry served three years of a six-year term in the Women's State Prison in Sacramento, California. Then she went over the fence."

"She escaped!" I exclaimed.

"Yeah—she and three others. They were captured, she got away. Surprise, huh?"

God, what a mess. I chewed on my lip.

Blackie went on. "It's clear that Donna was willing to take the rap to keep her sister from going back to jail in California—in addition to whatever time she'd get for Swenson's death. Which could turn into a pretty stiff penalty, especially if she'd been drinking when she hit him."

"Drinking?" I asked sharply. "What makes you say that?"

"There's no evidence, of course. But the more I study the situation, the more it looks like drunk driving—either that, or a deliberate hit. Swenson was working along the fence, China, almost ten feet off the road. Visibility was good, and there's no underbrush in that area. No sign of braking, either. It's hard to make a case for a simple accident. Either the driver was drinking—which explains the hit-and-run—or it was intentional." He paused and added: "Meaning vehicular homicide."

This was not what I wanted to hear. If there was a suspicion of drunk driving or an intentional hit, Dutch Doran would jump on it, especially since Terry was a prison escapee. As far as he was concerned, he couldn't lose on this one. I gave a resigned sigh. "What was Terry doing time for?"

"Growing and selling marijuana. While she was in prison, they put her in charge of the garden." Blackie chuckled. "It makes a certain kind of sense, I suppose."

Marijuana. *Damn!* That threw the affair into an entirely different context. Doran never missed a chance to showboat on a pot case. He wouldn't just jump on this, he'd fling himself into it with wild enthusiasm.

"Terry's name hasn't turned up in connection with Swenson's pot-growing activities, has it?" I asked apprehensively.

Blackie hesitated so long that my stomach knotted. When he finally spoke, he sounded disgusted. "What makes you think that turkey Talbot would tell me anything material? I'm not one of his inner circle. But I've formally requested that he keep me informed on the progress of his investigation and specifically that he include me in the action if he busts any locals. If I haven't gotten anything from him by this afternoon, I'll give him another call."

I thought for a moment. "What about the prints on the truck door?"

"What about them?" Blackie replied dismissively. "Like I say, they're unidentified. Could be anybody's."

"Did you try for a match?"

"What'dya think? On a hunch, I even had them compared to Swenson's. No dice." He paused and added hopefully, "They aren't yours, are they? You didn't pull that door open when you found the truck in the shed?"

"Hey, I know better than that. I looked through the window to see if the key was in the ignition, but I didn't touch the door."

"How about Ruby?"

"She didn't even go into the shed."

"Oh, well. They probably belong to one of Talbot's crew. Or the guy operating the tow truck. They're all supposed to know better, but they don't always follow strict procedure."

"Wait a minute," I said, frowning. It didn't seem to me that Blackie was taking the fingerprint evidence as seriously as he should. "Doesn't it strike you as odd that Terry's are the *only* prints on the steering wheel or the gearshift? Donna drove that truck regularly, and her aunt occasionally. You'd think their prints would be all over it, not just on the dash or the seat."

"Who knows? Maybe somebody cleaned up the truck recently. Maybe Terry wiped them off."

"That truck?" I laughed skeptically. "It's a ranch truck, for Pete's sake. It hasn't been cleaned in the past decade. And Terry wouldn't have wiped Donna's prints—if anything, she would have wiped her own, after she parked that truck in Swenson's shed."

"Not if she was convinced that nobody would find it," Blackie said. A stubborn tone had come into his voice. The sheriff is a very nice guy, but he's still a cop. He'd come up with a solution to his crime of the week, and he was going to stick with it.

"Look, China," he said flatly, "I'm letting you in on all this as a courtesy, because you were the one who told me that the Fletcher sisters were having trouble with Swenson, and because you located the truck. I also thought you'd want to notify Wyzinski that her client's prints aren't on the vehicle." That last sentence was spoken with some sarcasm. Blackie is not one of Justine's fans.

I hesitated. "Have you had any communication with Terry today?"

"Not since last night. She visited her sister here at the jail about eight o'clock—that's when we took her prints."

I was beginning to feel very uneasy about this. When Terry was asked for her prints, she probably figured the game was up. I wouldn't be surprised if she'd already fled. Come to think of it, though, she didn't have a vehicle—unless she'd finished repairing the van, or was willing to steal her friend's car.

"When are you picking her up for questioning?" I asked.

"I'm heading out there as soon as I can get hold of a social worker who can make some arrangements for the old lady's custody. We can't leave the aunt alone at the farm, not in this weather. They're forecasting freezing rain. If we get much more ice, there's no telling how long the utilities will hold up."

"How about sending Donna home to take care of her aunt?"

"I sure as hell would if I could," Blackie growled. "If I could get her to recant her confession. Which is why I want you to talk to Wyzinski. She needs to instruct her client to come clean. Until that happens, Donna's staying right where she is, and that's that. Damn, I wish that social worker would call."

I thought for a minute. "How about if Ruby and I go out to the flower farm with you? We can stay with Aunt Velda until the social worker gets there."

Blackie didn't hesitate. "Best idea I've heard all day. Stay where you are, China. I'll be there in ten minutes."

CHAPTER SIXTEEN

In Teutonic mythology, it is believed that if mistletoe is found growing on a hazelnut tree, a golden treasure trove will be discovered nearby.

German folklore

"So Terry was running from the law," Ruby said sadly, when I'd told her the whole thing. "That explains why she was so fanatical about privacy. And why she refused to involve the police when Swenson was giving them trouble at the farm."

"Yes. It also explains why Donna was willing to take the blame for Swenson's death, and why she was so insistent on avoiding trial." I wondered whether Donna had known all along that Terry was a fugitive. It was my guess that she had, for I couldn't imagine how two sisters could live with a secret like that between them. But maybe not. Maybe Terry hadn't told Donna anything about the escape until after she'd hit Swenson, panicked, and hid the truck.

For that was what had happened, I'd concluded. Unless Terry chose to make a clean breast of things, no one might ever know exactly what had occurred on that lonely stretch of road on Sunday: whether she had been drinking, or was full of rage at Swenson, or had somehow lost control of the vehicle. And I couldn't guess whether Terry had been involved in Swenson's marijuana operation. I wouldn't have thought so—but then I'd never suspected her of being a prison escapee, either.

However, it certainly wasn't hard to figure out what happened after Terry had hit Swenson. Believing that she'd go to jail for manslaughter in Texas and then be extradited to California to serve out the rest of her prison term, she'd decided that she couldn't get help for the victim or confess that she'd struck him. Panicky, scared, not thinking very straight, she'd run through all the possible places she could dump the old truck and hit on the idea of concealing it in Swenson's shed.

Once the truck was safely disposed of, she'd hiked home across the ridge to tell her sister what had happened—and perhaps, for the first time, the truth about her prison escape. Together, the two of them had cooked up that absurdly improbable story about Aunt Velda taking off with the truck and appearing later that afternoon without it—the same explanation they gave to Blackie and me when we went out to the farm on Monday. On Tuesday, when Donna learned that the truck had been found, she realized that their story would never hold up under scrutiny, so she had impulsively taken the blame for herself. A brave and generous act—but very, very dumb.

I frowned. I had constructed a reasonable theory, but it left two things unexplained. The perplexing fact that Terry's were the only prints on the steering wheel and the gearshift, and the troubling fact of those unidentified prints.

But there wasn't time to think about that now. I reached for the phone and dialed Justine's number. She was in court, so I left a detailed message with her secretary, summarizing what Blackie had told me and suggesting that she talk to her client as soon as possible. She needed to convince Donna to retract her confession so she could go home and take care of her aunt. It was a lost cause, anyway. Donna would have to be crazy to stick to her story, in the face of the fingerprint evidence. And once Blackie had booked Terry, Donna would be released, whether she wanted it or not.

Ruby had gone to change into jeans and a sweater and lock up her shop. Returning, she said: "The sheriff's car just pulled up out front. Ready?"

"Tell him we'd better take two cars," I said. "He'll be taking Terry back to town, and we don't want to be stranded."

"I'll drive," Ruby offered.

"Okay. I'll finish locking up." I picked up Mrs. K's reference guide. "I'll take this home with me. We've got to figure out how to handle the cooking."

I was getting my parka and muffler when the phone rang. I almost didn't answer, figuring that it was only a customer calling to see whether we were still open. On the other hand, it might be Justine, checking in. I picked it up.

The gruff voice on the other end of the line was Terry's. "We've got big trouble out here, China."

You don't know the half of it, I thought. But at least she was still at the farm—she hadn't hightailed it. Or had she? "Where are you? What kind of trouble?"

"I'm at home, where else? Aunt Velda's gone."

"Gone?" I asked blankly. "Gone where?"

"How the hell should I know?" Terry was brusque and angry. "If I knew, I'd go find her, wouldn't I? I've searched every damn place I can think of. There's not a sign of her."

"When did she leave?"

"Some time between ten and twelve." There was a brief

silence, and when she spoke again, the anger was gone and in its place was a quiet desperation. "I went out to the barn to work on the van. When I came back, her coat and her boots were gone. I've been searching ever since."

I shivered, thinking of the old woman wandering through the woods on a day when younger, able-bodied people had chosen to stay indoors.

"The weather out here is wicked," Terry went on. "Icy rain and bitter cold. Aunt Velda is a tough old bird, but if she's broken a leg or a hip, she can't last the night. Can you come out and bring Ruby?"

"The two of us won't be enough. Have you called the police?" I glanced up at the clock. It was after three o'clock. In December, the Hill Country is dark by six. Given the rugged terrain, it would take more than the three of us to mount a full-scale search-and-rescue operation before it was too dark to see. We needed help.

"I don't want to take the time to explain why, but that's a last resort," Terry said. "However, if we haven't located her by five, I'm planning to call the cops. Please don't—"

"We're on our way," I interrupted, and hung up before she could ask me not to notify the sheriff.

Terry's face darkened when she saw Blackie's official car pull in behind Ruby's red Toyota in front of the gate. "I thought I told you—" she began furiously.

I held up my hand. "The sheriff was already on his way out here when I got your call. He wants to talk to you, Terry. It has nothing to do with your aunt."

Terry's eyes suddenly went dead. "He knows, huh?"

Pulling my parka tighter around me, I replied shortly, "Yes, he knows." I didn't want to go into it with her. The sheriff gets paid to do that kind of dirty work.

"Where have you looked for your aunt?" Ruby asked.

"Just about everywhere," Terry said dully, thrusting her bare hands into the pockets of her coat. "I'm afraid she's gone to look for that stupid cave she keeps talking about. Or maybe she's hunting for that blasted spaceship." She threw a resigned glance at Blackie, who was striding up the path toward us. "Now that the cops are here, there's no point in delaying the search. Who do I call?"

"That's been taken care of," I said. "The sheriff has put an EMS crew on standby alert and radioed the volunteer fire department over at Deer Springs. They're only ten miles away, so they'll be here before too long. In the meantime, Ruby and I can start looking."

Look where? Beyond the well-kept fields, past the fences, we were surrounded by thousands of acres of impenetrable cedar brakes, dense thickets of scrub oak and elbow brush and unruly wild grapevines, rocky ridges littered with stones weathered loose from the thin caliche soil, steep canyons, eroded slopes, wilderness. The old lady could be anywhere, everywhere. I shivered in the cruel wind knifing down from the north. Exposure kills fast in weather like this. She could be dead.

Blackie reached us. His eyes were watchful and his mouth was firm, but when he spoke his voice was deceptively mild. "Ms. Fletcher, you and I need to have a little talk about some unfinished business you've got in California." He paused. "And about Carl Swenson's death."

Terry sucked in her breath, straightened her shoulders, and came to life again. "You're not getting anything out of me," she growled. "I'm not talking until I get a lawyer." She looked at me. "How about that Wyzinski woman? Will she represent me?"

"You'll have to ask her," I said. Justine had been sympathetic toward Donna, but I wasn't sure how she'd feel about Terry, who'd been willing to let her sister go to jail in her place. A lawyer doesn't have to like a client in order to represent her fairly, however. Some of my best work had been on behalf of people I detested.

"I know you're concerned about your aunt," Blackie went on, "so we can wait until the search team arrives and you can give them some idea where to look. I'll also arrange for someone to let you know as soon as she's found." He paused. "I suggest, though, that you wait in the car."

Terry lifted her chin. "I'll wait out here," she said defiantly. "I'm not cold."

"That's not an option," Blackie said. He took Terry's elbow firmly, steered her down the path, and locked her into the back seat of the squad car. He opened the front door and reached for his mike. I knew he was letting the dispatcher know that he had the suspect in custody.

Ruby and I stood looking after them. I had plenty of mixed feelings about Terry's arrest—mostly regret for the way things had turned out and for my part in it, combined with relief that Donna would be cleared, whether she wanted to be or not. More than anything else, though, I was glad the whole thing was over. Now if Aunt Velda would just turn up unharmed.

"I wish I could feel sorry for Terry," Ruby said sadly, "but I don't. It's all very karmic, don't you think? She messed up her own life by getting involved with drugs, then she made trouble for her sister, running to her after she escaped from prison. Now she has to pay for what she did." She made a disgusted noise. "I'll bet Donna didn't know a thing about the escape. Terry probably told her she got out early for good behavior."

I drew my wool cap down over my ears. "You think that's what happened?"

"Don't you?"

"I don't know," I said slowly. "It's possible. Terry is pretty coercive. And Donna strikes me as being the kind of person who invests a lot of herself in taking care of others, like Aunt Velda, for instance. Maybe Donna felt she needed to take care of her sister. Maybe she even helped Terry escape." I made a wry face. "Sounds like I'm describing a couple of dysfunctional co-dependents. I have no way of knowing whether it's an accurate description."

"It's hard to know what's really going on with people," Ruby agreed. "Just when you think you've got them figured out, they show you another side of themselves, and it changes your whole view." She pulled her hood forward and fastened it under her chin. "Where do you think we ought to start looking?"

"There's a spring near the top of that ridge," I said, pointing. "Mistletoe Spring. Donna and Aunt Velda talked about it when I was here on Saturday. The area was the source of their disagreement with Swenson. Aunt Velda mentioned that she'd found some arrowheads there and said she wanted to look for more. I suppose it's as good a place to start as any."

"Should we walk?"

I nodded. "There must be some kind of a road, but I have no idea what shape it's in. I don't want to drive on it." I glanced at my watch. It was almost a quarter past four. "We'd better get started. It'll be dark in less than two hours."

I had brought a knife, two flashlights, and a couple of wool blankets, tightly rolled and lashed with a bungee cord. I had considered bringing other equipment—a rope, first-aid supplies, and so on—but decided it would be better not to load ourselves down. If we found Aunt Velda, one of us could stay with her while the other went back for help.

I fastened the rolled blankets over my shoulder and we stuck the flashlights in our pockets. We left Blackie and Terry to wait for the search-and-rescue crew and headed off down the narrow gravel lane that ran beside Mistletoe Creek, calling Aunt Velda's name every few minutes and stopping to listen for an answering cry. The arctic wind flung flecks of stinging sleet in our faces and numbed our hands and feet. Ice was already beginning to embrace the exposed tree branches and twigs, and the rocks underfoot were treacherous. It was one of the coldest days I could remember. Terry had said that Aunt Velda had worn her coat and boots, but that wouldn't be enough to save her from hypothermia.

Despite the body warmth generated by the exercise, I was bone-cold before we had hiked half a mile. Ruby was shivering and out of breath, and her nose was as red as a berry. I gave her a concerned look.

"You sure you should be doing this?"

"I'm sure," she said emphatically. "I keep telling you, China, I am *not* sick. There's nothing wrong with me that a little surgery won't cure." She threw me a sidelong look. "You sure you know where we're going?"

"We're headed in the right direction," I said, stopping to adjust the blankets I was carrying. "The spring has to be up this way, because the creek is down that way." I pointed. "*Way* down."

In the last few minutes, the road—twin tire tracks in the frost-killed grass—had angled diagonally upward across the densely wooded shoulder of the ridge. Mistletoe Creek, on our right, was now at the bottom of a ravine that was probably sixty feet deep, lined with cedar trees and tumbled limestone boulders.

Ruby stopped, put her hands around her mouth, and called Aunt Velda's name again. We paused to listen, but all we could hear was the sound of the wind and the brittle rattling of the live-oak leaves.

"Let's keep going," Ruby said determinedly. "We've got to be close to the top of the ridge." She frowned. "What did you say Aunt Velda might be looking for up here?"

"Arrowheads. Donna and Terry were cleaning out the spring, and Aunt Velda found a cache of them. She claims she found a cave, too, with arrowheads and skulls, stuff like that."

I stopped, cupped my hands, and gave another loud yell. A flock of twittering robins, migrants from an even colder north, flew up from the creek bottom, and somewhere a tree branch crashed with a splintering sound. At the rate the ice was forming, there would be a great many more downed limbs by morning.

We started walking again. "A cave," Ruby said thoughtfully. "There's a big one on the other side of Austin—Inner Space Cavern or something like that. But I've never heard of one around here."

"The ones in this part of the Edwards Plateau are pretty small," I said, "mostly sinkholes. The bedrock is limestone, formed from ocean deposits. Like this—see?" I picked up a pitted piece and showed it to her. "Wherever rainwater runs into a crack, the stone dissolves. What you get over time is a honeycomb of fissures and holes." I tossed the rock into the ravine and watched it bounce all the way down to the creek. "Underneath all these trees and bushes, the limestone probably looks like a piece of Swiss cheese."

We stopped and the both of us called out together. After

a moment, we moved forward again. To our right, the ravine fell away steeply; to our left, the ground rose to the top of the ridge, maybe fifty feet higher than the old road. The spring must not be far ahead.

"There's a big cave over near Marble Falls," I went on. "Longhorn Cavern. When the area was first settled, some Comanches kidnapped a girl and took her there. Three Texas Rangers came after them, and there was a fight. The Rangers got away with the girl. She married one of them."

"How romantic," Ruby said with a grin.

"There's more, only not so romantic. During the Civil War, the Confederates used the cave as a gunpowder factory. They dug up bat guano from the cave floor to make saltpeter, and stored their munitions in some of the back rooms. Sam Bass hung out there too, in the 1870's. You know, the guy who almost robbed the Pecan Springs Bank."

"Sounds like a busy place." Ruby stopped and called for Aunt Velda. All we heard was the crash of another icy limb.

"There's even more," I said, when we were moving again. "In the twenties—"

But Ruby, head cocked, wasn't listening to me. Somewhere in the woods we suddenly heard a yelp, wild thrashing sounds, and loud cursing.

We yelled. There was a wavering call in reply.

"China? That you, China Bayles?"

"It's Aunt Velda!" Ruby cried excitedly. "We've found her!"

A silence, then more furious thrashing. "Goldurn grapevines! Stupid-ass, piss-ant grapevines! Tie up a person's feet so's she cain't walk."

"Keep talking," I called. "Where are you?"

"I'm in the clutches of these goddamn vines, that's

where I am," Aunt Velda replied bitterly. "Git the hell up here and cut me loose!"

We found her a few minutes later, just below the top of the ridge. She was sitting on a large hunk of weathered limestone, wearing purple sweatpants, old leather Army boots, a dirty red jacket with a torn sleeve, and a yellow wool cap. Her gray hair straggled around her face, her cheeks were scratched and filthy, and her feet and legs were hopelessly tangled in a snarl of wild grapevines.

"Oh, you poor thing," Ruby gasped, as I took out my knife and knelt down to cut the vines. "You must be freezing!"

"I bet I'm not as cold as you," Aunt Velda said, eyeing Ruby critically. "Yer nose is red as a beet, girl. What the hell you doing, traipsin' across this ridge on a day like this?"

"We've been looking for you, Aunt Velda." I freed her from the last of the unruly vines and put a hand under her elbow to help her up.

"Lookin' fer me?" She shook off my hand and stood. "I ain't lost."

"Terry thought you were," I said. "You left without telling her where you were going."

"Huh!" the old lady grunted. "I'm growed, ain't I? Do I gotta sign my name ever' time I walk out the door fer five minutes?"

"You've been gone more than five minutes," Ruby replied. "You've been out here for hours."

Aunt Velda shook her head. "Uh-uh. I bin down *there* for hours." She pointed toward the boulder.

"Down where?" I asked.

"In that hole," Aunt Velda said. She lowered her voice conspiratorially. "It's a cave."

"A cave!" Ruby exclaimed.

"Sure 'nuff," the old lady said. She turned and pointed. "Right there. See fer yerself."

I looked at the tumble of boulders. Between the two biggest rocks was an opening about the size of a large watermelon, overgrown with an almost impenetrable jungle of elbow bush and wild grapevines. A couple of old hackberry trees leaned over the site, their leafless limbs laden with the prettiest clumps of fruiting mistletoe I had ever seen.

Ruby sucked in a breath of surprise. "You crawled in through that little hole?"

"Nope." Aunt Velda was emphatic. "I crawled *out* through that little hole. I crawled in through a bigger one, over that way. The Klingons showed me where." She turned and pointed off to the left. "When I was in, I turned on my flashlight and snuck around, lookin' at stuff. I got sorta turned around after a while, though. Lost my bearin's. Lost my flashlight, too. That's how I come to crawl out here. I could see the light comin' through them rocks." She showed us a snaggle-toothed grin. "Good thing I came out this way, too. Guess whut I found, right inside that there hole." She grinned again, excitedly. "I found me a treasure trove. Real gold."

"Gold!" Ruby exclaimed.

The old lady cackled. "Ain't it a hoot? Here them poor girls've been workin' their fannies to the bone growin' flowers, and all the while there wuz enough gold in that there cave to make the whole durn lot of us rich as thieves."

I frowned. "I really doubt that you'd find gold in the caves around here, Aunt Velda. The bedrock is mostly sedimentary limestone, and gold is formed in igneous rock, where it—"

"I dunno about any iggy stuff. All I know is I found

gold." And she reached into her pocket and produced a gold coin. "A whole big bunch of it."

Ruby gaped at the coin. "It *is* gold!"

"Din't I tell you?" Aunt Velda demanded. "Gold, sure as yer born. Worth ten whole dollars," she added. "Says so right there, under th' eagle."

I took the coin. It was a ten-dollar gold piece, with an eagle on one side and a Liberty head on the other. I gulped when I saw the mint date. 1879. "And how many of these did you find?"

Aunt Velda pulled a handful of coins out of a pocket. "A bunch. But I dunno's I got 'em all. Some critter went 'n' chawed big holes in the leather saddlebag and drug it around in there. Could be a few more, here'n' there."

I grinned. I was betting that there were more—a *lot* more. For if I was right, that hole in the ground was where Jess Newton had stashed the loot that he and his two brothers stole from the Ranchers State Bank.

And what was more, that gold eagle Aunt Velda was holding was no longer worth just ten measly dollars. On the collectors' market, it would go for twenty or thirty times that much, maybe more. It didn't take a Ph.D. in higher math to figure out that the gold in Jess Newton's long-forgotten hidey-hole might be worth something on the order of a million dollars.

CHAPTER SEVENTEEN

The yellow colour of the withered bough may partly explain why the mistletoe has been sometimes supposed to possess the property of disclosing treasures in the earth; for on the principles of homoeopathic magic there is a natural affinity between a yellow bough and yellow gold.

Sir James George Frazer
The Golden Bough

It was dark by the time Ruby and I got Aunt Velda back to the farm, where we met the search-and-rescue party just as they were preparing to fan out across the hills in a full-scale search pattern. An hour later, after a hair-raising drive on glazed roads back to Pecan Springs, we checked the old lady into the Manor Nursing Home, where her social worker had arranged for her to stay until she was released in Donna's care, probably the next morning. Then we said good night to one another and went home. There wasn't anywhere else to go. Seized in the icy grip of a full-blown winter storm, Pecan Springs was totally shut down. The Diner was closed, the lights were off at Beans Bar & Grill, and the Sweet Adelines Women's Barbershop Group had canceled its concert in the high school gym.

By the time I got home, our electricity and the phone lines were down, victims of fallen branches. McQuaid and Brian had already eaten, but the scene in the kitchen was reminiscent of times long gone: father and son, wearing heavy sweaters against the cold, sat at the kitchen table in the golden glow of a kerosene lamp, playing Scrabble and snacking on popcorn and hot chocolate as Howard Cosell snored peacefully at their feet. While I made a tuna salad sandwich and warmed up some leftover sausage soup, I reported what had happened that afternoon—Terry's arrest and the fortune Aunt Velda had discovered in the cave.

I had expected Brian to be excited about the discovery of long-buried loot from a 1920's bank robbery, but he had other booty in mind.

"Awesome!" he breathed. "A cave that nobody knows about! I bet I can find some blind salamanders for my collection!"

"Just what we need," I said, dipping into my soup. "A pair of blind salamanders to hang out with those light-footed lizards."

McQuaid frowned. "Best to leave the salamanders where they are, Brian. If they're not on the endangered species list, they should be."

"They'd certainly be endangered if you brought them home," I observed, thinking of the lizard that had just missed being drowned in the drain. When I saw Brian's crestfallen look, I patted him on the shoulder. "But it'll be fun to explore that cave. After the gold has been recovered, we should let the University Caving Club know that it's been found, so they can organize a mapping expedition. You can go along." I'd have to check that out with Donna, but I was sure she wouldn't have any objection to mapping the cave. Aunt Velda could supervise.

McQuaid turned to me. "Speaking of gold, I hope you didn't just go away and leave all those coins lying around. Did you think to post a guard?"

I started on my tuna sandwich. "And who would guard the guard? Anyway, that opening is so well hidden that nobody's going to find it—even if they believe Aunt Velda's story about the stash, which they won't. She tried to tell the volunteer firemen about this wonderful pile of gold she'd found, but when she let it slip that the Klingons were the ones who led her to the cave, they just sort of naturally tuned out. I confiscated her gold eagles so she wouldn't be using them to prove her case. Here they are." I went to my bag, took out the coins, and piled them on the table, where they gleamed dully in the lamplight.

"Cool!" Brian said, picking up a coin and flipping it in the air. "Real bank robbers, huh? Wait'll I tell the kids at school that my mom found a cave full of gold!"

"I think," I said judiciously, "that we'd better swear ourselves to secrecy—for the moment, anyway." I turned to McQuaid. "I told Blackie about the cave, and promised to take him up there tomorrow. I figured he ought to take a look before any salvage operation gets underway."

With a thoughtful look, McQuaid took the coin from Brian and turned it in his fingers. "I never believed that old tale about Jess Newton getting drunk and losing the money." He grinned. "I always figured his girlfriend made off with it, and he was too embarrassed to admit it. Either that, or he told his brothers he lost it in order to keep from splitting it with them."

"Will the bank get the money back?" Brian wanted to know.

"The Fletchers own the land where the cave is located," I said, "and the landowner generally has a superior claim.

Anyway, it probably won't be possible to prove where the coins came from." I thought for a minute. "Carl Swenson's family owned that land for a long time. Maybe he knew there was a cave up there someplace, and suspected that Newton had left the money there. Maybe that's why he was so furious about the way the survey turned out." I finished my soup and pushed back my bowl.

"Oh, yeah. I forgot." McQuaid put the coin down. "Lila Jennings' granddaughter called here earlier this evening, before the phones went out. Said she wanted to talk to you. Something about Swenson."

I leaned forward. "Did she say what?"

McQuaid shook his head. "She wasn't very clear. She seemed nervous and kept talking low, as if she was afraid somebody was going to hear her." He raised an eyebrow. "Think it's important?"

"I don't know. It might be. Did she say where she could be reached?"

"Yeah, she left a number. But you can forget that. It may be tomorrow before they get our phone operating. Maybe even the day after."

"You could use the cell phone," Brian suggested. "The phones in town might still be working."

"Good idea," I said, and stood up. "I'll give it a try."

McQuaid cocked his head curiously. "What does Lila Jennings' granddaughter have to say that's so important that you need to hear it tonight?"

"I have no idea," I said. "But I'd like to find out. Anyway, I've got something to ask her, and the sooner the better."

Earlier that evening, during the difficult drive into town, I'd had a brainstorm. We needed to find somebody to replace Mrs. Kendall in the tearoom, and Lucy needed to escape from the Diner, where her mother and grandmother exercised an unhealthy control over her. She was an experienced cook, give or take a regrettable lapse or two. We needed help, and we could help her. It seemed like a good solution all around, and I was glad I'd thought of it. Ruby had agreed enthusiastically.

"Talk to her as soon as you can," she'd said. "It would be wonderful if we could hire somebody before Mrs. Kendall leaves town. I know you've got her recipes and shopping lists and stuff, but it would help if Mrs. K was still available to answer questions."

Now, I picked up the cell phone and Mrs. Kendall's reference guide, which I'd brought home, and went into the living room to make the call. McQuaid had built a fire in the fireplace and I lit the fat red Christmas candle on the coffee table. I put the binder on the coffee table and punched in the number on the slip McQuaid had given me. Lucy answered on the third ring.

"Hi, Lucy," I said. "This is China. I'm glad your phone's still working. Is your electricity off?"

"It's off all over town," Lucy said. "Which means that we can't watch TV. I'm sitting here with a candle, and nothing to do but twiddle my thumbs. Mom and Gramma have already gone to bed."

I was glad to hear that Lucy was alone. She might be more willing to talk if nobody was listening. "My husband said you called earlier," I prompted.

"Uh-huh. Well, I been thinking about what you asked me this morning—about whether Carl ever got any threats from anybody. Well, there was one, although maybe it didn't amount to much." She paused. "I wouldn't even bother telling you about it, except for the fact that Donna Fletcher has been arrested. I can't believe she would've done what they say. Why, she's just about the sweetest person I know. When she comes in the Diner, she always smiles and talks and leaves a nice tip, even though I bet she can't afford it. She and her sister can't make a lot of money out at their flower farm, and she takes care of that old aunt. You've got to admire somebody who works as hard as Donna does and still keeps smiling. That warms your heart real good, you know? I hate to see her in trouble. I'd like to help her, if I could."

I could have told Lucy that Donna was being released and her sister was taking her place in jail, but she might be more willing to talk if she believed that Donna was in danger. And she obviously felt much less inhibited when her mother and grandmother weren't there to boss her around. Maybe she wasn't as taciturn and uncommunicative as I had thought—just repressed.

"You believe that somebody else might have wanted to kill him?"

"I don't know the details about how he died, except what's in the newspaper. But I've been thinking about it, and yes, there was somebody who didn't like him. Hated him, even." Her voice grew tighter. "I was out to his place on a Sunday night, you see, the week before he got killed, and there was this phone call. It made him pretty uncomfortable. And sad. I don't know that he was scared or anything like that, but he was sure sad."

I listened with more attention. "Do you know who called?"

"You mean, do I know the name? Uh-uh. I happened to pick up the call, but I can't tell you much about it, really. All Carl said was it was about something he'd paid for already, and it would be better off forgotten because there was nothing he could do to change things." Her tone became philosophical. "Life is like that, you know? Sometimes we do something we wish we hadn't, but we still have to live with it. I got the idea that Carl had done something he was really sorry for, but he was putting it behind him and getting on with his life the best way he could. You know what I mean?"

All I knew was that if I didn't hurry this along, we could be on the phone all night. "You said you picked up the call. Maybe you could start there and tell me exactly what happened."

"That's what I'm doing. Telling you what happened. You see, he was cooking in the kitchen, making hamburgers, when the phone rang. I offered to do the burgers, but he said I had to cook all the time for people, and somebody oughta cook for me once in a while. He wouldn't even let me make the salad. Wasn't that sweet? You couldn't tell it from looking, but there was a caring side to Carl, more than you'd guess. Lotta times people don't show you their secret sides because they're afraid you'll think they're silly or bad or—"

I cut in, hoping to get her back on track. "So he was cooking when the phone rang. Then what?"

"So there was Carl, with a towel tied around him and the burgers in the pan. When the phone rang, he told me to answer it for him, so I did. The person didn't tell me her name, but I remember what she sounded like."

I frowned. "What she sounded like?"

"Sure. Different people talk different, haven't you ever noticed? This one sounded like that woman who cooks for you. She comes into the Diner sometimes, like today. I don't like to wait on her because she's always making fun of our food, like there's something humorous about okra and black-eyed peas and biscuits. Like maybe we're hillbillies or something. But I like to listen to the way she talks. It's classy, you know? Like old British movies." Lucy gave an envious sigh. "Anyway, that's how the woman on the phone talked. Classy. I bet if I talked like that, people would listen to me."

A log fell in the fireplace, sending up a sudden shower of sparks. "This caller," I said slowly, thinking of Mrs. Kendall. "What did she say that made Carl uncomfortable?"

"I can't tell you exactly," Lucy said, "because of course I only heard one side of the conversation, and when I asked Carl about it later, he wouldn't tell me. It was about something that happened a long time ago. To her cousin or her sister or somebody. Carl didn't want to talk about it. He said that she—this person who called, I mean—was a little weird. Like, crazy. She'd called him before, and sent him a letter or something, and she'd even come out to his place. He said it didn't matter and I should forget it, but it made him real sad, I could tell. It pretty much spoiled our evening. We ate the hamburgers, and then he took me home." She sighed. "I was kinda hoping we might get . . . well, get closer. But it didn't happen. He just took me home, and that was the last time we were together, except when he brought that mistletoe into the Diner last week and gave me a big kiss. Made my mom mad."

"I see," I said.

She cleared her throat. "I want you to know that Carl and me, we weren't engaged or anything, China, like my grandmother says. I don't want to marry anybody. I'm not that kind of person, to get married and have kids and stuff like that." She gave an awkward little laugh. "But Carl was good to me, you know? Sort of like I was his sister or something. I liked being around him. He'd been places and done things and he knew stuff. Sure, he'd been in trouble with the law, he'd even been in prison, which is why my mother keeps saying I should forget him." Scorn crept into her voice. "She thinks I ought to go out with Orville Pennyman. But Orville's not near as *interesting* as Carl."

I didn't doubt that. Orville Pennyman is about as interesting as a cold potato pancake. "I understand," I said sympathetically.

"Since Carl was killed, I've been kinda blue, just thinking about things," Lucy said. "Like, maybe it's time for a change." She stopped. "I just heard Mama upstairs. Hang on a minute, okay?" There was a longer pause, as if she were checking on something, and when she spoke again, her voice was lower. "That woman who works for you, the one that talks classy? Well, she was in the Diner this afternoon. She said she's leaving town, and there might be an opening in the tearoom, and maybe I'd be interested."

"What a great idea!" I exclaimed, thinking how nice it was of Mrs. Kendall to help us look for her replacement. But Lucy was going on.

"I said I didn't think so, because I want to do something different from cooking, but what she said got me thinking. It's time I got me another job. A different line of work, you know? And a different place to live, away from Mom and Gramma." Lucy's voice became earnest. "I thought maybe you might have some garden work I could do out at your place, China. I've always liked working in Gramma's garden, and I'd love to live in the country. I'm a fast learner and a hard worker. And I'm strong. I'd do anything you told me to do, and I'd do it without complaining."

Lucy's request for work was one of the most straightforward and wholehearted I had ever heard, and I was impressed. But if she wasn't interested in working in the tearoom, I couldn't offer her anything.

"I'm glad to hear you're looking for something different," I said. "But there won't be much to do in the garden for another six weeks or so. Even then it'll be part-time work. But I'll keep my ears open and let you know if I hear of something. One of the local nurseries might be hiring after the holidays."

Before Lucy could reply there was a click on the line, and an acrid voice demanded, "Lucy, it's after nine. Who you talkin' to all this time?" The voice sweetened. "That you, Orville? You and your mama got lights over on your street?"

"No, it's not Orville, Mama," Lucy said quickly, before I could speak. "Talk to you later, Charlene. 'Night, now." The line went dead.

I sat for a while in the darkness, watching the firelight flickering across the ceiling and listening to the storm sounds outside—the hiss of the sleety rain against the window, the pop and crackle of breaking limbs. I thought about the afternoon that Carl Swenson was killed, and the various stories that Aunt Velda and Donna and Terry had told about what happened, and where they were and what they were doing that afternoon.

And then I thought of something else, and I began to turn the pages of the notebook that Mrs. Kendall had assembled: recipes, menu ideas, procedures, shopping lists— all neatly written out in her careful block handwriting on sheets of paper inserted into plastic sleeves. Some of the sleeves also held menus collected from English tearooms and several held sample paint chips and swatches of cloth labled as tablecloths, napkins, and curtains. Perhaps, once upon a time, Mrs. Kendall had had her own tearoom, or dreamed of it. Perhaps she had come to us in the hope of realizing her dream. Perhaps—

And then, at the very back of the binder, loose between two pages, I found a newspaper clipping, old and yellowed and much folded. It caught my eye because it didn't seem to belong. And then I realized that it *didn't* belong—that Mrs. Kendall had inadvertently left it in the notebook. I glanced over it quickly, thinking I should return it to her. And then I read it more slowly, twice, three times.

And then I sat back and thought some more about Sunday afternoon, and possibilities I hadn't considered before. And about the way people are never who they seem to be, and how hard it is to know what's going on inside someone else. I thought about Mrs. Kendall's classy voice, and the call to Carl. Finally, I sat up straight and punched Ruby's number into the cell phone and told her what I'd been thinking. Then I hung up and went to the kitchen to consult with McQuaid.

"I don't believe this," Ruby said, when she got into the car a little while later. "It's incredible, that's what it is."

"I agree," I said. "The scenario seems unlikely, and there's no proof. My idea could be way off the mark."

That had been the trouble with this hit-and-run killing from the very beginning. There was no proof of anything, just one conflicting story after another, created to explain something totally inexplicable. If my implausible conjecture held any validity, not even the fingerprints on the truck proved what they seemed to prove. But there was still that unidentified set on the door of the truck. Maybe—

"We went off half-cocked about the money that was missing from the cash register," Ruby said, frowning.

"What makes you think we're not going off half-cocked now?"

"Here," I said, handing her the clipping I'd found. "Read it." I turned on the dome light so Ruby could see.

She read the clipping slowly, her eyes widening. "Oh, God," she whispered, aghast. "So *that's* what happened to her sister! No wonder she felt so bad about it."

"It suggests a motive," I said. "A very strong one."

Ruby let out her breath in a puff. "What do you intend to do?"

"Talk. Ask questions. Listen." I paused. "Look. I wanted you to read that clipping, but you don't have to come if you don't want to. It's late, and you must be tired. And if I'm wrong, this session might get a little uncomfortable." I made a face. "Hell. If I'm right, it could get a *lot* uncomfortable."

"Of course I'm coming," Ruby said. "You're not going off half-cocked without me." She pulled back her sleeve to look at her watch. "Anyway, it's not even ten o'clock yet. It just *seems* like midnight—probably because my power has been off ever since I got home."

I shifted into first gear and accelerated slowly, trying to keep the Datsun from fishtailing. The glazed streets and sidewalks were so eerily empty it might have been four in the morning. Along a few blocks in the center of town, the street lights and Christmas lights shone brightly, but the rest of Pecan Springs was pitch-black. When we turned the corner onto Pecos Street, the power was off there too, and there wasn't a glittering Santa or reindeer to be seen. I made a right turn off Pecos and another right into the alley, and spotted the car I was looking for. Where the alley crossed the next street, I made another right, then another back onto Pecos. I swung into the drive and parked next to Mrs. Kendall's white Plymouth.

A moment later, Ruby and I were climbing the stairs to her apartment, where we could see a faint golden glow through the window. The Duchess was still up, and burning a candle.

I rapped at the door, waited a moment, and rapped again. A low voice demanded, "Who is it?"

"It's us, Mrs. Kendall," Ruby replied loudly. "Ruby and China. We're sorry to bother you at this hour, but we'd like to visit for a few minutes."

The door opened slowly, on its chain, and Mrs. Kendall, wrapped in a floral dressing gown and holding a candle, peered out. "My gracious," she exclaimed crossly. "What are you two doing out on such a dreadful night?"

"We need to talk to you," I said. "It's important."

"It must be, to bring you out on such a wretched night." Reluctantly, she unhooked the chain and opened the door. "Although I dare say this visit could wait until morning. As you can see, I am quite busy with my preparations for departure."

In the wavering light of the candle, I could see that the apartment had only two rooms, a living-sleeping area and a galley kitchen with a back door. There was a large suitcase on the daybed and two smaller pieces of luggage on the floor, half-packed. Stacks of folded clothing lay on the chairs, and I caught the sharp fragrance of lavender sachets.

Mrs. Kendall put the candle back on the table, next to a copy of today's *Enterprise*. She turned. Her face was pale, her eyes red, and I saw to my surprise that she had been weeping.

"What is it you want to talk about?" she asked. She took a tissue and blew her nose. "If you're hoping that I'll change my mind and stay, I'm sorry to tell that's not possible. I really must go back to England and take care of—"

"We've come to return this," I said, extending the newspaper clipping. "I found it in your reference guide. I'm sure it's very important to you. I don't believe you meant to leave it there."

Mrs. Kendall stared at the clipping. "How . . . careless of me," she said. She lifted her eyes to me, then to Ruby. "You've read it?"

"Yes," I said. "It's helped us to understand a great deal about—"

Ruby put her hand on my arm. "We're so sorry about your sister's death in that automobile accident," she interrupted sympathetically. "It must have been tragic for you. It's so hard to lose someone you love."

Mrs. Kendall's face began to crumple and she half turned away. "Amanda was a young woman, and beautiful," she said brokenly. "So very, very beautiful. Like a blond goddess." She turned and pointed to a gold-framed photograph of a young woman with luminous dark eyes and a halo of light hair. "She didn't deserve to die." Mrs. Kendall clutched her dressing gown at her throat and her voice was harsh. "You can understand that, can't you? My sister didn't deserve to die!"

"I can also understand," I said quietly, "why you decided that Carl Swenson didn't deserve to live."

She threw back her head and whirled toward us, eyes wide, mouth twisted, face transformed with anger and hatred. "Swenson murdered her!" she blazed. "He was driving while he was intoxicated. It was no accident that she died, don't you see?" Her voice rose. "He took her life just as surely as if he had shot her with a gun. He should have paid for her murder with his own worthless life, but your courts saw fit to slap his wrist and let him go. It took me a very long time to see that he paid his debt to Amanda's memory. But it's done, and I'm not sorry." She stamped her foot, hard. "I'll never be sorry that justice has been done."

Ruby pointed an accusing finger at the newspaper that lay open on the table. "But aren't you sorry for Donna Fletcher?" The stark headline was illuminated by the flickering candle. *Woman Arrested for Hit-and-Run.* "How can you allow her to pay for something you did? Is that your idea of justice?"

Mrs. Kendall's shoulders slumped, and she gave a low, desolate cry. "I didn't intend for anyone else to suffer," she said. Her voice had dropped to a whisper and the hatred and anger had left her face. "How could I have known they would arrest someone else?"

"What did you expect when you took that truck?" I asked sharply. "Didn't it occur to you that its owner might be charged with your crime?"

"But I thought it was *his* truck!" she exclaimed vehemently. "Don't you understand? I saw him on the ladder, doing something to the trees, and a little further on, around the curve, there was that old red truck, parked on the same side of the road. The keys were in it. How was I to know that it belonged to somebody else?"

His truck. In all my speculations about what might have happened on Comanche Road that Sunday afternoon, this possibility had never once occurred to me. But I could see now how Mrs. Kendall could have mistaken Aunt Velda's truck for Swenson's.

Mrs. Kendall looked up. "I'd planned to do it with a gun, you see." She grimaced. "I bought one, and I had it with me. I had decided to go to his house and find him and shoot him. But I dislike guns intensely, and when I saw him working beside the road, and his truck sitting there, it flashed into my mind that I should kill him with the same weapon he'd used to kill Amanda—his vehicle. It would be poetic justice." Her voice became pleading. "It wasn't a crime! I was only doing what was *right*. You can understand that, surely. You can't blame me for killing the man who killed my sister!"

"And since you were an agent of justice," I said, "you didn't want to be charged with the crime. So you were careful not to leave any evidence."

She nodded numbly. "After it was done, I left the truck where it was. But I wiped my fingerprints off the steering wheel and the gearshift."

But not the inside of the door, I thought. Those were the careless prints that would convict her. Aloud, I asked, "You didn't see his green pickup beside the mailbox?"

"Afterward. But I didn't think anything about it." She sank down in a chair and put her face in her hands. "It wasn't until just now, when I read the newspaper article, that I realized I'd made a mistake about the truck. And now they've arrested the owner. I don't understand why. But surely she has an alibi." She looked from Ruby to me, her eyes filling with tears. "Surely someone will speak up for her, and they'll let her go."

Ruby knelt down beside her and took her hand. "You can't allow another person to be charged with your crime, Mrs. Kendall," she said gently. "*You* have to speak up."

Mrs. Kendall made a whimpering noise.

"In the days and weeks we've known you," Ruby went on, "we've learned that above all else, you're a fair person, with extraordinarily high standards. That's why you felt you couldn't let Carl Swenson live, of course. And that's why you can't participate in *any* injustice."

Mrs. Kendall sniffled. "I suppose you're right," she said, "but—"

"So it's only logical," Ruby continued, "that you should go to the police and explain what really happened. You can't permit Donna Fletcher and her family to take the responsibility for something you did—something you felt you *had* to do."

"Thank you," Mrs. Kendall said. She fished a tissue out of her pocket and blew her nose. "Yes, of course, you're right. I must exonerate that poor, unfortunate woman who has been so unjustly accused. I shall go to the sheriff tomorrow morning and tell him everything."

I cleared my throat. "I'm sure you don't want to put off your talk with the sheriff until morning, Mrs. Kendall. It wouldn't be fair to let Donna Fletcher stay in jail a minute longer than necessary. You need to take charge of the situation and straighten things out."

Mrs. Kendall blew her nose once more. "You're right," she said decisively. "That's exactly what I must do. Straighten things out."

"And I think," Ruby went on in her tactful way, "that you'll feel better if you let us have your gun."

"Oh, no doubt," Mrs. Kendall said, almost relieved. "I couldn't decide what to do with it. I couldn't take it back to England with me." She got up and went to a chest of drawers. A moment later, she came back to the table, the gun in her hand. "Nasty thing," she said. "I'm glad I didn't have to use it."

I went through the galley kitchen to the back door and opened it. Blackie was standing on the stairs outside. It had been his car I had spotted in the alley when we drove in.

"Thank you for being so prompt, Sheriff Blackwell," I said. "Mrs. Kendall would like to arrange for her surrender."

CHAPTER EIGHTEEN

After the sun god Balder was killed by the wicked Loki's mistletoe dart, the plant was feared and hated by all as the wicked instrument of death and betrayal. But Balder's mother, the goddess Freya, redeemed it in honor of her son, decreeing that mistletoe should became a symbol of peace and reconciliation. From that time on, enemies who met under a clump of shining mistletoe would lay down their arms and declare a truce. That is why it is hung in doorways to this very day, and a kiss of peace and loving kindness bestowed on all who enter.

Scandinavian folklore

The four of us—Justine, Ruby, Donna, and I were sitting in the visitors' room of the Adams County Jail. It was a few minutes past nine in the morning and we were waiting for Donna's release. As soon as the paperwork was finished, she'd be a free woman. Donna had changed her jail coveralls for street clothes, and you'd have thought that she would be celebrating. But her face was drawn and bleak and her voice despairing.

"I don't know what to say, Ms. Wyzinski," she said. "I suppose I ought to thank you, but—"

"Don't thank me," Justine said firmly. "Thank China and Ruby. They're the ones who persuaded Mrs. Kendall to turn herself in and confess to Swenson's murder. As far as you're concerned, the whole thing is over. You're in the clear, and the sheriff has decided not to charge your sister with concealing the truck." She drummed her fingers on the table, frowning. "Aren't you pleased—or at least relieved?"

Donna's eyes suddenly filled with tears. "But how can I be glad about anything when Terry—" She stopped and bit her lip. Her question was barely a whisper. "What's going to happen to her when she's returned to California?"

The Whiz pursed her lips. "That's entirely up to the California authorities."

Donna clasped her hands together, pleading. "You don't suppose they'll let her go, do you? I mean, the prisons are so crowded, and she's been totally and completely clean ever since we came here."

"No, I don't suppose they'll let her go," the Whiz said sternly. She stopped drumming and said, in a softer voice, "But I happen to know an attorney in Sacramento who might help her work out some sort of deal. Anyway, she won't be incarcerated forever. When she's released, I'm sure you'll be there for her."

Donna lifted her chin resolutely. "I'll *always* be there for her. She can count on me."

Ruby leaned forward and patted her hand. "I'm sure she knows that, Donna. It will make the next few months a lot easier for her."

Personally, I wasn't convinced that this was an entirely healthy approach to the situation. It seemed to me that Donna needed to make a life that wasn't entirely centered on somebody else. It might also be better for Terry if she had to fend for herself, rather than depending on her sister to shelter her. But now wasn't the time to express my opinion—and anyway, it was only my personal view. I couldn't help solve this problem, or even suggest a solution. As Ruby would say, Donna and Terry would have to find their own personal paths.

"But that's not all of it." Donna did not look comforted by Ruby's assurance. "If Terry won't be here to help with the farm work, I don't know how I'll manage. Even in the winter, there's a ton of stuff to do, especially in the greenhouses. And there's the equipment to maintain—" She broke off miserably, shaking her head. "I'll never be able to handle it alone, and Aunt Velda isn't much help."

"Can't you hire somebody?" Ruby asked, concerned.

"The person would have to stay on the place to help me look after it," Donna said. "And since the only living space is our spare room, she'd pretty much have to be a woman. But flower farming isn't glamorous work, under the best conditions." She spread out her hands so we could see the scratched fingers and chapped hands and ragged nails. "In the winter you're cold, and in the summer the heat is so fierce you just shrivel up. I'd have to find somebody who's strong and willing to learn, and willing to live with us. There aren't many women who fit that description."

Now, *that* was a problem I could help to solve. I leaned forward. "I know one who does," I said. "Lucy, from the Diner. She's looking for work."

Donna looked confused. "But she's a cook. A good one, too. I don't think she'd be the least bit interested."

I shook my head. "I talked to her just last night. In fact, she's the one who gave me the idea that Mrs. Kendall was somehow connected with Swenson. Lucy is looking for gardening work, and she wants to find a new place to live, away from her mother and grandmother. She said she'd love to live in the country, and she spoke very highly of you. I'll bet you could work something out."

Donna looked at me, a new hope in her eyes. "Do you think so? I like Lucy, and I think Aunt Velda would, too. If she's willing to give it a try, so am I."

The Whiz moved restively in her chair. "Speaking of the Kendall woman, China, what put you onto her? Was it just a lucky guess?"

"Maybe," I said. "But Lucy told me that the voice on Swenson's phone sounded like Mrs. Kendall's voice, and I put that together with an odd discrepancy. Mrs. K told me once that she had no living relatives, but when she gave me her resignation, she said she had to take care of an elderly aunt. I knew something was going on, although I had no idea what it was—until I found the newspaper clipping about her sister's death. Swenson was named as the driver who caused the accident."

The Whiz frowned. "Then it's true that Mrs. Kendall came to Texas from England with the intention of getting revenge?"

"That's what it looks like," I said. "She'd been trying to track Swenson down ever since he was released from prison, and was successful only a few months ago."

"So she began calling and threatening him," Ruby said.

"She even bought a gun," I added. "She had it with her when she drove out there on Sunday."

"So Carl's death wasn't an accident," Donna said.

"Not hardly," I replied. "She told the sheriff that she went out there with the intention of finding Swenson and shooting him. But instead, she found the truck, parked beside the road where Aunt Velda had left it when she went to look for the cave. Mrs. Kendall thought it was Swenson's truck, and she was suddenly possessed of the desire to kill him with it."

"Suddenly and irrationally possessed?" the Whiz asked, with a gleam in her eye.

"I suppose some wily defense attorney will try to cop a temporary insanity plea," I replied dryly. "But don't forget that she'd purchased a gun and she had it with her, which clearly indicates premeditation."

The Whiz cocked her head, her eyes narrowing. "Perhaps she intended only to threaten him with the gun." She leaned forward in her chair. "Perhaps she intended only to give clear and substantive expression to her quite understandable feelings of grief and despair over her sister's tragic and untimely death—her beautiful sister, crushed beyond recognition under the wheels of a drunken driver ten years before. Ten years, mind you, to the very day!"

"Don't get carried away, Justine," I cautioned. "This isn't what you—"

"But when my client saw the truck," the Whiz said, rising dramatically, "she was instantly seized by the maniacal and irresistible urge to kill."

Donna looked confused. "I thought I was your client."

"This is just something that happens occasionally," I said in a stage whisper to Donna. "She'll get over it."

The Whiz ignored us. "Suddenly and unexpectedly bereft of her reason, robbed of all normal sense of right and wrong, Mrs. Kendall leaped into the truck, accelerated crazily, and ran down the man who had run down her sister." She dropped her voice almost to a whisper. "And when it was all over, this poor woman had no recollection of what she had done in her crazed state. She—"

"When it was all over," I said, "Mrs. Kendall left her victim lying beside the road while she coolly and deliberately wiped her fingerprints off the steering wheel and the gearshift. Then she abandoned the truck, returned to her car, and calmly drove home, where she told the landlord that she was vacating her apartment." I paused, thinking I'd better include the exculpatory fact I had reported to Blackie. "On the other hand, she *had* been drinking."

"Drinking!" the Whiz exclaimed. She smacked her fist against her hand. "Aha! She definitely wasn't in full possession of her faculties!"

I shook my head. "Nice try, Justine, but that dog won't hunt. Mrs. Kendall is one cool character, with an extraordinarily strong sense of fairness. She will never let her attorney portray her as losing her wits, even for an instant, and she certainly won't admit to being so drunk that she didn't know what she was doing. No doubt about it—Dutch is going to go for vehicular homicide on this one, and he'll get it."

The Whiz thought about this for a minute, then sat back down in her chair. "You're probably right," she said, in her normal voice. "Anyway, I've got a bigger case load than I can handle right now." She looked at me. "If you've got any time to spare, China, I could use some help in the office. And I hate to see your investigative talents go to waste."

"Thanks," I said, "but I like what I'm doing. Besides, we just lost our cook. Ruby and I are going to need some help ourselves."

Ruby tilted her head. "So what happened next, after Mrs. Kendall drove away?" She turned to Donna. "How did the truck get into Swenson's tractor shed?"

Donna flushed. "We're to blame for that," she said. "When Aunt Velda wandered out of the woods, the truck wasn't where she'd left it. She went looking and found it up the road, around the corner. She also found Carl, dead. She left the truck—I guess she figured she didn't want to touch it after that—and walked home. She gave us this lunatic story about the Klingons borrowing it to take care of Carl, and that he was dead, or gone, or something. We didn't believe her, of course. We just figured it was her usual crazy talk. But we needed to get the truck off the road. It doesn't have any plates."

"So that's when Terry found the body," I said.

Donna nodded sadly. "It was dark by that time, and he'd already been dead for a couple of hours. Terry saw the broken headlight, and the blood on the grille. She thought Aunt Velda had run Carl down, either accidentally or on purpose."

"From the evidence, a natural assumption," the Whiz observed.

Donna bit her lip. "You never can tell about Aunt Velda. Sometimes she's really level-headed, other times she's just plain goofy. Anyway, when Terry saw the truck, she got scared. She figured that if we said Aunt Velda ran Carl down, nobody'd believe us." She shifted position to look at me, and her wooden chair creaked. "Like you said, China. They'd think we were using her to shield one of us, because she isn't—well, because any jury could see that she's not all there. She couldn't really be held responsible."

"So Terry was afraid the sheriff would suspect one of you," the Whiz said.

"Right," Donna said. "He might even think we'd done it on purpose, because we'd already told China about Carl making all that trouble. And China had heard Terry threaten to shoot him if he didn't stop." She dropped her eyes. "Terry also knew that her criminal record would turn up if they did a background check on her, and they'd find out about California."

"Did you know about that?" Ruby asked gently. "The escape, I mean."

Donna gave a rueful sigh. "Yes, but not until after it happened and the California police came looking for her. The escape wasn't Terry's idea, you know. There were some other women, and they were all in a prison truck with a bunch of plants they were supposed to be taking somewhere. One of the women had bribed a guard to leave a gate open and the driver just went right on through. They drove for a while; then they all jumped out of the truck and scattered. Terry went with them. She knew the authorities wouldn't believe she hadn't been in on the escape."

I wasn't sure I believed it, either, but I could see that Donna did, so I didn't say anything. Donna took a breath and went on with her story.

"She hid out for a while so they wouldn't trace her to us. Then Aunt Velda and I moved to Texas, and she joined us. Aunt Velda had some money saved up, and we used it for a down payment on Carl's place. We wanted to grow flowers, which was what Terry did when she was in prison." Her smile was twisted. "We figured that California would give up on her after a while. The prisons are really crowded out there, and drug users are a dime a dozen."

"So it was Terry who put the truck in Swenson's shed," Ruby said.

Donna nodded. "She was scared that the sheriff would show up and start asking questions, so she knew she couldn't bring it back home. The only thing she could think of was to drive it to Carl's place, where we could get it when the excitement died down. So that's what she did. Then she walked home across the ridge."

"Why didn't she wipe her fingerprints off the truck?" I asked.

Donna gave a little shrug. "I guess she just didn't think of it. She was pretty panicked. Anyway, she was hoping that no one would notice, that anybody looking at it would think it belonged to Carl. The truck didn't have plates, so it wouldn't be easy to trace."

Ruby turned to me. "Those unidentified fingerprints the sheriff found on the door—I suppose they'll match Mrs. Kendall's."

"They already have," I said. Blackie had told me that much.

"Well, I guess that about wraps it up," the Whiz said decisively. She looked at her watch. "Where the hell is that paperwork? I have to get back to San Antonio."

"Hey," I said, "don't you want to go with us to pick up Aunt Velda at the nursing home?"

"I think I'll pass," the Whiz said.

"What? And miss a chance to get your picture in the paper?" Ruby asked. "Hark is going to be there with a photographer when we check her out." She grinned. "Can't you just imagine the headlines? *Woman Finds Long-Lost Bank Loot. Secret Cave on Mistletoe Creek Yields Treasure.*"

"Aunt Velda is hot news," I remarked. "Hark says the wire services will jump on this one."

Donna managed a small smile. "Aunt Velda's certainly enjoying the attention. I talked to her on the phone a little while ago. She was getting her hair fixed for the photographer."

"Well, maybe I should go along after all," the Whiz conceded. "Has she filed a writ of possession under Chapter

72 of the Property Code? She'll need to do that in order to ensure her title to the abandoned property."

"Maybe you can take care of that," I said. "What's your fee for something like that?"

The Whiz frowned. "The standard commission is five percent. And I *have* lost some expected income, now that I've managed to get my client"—she nodded at Donna—"cleared of all the charges against her." She gestured expansively. "Tell you what. I'll file the writ and take care of all the paperwork for the standard commission, and consider it payment for my work on Donna's case."

"Five percent!" Ruby hooted. "What nerve!" She turned to me. "China will do the paperwork for nothing. Won't you, China?"

"Oh, yeah, sure," I said. "Right after I've finished making the party food for the Christmas Tour." I made a face. "And with no Mrs. Kendall to help, either."

A broad grin split Justine's face. "And whose fault is that? You were the one who was in a big hurry to catch a killer."

As it happened, Lucy offered to cook for the Christmas Tourists, and that event came off without a hitch. Then Ruby's friend Janet called and said she was back from Dallas and looking for work, so we were able to fill Mrs. K's empty place in the kitchen, after all. And since Mrs. Kendall had so conscientiously prepared the reference guide for her replacement's use, our customers never knew the difference.

But the big event was Ruby's surgery, two days after Christmas. Sheila and the Whiz and I, along with Amy and Shannon and Ruby's mother, sat in the hospital lounge, chewing our nails and drinking coffee and waiting nervously for the surgeon to tell us that everything was okay. It took longer than we expected, but at last the word came. The surgery was successful, Ruby was recovering nicely, and there was every reason to believe that the cancer would never recur. Relieved and jubilant, we trooped to Ruby's bedside with armloads of flowers and a bootleg bottle of champagne.

But the real celebration didn't come until early February—Friday night and Saturday, February first and second—when a dozen of Ruby's closest friends gathered at her house for an all-night, all-day body-painting ceremony. Of course, most of Ruby's friends are in tune with her unusual interests, but some of us aren't, and had to be persuaded. The Whiz, for instance, who frowned severely when I told her what we were planning.

"A *body-painting* ceremony?" she asked suspiciously. "It sounds really weird. What is it?"

"It's an ancient form of herbal body-art called *mehndi*," I said. "On Friday night, we make up a paste of henna and water and tea and eucalyptus oil, and we paint it on our bodies in ritual designs. Then we let it dry, and on Saturday, when we take it off, we're beautiful."

The Whiz made a face. "Sounds like we're messy and weird. Isn't henna that funny herbal stuff that Ruby puts on her hair to make it redder?"

"Right. For centuries, people have used it to dye hair and paint their fingernails and color textile fibers. It's probably the most popular cosmetic herb of all time."

"I'm not much into cosmetics," the Whiz said with a disdainful look. "Anyway, I can't go into court with funny-looking squiggles painted all over my face. Judges have no sense of humor."

"Paint the squiggles on the soles of your feet," I said. "The judge won't ask you to take your shoes off. Ruby will be really disappointed if you don't come and join the fun, Justine."

"But what happens if I can't get this henna stuff off?" The Whiz was plaintive. "I could be marked forever."

"It'll come off," I retorted. "After three weeks, maybe a month, you won't be able to tell it was there." I frowned. "I'm not asking you, I'm telling you, Justine. This is for *Ruby*. Stop being a jerk and put it on your calendar. Friday and Saturday, February first and second."

The Whiz pursed her lips. "February second? That's Groundhog Day, isn't it?"

"It is. It's also a Christian celebration for the purification of the Virgin Mary and the blessing of candles, called Candlemas. And in pagan cultures, it's a festival called Imbolc, halfway between the winter solstice and the spring equinox. It celebrates the return of spring and new life. Which is why we're having the party that day. To celebrate Ruby's recuperation and to wish her continued good health."

"Okay, okay," the Whiz said with a resigned sigh. "You don't need to make a federal case of it. I'll be there."

"And you'll paint?"

"My feet," the Whiz growled.

Ruby's body-painting party went on all night—we camped out in sleeping bags on the living room floor—and most of the next day. We brought our favorite party foods and drinks and flowers, and there was lots of story-telling and dancing and listening to music and lollygagging and laughing—the sorts of things women do when there're no men around to make them feel self-conscious.

But the most important part of the party was the body-painting itself. Each of us tried out different designs on paper until we had something we liked, then we mixed up the henna paste and painted it on ourselves. If there was a place we couldn't reach, we painted it on each other. With Sheila's help, I painted an arm band and a bracelet on my left arm (because I'm right-handed). With a little help from me, Sheila painted concentric hearts and stars around her belly button. With no help from anybody, the Whiz painted a geometric design on her instep, and Amy and Shannon and the others painted their ankles and wrists, or the palms or the backs of their hands.

But the most important body-painting was Ruby's body—which was why we were there in the first place. Ruby was wearing scarlet tights and a silky white off-one-shoulder tunic. It covered her left breast and revealed the empty place where her right breast had been, where the diagonal scar, almost completely healed now, curved sinuously from her underarm to her breast bone. She had already drawn the design she wanted us to paint, a delicate tracery of feathery lines and flowers. Her daughters were first, then each of us took a turn, lovingly and reverently painting a part of the pattern until the whole design was completed on our friend's bare, breast-less chest. When we were finished, she sat in the middle of the floor while we made a circle around her, holding candles and flowers and incense, each of us offering our prayers and best wishes for her vibrant health and a long, long life. As I stood there, I was swept by a complicated mix of feelings. I felt a deep sadness for Ruby's loss, relief because it wasn't mine, and guilt because I felt relieved. Glancing around at the women's intent faces, I was sure that we all shared these same feelings, and something more—a deep realization of what is really important in our lives: the grace of friendship, the joy of caring for one another, and the resolute strength to care for ourselves.

• • •

"Well, another great party comes to an end," I remarked, as we said goodbye to Amy and Shannon and shut the door. It was Saturday afternoon and Ruby and I were all alone, with the usual aftermath of a party—food to put away and a couple of rooms to straighten. "I think everybody enjoyed themselves, don't you?"

"Even Justine," Ruby said with a laugh. "Did you notice that she got carried away with the spirit of things and painted a flower on the back of her hand?"

"No kidding!" I exclaimed. "What's the judge going to say?"

Ruby's answer was lost in the peal of the doorbell. "I'll get it," I said, with a glance at her newly ornamented bare chest. She'd probably want to put on a blouse before she met the public.

"It's one of the girls," Ruby said, "coming back for something she forgot."

But it wasn't one of our friends. Instead, it was a plump, pretty woman with a halo of fluffy blond hair, a carefully made-up doll's face, and beautifully manicured nails. She was wearing a pastel yellow suit and yellow pumps and carrying a yellow shoulder purse the size of a diaper bag. Beside her on the porch was a yellow plastic case with Sherry Faye Cosmetics printed on it in large red letters.

"Hello." Her voice had a built-in artificial lilt. "I'm Tiffany. I'm here for the party."

"You're a little late, Tiffany," I said. "Everybody's gone."

Tiffany's eyebrows registered surprise, her mouth consternation. She looked at her watch. "But it's not due to begin for another half-hour!" she exclaimed. "I've come early to set up the sales table."

Ruby stepped forward. "You've got the wrong house," she said. "You're looking for June Cook. She lives across the street." To me, she added, in an explanatory tone, "June is hosting a Sherry Faye cosmetics party. She does it once every couple of months. She said we could come if we wanted to."

"Oh," I said. I grinned. "Maybe we're not beautiful enough yet. Maybe we should go and buy some lipstick and stuff." I turned back to Tiffany to say that we'd drop in a little later, but I was stopped by the expression on her face. She was staring at Ruby's bare and beautifully decorated chest. She started to say something, but whatever it was, we couldn't hear it. She tried again, blinked, gulped, and gave it up.

Ruby smiled sweetly. "I'll bet you're wondering why I'm dressed like this," she said, gesturing at her scarlet tights, her one-shouldered tunic, and her henna-painted chest. "Actually, we've been having our own party. A celebration. I've just been initiated."

Tiffany found her voice, or part of it. "Initiated?" she squeaked.

"Yes." Ruby lifted her chin. "I've just joined the Tribe of One-Breasted Women. It's a very elite group, you see. Membership is limited to women who are willing to sacrifice—"

But Tiffany wasn't waiting around to hear the prerequisites for membership in Ruby's tribe. She had snatched up her yellow plastic sales kit and was fleeing as fast as her yellow pumps could take her, down the walk and across the street, to the refuge of the Sherry Faye cosmetics party, where the women covered their breasts and painted only their faces.

The Mysteries of Yuletide Herbs

Our modern Christmas is far removed from its ancient roots as a solstice festival, and Christmas as we know it in America today owes much to the story of the birth of Jesus of Nazareth and to the Church's influence on the holiday. But the celebration of yuletide dates back to times and cultures before the spread of Christianity, and the familiar herbs of the Christmas season hold ancient mysteries that may surprise you.

Ancient peoples of many cultures observed the winter solstice on the shortest day of the year (around December 21), when the sun, worshiped as a deity, seemed almost to disappear from the sky. Particularly in the northern regions, the solstice was celebrated in both fear and hope: fear that the dark would triumph over the light; hope that the light would be born from the dark. This darkest day, paradoxically also the birth of the light, was a time for revelry, for feasting and drinking. In these festivals, a number of plants took on special symbolic meanings, some of which linger, transformed, to this day.

Oak and Holly

In Celtic myth, the Oak King (symbolizing the new solar year and the waxing sun) ruled from the winter to the summer solstice, while the Holly King (symbolizing the old solar year and the waning sun) ruled from the summer to the winter solstice. An oak log (the yule log) was burned to herald the coming of new light, while holly was brought into homes and places of worship to bid farewell to an old year and a dying god. In early Rome, the oak was dedicated to Zeus, because its hospitable leaves shaded the god's cradle in his birthplace in Arcadia, and oak-leaf crown was awarded to anyone brave enough to save the life of a Roman. At first, the Church forbade these pagan practices, but when the people persisted in their celebration, the priests gradually assimilated the plants into Christian rites and Christian myths emerged to explain their meaning. The oak was said to symbolize the hospitality offered to the Holy Family, while holly (now called the holy tree) sprang up in the footprints of Jesus, its thorny leaves and scarlet berries symbolizing the crown of thorns and the dying Christ's blood.

Ivy

Ivy was held in high esteem in the ancient world. Its leaves formed the crown of Bacchus, the god of wine to whom the plant was dedicated. (In Roman times, the practice of binding the head with ivy was thought to prevent intoxification, and holiday hangovers were eased by drinking an infusion of ivy leaves in wine—something like the hair of the dog that bit you.) During wedding celebrations, Greek brides wore an ivy wreath as an emblem of fidelity, a significance reflected in an old Christmas carol: "Christmastide comes in like a bride, with holly and ivy clad." Revelry was an important part of the yuletide festivities, in whatever culture they were celebrated.

Mistletoe

To the Druids, this plant was neither herb nor tree but something of both. Since it grew in midair, often on the branches of the sacred oak, they thought of it as a gift of the gods and believed that it was suspended over the magical threshold between this world and the spirit world. In Scandinavian mythology, the sun god Balder was killed by a dart made of mistletoe (Shakespeare calls it "the baleful mistletoe"). The god's death symbolized the end of the waning year, and his restoration to life (at the plea of the other gods) the beginning of the new. Mistletoe was given into the keeping of the goddess of love, and it was ordained that all who came under it should exchange a kiss of peace and reconciliation. By Victorian times, this tradition had evolved into the ritual of the Christmas kiss: Each time a gentleman kissed his lady, he was required to pluck one of the mistletoe berries. Since the kissing ended when the berries were gone, it was to everyone's advantage to hang a sprig with a great many berries.

Evergreen herbs

In the British Isles, wood sprites were thought to take refuge in the branches of evergreen herbs that flourished even during the darkest days of the year: rosemary, cypress, yew, juniper. As garlands and wreaths, these branches were brought into the house to signify hospitality to the spirits of the woodland and to keep them from casting unpleasant spells over the new year—a practice we continue in the form of our "Christmas tree." The Church attempted to keep evergreens out of its sanctuaries but yielded during the Renaissance, when the "decking of the hall" became an essential part of the religious celebration. The significance of rosemary as a part of holiday festivals was explained by another legend: that Mary washed her blue cloak and spread it over a rosemary bush to dry, turning its white blossoms to blue, the color they have been ever since.

Frankincense and Myrrh

These two plants (originating in Arabia, Somalia, and Ethiopia) produce valuable gums that are used as incense in ritual purification ceremonies by many peoples, including Hebrew, Egyptian, and Arabic. The biblical author Matthew names them as gifts brought to the Christ child, from which Christmas gift-giving is said to derive. But this practice has other origins, as well. The Roman feast of Saturnalia honored the god Saturn and was celebrated from December 12 through 17. Candles were exchanged, symbolizing the coming of the light, as well as gifts of honey, figs, and coins.

One of the very great pleasures of learning more about the mysteries of the "useful plants" lies in recognizing the many different roles they have played in the history of human cultures. While the early magical origins of our familiar Christmas plants may have been hidden by later cultural forces, it is fascinating to uncover them and to know that the herbs and plants that play such an important role in our favorite celebrations were loved and respected by people who lived millennia ago, in a time and place very different from our own.

REFERENCES AND RESOURCES

If you would like to receive the most recent issue of the Alberts' newsletter, *Partners in Crime* (including a list of their books), please write to Partners in Crime, P.O. Box 1616, Bertram, TX 78605. Or you may visit the Partners in Crime Web site at http://www.mysterypartners.com, where you may download the recipes and subscribe to a free E-mail newsletter. (Susan Albert's herbal newsletter, *China's Garden*, is no longer being published.)

Breast Cancer Survival Manual, by Dr. John Link, Owl Books, 1998.

Flora's Dictionary: The Victorian Language of Herbs and Flowers, by Kathleen Gips, TM Publications, 1995.

The Golden Bough, by Sir James George Frazer, Macmillan Publishing Company, 1922.

Herbs Against Cancer: History and Controversy, by Ralph W. Moss. Equinox Press, 1998.

The Meaning of Flowers, by Claire Powell. Shambhala, 1979.

A Modern Herbal, by M. Grieve (2 vols.). First published in 1931, Dover reprint edition 1971.

Mehndi: The Art of Henna Body Painting, by Carine Fabius, Three Rivers Press, 1998.

And now an exciting preview of
BLOODROOT

the newest China Bayles Mystery from
SUSAN WITTIG ALBERT

*Many wild flowers which we have transplanted to our
gardens are full of magic and charm, while others are
full of mystery. In childhood I absolutely abhorred
Bloodroot; it seemed to me a fearsome thing. I remember well my dismay, it was so pure, so sleek, so
innocent of face, yet bleeding at a touch, like a murdered man in the Blood Ordeal.*

Alice Morse Earle
Old Time Gardens, 1901

For a long time, it has seemed to me that every chapter in
my life's story has held a meaning I'm meant to understand,
a lesson I'm meant to learn—and this one is no different.
Before I went to Jordan's Crossing, I believed it was possible
to cut myself off from a past I had rejected, to disinherit
myself from my family and renounce its unhappy legacy. But
the past, as someone has said, is always present, no matter
how completely you reject its mysteries or pretend that they
don't exist. I think now that everything that happened during
those difficult days at Jordan's Crossing was meant to make

me come to terms with what is in my blood, to force me (if you'll pardon the metaphor) to dig out my roots. But perhaps the lesson was even more specific than that: I was meant to rediscover the legacy I inherited from the women who bore me—as my friend Ruby Wilcox would say, from the motherline.

Whatever the reasons, I had a lot to learn during the days I spent with my mother at the place where she grew up, at Jordan's Crossing. Now, it seems to me that we were able to resolve only a very few of the mysteries. Yes, we found out who killed Wiley Beauchamp, and why. We discovered an unsuspected branch of the family tree. And we learned far more than it is comfortable to know of the ugly truths wrapped in the bloody history of the Mississippi plantation where as a child I spent the hot, still summers, rich in the resinous scent of pine trees and the moist green smells of the swamp. But the deeper shadows in that house, the darker enigmas, the most puzzling mysteries—these ghosts haunted my childhood, and haunt me still.

I think they always will.

In Texas, April is a spectacularly beautiful month. The meadows are an exuberant wildscape of bluebonnets, orange-red Indian paintbrush, and white prickly poppies—one of those hands-off plants that is defended by so many thorns that even a starving longhorn won't touch it. By the thousands, the tourists congregate in the Hill Country to warm their winter-chilled bones in the spring sunshine and marvel at the wild-flower meadows, and when they've seen enough bluebonnets and Indian paintbrush to last for a while, they drive to Fredericksburg for Bill and Sylvia Varney's annual herb fair, or to Kerrville for the arts and crafts festival, or to Pecan Springs. And while they're hanging around Pecan Springs, they have lunch at Thyme for Tea and buy lots of pots of herbs and herbal products at Thyme and Seasons—enough to ensure that April is not just beautiful, it's profitable. You can't beat that.

My name is China Bayles. I'm the owner of Thyme and

Seasons and the co-owner, with Ruby Wilcox, of a new tea-room called Thyme for Tea. In April, I'm lucky if I can find enough free time to scrub my teeth and flip a comb through my hair. In addition to the daily work in the shop and the tearoom, somebody's got to look after the herb gardens. April showers (definitely a good thing) are guaranteed to bring a fine flowering of May weeds (definitely bad) so the spring battle plan calls for me to show up at the shop around dawn and get started on the day's planting, mulching, and weeding chores. I try to leave by six in the evening so I can have dinner with my husband McQuaid, and our thirteen-year-old son Brian, but during the intervening hours, I go at a dead run all day.

In fact, April is so wild and woolly that Ruby and I often threaten that one of these years we're going to give ourselves a Spring Break of our very own. We'll throw our suitcases in the car and drive as far and as fast as we can, away from the tearoom and our shops and the gardens, far away from Pecan Springs. Who knows how far we'll go? The still-snowy plains of Manitoba, maybe, or the steamy jungles of Mexico, where there are no bluebonnets and no tourists.

Ruby Wilcox—six feet tall in her sandals, with an unruly mop of curly red hair, a face full of freckles, and an arresting sense of style—is the proprietor of the Crystal Cave (Pecan Springs' only New Age shop). Ruby is also my partner and very best friend, and while she frequently displays certain personal characteristics that can only be called, well, weird, I know I can always count on her to listen when I've got something on my mind.

On this bright, breezy morning on the last Tuesday in April, I had something on my mind. Her name is Leatha Richards, and she's my mother—although we haven't always been on the best of mother-daughter terms. While Ruby couldn't offer much help, she was willing, as always, to listen.

"Leatha's gone *where*?" Ruby sat down on the garden bench, folded her legs under her à la lotus, and closed her eyes. Ruby has taken yoga classes for years and is as foldable as a piece of rice paper.

"Mississippi," I said, slowly getting down on my knees. I'm not as supple as Ruby, who can bend straight over and touch her nose to her knees. (If you think this is easy, I invite you to try it.) I popped a dill seedling out of its plastic six-pack and snuggled it into an open space at the back of the kitchen garden. Dill is not only a tangy culinary herb (fine with fish, zippy in scrambled eggs, and especially famous for what it does to pickles) but is also useful in repelling witches—something to keep in mind if you have a problem along those lines. "She's at Jordan's Crossing," I added. "She's been there about two months."

Ruby opened her eyes. "You don't mean she's left Sam?" she asked, startled.

A few years ago, some fifteen years after my father's death, my mother married Sam Richards, who owns an exotic game ranch near Kerrville: exotic as in buffalo, antelope, wild sheep, and wild boar—animals whose bloodlines are almost extinct in the wild. The two of them live on Sam's ranch, which is a far cry from the palatial home in the affluent Houston suburb bequeathed to her by my father. And they seem to be happy together, which has come as some surprise to me. In the beginning, it was hard for me to imagine Leatha trading in her hairdresser and beauty spa for a home on the range, but so far it seems to have worked out.

I pulled cedar-chip mulch around one seedling and reached for another. "Aunt Tullie is sick," I said, pushing the trowel into the dirt. "Leatha's gone back to the plantation to help out."

My grandmother, Rachel Coldwell, died when my mother was born, and Leatha was raised by her father Howard and his sister Tullie at Jordan's Crossing, in a plantation house built during the bitter years following the Civil War. Aunt Tullie stayed on at Jordan's Crossing after her brother died in 1963, managing the plantation in the sternly autocratic style of her father and grandfather, keeping the place pretty much as it had been during her parents' lifetimes. (Or so Leatha told me—I hadn't been back since my early teens.) Tullie had to be in her mid-eighties now, and while I could not imagine her as anything less than absolute ruler over the kingdom of Jordan's Crossing, it sounded from Leatha's report as if she wasn't well. Not dying, exactly (at least not yet), but suffering from some sort of debilitating illness.

When the end finally came, Aunt Tullie's death would also be the death of an era—an era that had its roots in the bloodiest period of our nation's past and in the darkest depths of the Coldwell family history. *My* family history, although I had already and quite deliberately cut the Coldwell connection, leaf, branch, and root—which accounts for the fact that I've had little communication with Aunt Tullie. Except for the obligatory exchange of Christmas and birthday cards, I put my mother's family into a box, closed the lid firmly, and slid it onto a shelf in the back corner of my mind. It's not personal, mind you. After I entered high school and began thinking seriously about such matters, I began to hate the plantation and everything it stood for. I declared that I would no longer imagine myself in any way as a product of the Old South, with its brutal treatment of slaves, its contradictory veneration and exploitation of white women, its utter disregard for the dignity of human life. Like other women of my era, I decided to repudiate the patriarchal past and reinvent myself as a new kind of Southern woman, free to make her own choices, build her own life, write her own personal declaration of independence.

Ruby adjusted her orange tunic over her silky brown harem pants and closed her eyes again. The morning sun glinted off her bone-and-bead necklace, an African-style bib affair that made her look like a shaman.

"Mississippi in the spring." She sighed softly. "I did that once—Natchez. It was gorgeous. Azaleas, magnolias, live oaks draped with Spanish moss. Beautiful antebellum mansions, Greek Revival architecture, wide verandas, tall white columns." Her eyes popped open. "I've got it, China! Next year, let's go to your plantation for our Spring Break. We'll wear white dresses and Scarlett O'Hara hats and sit in the shade and sip frosty mint juleps and pretend we're Southern belles with a dozen adoring beaux."

"Whoa," I said, clambering to my feet. "You've got the azaleas and magnolias right, but the rest of it's all wrong.

For one thing, it's not *my* plantation, it's Aunt Tullie's. For another, the Mississippi you have in mind is southern Mississippi, between Natchez and New Orleans. Jordan's Crossing is in the delta of the Yazoo River, too far north for live oaks and Spanish moss. And while the house is definitely antebellum, there's nothing even remotely Greek about it. There was a place like that once, but it burned. This house started out as a trading post, you see, on Choctaw Indian land. It's—" I stopped, thinking what I could say. "It's big," I said, imprecisely. "And old, and built out of native cypress, cut and milled on the plantation. But it doesn't have Greek columns and—" I stopped again, remembering my Sunday phone conversation with Leatha. "Anyway," I added, "There might not be a next year. Aunt Tullie's sick. And there are . . . well, complications."

Ruby cocked her head, curious. "What kind of complications?"

I smiled teasingly. Ruby tends to get excited about anything that sounds even vaguely supernatural, and I sometimes like to lead her on just a little. "Leatha hasn't been very specific," I replied, bending over to pull a weed out of the chive border. "But I think it's got something to do with Uncle Jed."

"And who is Uncle Jed?"

"Who *was* Uncle Jed," I amended, surveying the luxuriant rosemary that had flopped across the path like some loose-limbed Jezebel. The plant needed shearing, or people would break branches as they brushed past. Here in Pecan Springs, rosemary can grow five feet high and just as wide. I should have planted it farther away from the path in the first place. Now, all I could do was trim it back.

Ruby's orange eyebrows went up. "Uncle Jed isn't around any longer?"

Another teasing smile. "Yes and no," I said. "He's a ghost. At least," I amended, taking my clippers out of their pouch at my belt, "that's what people say he is. You can't prove it by me."

Which isn't exactly true, I thought, remembering a little uneasily the shadow like smoke twisting in a moonlit corner of my bedroom at Jordan's Crossing, when I was five or six. I might have been dreaming, of course, but I don't think so. I had seen Uncle Jed's smoky shape as clearly as—a few years later—I had seen Aunt Tullie and the witch woman and the skeletal hand reaching up out of the earth. The stuff of nightmares.

"A ghost?" Ruby's heavy bead bracelets jangled excitedly. "You have a ghost in the family and you've never even mentioned it?"

"It's just a story Aunt Tullie used to tell," I said drawing it out, leading her on. "Anyway, all old Southern houses have a resident ghost."

Ruby leaned forward. "Tell me, China," she commanded in an imperious tone.

"Well, if you insist." I clipped as I talked. "Jedediah Coldwell was my great-great-grandfather's older brother, you see. He acquired Jordan's Crossing back in the 1830s, when it was nothing but a log trading post on the Bloodroot River, plus a couple hundred acres of rich bottom land and wild swamp—Muddy Bottom, it was called."

The words began to come easily now, and the rhythms— Aunt Tullie's familiar words and rhythms, remembered from hot summer evenings on the veranda, when she was in a storytelling mood and I had been an eager audience.

"The land had been open to white settlement for only a few years, after the federal government—Andrew Jackson was president then—talked the Choctaws into trading their lands east of the Mississippi for territory in Arkansas and Oklahoma. The Yazoo Delta was the frontier in those days, and wild. The piney woods were full of game, and you could still find hold-out Choctaws and Chickasaws who had refused to leave, and bears and panthers too, which the old-timers called "painters" and whose scream sounded like a dying woman. The river bottoms were flat and fruitful and seductive, and the promise of rich soils and plentiful water enticed settlers from their worn-out fields in Virginia, Georgia, Carolina. It lured land speculators, too, and bad money and—"

"So?" Ruby demanded impatiently. "Cut to the chase,

China. What happened to Uncle Jed? How did he get to be a ghost?"

"There was a fire at the trading post," I said, scooping the rosemary clippings into a basket. *'There's rosemary, that's for remembrance,' Ophelia says; 'pray, love, remember.'* This was one of the family stories I'd never been able to forget. "Uncle Jed and some of his drinking buddies had been carousing all night in front of the fireplace. After they stumbled off to bed, the soot in the chimney ignited the shingle roof. That's how some people tell it, anyway. Others say that Uncle Jed had cheated a Choctaw out of a section of land that was rightfully his under the terms of the treaty—that would be the Treaty of Dancing Rabbit Creek—and the man got even by putting a torch to the back wall. However it happened, Uncle Jed's cronies managed to escape, but he burned to death."

Aunt Tullie always concluded the story at this point with a grim smile and evident relish, as if she were saying to herself, *Good riddance to bad rubbish!* I was obviously too young to be entrusted with the unseemly details of Uncle Jed's riotous life, but I was old enough to realize that he did not occupy an honored place in Aunt Tullie's bloodline, her pantheon of paternal ancestors. Or perhaps she was smiling because his unfortunate ending had led to a fortunate outcome, at least as far as the Coldwells were concerned. For at Uncle Jed's death, Jordan's Crossing had come into the hands of his brother Abner, her grandfather, a Memphis lawyer who wanted to become a wealthy planter. Abner took possession of his new property and promptly married his rich neighbor's only daughter, Samantha, thereby adding nearly thirteen hundred acres and fifty slaves to his holdings. From Abner, the plantation (five sections at that time, or thirty-two hundred acres) had come to Aunt Tullie's father Clancy, who was still a boy when the Civil War broke out, and on Clancy's death in the 1940s to her brother Howard, my grandfather. When Howard died, he passed it on to her, in gratitude for taking over the care of his motherless child. Perhaps Aunt Tullie's enigmatic smile was not a judgment on Uncle Jed but merely the expression of an understandable satisfaction with the way things had turned out.

"And now he's come back?" Ruby asked excitedly. "Uncle Jed, I mean?"

"He comes back periodically, when something happens to threaten Jordan's Crossing." I picked up the basket of rosemary clippings. "At least, that's what people say. But it's really just a story, Ruby. *I* certainly don't believe it."

Just a story. But there were those spiraling wisps in the shadows of my room and the faint but unmistakable odor of green cypress logs burning. And Leatha's odd comment, in our phone conversation on Sunday, about the past coming back to haunt the present. When I'd asked her what that meant, she only said, "There are ghosts here, China. This is an unhappy place. And some of those ghosts are coming to life."

Ruby unfolded her long legs and stood up. "Why don't we get in the car and drive to Mississippi?" she said impetuously. "We could see for ourselves whether there's any truth to—"

"I don't think so, Ruby," I said. "Leatha's already been after me to come, but I told her that I've got too much to do here to go digging around my family tree."

Which is more or less what I'd said to my mother when she'd phoned from Jordan's Crossing the night before, to extend Aunt Tullie's invitation.

"Just for a few days, darlin'," she'd said, in that slow, sugar-sweet Mississippi drawl that she's never lost. (*Was it my imagination, or was her drawl flavored with gin and tonic?*) "You can relax and have plenty of time for yourself. It's lovely just now, with the azaleas in bloom." She'd paused and given an extra weight to the next few words. "Aunt Tullie is 'specially anxious for you to come, China. She's got something important she wants to talk to you about."

And then, uneasily, she'd added that enigmatic comment about the past haunting the present, and old ghosts coming back to life. Uncle Jed, no doubt, although he wasn't the only one. There was Great-grandmother Pearl, for instance, who committed suicide in 1918 by taking some sort of poison—digitalis, perhaps—a deeply mysterious event that has troubled the family down through the years. I've never seen Pearl's ghost, of course, although as a girl I often liked to think I caught a whiff of her lily of the valley scent on sultry evenings in the upstairs hall. Given the age of the Big House and the tumultuous times through which it has come, it would be something of a surprise if there weren't quite a few more ghosts lurking in the attic or the cellar or the family graveyard.

Aunt Tullie's invitation came as a surprise, too. I hadn't been back to the plantation since I was a bored, rebellious kid, and I couldn't think of a single reason why my mother's elderly spinster aunt should be anxious to entertain a grand-niece whose obstreperous preteen behavior she had clearly considered unacceptable. I knew I'd enjoy the gardens, if they'd been kept up, and it was tempting to imagine myself in a rocking chair on the old veranda, iced tea at my elbow and a novel on my lap. But I subscribe wholeheartedly to Margaret Mead's observation that while there is such a thing as familial duty, it is not necessary to be intimate with one's blood relations. I remembered Aunt Tullie as stern and joyless, her step firm and unhesitating, her back straight as a poker, her dour spirit casting gloom over the whole place. I doubted that age and ill health had sweetened her temper, and I hoped that her legendary tantrums weren't driving my mother to drink.

"I couldn't go anyway," Ruby said, being realistic for a change. "Shannon's birthday is next week, and Amy and I are planning a big bash. And my checkup is scheduled for the day after the party."

Ruby had surgery for breast cancer at the end of December, a traumatic event that brought her and her two grown-up daughters, Shannon and Amy, closer together. It's brought us closer, too. The possibility of losing her—breast cancer is such a frightening thing—made me value our friendship in a new way. My eyes went briefly to her loose, gauzy top, which completely disguised the fact that she has only one breast. With a defiance that was typically Ruby, she'd refused reconstructive surgery, preferring, she said, to belong to the Tribe of One-Breasted Women. If I asked, she would be glad to lift her top and show me the permanent fern-and-flower tattoo she'd gotten recently to embellish the scar that arched across the flat half of her chest.

But I didn't. I said, instead, "Shannon is how old now—twenty-six?"

"Don't rush it," Ruby said, pushing her hair out of her face with both hands. "She'll be twenty-five." She took two deep breaths and added, "And don't let McQuaid forget about the party. It's Wednesday night, and he's definitely invited."

"I'm sorry, but he won't be there," I said, as we started down the path together. "He's scheduled to give a talk at a law enforcement conference in Baton Rouge." Brian and I would be batching it, and McQuaid's absence would give me a little extra catch-up time. I planned to finish my taxes, instead of waiting until the extension ran out. And when that was finished, I could write a couple of Home and Garden pieces for the next few issues of the *Enterprise*—in addition to all the daily stuff, of course. When you're self-employed, you work around the clock.

"Hey, China, it's your mother!" Laurel Wiley, my shop helper, had stuck her head out the back door and was holding up the cordless phone. Cupping her hand over the mouthpiece as she gave me the phone, she added, "She sounds sort of upset."

"If I know Leatha," Ruby said, "you're on your way to Mississippi after all." She waggled her fingers sympathetically, and she and Laurel went inside.

I put my basket on the step and sat down beside it, feeling uneasy. When I was a girl, my mother's lack of personal authority, her apathy, her alcoholism, had filled me with confusion and pain. Like many daughters of my generation, just beginning to sense the possibilities of a new kind of power, I feared that my mother was a mirror of the self I would inevitably become. So I turned myself into my father instead—until I found the flaws in that pattern and was forced to begin inventing my own life, free of both of them (or so I thought).

But a few years ago, Leatha began going to AA and got control of her drinking, more or less. Since that time, the two of us have moved a long way toward repairing and refloating our derelict relationship. I've even begun calling her Mother when I speak to her, although she is still Leatha when I *think* about her. But her ongoing recovery hasn't been entirely without incident. A couple of times—when she and Sam had a crisis, or one of Sam's several children made life difficult— she's fallen off the wagon, and when that happens, the ghost of the woman she was comes back to haunt us both. I thought back to last night's telephone conversation (*Had she been drinking when she called?*) and felt a swift apprehension. Was there a crisis now?

"Hello, Mother," I said into the phone, as lightly as I could. "What's up?"

"I need you, China." Her voice was taut and urgent, and low, as if she were afraid of being overheard. "I want you to come right away. Come *today.*"

I cleared my throat. "How's Aunt Tullie? Is she—"

"Some days are better than others. But that's not why."

"Well, then, what *is* it? I told you last night: Unless it's really important, I can't just drop everything and—"

"I wouldn't ask if it wasn't important," she said, and I thought that the longer she stayed at Jordan's Crossing, the more Southern she sounded: *I wudn't ask if it wa'n't im-pawt'nt.* "There's trouble here, China, and there's nobody to talk to. Nobody I can trust, anyway. And you're a lawyer. You can help."

Uh-oh. *That* kind of trouble. "Mother," I said carefully, "you know I don't practice now. And I've never done wills and estates, if that's what this is about." I used to be a criminal defense lawyer before I cashed in my retirement fund, moved from Houston to Pecan Springs, and bought Thyme and Seasons. I keep my bar membership current, just in case, but the old life has no appeal for me, and I hate it when people ask legal questions. "If you and Aunt Tullie need property advice or help with her will or whatever," I added, "you should find somebody local. Anyway, you must have a family lawyer. Can't he—"

"China," Leatha snapped, "this has nothin' whatsoever to do with your great-aunt's will, and the fam'ly lawyer is part of the problem. And if you keep on ditherin' back and forth and draggin' your feet, Aunt Tullie could be in *jail* by the time you get here. Is that important enough for you?"

I sucked in my breath. "In jail?"

"It's a distinct possibility," Leatha replied darkly. "The police haven't been here yet, but . . ." Her pause was pregnant with significance. "Well? Can you leave today?"

"I suppose, if Mother McQuaid is available to stay with Brian. McQuaid is going to a conference." I scowled. "What do the police have to do with anything? What the *hell* is going on there?"

"I can't go into it on the phone," she said evasively. "What time can I look for you?"

I glanced at my watch. It was just after nine. "If I leave in a couple of hours, I suppose I could be there by ten or eleven—midnight at the latest."

"Good," Leatha said, and I could hear the relief in her voice. "I'll wait up. Do you remember how to get here? Take Route 61 north from Vicksburg. When you get to Middle Fork, go east to Chicory."

Middle Fork. Chicory. The names brought back images of dusty towns, unpaved streets arched with green trees shimmering in the summer sun, barefoot kids in straw hats, cane fishing poles over their shoulders, heading for the river.

"If I get lost, I'll call," I said.

"Drive safe, dear." The urgency came back. "But please hurry."

I turned off the phone and went into the tearoom. "You were right," I said with a sigh to Ruby, who was checking the menu. Thyme for Tea doesn't open until eleven-thirty, but Janet, our cook, was already in the kitchen, getting things ready for the day.

Ruby glanced at my face. "When are you leaving?"

"As soon as I can arrange it, if it's okay with you. McQuaid will be out of town too, so I've got to call his mother and see if she can come and stay with Brian. I'm sure Laurel can manage the shop by herself, though, now that things have slowed down a little." I looked around at the tearoom, with its original limestone walls and hunter-green wainscoting, green-painted tables cheerful with floral chintz napkins and terra-cotta teapot centerpieces, pots of lush ivy and philodendron hanging from the ceiling. Janet was humming happily in the kitchen, the tables were laid for lunch, and I knew that Ruby could handle anything that came up.

"Of course it's okay," Ruby said. "You don't have to worry about this place. Just be sure to leave a phone number where I can get in touch with you." She gave me an intent look. "Has Aunt Tullie taken a turn for the worse?"

"I don't think that's it," I said. "This is . . . different." *Jail*? I turned on the phone and punched in the McQuaids' number.

"Well," Ruby said, "if it turns out that Uncle Jed is causing trouble, you can always give me a call. I'm sure I can come up with something that will help, even long distance."

"Thanks," I told her, tapping my fingers impatiently. "But I'm sure I'll be able to manage."

Yeah, right. If I'd have known how the trip was going to turn out, I would have insisted that Ruby get in the car and go with me. She's the only one I know who's qualified to handle the weird things that happened in Mississippi.

"Are you sure you don't want me to drive you?" McQuaid asked as I sat at the kitchen table, making a list for his mother, who'd said she'd be delighted to come and stay with Brian for as long as necessary. "I could drop you off at the plantation and then go back to Baton Rouge. It can't be more than a hundred and fifty miles extra."

"But then I wouldn't have a car," I objected. "I'd have to borrow Leatha's." At the disappointed look on his face, I added quickly, "It would be great if you'd come up after the conference, though. You've never seen the plantation, or met Aunt Tullie." A few years ago, on a visit to New Orleans, I'd introduced him to my father's mother, Grandmother Bayles, the China Bayles for whom I'd been named and from whom I inherited my love of gardening. But Grandmother Bayles was dead now, and there was no one left on my father's side of the family. Besides Leatha, Aunt Tullie Coldwell was the only relative I had left, and this might be McQuaid's last chance to meet her.

McQuaid chuckled. "Your aunt sounds like one fearsome lady. Is that where you get your determination?" He put his hand over mine. "Listen, China. With Mom here to look after Brian, we wouldn't have to rush right home. We could check into a nice private B and B with a Jacuzzi, lock the bedroom door, and take off all our clothes." He waggled his eyebrows suggestively and put on an exaggerated leer. "Whad'ya say, babe? Just you and me and some good wholesome sex."

I love my husband's face. It's not handsome, but it has a certain rakish appeal that's emphasized by his crooked nose and the scar that zigzags across his forehead, under the loose thatch of dark hair. McQuaid is an ex-cop who is now an associate professor in the Criminal Justice Department at Central Texas State University, on sabbatical leave this year to recuperate from a shooting that happened when he was doing undercover work for the Texas Rangers. When he's feeling good, he walks slowly, with a limp; when he's tired or the pain gets bad, he leans on a pair of aluminum canes. But I'm thankful that he's walking at all. I still shiver when I think how much worse it could have been.

I picked up his fingers and kissed them. "All our clothes, huh? Now, that's something a girl can look forward to."

Holding my hand, he gave me a quizzical look. "Leatha didn't say what the problem was, or why the big rush?"

I shrugged my shoulders, being casual about it. "Just that if I didn't hurry, I might find Aunt Tullie in jail."

"Jail?" McQuaid exclaimed incredulously. "She wasn't serious, I hope."

"Probably not," I said. Thinking about it on the way home, I'd come to the conclusion that Leatha must have been overstating her concern, just to get me there. I couldn't believe that Aunt Tullie could be in any danger of arrest—unless she'd been driving the car and had hit somebody. That was possible, I supposed, and it would explain the business about legal advice. Criminal charges aside, Jordan's Crossing was a substantial financial asset, and under the right circumstances, Aunt Tullie would make a damned good target for a lawsuit.

I frowned. There was no point in worrying, since I had no idea what to worry about. I went back to the list, jotting down *Pick up Brian's band uniform at Jake's Dry Cleaners* and *BRIAN: NO OVERNIGHT GUESTS!*, then added the phone number at Jordan's Crossing and a big heart with an arrow through it, hoping that Brian wouldn't give his grandmother a hard time. But he's a good kid, usually. And Mom McQuaid raised his father with great success. She probably knows how to handle boys better than I do.

A half hour later, my suitcase was loaded in the trunk of my shiny white two-door Toyota (a replacement for my beloved old blue Datsun, which had rattled itself to death) and McQuaid was giving me a lingering good-bye kiss and wishing me a safe journey.

And then I was on my way, back to the blood relations I had repudiated and the past from which I had resolutely turned away. Back to the women who had gone before me. Back to the motherline.